Also by Bonnie Shiloh

The One, the Only, the Amazing...

The Sunset Girl

The Sunset Girl

Bonnie Shiloh

About the author
Bonnie grew up in a small town in Texas and hung around long enough to date everybody in the tri-county area and snag a few college degrees before bolting for the big city. Full of work ethic and determination, Bonnie climbed the corporate ladder to a comfortable position outwardly giving the appearance of a hard, but fair corporate manager. Bonnie remained single until late in life, concentrating on the career, traveling and expanding the social circle. Inwardly, Bonnie yearned to be more creative. Unable to paint, sing, play an instrument or do photography, Bonnie began to write with the final goal being a collection of three books about exceptionally uncommon people. Not super-heroes, but flesh and blood men and women who feel physical pain and whose hearts break. The Sunset Girl is the second novel in this collection.

The Sunset Girl
Copyright © 2020 by Bonnie Shiloh

Published in the United States of America by
O•Zone Press, El Paso, Texas

ISBN-13 978-0-9976760-3-7
ISBN-10 0-9976760-3-5

Published 2020

To my family and my real friends, thanks for sticking
with me. It was a long road.

Contents

Contents Continued

Contents Continued

Chapter 1

It was probably a mistake. Almost always was, having sex with a co-worker especially when he was the new resident bad boy and lived next door. John Luke just left her cabin and she was already regretting what happened, mostly because it was the second time and swearing after the first, she needed no more of him. Wanting a 'one and done' just to satisfy her curiosity, now thinking a 'two and through' was in order. *He's such a mean and selfish lover,* she thought. *Why did I do this twice?*

Naked and a mess on her bed, she needed to get up and get ready for the boisterous breakfast crowd at the Hill Top Hunting Lodge. She was a waitress and the boys were up early during deer season. It was 3:35 am and she was already running late.

The Hill Top Hunting Lodge was an East Texas legend, located on one of the largest hills in the area somewhere in the vast woods between Jacksonville and Nacogdoches. The resort had nearly 20,000 acres of hunting leases, a medium sized, spring-fed lake and access to flowing water called Mud Creek. Ten cabins were built in the shape of an L, seven on the long side and three on the short side. There was a restaurant at the other end of the L. The veranda of the restaurant faced west and caught the sunsets.

Walking from her cabin (No. 8) to the restaurant, dressed in her mini-skirt waitress uniform, she was wondering what kind of cruelty was in store for her today. She walked through the front door of the restaurant and met face-to-face with the head cook and owner of the lodge, Big Al. He looked exactly like his name, tall and fat. Big Al never really sexually harassed her but he was always giving her those sideways looks and muttering to the good old boys and other "bubbas" in the restaurant.

"Where's your nametag?" Big Al grunted at her like he did almost every morning.

She reluctantly pulled it out of her skirt pocket and pinned it to her blouse. The name on the badge was "Orange". Her real name was Whisper Jenkins, born in Texas near the Louisiana border. Her parents were dirt poor, didn't want kids and especially didn't want her. As a baby, Whisper wouldn't cry loudly like most babies, but whimpered almost all of the time. Her father wanted to call her "Whimper" but her mother insisted on "Whisper".

When Whisper was born, she had a red hue about her. The midwife said it would change as the baby got older and the midwife was right. By the time Whisper was six months old the red hue changed to orange. Whisper's parents didn't want her to begin with and as the baby turned orange, they wanted her even less.

Just before Whisper's first birthday, she was given up to the Belmont School for Wayward Girls near Dallas. Belmont was basically a place where knocked-up teens went to have their babies. After birth, the teen left and the baby stayed. Whisper grew up there, suffering almost every indignation one could imagine.

Being called "Orange" was the best of it. "Dreamsicle" and "Orange Sherbet" were two of the other nicer nicknames. In front of the matrons, the mean girls called her "Yesterday", in private they called her "Yesterday's Kotex".

By the time Whisper was old enough to attend classes at Belmont, even the teachers called her "Orange". She accepted this because that is what she was. Her skin was as orange as could be.

Her blonde hair looked yellow against her orange skin. Her lips were blood orange colored, almost red. Nails were bright yellow compared to her hands and feet which were a duller yellow. She had sky blue eyes and looked like an Andy Warhol painting.

At sixteen years old, she ran away from Belmont and got as far as Tyler which was only a hundred miles away. Whisper hitchhiked southeast and was picked up by Glyna, Big Al's wife. Glyna ran the household and stayed away from the lodge while Big Al ran the business. Glyna knew Whisper didn't have any prospects so she made Big Al give her a waitress job, a cabin to stay in and meals at the restaurant. Big Al paid Whisper next to nothing because expenses were deducted from her pay. However, Whisper got to keep her tips, as little as they were.

When Whisper told Big Al about Belmont and the other girls making fun of her, he didn't much care. Big Al decided having an "Orange" girl as a waitress could be good for business. Maybe a few extra people a month would come to the restaurant just to see the freak. For Whisper, it was Belmont, all over again. Whisper "Orange" Jenkins has been a mainstay at the Hill Top Hunting Lodge for the last five years.

By 4:00 am the restaurant was packed with hunters. Each one was trying to outdo the other with their camouflage and weapons. Why anyone had to kill a 140-pound deer with an AK-47 assault rifle was beyond Whisper's comprehension.

Whisper and Molly, the other waitress, who lived two cabins down from Whisper, were running around like chickens with their heads cut off. Hunters could be demanding, especially when they wanted to get out to their stands and shoot something. There really wasn't any hurry because after putting out feed all year long, with tall stands pre-positioned about 50 yards away from the feeder, there was no missing the shot and deer were always there. The deer became dependent on the humans feeding them so they didn't know how to go anywhere else.

Molly was a down-on-her-luck lady also. She was a few years older than Whisper with larger breasts, dark hair and was reasonably good looking although the guys didn't look much beyond her boobs. Molly always showed a lot of leg and cleavage while touching the men on the back, shoulder or arm every chance she got. Whisper never touched any of them and never showed cleavage because her small breasts with blood orange colored nipples would only be cause for more ridicule.

Molly's gamesmanship got her five times the tips Whisper earned. Also, Whisper often found oranges, tangerines or "Cuties" on the table instead of a tip. Every blue moon, some idiot would leave a grapefruit because they didn't know the difference between that and an orange.

About 6:00 am, after all the hunters finished breakfast and ventured off to be real men, John Luke walked in the restaurant wearing his overalls and T-shirt looking all Ryan Gosling only taller and bigger. He glanced over at Whisper, smirked a little laugh and joined Big Al at the back booth. Whisper blushed but no one could tell with her complexion. Molly moved over close to Whisper and asked her if she's had any of that yet. Whisper lied and said she didn't want any part of him. Molly scoffed and said, "Yeah, me either," and walked away.

Whisper and Molly prepared for the regular breakfast crowd which consisted of a few locals and the wives of one or two of the hunters. The wives usually slept in on hunt days. John Luke stood up, drained his coffee cup, flashed the girls a devilish smile and the girls let out an audible sigh. Whisper hated herself the instant she did it. Big Al watched with a little too much interest and Whisper was afraid she discovered John Luke was the kiss and tell kind of guy.

By noon, the hunters all returned, some having dead deer strapped across their ATV's which were provided by the Hill Top Hunting Lodge. The lunch crowd was rambunctious, the beer (for unarmed customers only) and beef brisket were on special, and the waitresses were flying around the restaurant trying to keep up with the demands. The hunters from Cabins 3 and 4 broke out in a shoving match when one of them insulted the other's Remington Model 700 in favor of a Winchester 94.

Molly, with her hands full of dirty dishes, swung by Whisper and asked already knowing the answer, "Are they fighting over guns again? That usually means they have short barrels themselves. You know what I mean?" Whisper laughed, scraped food off a dish and threw an orange into the trash.

In the middle of the afternoon, all the hunters went to take a nap, because the manly art of hunting was hard work. They got up early, ate a big breakfast, drove an ATV right up to their stand, climbed a short ladder, sat on their asses, shot a deer, drove it back to the lodge, ate lunch and drank beer. They probably burned a whole hundred calories all day long.

This was Whisper's favorite time of the day because John Luke was about to take his break and come into the restaurant for an iced tea. Both girls were waiting anxiously when the door opened and a sweaty, dirty John Luke walked in. He sat in the back booth with Big Al and Molly went over to wait on him. John Luke ordered his tea and he touched her arm. Whisper saw this and felt a ridiculous pang of jealously. Molly came back to Whisper and said, "I hope he's good in bed because it would be a real waste if he's not." Whisper wasn't about to say anything but she knew he was not the best in bed because his equipment was too big to really enjoy and John Luke didn't care one iota about satisfying his partner. John Luke finished his tea and left the restaurant but only after giving the girls a once-over.

Molly and Whisper sat with Big Al and enquired about John Luke's background. Big Al enjoyed the attention and drew out the story as long as possible. After an hour of prying and prodding, the girls learned John Luke was twenty-seven years old, divorced, came from Baton Rouge originally, was in jail or prison at least once before on an assault conviction and he was good with his hands.

Molly said, "I bet that's not all he's good with." Whisper gave her an elbow.

A 5:00 pm, their day was done. Young college girls from Stephen F. Austin University came in to work the supper crowd. Big Al couldn't get college kids to wake up early enough to work breakfast so the resident waitresses were stuck with the early morning breakfast service and lunch. The college kids always got the biggest tips because the evening crowds were bigger, the drinks flowed and the meals were more expensive.

At 7:00 pm, Whisper was lying on her bed in her underwear and thick socks, wrapped in a comforter, trying to read. Mostly she was looking out the window of her cabin watching for John Luke to finish his work day. A few minutes later she heard him stomp his work boots on the planks of the front porch of his cabin next door to hers. She quickly put the paperback down and peeked out the window. John Luke always left his curtains open and Whisper could see into his bedroom and down the hall a little.

John Luke went into the kitchen, grabbed a beer and stripped naked in his bedroom. He walked down the hall to the shower drinking his beer. Although she had him between her legs just fifteen hours ago and it wasn't good at all, seeing him naked thrilled her. She couldn't help it, even knowing he was the king of the bad of boys and could care less about her needs. She slid her hand under her panties and rubbed herself anticipating his exit from the bathroom.

In a few minutes, John Luke came down the hall drying himself with a towel. He stopped in the doorway of his bedroom and paid particular attention to what was between his legs. Because of the way he exposed himself, Whisper was pretty sure he knew she was watching. Drying himself off with so much vigor was making him noticeably excited. This was enough to allow Whisper to finish masturbating and fall back on the bed, satisfied, but feeling guilty. John Luke dressed and went to the restaurant to drink beer with Big Al and hit on the college girls. Whisper slipped into a state of deep relaxation.

Molly went to her cabin (No. 10) on the other side of John Luke's and was met there by the hunter from Cabin 4. He was a big, pot-bellied good ol' boy who offered her just enough money to get him in her front door. They drank a few beers and when drunk enough, she told him he could have a hand job for the money he offered. He wasn't thrilled with the prospect but she wouldn't agree to anything else for that price.

He was so fat he had to lie down with a pillow under his butt so she could find his thing. It was a nice one but what it was attached to was disgusting. Finished with her business and fifty bucks richer, Molly sent him on his way with a beer in hand. He stumbled back up to the restaurant to tell Big Al all about his conquest. Molly took a shower and went over to talk to Whisper.

The two girls sat at the table and drank hot tea. Molly told Whisper it was a good night with tips especially with the fifty bucks she got for her extracurricular activities. Whisper didn't say anything because she only received $11.00 in tips, three oranges, one invitation to Cabin 7 and a note on a credit card receipt that said, 'Knock, Knock. Who's there? Orange. Orange who? Orange you glad to see me?'

Molly asked about John Luke and Whisper said he got cleaned up and went back to the restaurant, probably to try to pick up one of the evening waitresses. Molly looked like she was in deep thought, trying to figure out if she should chase after him but decided against it. After a second cup of tea and all of Molly's fantasies about John Luke on the table, it was time for bed. Molly and Whisper hugged at the front door and Molly went to her cabin on the other side of John Luke's.

Whisper went to bed thinking John Luke might come by if he struck out with the evening college waitresses. She really didn't want to be the hollaback girl and needed to catch up on her sleep because he kept her up late last night assaulting her with his big member, the biggest one she'd ever seen. John Luke was going to be a real complication if she didn't break it off, knowing in her heart and mind John Luke was all dick. Physical and personality, nothing but a dick.

A little after midnight, she heard some voices in front of the cabin next door. It was John Luke and the short, cute, dark-haired evening waitress, name unknown. Whisper was wide awake and peeking through the windows into John Luke's bedroom not knowing if she wanted to watch the show or not. All she could think about was how big John Luke's equipment was and how little this girl looked.

Whisper could tell they went in his front door but never saw them come down the hall to the bedroom. She secretly hoped they were going to do it on the couch in the living room so she wouldn't have to make the decision to watch or not. In a few minutes, the girl and John Luke walked down the hall. They were both fully naked with the little girl pulling him along by his giant pole. For no reason whatsoever, this pissed off Whisper to the point she didn't want to watch anymore. She flipped over on her back, crossed her arms in disgust and stared at the ceiling.

Whisper started hearing the girl call out John Luke's name and she knew he was inserting himself into her. Whisper covered her ears with pillows, still hearing the girls muffled cries. This went on for five minutes. Finally, when all fell silent, Whisper drifted off to sleep.

At 3:30 am, the alarm went off and a new day started. Whisper slept a total of three hours. She was going to have to let go of this John Luke fixation or it would ruin her health. More sleep was desperately needed.

In the restaurant by 4:00 am, wearing her mini-skirt, looking like she hadn't been to bed at all and wanting a cup of coffee, she met up with Molly who was frantically putting set-ups on the tables. The hunters were starting to flood in.

"What time did John Luke get in last night?" asked Molly as she handed Big Al the first order of the morning.

Whisper said she didn't know, she was asleep. A boldface lie.

Molly said, "I think he took that little bitch from evenings home with him."

"What makes you think that?" Whisper asked as she was picking up a plate of bacon, eggs and grits.

"Because I saw her walk out of his cabin at nearly one in the morning carrying her bra in her hand."

"You saw that and you still *think* he took her home?"

"Well," said Molly. "I guess there's really no doubt, huh?"

"Why do you care?" asked Whisper as they met up at the condiments station feeling like a hypocrite.

"I don't know. I guess I wanted to be first I suppose. Now I've got to hurry things along to come in second."

Whisper didn't tell her she was already running third because Whisper was first, twice, and then the little girl from evenings was second. John Luke was going to be a major player. Bastard!

A little before 10:00 am, John Luke strolled in the restaurant, ready to start his day. He looked fresh, well rested and certainly well laid. Whisper thought it wasn't fair John Luke got to sleep in while the girls had to get up at 3:30 am. Whisper went to wait on him.

"What else will you have?" asked Whisper.

John Luke smiled, "Besides what I had the last two nights? I'll take the Hunter's Special with four bacon strips and a glass of juice."

Whisper didn't want to ask, but she did, "What kind of juice?"

"I've just had orange and it wasn't that good," he said with a stupid look on his face, "I think I want something different."

"Was that supposed to be your idea of an insult?"

"No, I just think I want cranberry this morning,"

"You're an ass." Whisper walked off to deliver the order to Big Al.

Molly came to the service counter and asked Whisper, "What's up with our boy today?"

Big All was standing at the grill listening to every word. "Nothing," said Whisper. "He's just being himself."

In a few minutes John Luke's order was ready. Whisper carried it to his table, set it down in front of him, took a piece of bacon off his plate and ate it in one bite, handing him his glass of cranberry juice.

"What are you doing?" John Luke asked with mild irritation.

Whisper replied. "I tried some strange meat recently but it wasn't any good. This bacon is so much better." She turned around and walked off.

John Luke dove into his meal thinking he didn't care what she thought, he'd already had her. He laughed to himself. *How preposterous? Any woman not liking what I've got. I'll have the orange bitch again. Real soon too.*

It was only the second day of deer season and the Hill Top Hunting Lodge was already running rampant with sexual overtones, innuendos and outright libidinous acts. Typical. Big Al was loving it.

Chapter 2

When Whisper and Molly finished their shift, they sat at the back table to count tips. Molly had $62.00 and Whisper had $13.00 plus a tangerine, an orange, a peach, a second offer of sex from the guy in Cabin 7 and another Knock-Knock joke on a receipt.

After the tally, Molly asked, "Who do you think the flavor of the day will be?"

"Well, it won't be me," said Whisper.

"It better be me," said Molly. "I don't think I can take it if I see some other bimbo coming out of his cabin at one in the morning."

"But you would be willing to be that bimbo tonight?"

"I know it sounds like a double standard but I really want to get some of that now. It's like being chosen for teams in junior high and the captains are picking everybody else and you end up being taken last by default. I don't want to be last."

Whisper just shook her head and wished she wasn't chosen first. She didn't know how long the John Luke parade was going to be but felt sure they were just seeing the tip of the iceberg. Every time he scored it cheapened the quality of their tryst. It's like thinking you're winning first place but when you receive the award it's just a participation ribbon printed on construction paper.

Big Al came over to the booth and sat down next to Whisper preventing her from getting out.

"What are ya'll girls talking about. John Luke, I bet."

Molly asked, "Were you listening?"

Big Al laughed and said, "What else would two hens be talking about but the rooster." He laughed so hard his body shook all over.

"Let me out, Al. I need to go get some sleep." Big Al begrudgingly slid off the seat so Whisper could leave. Once out the door, Big Al asked, "Hey, do you think she's orange all over?"

Molly didn't know what to make of the question. "Well Al, she's orange."

Molly's answer didn't make any sense to Al, but they left it like that.

Whisper was just about to collapse on her bed in her flannel pajamas and fuzzy socks when she heard a noise coming from John Luke's cabin. She peeked through her curtains to see John Luke rolling around in the sack with the wife of the hunter from Cabin 6. Whisper saw her around the area and in the restaurant yesterday for lunch.

John Luke was really putting it to her. This woman was not little and she wasn't particularly attractive. Whisper surmised John Luke was nothing more than a horn-dog and would do it with just about anybody which made her feel cheaper than she did last night. Whisper rolled over with the pillows covering her ears.

After the better part of an hour, Whisper heard the woman leave and peeked through the curtains again to see John Luke walking down the hall toward his bedroom. His heavy manhood swinging between his legs as he walked.

"Damn it," she said to herself watching him climb into bed. Cursing, because as much as she hated him, in that moment, all she could think about was wrapping herself around that mass of flesh. "Damn it!"

The alarm startled her awake from a rare full night's sleep. She dressed in her uniform and went to the restaurant. It was much colder out than the previous day. Winter was coming. In East Texas, winter sometimes didn't amount to a hill of beans but this morning a northeast wind blew a chill into her bones.

Molly and Whisper reached the restaurant front door at the same time and walked in together. They took off their light jackets exposing their very erect nipples, easily seen through their thin uniform blouses. Big Al stopped cleaning the grill and stared. He loved the cold weather. The girls said "Good morning" to Al and started their day.

The hunters came through the restaurant in a hurry and the girls frantically served the meals. By the time the sun was up, the restaurant was completely empty. Big Al sat in the back booth and the girls sat across from him. Big Al was telling them how he used to drive all the way to Dallas in his Mustang just to go dancing when suddenly, the front door swung open.

Myles Carter walked in wearing an olive drab hunting outfit with a bomber jacket. He took off his aviator sunglasses and scanned the room. Tall, broad shouldered and thin, handsome would be an understatement and he was rich beyond compare. A local, well known in all the right circles.

Molly flew out of the booth to take care of 'the customer' and Whisper noticed an extra button on Molly's blouse was undone. Whisper never saw Molly unbutton it.

"Mr. Carter, welcome to the Hill Top Hunting Lodge Restaurant. Please sit anywhere." Molly waved her hand showing all the empty booths.

"Do I know you?" he asked as he sat at the nearest booth.

"No sir, I've seen your picture in the paper. I'm Molly."

"Hey Molly, what's good today?"

Molly's mind was racing for a snappy comeback about her being the best thing in the place but she said, "The Hunter's Special is always good."

As Big Al cooked the order, Molly and Whisper sat in the corner booth trying not to stare at Myles. They discussed how incredibly good looking he was and estimated his wealth to be in the hundreds of millions. He was 31 years old, unmarried, not engaged and educated at the best schools. He would be any mother's dream for their daughter. Myles Carter was the next thing to royalty.

As Myles ate, two of the hunters' wives walked in and sat in the booth next to Myles even though every seat in the restaurant was open. Whisper went to wait on them and she recognized one of the women as the one being with John Luke the night before.

When Whisper asked them what they wanted, they turned to Myles and asked him what he was having. They both ordered the Hunter's Special even though women almost never ordered that meal. When Whisper went to deliver the order, Myles could hear the two women talk about how freakish Whisper looked. He heard one of them say, "Could you imagine, a man waking up next to that every morning?"

Myles paid with cash, leaving a $20 tip, more than the cost of the meal. As soon as Myles stood up, Molly snatched the twenty off the table top and stuffed it in her bra. She made sure Myles saw her do it. Myles turned to go out the door at the same instant John Luke was coming in. They stood face-to-face in the doorway seeing which one would back down.

Molly stood by Myles' booth holding her breath with her hand to her chest. The wives were staring, frozen in mid-chew waiting for something to happen and Whisper held a coffee pot in her hand standing stationary by the pick-up counter. Big Al was watching from the kitchen. The only thing moving in the entire restaurant was steam rising from the grill.

The two gorgeous men stood their ground. It was like watching a lion and a tiger stalk each other. Finally, after an eternity, Myles took one step back and let John Luke enter the restaurant. John Luke triumphantly took a seat in the back booth and Myles exited, got into his Range Rover and drove off.

Molly went to wait on John Luke. "Bring me a cup of coffee and who was that asshole?"

"That 'asshole' was Myles Carter, the richest man in East Texas."

"I don't give a shit if he is the richest man in the world, he's still an asshole."

"If you say so." Molly poured him a cup of coffee, black, like real men drink it.

Whisper took her pot of coffee to the wives and asked them if they needed a warm up. The one who wasn't with John Luke last night asked Whisper why she was so orange. Whisper told her she was born this way. Then the lady asked. "Are all orange girls like you?"

"What? Orange?" Whisper replied thinking it was a stupid question. "I don't know any other orange girls," and she walked off.

As John Luke was finishing up his cup of coffee, the wives were trying to time it so they could walk out with him. They called for Whisper to bring them the check. As she neared the table, Whisper heard the woman who was with him last night say, "It's so big, Jill. It's like this." Whisper saw the lady hold her hands about a foot apart on the table. Both ladies got up and literally chased John Luke out the door.

The meal cost $18.79 and the ladies left a twenty-dollar bill. Whisper got a $1.21 tip and an insult about her skin color. It was the start of a fairly typical day for Whisper "Orange" Jenkins.

Chapter 3

The day after seeing Myles Carter for the first time, Molly and Whisper sat with Big Al in the corner booth during the after-breakfast lull.

"What do you think of Myles Carter?" asked Big Al.

Whisper didn't say anything but Molly jumped right in. "I think he's a dream and is going to give John Luke a run for his money."

"You mean John Luke won't be the stud around here anymore?" Al shoved a sausage in his mouth.

"A good looking ex-con handy-man at the Hill Top Hunting Lodge or a good-looking, college educated man with a hundred million bucks. Who would you choose, Al?" Molly asked.

Big Al shrugged and bit down on another sausage speaking with his mouth full, "Girls will marry the good guy but they will always want to play with the bad boy. John Luke will be the stud around here for a long time if I can get him to stay."

"He's not planning on leaving, is he?" Molly looked worried.

"He hasn't said as much but when he fishes out the water, there won't be any reason for a guy like that to stay."

"What do you mean 'fishes out the water'?" Molly's eyebrows furrowed.

Big Al snorted a little. "He told me he already screwed one of the guests and two of the staff and he's only been here a week! When he runs through all of them, he'll want to hit the road."

"I knew he was screwing those college kids!" Molly looked at Whisper when she said it. Whisper was blushing hard from guilt and shame but no one could tell.

The door opened and in walked Myles Carter, right on cue. Molly shot out of the booth, grabbed a menu and directed him to a seat. Big Al was watching with a serious intensity. Big Al's life was basically over. He was relegated to cooking up hash on the grill and living his life vicariously through the young employees at the Lodge.

Myles was looking over the menu when Molly sat in the booth across from him. He looked a little surprised. He couldn't find anything so he asked, "What's good, besides the Hunter's Special?"

Molly swung around to the other side of the booth and sat beside him so she could point out suggestions on the menu but really just wanted to rub herself up against him. After dragging her boob across his arm twice and letting her hand brush his thigh once, he chose the Eight-Point Omelet. Molly looked down between his legs and imagined she could see a growing interest developing.

Molly gave the order to Big Al and he began cooking the large omelet with eight ingredients. Molly sat with Whisper in the corner booth and told her that she thought Myles started getting an erection.

Whisper responded, "Well imagine that. You did everything but give him a blow job."

"I've got to think of some reason to go back over there."

"A hard-on wasn't invitation enough."

"You're right." Molly went right over a sat back down next to him.

Myles asked, "What are you doing?"

"I thought this was an invitation," she said reaching over and squeezing him right between the legs.

He let out a low grunt but grabbed her hand and pushed it away. "I don't think this is the time or place."

"Just name when and where."

Big Al nearly burned the omelet staring at the action and Whisper tried hard not to look.

"Just like that?" Myles asked.

"Sure, why not. I'm easy for the right guy."

"What kind of guy is the right guy?"

"Well, you, Myles."

"What's your name?" Myles had completely forgotten.

"Molly," she said. "Isn't that cute, Myles and Molly?"

Myles looked up at Big Al and hollered, "Hey, can you make that order to go. I've got something I need to do."

Molly squirmed on the seat, "Am I that something you need to do?"

Myles laughed a little, "I'm afraid not."

Big Al hit the bell and Whisper went to get the omelet in the Styrofoam container. Molly still had Myles trapped in the booth and wouldn't let him out. Whisper set the container down on the table and said, "Here's your order."

Nobody moved. Finally Whisper said, "Molly, let the man out." Molly slowly stood and Myles grabbed his food, threw a twenty on the table and ran for the door.

Molly said, "I think he's gay," and grabbed the twenty off the table.

Whisper responded with, "I think you scared him."

"He's a pussy if that scared him."

"Who's a pussy?" John Luke walked in the restaurant through the back door.

Molly said, "I think that rich guy might be gay."

"Oh, I know that already. You can tell by looking at how soft he is all over." John Luke sat in the back booth. Molly sat down next to him.

Whisper asked, "What do you want to eat?"

John Luke said, "The special with a cup of coffee."

Whisper delivered the order and Molly rubbed herself on John Luke.

Whisper was standing next to the grill when Big Al said, "I think that is going to be trouble."

Whisper couldn't agree more.

Chapter 4

When John Luke left to go do some work, Molly came over to Whisper and pulled her off toward the restrooms.

"What are you doing?" Whisper asked.

Molly was so excited she could barely talk. "First of all, let me say that John Luke has got the biggest cock I've ever seen. It goes half way down his thigh. Second, he says he's willing to do us both at the same time."

Whisper was stunned. She just froze.

Molly asked, "What's wrong. I know you want him too. I can see it on your face. He said he felt sorry for you and would throw you a bone so to speak but only if I was there too. He didn't want you getting the wrong idea or falling in love with him or anything like that."

Whisper was stunned at the offer, especially since he'd been with her twice already. This re-affirmed to her that John Luke was a master manipulator and a plain old asshole.

"I'll have to pass."

Molly was shocked. "This is the opportunity of a lifetime."

"Really? Pulling a threesome with John Luke is an opportunity of a lifetime? I'm out. Tell John Luke I appreciate his "pity fuck" offer but trust me, you getting laid is not contingent on my participation. Just tell him I'm out and see what happens."

John Luke exited the restaurant, leaving a piece of paper on the table. Molly went over and read the note. "My cabin. 10 pm tomorrow," was all it said. Molly was hoping if she showed up alone, John Luke would take her anyway.

The early supper crowd was starting to come in and the excitement was apparently over for the day. Molly kept telling Whisper she was already wet and couldn't wait for tomorrow night. Whisper nearly gagged every time she said it.

Right before the change-of-shift, a guy walked into the restaurant and took a seat in the booth by the far window. He was medium height, strong and broad shouldered, brown haired, wearing green Dickies work pants and a long sleeve khaki shirt with a State of Texas seal over the pocket and a Texas flag on the shoulder. He was handsome and looked rather Indiana Jones-ish. Whisper brought him a menu.

The guy scanned the menu, but couldn't concentrate enough to read because he was fixated with Whisper's orange coloring. Finally, he set the menu on the table and looked at her. "You might be the most fascinating person I have ever seen."

"What, never seen an orange girl before?" she said with a smile.

"No, I haven't. It's like discovering a new species of rare and beautiful animal."

"How beautiful?" she asked.

"Like a snow leopard."

Whisper sat down across from the man. "Most of the time I find what men say about me disgusting, derogatory or just plain mean. For some reason, I don't think you have a mean bone in your body."

"I'm usually not very good with people and I don't want you to take this wrong, but I really do find you rare and beautiful and I won't be able to take my eyes off of you. So, forgive me in advance for staring."

"Well, let me think about it….okay, you're forgiven."

"My name is Ross Evans." He stuck his hand out across the table.

Whisper took his big rough hand in hers and said, "Whisper Jenkins."

While they were still holding hands, Ross said, "But your nametag says, Orange."

"A very non-imaginative nickname that has stuck with me all of my life." Changing the subject, she asked. "What do you do for the State of Texas?"

"I have chosen to pursue the lucrative career of wildlife biology."

"Oh, there's money in that?"

Ross laughed and said, "If I'm lucky, I mean really lucky, I can pay off my student loans in four more years. Then I can live the lower middle class life I so deserve."

Whisper said, "Well in four years I'll have about $200 saved up so I guess I win." They both chuckled a little and Ross told her about how he was sent to the Hill Top Hunting Lodge to check on the deer herd this year to make sure they were abundant and healthy and to do some other routine biological tests.

"Today I will mostly look for scat, bag it up and take it to the lab to check later."

"I've seen a lot of cowboys and cowboy wannabe's come through this restaurant but I've never seen a real live 'shit picker' before." She raised her eyebrows upon finishing the sentence.

Ross held his eyes down, smiling……. "Orange!" Big Al called out across the room. Whisper looked up with a scowl on her face. Al admonished, "There's other customers besides the Texas Ranger."

Whisper looked at Ross, "They are equal opportunity discriminators here. Nobody is safe."

Ross looked Whisper right in her sky-blue eyes and said, "Hell, Texas Ranger is a compliment, I was called a 'shit picker' just a minute ago."

"I've got to get back to work but I'll be off in twenty minutes."

"When I finish my supper, I have a date with that balcony to watch the sunset." Ross pointed to the veranda facing west.

"I'll see if I can squeeze that into my schedule." Whisper walked off to clear some tables and settle some bills before her shift ended.

Ross Evans ate his Whole Hog Hamburger and migrated out to the veranda. It was a wooden deck built over the side of the hill with an expansive view. The chairs and tables were made of metal and looked like cheap patio furniture, but the view was priceless.

Ross sat in one of the chairs and tried to read messages on his iPhone which barely worked. Connection was spotty at best. A college aged waitress came out and asked him if he needed anything, but he declined. Giving up trying to read his messages he walked to the edge of the balcony and stood by the rail. The sun was just above the horizon and the clouds were such that a spectacular sunset was in in the making.

Several of the patrons joined him on the veranda to watch the sunset. They all lined the rail. Right when the edge of the sun touched the horizon, Whisper put her hand on the rail touching Ross's hand. He didn't look at her. "Thought you were going to miss this," he said nonchalantly.

"Not for the world," she replied. They both stared at the descending sun and the sky turning pink, yellow and orange.

"It looks like fire," Whisper said to no one.

"It looks like you," said Ross. They turned towards each other. She looked beautiful with her flowing yellow hair, blue eyes and sunset skin. If there was ever a 'moment' between a man and a woman, this was one.

"Doctor Evans!" Somewhere in the back of his mind Ross thought he heard his name being called. "I've been looking all over for you."

Ross turned to see his graduate assistant, Shelby Garrison.

"I've been looking everywhere for you," he repeated.

"Now you have found me."

"What time do we get up tomorrow? I want to know if I can go into town." Shelby was a tall, thin, lanky character. He reminded Ross of Ichabod Crane.

"I think we need to be at breakfast by 4:00 am."

Shelby looked stunned. College kids didn't like getting up early.

While Shelby was trying to comprehend a 4:00 am work call. Ross said, "Shelby, this is Whisper Jenkins."

Whisper said, "Pleased to meet you. Just to let you know how lucky you have it, I have to be at work by 4:00 in the morning. I get up at 3:30 am six days a week." Whisper smiled.

Shelby said, "Bummer." Then he stared at Whisper as if he was seeing her for the first time. She put her hands on her hips and stared back. He even cocked his head a little to the side. Then he turned and walked off.

Whisper turned to Ross, "So, 'Doctor' Evans, huh?"

"Don't get all excited. I'm officially a Research Veterinarian. My main project right now is mapping disease patterns across the state. I know it sounds like riveting entertainment," he said facetiously, "but it will help the herds over time."

They turned back to watch the last of the setting sun.

Chapter 5

At 4:05 am Whisper was rushing to the restaurant, late as usual. As she passed Cabin 2, she saw Ross standing on the porch, shirtless, drinking a cup of coffee. She stopped dead in her tracks, he was built like a boxer. "Doctor Evans, I didn't expect to see so much of you this early in the morning."

Ross raised his finger as if to say, 'wait a second' and turned to go into the cabin. When he turned, she could see some horrible scarring on his back, like a bad burn or acid spill. He appeared in a few seconds and was putting on his khaki uniform shirt. He bounded down the steps and started walking with her to the restaurant.

As they got near the restaurant entrance, she said, "I'm late, they'll be scrutinizing me like they always do and if I walk in with you, they will assume we've been together all night."

"But we weren't."

"It doesn't matter. It will give them something to talk about and I am usually that something every day anyway. Could you please just walk in a few minutes after me?"

Ross shrugged, "Sure."

"Thanks." She rushed inside to jeers from Big Al and shouts from the customers for more coffee and service. They were all in a hurry. Killing deer couldn't wait.

Ross stood in the cool morning air for five minutes before he went in and took one of the few seats available. Molly was his waitress. "Hey, if it ain't the Texas Ranger," she said giving him a menu. She poured him a cup of coffee automatically. "What'll it be?" pulling a pen from behind her ear and standing impatiently. He studied the menu.

"It's real simple," she said as she leaned over touching her boob to his shoulder and putting her hand on his back. Whisper was watching as Ross stiffened when Molly touched him. Molly didn't think anything about it because men reacted in all different ways, some leaned in, some grabbed, some stiffened.

"Most men get the Big Breakfast, but you can have any of the candy-ass ones if you want."

"I suppose I'll have the Big Breakfast then." The Big Breakfast was the most expensive meal on the breakfast menu. Molly always encouraged the purchase of the Big Breakfast because it assured her a larger tip.

"Good boy," Molly said as she stroked him across his broad shoulders. He stiffened again as Molly retreated to the kitchen.

Ross caught Whisper's eyes from across the room and they gave each other a slight head nod of acknowledgment.

The Big Breakfast arrived at the same time Shelby did. Shelby looked like he just woke up. His shirt was buttoned the wrong way and his hair was matted into a rooster tail. Ross and Shelby watched as the Big Breakfast was delivered. It was three of everything: three pancakes, three sausages, three bacons, three eggs, three biscuits and gravy, three toasted slices of bread, a mound of hash browns, a bowl of cheese grits and about a quart of orange juice.

"I think we can share the breakfast, don't you?" Ross asked, knowing it could easily feed six normal people.

Shelby looked up at him, "Do I still get my breakfast per diem if I don't spend any money?"

"The State of Texas is very generous that way. You could eat nuts and berries found in the woods and the State would still give you per diem just to ensure a growing graduate assistant got properly reimbursed for any out-of-pocket food expenses." Shelby wasn't awake enough to comprehend what Ross just said. "Yes, you'll get your money. So, dig in."

Like all twenty-two year olds, Shelby was starving. He grabbed the pancakes, loaded them with butter and syrup and woofed them down in no time. He started on the biscuits and gravy. They were gone in minutes. Shelby grabbed a couple of slices of bacon, a sausage and a forkful of eggs, placing them in between two pieces of toast. Gone. Then he drank the entire carafe of orange juice. The kid could eat.

Ross managed to eat one egg, one piece of bacon, one sausage and a piece of toast. Shelby started on the grits and hash browns.

Molly came back around, "I see the Junior Ranger didn't want to order." She was mad she didn't get a chance at a larger tip. She sat down next to Shelby, gave his boney knee a squeeze and asked if there was anything else she could get him. He was stunned, girls never made a move on him.

"No?" she said. "Okay then, here's the bill. I'll be your cashier." She got up and left but not before sliding her hand way up into Shelby's crotch. He noticeably jumped. Ross just smiled.

The price of breakfast was outrageous, but Ross forked over the cash with a 20% tip. As the state boys were leaving, Whisper and Ross made eye contact again. Shelby stared at her too, then Whisper noticed half the men in the restaurant were staring at her. But that wasn't unusual.

When Molly and Whisper had a break in the action, they stood by the condiments looking for signs of patrons wanting service. Molly asked, "What do you think of the Ranger?"

"Oh, I think he's nice enough."

Molly looked at Whisper and laughed a little, "And he's hot as fuck, but I think he's married."

"Why would you think that?"

"One, he didn't even look at my tits and believe me, I dropped them on him too. And two, it didn't seem like he wanted me touching him."

"That would make him married?" Whisper scrunched her face up as she asked.

Molly thought for a minute, "Or maybe gay. But I can tell you this, the kid isn't gay. He got a boner in the thirty seconds I sat with him."

"Well, wasn't he lucky?" Whisper added playfully.

As their day at the restaurant came to a close, all Molly could talk about was the two of them meeting up with John Luke later that night.

Whisper reminded Molly a dozen times, "I haven't committed to this, you know. I'm not sure a threesome with John Luke is going to be my thing."

"You'll go for it. Who wouldn't, it's John Luke? Just think about those overalls sliding down, you on your knees and that big, giant cock poppin' out right in your face. He is so big. You're just not going to believe it, Orange." Molly was shaking her head like she could see him now and couldn't believe what she saw.

Whisper had already been on her knees in front of him once before and wasn't about to admit it to Molly. Whisper hoped John Luke wouldn't tell. "I don't think it will be a good idea for us to get involved with him." Whisper felt like a hypocrite.

"Why, because he works here, he lives next door, has a prison record and screws everything that walks and talks?"

"I think that just about sums it up."

"Don't be silly Orange, we're not going to marry him."

The girls went to their respective cabins to relax a while. Whisper threw on some flannel pajamas and thick socks and curled up with a book. She fell asleep in ten minutes. Molly showered, washed her hair, and shaved her whole body, except her pubic hair, which she spent the next hour grooming until it was in the perfect shape. By 8:00 pm Molly was parading around her cabin, naked, with tissues stuffed under her arms and in her crotch. She was nervously perspiring.

At 9:00 pm, Whisper woke up and was hungry. She fixed a bowl of oatmeal and some multi-grain toast, sat at her little table and turned on the radio. A local news program came on and the feature story was about Myles Carter, the rich philanthropist and his donations to the Texas communities of Lufkin, Jacksonville and Palestine. He'd evidently given away over a million dollars to hospitals, libraries and law enforcement in those towns.

Finishing with supper, Whisper heard a knock on the door. Opening the door, she found Molly standing there in some very high, black heels and a long coat, like a trench coat. Molly opened her coat a few inches and showed Whisper she wasn't wearing anything underneath.

"Certainly dressed for the occasion, aren't we?" Whisper said. Molly laughed.

"Do you think it's too obvious?" Molly opened her coat a little again.

"I think that's about what he's expecting."

Molly stepped in and asked, "When are you getting ready? It's almost time."

Whisper outstretched her arms and looked down at her flannels and socks. "This is it for the night. I'm not going."

"You have to! John Luke said he wouldn't do it unless we were both there."

"Oh, you just show up on his doorstep with that outfit on and I can guarantee you won't get turned away."

"C'mon Orange, it'll be a sure thing if you come with me. It'll be fun. He's got a huge cock! It'll be worth getting dressed just to see it."

"There's more to life than big dicks, Molly."

"Yeah? Like what? Well, maybe money. Big dicks and money."

"You're impossible. Go have a good time. Go on, now." Whisper gestured for her to get out.

Molly stood in the doorway, "I'll tell you all about it later."

"I'll see you tomorrow." She shut the door and leaned her back against it thinking of John Luke's big cock sliding into Molly and felt another ridiculous pang of jealousy.

Whisper got in bed, tightly shut the curtains and turned on a CD of relaxing Native American flute music so she wouldn't hear any of the noises coming from next door. She went to sleep.

Molly stood on John Luke's cabin porch and lightly knocked on the door. The door seemed to open by itself. The cabin was dark and Molly slowly stepped in calling John Luke's name. Suddenly a bright spotlight shown at her from the back room. It completely blinded her. "Where's the orange bitch?"

Molly was shielding her eyes with her hands, "She's not coming. She doesn't feel good."

There was a long pause. Molly thought John Luke was going to ask her to leave. "What did you bring me?" he finally asked.

Molly let her coat drop to the floor. She was really quite attractive. "I see," said John Luke.

He turned the light out and said, "Come here." Molly started feeling her way toward John Luke. Seeing she was struggling to find her way, he lit a candle. John Luke was lying on his back in the bed with his huge, hard cock slanted over to one side. Molly nearly lost her breath when she saw him.

Actually seeing his dick in the flesh nearly frightened her, not sure she'd be able to take it all. She kicked off her shoes and knelt by the bed, reaching out and grabbing his cock with both hands. "My God, John Luke."

She tried to put it in her mouth but could barely handle the tip of the head. John Luke showed no sign of enjoyment. He just stared a hole in her while she was working on him. After a minute, John Luke scooted over and told her to get on the bed. She laid down beside him, heart pounding so hard she thought it might burst.

John Luke got between her legs and was positioning himself to insert his huge cock when she said, "Don't hurt me."

John Luke's shoulders drooped and he looked up at the ceiling, expelling a deep breath. "Are you telling me how to fuck? Now you spoiled the moment!"

"I'm sorry, I just want you to be a careful. You know, go a little slow, be gentle."

"Now you're just trying to piss me off."

"No, John Luke, I'm a little scared. I've never had one so big and hard."

"Spread your legs and show me you still want it."

Molly spread for him and he started to put it in. The head inserted with no trouble but halfway down the shaft she realized taking all of it would be impossible. She put her hand on his chest and pushed back gently as an indication of being far enough.

He forced it in a little more and Molly cried out in pain. "John Luke, it's too much."

He tried to shove it in deeper but there was no way she could take another inch. The pain was excruciating. Molly pulled her knees up and put her feet on John Luke's chest and pushed hard, throwing him backwards, nearly off the bed.

"What the fuck?" he screamed not believing she really did that. Molly sat up in bed, wrapping her arms around her knees.

"I'm sorry I didn't mean to push you so hard but you were hurting me." She wasn't sure how he was going to respond.

The anger on his face quickly subsided and he said, "Maybe we can start over?"

"I'd like that." Molly started to relax. "How about I get on top? That way I can control how deep you go with that big beautiful dick of yours." She was trying to butter him up to keep his anger in check.

"Excellent idea. But you see there has been some damage here that needs repair." He was only half as hard as he was before.

"Oh, I think we can fix that."

John Luke laid down on his back and Molly got between his legs. She started fondling him and rubbing his balls. Then she ran her

tongue up and down the entire length of his shaft while gently twisting the head of his massive pole. In no time, his manhood was fully
engorged and throbbing.

"There," she said, quite proud of herself. Because he was so big, she
had to crawl way up on his chest to get in a position to start to put it
in. She was hoping he would encourage her to slide up a little further
and so he could kiss her between her legs but he showed no interest in
doing that. As a matter of fact, he showed no sense of wanting to give
pleasure during the whole episode.

She bent down and reached between her legs, getting it in the right
position. Her tits were inches from his mouth. She was hoping he
would nibble on her nipples. He laid there, staring at her but not paying any attention to her voluptuous breasts. She inserted the head and
worked it around in exaggerated undulating circles with her hips.

After each rotation, she slid down another half inch, gobbling up
his huge cock with her hungry, hot, pussy. With his cock inserted to
the maximum depth, she put her hands on his muscular chest and
pushed back, holding his big dick in her as far as it would go. It hurt,
but she could control the pain and wanted to give John Luke as much
as she could.

After a few bounces against his big cock, she looked up at him and
said, "That's it. That's as much as I can take."

John Luke, being tall and built like a bull, easily flipped her over
where he was on top. "Well, how about that," Molly said in a light-
hearted manner. John Luke still showed no emotion.

"You're going to take all of it," he said and started pounding it
into her. Molly knew at that moment she was trapped and was being
raped. There was nothing she could do about it. She tried to scream
but John Luke held his hand over her mouth. Molly bit his fingers
but he slapped her so hard she almost lost consciousness. He kept
pounding away.

She squirmed and kicked and tried to claw but he was so big and
powerful, taking exactly what he wanted. Molly prayed for it to be

over quickly before she was ripped open on the inside. After what Molly thought was forever, John Luke pulled out and shot a tiny load on her stomach. He smeared it around on her big tits and wiped his hand on her hair. Then he shoved her completely off the bed on to the floor, telling her to get out.

Molly slowly got up, grabbed her senseless high heeled shoes, limped to the living room and put on her coat. She walked out the door crying softly to herself, thinking how stupid could she possibly be.

Chapter 6

At 4:00 am, Whisper was in the restaurant, anxiously awaiting Molly's arrival. The place was crowded, as usual, and Whisper was doing double duty. In fifteen minutes, Big Al asked Whisper, "Where's Molly?"

"How should I know?" Whisper assumed Molly and John Luke went at it all night and her absence was to catch up on sleep.

A half hour later, Ross and Shelby came in for breakfast. "Hey guys," Whisper said as she handed them menus.

"Good morning Whisper," said Ross. Shelby responded nonverbally with a confused stare. Ross continued, "Okay, we know what the Big Breakfast is, do you have a Tiny Breakfast?"

Whisper laughed a little, "Tell me what you want and I'll get it."

"Two eggs over medium, hash browns and a slice of toast,"

"And Shelby, what can I get you?" Shelby was entranced and frozen. "I'll bring you something," said Whisper after a few seconds of silence. Ross and Whisper smiled at each other.

When Whisper was well away, Ross said, "Shelby, you've got to snap out of it. She's just a girl."

"Girls make me nervous, but an orange one really throws me off my game," was his reply.

"Like you got game, huh?" Ross chuckled not admitting he was nervous around her too.

Ross and Shelby ate their normal sized breakfasts and left to start their workday. Whisper was too busy to notice them leaving.

At midmorning, four middle-aged women came in to the otherwise empty restaurant. They were well-dressed and looked like upper-class locals. Whisper handed them menus and said, "I'll give you a few minutes."

As she was walking off, one of the ladies said, "See, I told you it was worth the trip over." Whisper felt sure they were talking about her, but it wasn't anything new. Everybody talked about her and this is why Big Al hired her, to attract those few customers that spent money needlessly just to get a look at the orange girl.

In a few minutes, Whisper went over to them and asked what they wanted. All of them studied her without trying to hide it. Whisper felt flushed although no one could tell and she fought back the urge to get angry. When the ladies were good and ready, they all asked for coffee. Whisper brought out a pot and placed it on the table. When she set down the pot she said, "Be very careful now, I touched the handle," and she walked to the condiment stand.

Whisper watched out of the corner of her eye as one lady wrapped the handle in a napkin before she picked up the pot and poured four cups of coffee. Whisper smiled watching them drink. About halfway finished with their coffee, Whisper went over and said, "Oh, sorry I forgot to tell you that I'm responsible for the set-ups and my yellow hands were all over those cups too." Whisper held her hands out over their table, yellow palms up and snapped the even brighter yellow nails of her thumb and middle finger together.

The ladies started mumbling and asked for the check. Whisper set it on the table and said, "I'll be your cashier."

The lady who brought them out to see the orange girl was frantically digging through her purse to find some cash. She didn't want Orange handling her credit card. Finally, she found her emergency twenty-dollar bill and laid it on the table by the check. "Keep the change." The lady didn't want to leave any tip, let alone one that large, but she sure didn't want to handle change soiled by the orange girl.

As they were leaving the restaurant, Whisper singled out the lady who appeared to be the most gullible of the bunch and said, "If you've already caught the orange disease, you'll know in a couple of weeks. It starts with the bottom of your feet. They'll turn yellow." Whisper held out her hands again, palms up. The lady ran out the door. Whisper laughed thinking about them checking the bottoms of their feet for the next several weeks. And, as a bonus, they'll probably never be back.

The lunch crowd was unusually large and there was no time for anything except serving the customers. It seemed Big Al was shouting instructions every few seconds.

At nearly 1:00 pm, John Luke strolled in wearing his overalls, t-shirt and distressed leather jacket. Whisper tingled thinking about what was between his legs. She hated herself for it but couldn't help it. *I'm getting more like Molly every day!* She didn't want to, but went over to wait on him.

As soon as she handed him a menu, he said, "We sure missed you last night. Where were you?"

"I got bored and went to sleep early."

John Luke laughed, "You just couldn't stand the thought of sharing. Since you weren't there, Good Golly Miss Molly got all of my attention. I think it was more than she could handle. She's not the woman you are, you know."

"What do you mean?"

John Luke leaned back in the booth so she could see his growing hard-on. "Let's just say she didn't take to it quite like you did."

Whisper was a little slow on the uptake but finally caught on, "What did you do to her?" John Luke just smiled and put his hands behind his head in repose.

Whisper went flying out of the restaurant toward Molly's cabin, winded by the time she reached the porch. Knocking on the door and hollering Molly's name produced no response. Whisper went to the windows and looked in but couldn't see anything. She went back and banged on the door again. After a long time, Whisper heard movement coming from within.

The door opened a sliver and Molly said, "What do you want?" Whisper tried to see through the inch-wide crack in the door but could only see a mass of matted hair hanging in front of Molly's face.

"John Luke was acting a little more strangely than usual and eluded to the fact there might have been a problem last night." Whisper waited for a response.

"*Might* have been a problem!" Molly slowly swung open the door and laid down on the couch wearing panties and a halter top. Whisper walked in trying to get her eyes to adjust to the dim light and when her pupils dilated, didn't like what she saw at all. Molly's face was bruised, her shoulders were bruised and there were even more bruises on her legs.

"Molly, what happened?" Whisper knew full well, John Luke is what happened.

Molly started to cry. Whisper sat on the edge of the couch and pushed the matted hair out of Molly's face. "Tell me what happened?"

Molly told the story without embellishing, not needing to exaggerate. John Luke's cock was too big for her and wouldn't take "no" for an answer. He did it anyway and finished by literally kicking her out of bed.

Whisper sat for a few minutes, unable to say anything, fuming, trying to formulate a plan for revenge. When nothing came to her, she jumped up and ran out the door headed for the restaurant not having a clue as to what she was going to do.

Whisper ran back to the restaurant, getting more and more furious with every step. She burst through the restaurant door and made a beeline to John Luke who was sitting in the booth with Big Al. Everyone stopped eating and fell silent waiting for what was to come next. The wait wasn't long, Whisper balled her fist, reared back and busted John Luke above his right eye.

Big Al tried to stop her but he couldn't get his giant frame out of the booth in time. John Luke punch her in the stomach from an awkward sitting position and she fell to the floor near the condiments. John Luke stood up looking like he wanted to hit her some more. Whisper had no breath left in her but she bounded up, grabbed a hot pot of decaf off the machine and was going to throw in on John Luke's crotch. Big Al managed to free himself from the booth and grabbed Whisper around the waist, picking her up. She flailed and kicked slinging hot coffee all over the floor. John Luke backed away.

Big Al said, "I think you better go John Luke." Whisper was still trying to get out of Big Al's grasp. John Luke turned to leave and Whisper threw the mostly empty pot hitting John Luke on the back of his leg. The pot bounced to the floor and shattered into a thousand pieces. John Luke paused for a moment, then walked out never turning around.

Whisper hadn't taken a breath in nearly a minute because of the punch in her bread basket and passed out right in Big Al's arms. Big Al put her in a booth with her head in her arms on the table. "Show's over!" he hollered to everyone else. Slowly, the patrons started eating again and talking amongst themselves.

Whisper finally took a breath and raised her head up looking around for John Luke. Big Al shoved a glass of water in front of her and took a seat on the opposite side of the booth. "You okay?" he asked.

"I think so. What happened? After I blacked out, I mean."

"What do you remember?"

Whisper thought for a moment then looked at the floor. "Well, I don't really remember but I must have done something with the coffee pot."

Big Al laughed. "Yeah, you did."

Whisper looked around the restaurant and everyone was glancing at her and quickly turning away. "Okay Al, was this good for business or bad?"

Big Al looked at the crowd's faces and saw nothing but dollar signs. "Definitely good. Lunch will be booming tomorrow."

"So, I still have a job?"

"Honey, you are the star."

"Since I've still got a job, I better clean this place up."

"Yeah you will. And I won't even ask what happened. I already know. John Luke stuck it in somebody and you didn't like it. And that somebody was probably Molly since she didn't show up for work today. Am I right?"

Whisper flashed her sky-blue eyes at him and slid out of the booth. Just another day at the Hill Top Hunting Lodge.

Chapter 7

The next morning, after all the hunters cleared out, a big black Range Rover pulled up to the restaurant and Myles Carter exited looking like an Abercrombie and Fitch advertisement. His long sinuous frame easily strode up the steps, two at a time. When he entered, Molly said to Whisper, "I've got this."

Whisper responded with, "You didn't learn a thing the other night, did you?" The comment fell on deaf ears as Molly moved forward with a menu and a pot of coffee in her hands to show Myles a seat.

"Welcome back Mister Carter," she said in a very professional manner.

"You weren't so formal last time."

"I may have been a little tacky before. Here's the best seat in the house." She sat him in a booth by the window, turned over a cup and filled it from the new coffee pot brought out of storage to replace the one Whisper broke. "What can I get you today, stud?"

Myles looked at the menu briefly and said, "I'm really hungry. Why don't you surprise me?"

Molly immediately interpreted that as meaning, *Let's fuck.* "Sure, Myles. I'll get you something that will satisfy you."

She returned to where Whisper was standing and handed Big Al an order for the Big Breakfast. "I'm pretty sure he's still flirting with me," Molly said.

Whisper looked doubtful, "What makes you say that?"

"He said it was up to me to satisfy him."

Whisper rolled her eyes, "He said those exact words?"

"No, of course not, he's got too much class to do that."

Whisper asked, "What were his actual words?"

"He said, 'I'm really hungry. Why don't you surprise me?'"

Whisper laughed. "Oh, and that's flirting?"

"Well, it wasn't *not* flirting."

The door opened. Ross and Shelby entered. Ross gave a slight wave to Whisper and Shelby stared.

Molly quickly said, "You can take the Texas Ranger and his side-kick Robin Ranger."

Whisper smirked a bit and headed to the guys with menus and a pot. "Good morning, boys."

Ross said, "Hello Whisper, good to see you again." Shelby stared. Whisper stared right back at him and tapped her foot. Finally, his trance was broken and he said, "Can I have a Big Breakfast again?"

"Sure, and for you Doctor Evans?"

"I'll take two eggs over medium, hash browns, toast and this coffee."

"You got it." Whisper turned to deliver the order.

"And......", said Ross.

Whisper turned back around.

"And I'd like to know if you would like to go out with me in the morning?"

"You mean 'go out' like a date?"

"Ah, well, yes and no. I guess I'm not saying this very clearly."

"No shit, Doc," Shelby said under his breath.

"I'm going out across the lake in the morning in a canoe and I was wondering if you wanted to go out with me?"

"I can't tomorrow morning, I work. But I'm off on Mondays."

"Okay then, we'll go out on the lake Monday morning."

Whisper looked at him and said, "Monday is my only day off and I get up at 3:30 every morning. Just how early do you want to start this little lake adventure?"

"You tell me."

"How about six?"

"Dress warmly. The only thing I've seen you in is a mini skirt and thin long sleeve flimsy shirt. The air on the lake is ten degrees colder than it is here and there's nothing to block the wind."

Whisper smiled and said sarcastically, "You're making this sound as fun as a barrel of monkeys."

"What? Freezing your butt off while I take water samples and try to catch a perch and a crappie for the ichthyologist doesn't sound like a great date?"

"So, it's a date?"

Ross blushed, "I would really like for it *not* to be a date. I don't want to be remembered as the worst first date you've ever been on. I mean, early morning wake-up, a turn-off for most women I know. A canoe ride on a freezing lake and spellbinding subject matter such as lake algae, pond scum and fish diseases."

"Wow, you're right. This better not be a date. I'll see you at six."

Ross and Shelby finished their breakfasts and went to do their work. Myles Carter finished half of his breakfast and barely managed to escape out the front door without Molly dragging him into the store room.

"Damn, I let him get away," Molly confessed to Whisper.

"Well, it wasn't from lack of trying."

When the morning lull rolled around, Whisper and Molly were sitting in the booth with Big Al. They had polite conversation but the underlying question on each of their minds was what was going to happen when John Luke walked in.

Molly was thinking she should act like nothing happened because she was a slut and deserved what she got. Whisper was mentally gauging how fast she could get out of the booth, grab the freshly made coffee in the new pot and deliver it with a high degree of accuracy to John Luke's sausage and biscuits. Big Al was conflicted with the thought of letting the brawl play out or somehow trying to make peace.

John Luke didn't take his morning break in the restaurant. Such an anti-climax. Instead, he was delivering "meat" to the hunter's heavyset wife in Cabin number 2. She was large, five foot eleven inches tall and weighed out at 275 pounds. She paid him $150 for the service and she wanted her money's worth.

John Luke pounded her until they both had orgasms. The big lady could take every inch of what John Luke had to offer. Her orgasm was first, thank goodness, because if he came first, he wouldn't have cared enough to finish her. John Luke wanted to do just enough to get the money and get away from the cow. However, to John Luke's surprise, the cow wasn't done! She said she paid good money for a service and wanted to be serviced thoroughly.

Try as he might, John Luke couldn't get himself up again. Not knowing John Luke's true nature, the woman took the nurturing route and said, "Come here, Sugar. Let Momma help with that," She started tenderly working him with her hands and mouth. There probably wasn't a twenty-something male on the planet that wouldn't have gotten erect again after receiving such attention, but John Luke didn't. He found her so revolting he loathed himself for stooping so low as to let her even touch his precious cock.

As she was manipulating him with her mouth and tongue, he contracted his pelvic muscles as hard as he could and shot an immense stream of urine down her throat. She choked, coughed and pulled away as he continued to piss on her face. She rolled away in disgust and shame, covering her head with a pillow.

John Luke grabbed the $150 off the night stand, opened her purse and took all the cash he could find, put on his clothes and walked out saying, "You don't know how lucky you are to have had my cock, you fucking fat cow."

Chapter 8

Ross was standing in the middle of the complex when Whisper bounded out of her cabin at exactly six in the morning. She was wearing jeans, brown knock-off UGG boots, a thin white work blouse, a crazy looking paisley button-up vest and a light wind-breaker jacket. She ran over to him and said. "Ready for action."

"I don't think so," Ross responded. "Wait here." He ran back into his cabin and came out with an army field jacket with liner, an army watch cap and a pair of army gloves. He handed the items to her. "Put these on."

The field jacket swallowed her up and the gloves were several sizes too big but the watch cap fit snugly on her head. "Now you're ready for action." Properly attired for lake canoeing, although dressed in the fashion category of 'I wouldn't be caught dead looking like this in public'. They started walking down the trail behind the cabins leading to the lake.

In the five years Whisper worked at Hill Top Hunting Lodge, she never went to the lake. It was about a mile walk and she was generally exhausted after work and never took the time. Whisper was surprised to see how large the lake was and the quality of the marina. Ten boat slips altogether. Eight slips moored bass boats of varying size and cost and one slip had a row boat. The last slip was occupied with a large canoe.

There were several boxes of gear and a fishing pole in rear of the canoe. On the center seat were three large pump coffee containers, two thermal travel mugs, a pint carton of heavy cream and a small metal container holding sweeteners and sugar packets obviously appropriated from the restaurant.

"You didn't tell me there was going to be a coffee bar."

"Well, one of the containers has hot chocolate, then regular and decaf of course, because I didn't know what you drank in the mornings." She was making some kind of face that he was hoping was her 'appreciation' face but it could have been her 'he's and idiot' face. "Alright, let's get aboard. I need you to sit up front and I'll be in the back."

She got in while he held the canoe steady and then he sat down pushing away from the pier with the paddle. They gently and silently glided out onto the water. Whisper was thrilled with the feeling, turning in her seat to gaze at him. Ross studied her face and interpreted her countenance as some kind of satisfaction. They stared at each other for a moment then Ross broke the spell, "I hate to be all official and I am loath to say these words but we have to put on orange hunter vests and life jackets which also happen to be orange."

"Really?" she said, halfway joking, he hoped. Ross pitched her a vest and a life jacket. They donned their safety equipment and set off across the lake. As Ross paddled, he described the shape of the lake. It was like a hand, a large flat area, being the palm and four fingers and thumb of narrow water extending from the palm. His mission was to test water in each finger and he already took samples from to the two south fingers. Today, they would go to the middle finger.

"So, is the coffee bar open?"

"By all means, help yourself."

Whisper carefully slid to the center of the canoe and began pumping a thermal mug full of regular coffee. She set it aside and ask him what he wanted. "Hot chocolate today. Something different."

She pumped a mug full and leaned forward handing it to him. Back on her seat facing him, she sipped on the hot, strong coffee. Ross sipped his chocolate. Finally, she said, "It seems to taste a little better out here."

"I agree."

Ross continued slowly paddling across the still lake. There was no hurry. Plus, he didn't want his time with Whisper to end too quickly. After some silence and a half dozen strokes Whisper asked, "Can I help you paddle?"

"No, I've got this."

"What do I do then? Just sit here and look….."

"Pretty," Ross finished her sentence.

"Well, no. What I was going to say was sit here and look very orange."

Ross smiled, "Never crossed my mind."

After another moment of silence and several sideways glances at each other Whisper said, "I know nothing about you."

Ross started his story. He graduated high school not 50 miles from where they were. At eighteen, he joined the army. One tour of Iraq was cut short by a mortar attack. He was in a forward operating base when the attack came and he wasn't wearing his body armor and a resulting fuel fire severely burned his back. He was medically discharged from the army after only two years. Half a year spent training, half a year in Iraq and one year in the hospital. Armed with a purple heart, 40% disability and government educational benefits, he started college at Texas A & M, going straight through to include veterinarian school.

"A short ten years later and here we are. After Iraq, I decided I'd rather work in a field where I didn't need to interact with other humans too much. Crowds of people get to me. Okay, how about you?"

"Simple," Whisper said. "Born orange. Nobody wanted me. Ran away from Belmont School for Wayward Girls and Big Al found me. I've been the main attraction at Hill Top Hunting Lodge for the last five years. I have no idea where I'm going or what I want to do. I just live day to day."

"You're young. An epiphany will come to you at the strangest time."

"You think there is something out there for me?"

"Sure. Just keep your eyes open so you don't miss the opportunity. Okay, here we go." Ross started down the entrance of the third finger. It was very narrow with over hanging branches. They ducked and pulled on the branches until they burst through the other side into a long wide canal that could easily pass as a lake by itself.

"Water looks nice and clear. This must be the finger with the spring." Ross reached in a backpack and pulled out a glass sample jar and scooped up some of the water, labeled the jar and put it back in his pack. I want to go all the way to the end to make sure a lot of trash hasn't accumulated."

Ross continued to paddle while Whisper took it all in. Whisper was never an outdoor kind of girl but was thinking she could be with the right encouragement. She involuntarily smiled at Ross. They reached the end only to find one twenty-ounce Styrofoam cup floating near the bank. Ross snatched it out of the water and put it in the bottom of the boat. "Good, no trash." Ross was not known to be the best conversationalist but there was enough non-verbal communication between them to fill the air with a palpable tension.

Ross took a couple of hard, long strokes with the paddle and ran the boat up on the bank. "Can you get out without getting wet?"

Whisper looked down and saw solid ground. "Yes, I can."

"How about jumping out and pulling the boat up about a foot."

She complied and Ross proceeded to get out with his pack. They discarded their life jackets but continued to wear their hunting vests. "This trail leads to a large hunting cabin, formerly the main house for the family who originally owned this land. They built the home near the spring. Of course, that was before the roads were surveyed on the higher ground where the lodge is now."

"I have to say I'm a little embarrassed. I've been here five years and have never been to the lake, let alone know anything about the history. You've been here, what? Three days and you're already canoeing on the lake and hiking the trail to the original homestead, taking water samples and plucking trash from the water."

"Oh, and don't forget that I picked up about a pound of deer dung yesterday. "

"My hero," was all she said as they started walking down the trail.

A half mile into the thick woods, they found the cabin. It was an old brown stone structure that looked very much like the Hansel and Gretel gingerbread house. They both agreed it looked creepy. Ross went right up on the porch to the front door and turned the knob but it was locked. He looked under the ragged welcome mat, under a very dead potted plant and above the door jamb but didn't find a key.

Ross said, "It doesn't look like anyone is using it right now. Which is surprising since this is the start of deer season and Big Al could rent this out for hundreds of dollars a night. Just think of the advertising. Hike to the lake, take a boat to the spring, hike to the original pioneer home and hunting. What an experience for a city slicker."

Whisper said, "In my five years at the lodge I've discovered that the easier it is to kill a deer the better the guys like it. More time to drink beer and be assholes."

"Maybe Big Al could advertise it so the hunter knows he can shoot a deer right off the back porch and he doesn't even have to get dressed to do it. Speaking of the back porch, let's see what's back there."

They walked around behind the house and saw a magnificent covered porch with half a dozen rocking chairs in a row. "There you go," Ross said. "Spit and whittle, drink, rock and shoot. A money maker if I ever saw one." Whisper rolled her eyes.

They walked around the structure while Ross looked for signs of animals…tracks, scat, hair, bones and as circumstance would have it, the animal itself. Not thirty yards into the woods, they saw a feral hog. One of the millions of them in Texas. It wasn't a hogzilla but it wasn't a small one either. The animal appeared to weigh between 250 and 300 pounds. Whisper was a little off-put by its size. She was not used to seeing a wild animal twice as big as she was with tusks four inches long. "What do we do?" she asked ready to make a run for it.

"We just amble on back to the boat."

"Does amble mean we run as fast as we can?" she said only half joking.

"No, we just stroll. He won't bother us unless we get in his face and he has no place to escape. Then he'll gore us from now until next Tuesday and maybe eat us too. They'll eat just about anything."

"Enough of the color commentary. Let's amble on out of here."

Back at the boat, they donned their life jackets and paddled out into the spring water. "Can you imagine what this place was like a hundred and fifty years ago?" Ross asked almost rhetorically.

"You mean paddling around in canoes, walking down isolated trails in the woods and confronting giant wild animals?"

"Yeah, just about like that I suppose." Whisper pumped them each another hot beverage and they paddled silently back to the marina.

Chapter 9

They walked back to the lodge in relative silence. Whisper gave Ross his coat, gloves and watch cap. "Now what?" she asked as she ran her hand through her hair.

"I didn't think past this point. I'm not sure what to do next."

"On most dates, it would be a dinner and a movie then the question of your place or mine. We just replaced a dinner and a movie with coffee and a canoe ride but I think we're still down to your place or mine."

Ross hesitated for a moment while that sunk in, then he said, "Shelby is asleep in my cabin."

"Well, I guess it's my place then." She grabbed him by the arm and led him down to her cabin. He was still holding the coat, gloves and hat. "Are you sure you want to do this?" he asked.

"Listen. If we don't do it now, we may never get another chance. You'll be assigned to some other area of Texas with new opportunities to pick up dung and meet other girls and I'll be forgotten. Better strike while the iron is hot. You do want to, don't you?"

"Of course, I do," Ross said as she opened her cabin door and led him in. He dropped the coat, gloves and hat on the couch and she literally jumped on him, wrapping her legs around him as he carried her to the bedroom. By the time they got there, she could feel he was already hard.

They kissed passionately on the bed for a few seconds before frantically beginning to strip. The process seemed to take forever. Boots and shoes with what appeared to be way too many laces, shirts, undershirts, bra, long pants, and socks were all discarded unceremoniously on the floor. Finally, down to the underwear.

They paused, sizing each other up. Whisper was doing it literally, staring at the impressive bulge in his Duluth boxers and mentally counting the inches. She shook her head trying to snap out of her trance and raised her eyes to his. He was staring at her beautiful, small orange breasts with very hard elongated blood orange red nipples poking out. Then he raised his eyes to hers. She almost melted. Her knees actually got weak. Then she thought, *just go with it.*

Her knees continued to fail as she went down to the floor in front of him. She reached out and grabbed his hips to steady herself, her face just a breath away from what was hidden in his shorts. She could smell the mustiness of what could only be considered the essence of a man.

Very rarely was she ever at a loss for what to do in any given situation but she just froze, trembling. Ross wasn't a whole lot better but he did take her hands and wrap her fingers inside the top elastic band of his shorts and she slowly started to pull them down, pausing for a deep breath and then continued to slide his underwear down in slow motion as if she were afraid of what was in them.

His long stiff cock made it difficult for her to maneuver the shorts down to his feet so he could step out of them. When she raised up, his cock was next to her cheek. While it was still in his shorts, she mentally measured eight inches. But now that it was loosed...something bigger. Not as big as John Luke's but big. *Dammit!* She told herself she wasn't going to make comparisons because, number one: she hated John Luke, two: nobody was going to be bigger than John Luke and three: she wanted to be the kind of girl where it didn't matter. Guys were born with what they had, she of all people understood that.

She instinctively reached up with both hands, cupping his big balls with one and grabbing the middle of the shaft with the other. His balls felt remarkably warm. His cock was hard as a fence post. Unable to wrap her fingers all the way around it, she touched the head to her lips. In contrast to the shaft, the head felt soft, like velvet. It pulsed in her hand causing a slight momentary swell of the head against her lips. A bead of anticipatory nectar appeared at the tip. She stuck out her tongue, looked up at him with her sky-blue eyes and licked the juice from the head.

That was all he could take. He picked her up, nearly threw her on the bed, literally ripped off her only pair of Victoria Secret panties and fell into her like they had practiced the maneuver many times before. It was way too easy and comfortable.

She was afraid he would cum too quickly because he seemed to be, let's just say, extremely excited. Whisper had an orgasm almost immediately and two more before he had his. He never lost his erection and seemed as hungry for a second one as he was for the first, but this time he was slower and more thorough. She came half a dozen times before he could tell she was wearing out. After the last one she said, "I don't think I can cum anymore."

"Then I guess it's my turn," and almost on cue, he had one second enormous orgasm before he rolled to her side. She held his cock as he lay there and it throbbed for a good five minutes before he settled down and he lost his hard on.

They fell asleep momentarily until Whisper snorted. Ross chuckled as he got up to get dressed. "Unlike you, I'm supposed to be working today so I better get going. Shelby will be wondering where I am." As he stood, she got a good look at the scars on his back. *God that must have hurt*, she thought.

After dressing, he turned to see her sitting up, entangled in a mess of covers, her yellow hair going in every direction. Ross smiled. "I've got to go."

"What? Can't stand to be around this gorgeousness?" She ran her hands through her matted hair.

Ross smiled again. "I've really got to go now or I'll never get out of here." He walked to the front door.

'Wait." She sprang out of bed, completely naked, ran to him and full body hugged him, wrapping one leg around his. She could feel him press into her. They kissed, deeply. His manhood swelled, again.

He pushed her away and said, "If you get me going again, I'll never get any work done today."

"So," she said looking very coy.

"Sooo, it was great." He quickly opened the door and stepped out on the porch. "I've really got to go."

"You owe me a new pair of panties by the way."

"Sorry I ripped them but it was a small price to pay, right? But I will buy you another pair. I promise."

"When?" she asked.

"Soon." Backing away and staring at her naked in the open door, he stumbled off the first step making her laugh.

Chapter 10

At zero dark thirty Tuesday morning, Molly and Whisper opened the restaurant. Big Al followed shortly. They made coffee and sat at the back booth sharing small talk initially. Then conversation got around to what Whisper did on her day off. Whisper told them her time was spent in bed and reading a book which wasn't really a lie.

In a few minutes two hunters came in wearing camouflage and carrying scoped rifles. They were large men with giant bellies. Molly easily sold them a couple of Big Breakfasts with additional coffee to go and a spare carafe of orange juice so 'they would have the nourishment to successfully hunt that ten-point buck they'd been dreaming about'. She sat beside the largest man, squeezed his massive thigh and convinced him he needed to order a couple of sandwiches for later in case they got hungry out on the deer stand. Afterall, hunting was hard work, squeezing high on his thigh once more when she said the word "hard". By the time she finished with them, they gave her a hundred-dollar bill and didn't ask for any change. Whisper just shook her head.

Three more younger hunters came in wearing camo and carrying rifles. Whisper waited on them. All they wanted was *one* order of avocado toast and coffee. *Who splits avocado toast three ways?* The bill was $11.18. They left $12.00 on the table.

Ross and Shelby entered next. Ross wearing his uniform and Shelby wearing jeans and a dirty, nondescript, grey sweatshirt. "Well if it isn't the Texas Ranger and his sidekick, Robin Ranger" Molly said to Whisper.

Whisper went over to wait on them. "What'll it be boys?"

"Oatmeal, toast and coffee for me and a Big Breakfast for Shelby, please."

Whisper was writing down the order on a little pad. "What's on the agenda today?" she asked.

Ross said. "We're going down to the lake to catch some fish for examination. I should have done this yesterday but I got sidetracked."

"Oh." Was all she said as she flashed her big blues at him over the note pad and walked off to hand in the order.

Shelby, still half asleep asked, "So, we're going fishing today?"

"Yep, we're going fishing." Ross couldn't keep his eyes off the beautiful orange girl as she glided across the room.

Finished eating, Whisper brought them the check. The breakfast rush was raging so she couldn't visit like she wanted. The state boys left money on the table (25% tip) and quietly exited the restaurant to do what Shelby described as 'fucking fishing when it's this cold and so damn early in the morning'. Ross had doubts about Shelby's future success in his chosen field.

During the between meal lull, Big Al and the girls were sitting in their booth waiting for the lunch crowd to start filtering in when Molly asked if anyone had seen John Luke. Considering the way he treated the girls and the ass kicking Whisper gave him, they decided he was just laying low. Big Al was giving him work orders which were getting completed. Big Al pinned the paper work orders on the bulletin board in the office and John Luke was sneaking in and getting them. No one had actually seen John Luke in two days. Both Molly and Whisper decided his absence was for the best and never gave it another thought.

The first two early lunch customers timidly entered the restaurant. Both were attractive housewife types in their mid-forties. MILF's as John Luke would call them. Molly had no interest in waiting on them so she gave Whisper the nod. Whisper didn't really want to wait on them either but she got up and put on her pleasant face. "What can I get for you ladies?" she asked. They both stared at her like she wasn't really a person. "Ladies?" she said as she snapped her fingers.

"Oh, um, we don't want anything to eat. We're looking for someone."

"Does this someone have a name?" They fell back into their trance and stared again. "A description of some kind....white, black, tall, short, man, woman, transvestite, maybe someone orange?" They just stared. "Oh, for Christ's sake ladies."

"Come on Beverly, let's go. I don't see him here."

"Oh shit. You're looking for John Luke aren't you?" Whisper was smiling.

"Yeah, you know him?"

"Of course, I know him. There are only four of us who work here full time."

The ladies were waiting for some more details but Whisper offered nothing.

"Is he here today?" the more attractive one asked.

"We were just talking about him. None of us have seen him for two days but we know he's around because Big Al says the work keeps getting done. Do you want me to tell him something if I see him? It'll be no bother. I've still got some things I'd like to talk to him about myself."

The most outspoken lady gave a little cough and said, "Probably not about the same thing we want to talk to him about." They giggled in their grownup sophisticated way, kind of like an adult talking to a child.

"Okay, I'll tell him when I see him," said Whisper as she turned to walk off.

"Tell him what, exactly?"

Whisper smiled, "That you came by to pay him to have sex with you. Isn't that why you're here? I mean, that's all he's been talking about, a couple of older, whore housewives who pay him because they can't get it any other way. Can I bring you some water or something?"

The women frantically grabbed their purses and ran out the door. Whisper sat down by Molly and said, "I guess I blew that tip."

"What did they say to you?" asked Big Al.

"Well, I think it was mostly what I said to them. But what they wanted was John Luke."

Molly burst out, "What do you mean 'wanted John Luke'? Wanted him for what?"

"Molly, don't be dumb," Whisper said. "They wanted to pay him for sex."

"Fucking bitches." Molly crossed her arms in front of her.

"Why do you care after he treated you like he did? He's a piece of shit."

"I can't help myself. I know he's a piece of shit but I still feel like he's my turd."

More legitimate customers started coming in and the girls got busy doing their thing. Foremost on Molly's mind all afternoon was *Where was John Luke and who was he with?*

Whisper, on the other hand, was thinking, *I hope Ross gets here before I get off work.* She wasn't wearing any panties and wanted to give him a hard time (more ways than one) about ripping up her only pair of sexy underwear.

After the lunch rush, Molly, Big Al and Whisper sat in the booth drinking tea. Molly was counting her tips which were plentiful. Whisper didn't have such a problem. Big Al asked, "Anyone see or hear from John Luke? I know he's around but I can't catch up with him."

"Do you really want to find him?" asked Whisper.

"I'd like to lay eyes on him to make sure he's not getting himself or me into trouble."

As soon as one of the evening college waitresses walked in, Whisper got up and said. "I've had it. I'm going to watch the sunset, then go to my cabin and read, sleep and repeat." Whisper walked out on the veranda and sat in one of the iron chairs. It was cooler than she wished and knew staying outside long enough to watch the sun go all the way down might not be feasible. She got goose bumps and her nipples turned to stone. They almost hurt. Then she saw Ross and Shelby walk into the compound carrying a crap-ton of fishing gear. She got goose bumps again.

The boys threw the gear down on the porch. Shelby started walking towards the restaurant and Ross went into the cabin. Whisper went down the stairs at the back of the veranda and met Shelby in the parking lot. "How was the fishing?" she asked.

"It was cold as fuck but we caught what Doctor Evans needed I suppose. It took all day especially when we had to drive into Tyler for lunch."

"Tyler? Why did you have to go there for lunch?"

Shelby scratched his head, "I don't really know what he did. He dropped me off at a mall and told me he'd pick me up there in an hour. I just ate mall food."

"Okay, I'm off work now. I'm going to my cabin."

Shelby said, "I'm still hungry. I told Doctor Evans I was going to eat before I did anything."

They went their separate ways, but instead of going to her cabin, she went to Ross's cabin where a pile of fishing rods and minnow buckers adorned the porch. She knocked on the door.

"Just a sec!" Ross yelled from deep in the cabin. Whisper waited patiently.

In a moment, the door knob turned and Ross peaked out. "Well, I didn't expect to see you. I thought Shelby changed his mind or forgot his key."

The door was barely cracked open. "Are you going to invite me in?"

He slowly swung the door open and said, "I just got through rinsing off." He was wearing a towel. Whisper stepped in, closed and locked the door behind her.

"And how was your day? She asked playfully.

"Productive and I got you something."

Something from Tyler I'll bet," she said.

"Damn. There are no secrets here are there?" Ross bent over and picked up a pink sack off the couch. "I didn't know what size you wore so I guessed." He handed the sack to Whisper.

She rifled through the pink paper and came out with a pair of red lace panties.

"I hope it fits," he said.

"It's perfect." She threw it on the floor, snatched his towel off, dropped it on the floor beside the panties and wrapped her arms around him. They began kissing and instantly felt him start to grow. Ross picked her up and carried her to the bed. He was about to get on top of her when she stopped him. "I've been working all day. Can I rinse off too?"

He made a groaning sound and said, "Sure, but hurry." Whisper jumped up, shucked off her clothes all the way to the shower, soaped and rinsed really quickly, in record time for her. Returning to the bedroom, she saw Ross naked, lying on the bed with his ankles crossed and huge cock poking straight up into the air. His torso was ten inches thick and his dick had to be ten inches long so the tip of that beautiful prick was flailing around at twenty inches above the bed.

If her body was not aching in every imaginable way, she would have paused to take in the view, but she was hungry, more like ravenous. She stepped up on the bed, stood straddling him with that big spear beneath her, right between her legs. She licked the palm of her hand, spread her shiny yellow pubic hair and rubbed her saliva on her engorged blood-red pussy lips. She slowly bent her knees until the head of his cock touched her pussy. Only half the large head inside her, she held there for moment, knees still bent and shaking with strain and anticipation.

Ross reached up and grabbed the slats in the old wooden headboard. His chest and arm muscles looked ripped. Whisper could feel him start to thrust his hips upward trying desperately to insert more of his large cock. Ross's world just shrank to two things: his dick and her cunt. There was nothing else. He closed his eyes inwardly pleading for her to give him more.

Whisper also urgently needed to feel him deep inside of her but was still in control enough to want him to beg for it. She knew he wouldn't beg verbally and didn't want him to. She wanted him to beg physically, coaxing her into submission with kisses, caresses and slow strokes of that wonderful large cock.

Whisper put her hands on her knees to help hold herself up. She was crouched over him with the tip of his dick still in her. As she got more wet, she began rotating her hips in a deliberate fashion like twerking but in slow motion. After several rotations she would lower herself and inch, eating up his dick with her pussy ever so slowly. Ross was about to cry out in a wonderful kind of aggravation.

He was tensing every muscle and pulled hard on the headboard. Whisper was half way down on his shaft, still ringing out his dick like a wet towel. Ross groaned from the immense sensation. He was trying not to cum. He strained against the headboard and the slat in his right hand snapped off with a loud bang. Ross let out a yelp of irritation, threw the piece of slat across the room and grabbed another slat with which he would vent his frustration.

Whisper was tiring out. A few more rotations and she would be on top of him with all his inches up in her. A twist, another turn, a final thrust and she was all the way down, sitting on him like squatting on a very short stool, except impaled with a large but friendly pike. Clit, at last, digging it into the pubic area at the base of his cock.

Ross let go of the headboard and grabbed her ankles. She wasn't sure what was going to happen next. "If you don't stop moving, I'm going to cum." Ross locked into her eyes.

She said, "Isn't that the point," and he exploded, thrusting his hips a foot off the bed, lifting her like she was nothing, feeling his dick swell in her with each squirt of cum. He raised her high into the air every time he shot another stream. She rocked back and forth like riding a bareback bronc to keep from falling off. After he finished the actual ejaculation, he still continued to thrust her up into the air in a rhythm. His juice was running down her thighs.

Finally, he settled down with her still riding him. Although his cock wasn't as hungry, it was hard enough to be useful. If she hadn't known he just came and seen his dick in this state, she would have thought it was his normal hard on.

Ross lay there breathing quickly trying to recover, jerking violently every time Whisper gyrated on the tip of his supersensitive cock. She continued to press her clit into him grinding it with the full pressure of her weight. She swirled around on him for a few minutes before she righteously began to fuck him for her own pleasure. Ross was at her mercy, floundering like a fish out of water. She bounced and thrusted and twisted and slammed her body down on his when she began to cum, falling on his chest with her yellow hair tickling in his face. She shuddered and moaned and cried a little as she came. Finished and becoming aware of Ross's movements, she noted he was again rock hard and starting to move inside her.

Without saying a word, Ross flipped her over and he was on top in a maneuver that took less than a half a second, Whisper was impressed. He began slow, deep thrusts, using every inch of his manhood. All the way in and all the way out. Every time he pumped, he extracted and reinserted every inch of his massive cock into her. They were so slick from all the fuck juice that it was easy. He did that for number of strokes then laid on top of her, keeping his cock all the way up inside and grinding. She thought his dick was going to come out of her mouth. He was pushing the base of his cock right into her clit and she knew she wouldn't last very long.

It was building and growing and building until Whisper said, "I'm cumming."

As soon as Whisper started to scream, Ross raised to his knees and pushed into her as hard as he could. Her hand went to her clit like lightening to enhance her orgasm. She strained so hard, she peed a little. When she was done and went limp, Ross pulled out and stroked the head of his big dick, He squirted another load right between her blood orange erect nipples and on her flat tummy. Milked dry, Ross stuck his cock back in her and pumped for a few dozen strokes until she came a little more. Exhausted, he fell over on the bed beside her.

They stared at the ceiling, catching themselves glancing at each other, wide-eyed. Finally Whisper said, "That might have been embarrassing if it wasn't so good." She reached over and held his sticky cock. It was still swollen but not hard.

"I think you're a little bit messy," an observation from Ross.

Whisper just responded with "Uh-Huh" as she drifted off to sleep.

Ross got up and went to the sink, soaked a hand towel in warm water and tried to give Whisper a crude sponge bath. He took a shower, put on his fishing clothes, left Whisper a note on the night stand and went to the restaurant.

The note read:

GONE TO THE RESTAURANT TO DELAY SHELBY. I'LL MAKE HIM PUT THE FISHING GEAR AWAY FIRST SO YOU SHOULD HEAR HIM BANGING AROUND ON THE PORCH BEFORE HE COMES IN. GOOD LUCK ON YOUR ESCAPE...OR SAY HELLO TO SHELBY FOR ME WHEN HE WALKS IN. R.

Chapter 11

Whisper immediately woke up, aware of someone walking on her porch. She saw herself naked, realizing this was Ross's cabin. *I hope it's Ross.* Then she saw the note. "Oh my God."

She threw her clothes on, grabbed the note and picked up her precious new, red lace panties. Cracking open the door, Shelby was seen loading the fishing equipment into the back of the big state truck. "Now or never," she said to herself, as she bolted out into the chilly night air, ran down the steps and around beside the cabin. Hiding at the corner, she watched Shelby work and mumble to himself. It was starting to get really cold and wished the dude would work a little faster. But it was Shelby and work ethic didn't mean a whole lot to him.

Holding herself in her arms and marching in place trying to keep the blood circulating, she thought about Ross tearing off the headboard slat and giggled to herself momentarily sending the cold to a distant place. Shelby made a third trip to the vehicle, this time carrying the heavy buckets. She knew he would go inside after this trip and could escape to her own cabin. Shelby closed the front door of the vehicle and locked it. Whisper heard something in the woods. It startled her. Shelby climbed up on the porch and unlocked the door. Whisper heard the noise again and thought it might be one of those giant wild pigs they saw yesterday. When she heard Shelby turn the shower on in the cabin, she flew around the corner and made a bee-line to her cabin shaking from the cold and the fear of nearly being eaten by a giant pig. Okay, the fear of maybe almost seeing a big pig.

As Shelby entered the cabin, he wondered why a towel was on the floor in the middle of the living room. Ross's bedroom door was open and he glanced in. It looked like a bomb went off somewhere near the bed. Shelby went to the bathroom and showered never giving it another thought.

Ross ate a leisurely supper with a grand smile on his face. Even the college girl waitress commented on his good humor that evening. He hoped Whisper managed to flee without incident. There was really no reason to keep their relationship a secret except for the ribbing Whisper might receive. Ross took the last bite of his chicken fried steak and paid the bill.

Back at the cabin, Ross saw Shelby in his bed with a laptop balanced on his stomach, ear phones on and a controller in his hand. Ross felt sure he would kill zombies until at least two in the morning. Ross picked up the towel out of the middle of the floor and threw it in the pile of used linen in the bathroom. The housekeeper was due to come in every third day and tomorrow was that day.

Ross shucked off his smelly fishing clothes, took another shower and went to bed early to read. The sheets were still damp from the sex fest they had earlier and he couldn't get comfortable. Not because of the messy sheets but because of who made them such a mess and how. He started to get excited again.

Ross began thinking he might want to masturbate. Strangely enough, Whisper was lying in her bed thinking the exact same thing. Shelby bumped around in his bedroom and Ross heard the bathroom door close. The thought of Shelby taking a crap in the next room ended any urge to get relief. Whisper on the other hand heard a sound. It was faint, but distinct and not far outside her bedroom window. *A giant pig!* She now, too, lost all desire for relief.

Whisper went to the window and looked out, thinking the giant pig stalked her down to her cabin. She didn't see anything. Opening the front door and looking out at the large parking lot garnered no new information. Most of the cabins had trucks parked in front of them with a few other vehicles scattered around elsewhere. She walked out on the porch to the corner and looked towards the woods between her cabin and John Luke's cabin, imagining what a giant pig would look like in the dark. No matter how much her imagination suggested it, a giant pig could not be seen roaming around. But suddenly, she heard the noise again. Definitely something walking. Her first instinct was to run to Ross but she stood her ground, back against the wall, peeking around the corner.

There it was! *Oh my God!* It was John Luke coming out of the woods, walking to the gap right between her cabin and his. She stood perfectly still trying to make herself small and invisible. John Luke walked past her, silently climbed up on his porch and went into his cabin. She breathed out a long breath and scurried into her own bedroom, jumped in the bed and pulled the covers up. *What was John Luke doing roaming around in the woods behind the cabins in the dark.*

Ready for work at four the next morning, she was a little afraid to go out of her cabin. It was cold and dark and besides giant pigs, now John Luke could be skulking around in the blackness. She opened her door, looked both ways and stepped out. She quickly shut her door and jogged out into the middle of the parking lot, away from the woods and John Luke's cabin. She looked at Ross's cabin and all was dark. He was still asleep. *Poor boy, must be exhausted.* She laughed a little as she nearly skipped her way to the restaurant.

Big Al and Molly were in the corner booth as usual. Whisper was coming in a few minutes late as usual too. As soon as she entered Big

Al told her to put her name tag on. He never looked up from his plate of biscuits and gravy.

"How the hell did you know I wasn't wearing my name tag?"

"I'm psychic," Big Al said as he stuffed a half a biscuit, sopped with gravy into his mouth.

"Well, if you're so psychic, tell me what happened to me just now."

Molly perked up and said, "You fucked John Luke."

"No," Whisper returned in an incredulous manner.

"You fucked Myles Carter, the rich guy?"

"No." she said again even more enthusiastically.

"Well who else is there?"

"God, Molly, you truly have a one-track mind."

Finally, Big Al asked, "What just happened?"

Whisper said, "It didn't really *just* happen, but last night on my way home, I heard something walking around in the woods. I thought it was just an animal but it scared me a little. And right before I went to bed, I heard the same kind of noises. I thought the animal wandered down by my cabin. I went outside to see what it was and saw John Luke coming out of the woods in the dark. No flashlight, walking quietly like he didn't want anyone to know. I hid and watched him sneak into his own cabin."

"First of all," Molly said. "Haven't you seen any horror movies? Why on earth would you go outside if you heard a noise and were scared?"

"Are you sure it was John Luke?" asked Big Al.

"Of course, he's unmistakable. Tall, broad shouldered, good-looking, walking, talking asshole."

"That's him," Big Al grunted as he shoved the last bite of a five biscuit and gravy breakfast into his mouth. "Orange, why don't you go back down there right now, knock on his door and tell him I want to see him up here in the restaurant."

Big Al wasn't really asking her to do it, he was telling her. She knew Big Al wouldn't do it himself because he didn't much walk anywhere let alone down to the furthest cabins. *Shit.* Whisper headed out the door down to the asshole's cabin. It was still cold and dark and she was a little afraid. The giant pig seemed like a pet compared to an unpredictable John Luke.

Whisper lightly knocked on his door frame in a way that gave the appearance of not wanting to wake much of anybody. She lightly rapped again. Finally, she decided to rip the band-aid off and banged on the door loudly enough to wake the neighbors if his neighbors weren't actually Molly and herself. She banged again, this time calling his name. There were no lights and no response of any kind. She concluded he wasn't there because if he were, any woman knocking on his door in the dark would have been reason to open up. Knocking once more for good measure, she turned and walked back to the restaurant.

Big Al was cooking and Molly was tending to two tables of hunters. Big Al looked up. Whisper shook her head "no". Another set of hunters came in and Whisper went to wait on them. The Hill Top Hunting Lodge restaurant was in full swing sans John Luke.

Just before eight in the morning, three men in suits strolled in. This was not the normal suit and tie kind of restaurant so all heads turned to stare. Molly recognized him first, "Oh shit, that's Myles Carter, the mega-millionaire and some of my filthy rich friends."

"Those are your friends?" asked Whisper doubting every word Molly said.

"I don't know them yet but I'll bet at least one of them is going to be my bitch before next weekend."

"I like your confidence but try not to make it where they won't come back."

"Whatever do you mean?" Molly headed to their table.

"Hello Mr. Carter," she said. "Welcome back to the Hill Top Hunting Lodge restaurant. What can I interest you in this fine morning?" She sat in the empty seat next to a guy and across the table from Myles.

The guy next to her asked, "What's good?"

She reached down and put her hand way up high on his thigh, extended her little finger and touched something in his groin. Molly thought it was his right nut but it could have been the head of his dick. It didn't really matter because the man nearly jumped out of the booth. The other two guys sniggered.

"Hey Molly," Myles said. "Why don't you bring us three coffees and one Big Breakfast. I want these guys to see just how enormous it is."

"Sure, Mister Carter, anything you want." She got up to deliver the order and get the coffee.

"See," Myles said. "I told you she was aggressive."

"For fuck sake Myles," the guy said. "We haven't been in here more than two minutes and she's already touched my dick. I think we need to get out of here." The other two guys laughed again.

Molly gave the order to Big Al, grabbed a coffee pot and pulled Whisper by her arm over to the side of the service counter. Molly spoke quietly, "Did you see that?"

Whisper was busy and didn't see a thing. "No," she said.

"I already grabbed his dick and he didn't do anything. I'm sleeping with him before this weekend, bet you five bucks."

"No bet. But what if this guy doesn't have a hundred million dollars like Myles Carter? Are you still going to go for it?"

Molly thought for a second. "He's got money. He wouldn't be friends with Myles if he didn't. It doesn't matter if he doesn't have hundreds of millions like Myles. So, what if he only has ten million, I'm still going to have him."

"Jeez Molly, only ten million? Are you really ready to stoop that low?" Whisper turned to carry a plate of food to hungry hunters.

Molly stood in front of Whisper. "Are you really going to wait on tables all your life? I'm going somewhere. I'm going to land one of these rich fuckers if it's the last thing I do." Molly went back to the booth, poured the coffee and sat down again. The guy next to her scooted over to the wall. She followed and pinned him in.

"Now boys, what is it ya'll do for a living, looking all Gentleman's Quarterly in those suits?" Molly picked up the guy's coffee, took a sip and left a lipstick ring on the cup.

Whisper watched Molly with absolute awe. Molly may be a bit of a slut but she sure was bold. Whisper let her play with the boys for a while before her table load became too much to give good customer service. Whisper picked up the Big Breakfast and went over to Myles's table, "I'm sorry gentlemen but I have to ask you to let Molly go for just a minute so we can take care of the other customers. Here's your meal. Enjoy."

Myles looked a little embarrassed. "Sure, we're sorry." Molly reluctantly got up and started working, glancing over at the rich guys' table every chance she got.

Sometime past sun-up, Ross and Shelby strolled in, Ross wearing his uniform and Shelby wearing jeans and a sweatshirt, probably the same clothes he wore yesterday.

"Hey, there's your Ranger and Robin right on schedule," Molly said to Whisper. Whisper instinctively flipped her yellow hair back, smoothed her uniform skirt and went over to wait on them.

"Good morning Doctor Evans," she said in a sing-song manner. "And you too, Shelby. What will it be today?"

"I'm really hungry and Shelby is always hungry so a Big Breakfast for Shelby and an Eight Point Omelet for me. Two coffees and one of those chocolate donuts under that glass dome on the counter, I feel like I need some energy. We have a lot going on today."

"Oh yeah, what?" asked Whisper. Shelby perked up also. He wanted to know how hard he had to work today.

"We're going deep into the woods, set up camp and spend three days in the wild."

Shelby looked like he was about to cry.

"Oh, I wish I could go." Whisper looked genuine.

Shelby said, "You can take my place."

"Can I really go with you?"

Ross thought for a minute, fighting his conscience, "No, I don't think I can let you do that."

Whisper looked extremely disappointed but acquiesced saying, "Big Al wouldn't let me off for three days during deer season anyway."

"How 'bout you and I get together when we return?"

Whisper smiled and her blue eyes gleamed, "I'd like that."

"Okay then. We'll get back in a few days, but I think I'll need some rest. How about after I rest one night and the next night, we drive into town, do that dinner and a movie thing you mentioned."

Whisper almost giggled. "I've never been on a real date before. This will be fun."

Shelby was watching with mild interest but mostly wanted Orange to go get his food. Finally, Whisper turned and went to deliver the order.

"So, Doc," Shelby said. "What in the great ape are we going to do in the woods for three fuckin' days and will there be internet access?"

"I don't think you'll have internet access out there. Hell, you barely have any at the lodge, but you might. I don't understand all the wi-fi, satellite, hot-spot, roaming ramifications. You're the expert, being born with an iPhone in your hand. And what we are going to do in the woods is trap a few animals."

"What kind of animals?"

"Deer, a male and female if we can catch them. We need blood samples and a visual inspection for parasites."

"I never knew this job was going to be so disgusting."

"We also need to catch a wild hog." Ross pulled a piece of paper out of his shirt pocket. Looking at it he said, "The order calls for 'a wild hog heavier than 150 kilograms' for a study being done in the United Kingdom."

"How big is 150 kilograms?" Shelby asked warily.

"Somewhere in the neighborhood of 330 pounds."

"That's twice as big as me!"

"How do you like your job now? Any better?"

Chapter 12

Ross and Shelby began preparing for their trapping adventure. Their truck was piled high with metal fencing brought in from Austin specifically for the wild hog capture. Camping gear was crammed in every nook and cranny of the pick-up bed. By mid-morning they were ready to go. Ready to go was an overstatement for Shelby because he plain just didn't want to go and Ross found himself wanting to spend some more time hanging around the restaurant.

Ross proposed an idea, "Why don't we wait about an hour before we take off and eat lunch in the restaurant. We'll be eating camp food for the next two and a half days?"

"Yeah. Okay." Shelby agreed almost as if it were an inconvenience. Ross smiled to himself. They went to their cabin to wait for the lunch service to begin.

Whisper was dreading the next few days. Ross had become the only bright spot in her otherwise dismal life. She was already missing him. Molly came up and stood next to her but Whisper just stared off toward the front door. "Damn, you got it bad."

Whisper jumped. "Shit, you scared me. I guess I was lost in my thoughts."

Molly laughed. "You don't have to explain because I've got it figured out. I know exactly where you were and it wasn't lost in your thoughts. You were underneath the Texas Ranger getting some afternoon delight."

"I'm not like you Molly." Although that was a perfect description of what Whisper was thinking.

Six hunters came in from the field and sat in two different groups of three each. Molly took the table with the biggest men. The bigger the men, the bigger the appetites. Whisper took the table with the more human size hunters. Two of these normal sized guys still had their rifles, all high-powered bolt actions with scopes. The deer never had a chance.

The big men somehow squeezed into a booth which Molly loved because she could sit by the man in the side by himself and give him the Molly special. The human size guys sat at a table. Whisper took the order and turned it in to Big Al at the window. Molly was still sitting at the booth. The biggest man sat by himself and she had her hand on his thigh. Whisper watched with an uneasy feeling. Things seemed off today.

After about a minute, Whisper went over to Molly, got the order slip and gave it to Big Al. Molly continued to sit at the booth. Whisper watched. Molly waved for Whisper to come over. Whisper approached the guys with a great deal of trepidation.

"They got some questions they want to ask you," Molly said as she leaned against the big man.

Whisper tried to give everyone the benefit of the doubt until she was proven wrong, which happened more often than not. She hoped they were just curious and wanted to ask the usual questions about growing up being completely orange skinned, yellow haired, red-lipped and blue-eyed.

"Okay, what's on your minds?"

Having their chance to ask questions somehow turned them into giggling pre-teens. As soon as they started to laugh, Whisper knew this was not going to turn out well. She put her hands on her hips and stared at each one in turn. Finally, the largest man by Molly said, "I think you are an abomination to God."

Whisper expected all sorts of childish remarks but this was a first. This was deep. It required a well thought out response. "Well, fuck me," was all she could muster at the moment.

The big man said, "Why did God make somebody like you anyway?"

"Funny you should ask," Whisper said, gaining her composure. "Just this morning God told me he was experimenting and said to himself, 'Let's just see what I can make out of these.' In front of Him was a stack of fresh fruit, oranges, bananas, strawberries, and a small bowl of blueberries. God waved his magic wand and said 'Behold, a girl,' and behold bitch, here I am."

The big guy just grunted.

Whisper was not done. "Then God went to a beautiful dairy farm in the country with green rolling hills and said, 'What can I possibly make with this?' God waved his magic wand and said 'Behold, a man,' and the three-hundred pounds of piled up cow shit turned into you."

The two guys on the other side of the booth simultaneously exclaimed, "Whoa" and laughed like a good-natured 'burn' just occurred. The big guy by Molly didn't find it so funny. He scooted out of the booth so quickly it shoved Molly on to the floor, falling flat on her ass. A lot quicker than anyone thought, the large dude was upright towering over everything in the restaurant. Big Al came out from the kitchen holding a spatula in his hand. Big Al hadn't been in a fight since he was in his twenties. He was not afraid of fighting but thought he was in serious danger of popping a hernia at the first sign of exertion or worse, having a heart attack.

"You ugly orange colored bitch! You think you're funny, don't you? You're nothing but an orange nigger!"

Whisper's brain went dim just like it did when she attacked John Luke. Whisper lunged forward and smacked the big guy right in the nose with her fist as hard as she could. It didn't even phase him. He grabbed Whisper by her hair, reached down and grabbed Molly by hers and pulled her to her feet. Both girls were holding the big guy's wrists trying to keep him from snatching out a large chunk of their locks. Whisper, being smaller than Molly was sometimes lifted completely off the ground. Molly just stood on her tiptoes.

Whisper was trying to kick him in the nuts and Big Al was screaming for him to let them go. The girls were screaming with rage and pain. The other human sized men were screaming for him to put the girls down. Two human sized men picked up their rifles and chambered a round. Big Al's thoughts were, *What a fucking mess.*

Ross stepped into the restaurant with nothing more on his mind than eating a Buffalo Burger and seeing his beautiful orange girl. Instantly dashed were his hopes for a quiet, semi-private lunch with Whisper. He quickly assessed the situation and acknowledged the need for action or maybe he misinterpreted the call for diplomacy. He walked directly up to the big man and knocked him right in the fucking mouth with a powerful roundhouse right-hand punch. The big guy dropped the girls and crumpled to the floor in a 300 pound pile of cow shit.

Whisper scrambled up and threw herself into Ross's arms. He held her tightly, staring at the big guy to make sure he didn't get up or to make sure his buddies didn't want to exact a little revenge or to make sure the guys with rifles didn't do anything stupid or to make sure Big Al didn't collapse from exertion or to make sure Molly got herself upright...too much. Ross just shut his eyes and became lost in Whisper's embrace. Molly got up and went to hug Big Al. He might be the only safe man Molly knew.

In a second, the three smaller hunters grabbed their gear and left the restaurant. The degenerate's two buddies kneeled on the floor and started trying to revive their friend. Big Al saw smoke coming from the kitchen. "Oh, shit!" and went to remove the contents of three chicken fried steaks and three hamburgers that were burning on the grill. Ross continued to hold Whisper closely.

The other hunters finally got their big friend on his feet and slowly guided him out the front door. On their way out, one of them said, "No one has ever knocked out Long John Locke before. Ever!"

Whisper raised her head from Ross's chest and said, "Until now."

Shelby walked in the front door after spending some alone time in the cabin restroom, "What did I miss?"

Chapter 13

Big Al encouraged everyone to sit down and relax. They sat in a booth with Ross and Whisper on one side and Shelby and Molly on the other. Ross continued to hold Whisper, she loved it. Molly took Shelby's arm. He was a little surprised but liked the feel of her big boobs against him. He was still clueless about what happened. Big Al hollered from the kitchen, "I don't know about you but a good fight always makes me hungry."

Molly and Whisper simultaneously hollered back, "You're always hungry!" They heard him laugh hardily. The kitchen doors swung open and Big Al pushed a food cart out, the cart they only used for formal banquets. It was piled high with food for six big lunches. He got everybody large glasses of iced tea. Big Al served the meal of choice to each person keeping the extra meal for himself.

Big Al sat at the table by himself and everyone began preparing their food and eating until Whisper broke the silence by saying, "You're welcome."

They all looked at her with the expression of 'Whatever do you mean?'

"I'm talking to Ross," she said.

Ross was still giving her the same look. Then she said, "You know when a person can't get a jar open, try as they might. And after many attempts, they give it to someone else who opens it with ease and the first person says, 'I must have loosened it for you.' I think I loosened the big guy for you. I hit him first."

"Oh," was Ross' response.

It was a slow roll but they all started to laugh and shoveled in food as if there were no tomorrow. Even Shelby laughed and he didn't know shit from Shinola about what happened.

Two hunters came in and took a seat at one of the tables. The waitresses said some version of expletive under their breaths and got up to go to work. When finished, Ross went over to Whisper and asked her what they owed. Whisper said it was on the house since it was what someone else ordered and half-way burned. "When will you be back?" she asked gazing at him with forlorn eyes.

"We'll be out two nights and return late the third day. If we actually catch a hogzilla, I have to take it to Austin the next day. I won't be able to see you until Saturday."

"Saturday!" she said with disappointment.

"I'm sorry but it's my job. It won't be so long."

"For you! You'll be off hunting giant pigs and driving into the city. I'll be serving sandwiches to Billy Bob and Jim Bob and Bob Bob and every other Cousin Bob in the county." She leaned her head on his muscular chest and he folded her in. She bounced her head against him a few times like she was symbolically hitting him, "Go on then, get on with you." She pulled away.

"Why don't you walk down to the truck with me and kiss me goodbye? Molly can handle the one table."

Molly was listening, as was Big Al, "Go do it, I got this," Molly said. Big Al nodded.

Ross looked at Shelby, "Come on, let's go." Shelby was still picking at his food. The three of them walked down to the truck, Shelby just strolling along, Ross and Whisper, arm-in-arm.

At the truck, Ross said, "Wait here. I need to get a few things out of the cabin." Ross kissed her on the lips. It was a peck and Whisper wasn't expecting it, missing her opportunity for a deep tongue rolling, tingling kiss before a five-day break. Ross returned carrying a small camouflaged shoulder bag and a lever action rifle.

"A gun? Why are you taking a gun?" Whisper seemed worried.

"It's just a precaution." Ross leaned the rifle against the truck, lever open. He threw the shoulder bag into one of the last remaining spaces in the pick-up bed. Whisper touched the rifle barrel. It felt cold. She slid her little finger all the way down inside the barrel.

Pulling her finger out quickly, "What kind of damn gun is this? It may be the biggest one I've ever seen."

"It's a 45-70, shoots a 405 grain bullet." Ross reached in his shirt pocket and pulled out a bullet and handed it to Whisper. She weighed it in her hand and mentally compared it to her middle finger. The bullet was bigger.

"I don't think I like this," she said.

"What, the bullet? The rifle?"

"No, you taking this cannon out there. Do you really need it?"

"I hope I don't need it but we are going to try to capture a hog almost twice my size. If things go sideways, I'll want to make sure Shelby and I will be safe. I do have a really good reason to come back."

Ross saw her lips turn up just a little when he said that. She looked up at him, "Long John Locke was nearly twice your size and you didn't need a gun to take care of him."

"Long John didn't have 5-inch tusks,"

"You Jerk. Please be careful."

"I will. We've got to go now." Shelby was already sitting in the truck, leaning back trying to nap. Ross leaned forward and they started kissing. A deep, long lustful kiss. They wrapped up in each other, her nipples sprang to fullness and she could feel him growing quickly. He pressed her against the truck then picked her up. She wrapped her legs around him and kissed more and deeper until Ross finally pulled his mouth away and just embraced her. "I've really got to go."

She released her leg grasp and started to slide down his body. His huge, rock hard erection straining against his pants caught her right between the legs. If not for the clothes, she would have surely been blissfully impaled. After another smoldering kiss, he lifted her off his swollen, painful cock and allowed her feet to touch the ground. "I really hate you leaving," she said giving the head of his cock a mean, twisting squeeze and running off to her cabin.

She threw herself on the couch, pulled her skirt up and panties down to her ankles, angrily rubbing her yellow haired, swollen, grapefruit red colored pussy until she came half a dozen times. Each time saying something like, "Damn you, Bastard, Asshole, Fucker." Terms of endearment for the man who just left her in this condition. Whisper momentarily fell asleep on the couch after relieving herself several times. When she woke, her panties were still down around her ankles. Cleaning up and splashing some water on her face she was ready to go back to the restaurant.

Ross had no such luxury of relief. He walked around the back of the truck half a dozen times inspecting the cargo to make sure everything was loaded properly. Mainly he was killing time praying his hard on would go down enough to be able to bend into the truck and not have Shelby notice. Finally, finally, finally, it started to dissipate. He stuck the rifle under the seat, jumped into the driver's side and upon bending over he squirted some juice out leaving a darkened wet spot on his OD green uniform trousers. "Well, crap." He looked over at Shelby who was fast asleep. Ross started the truck and drove for an hour, deep into the woods.

They drove down three dirt roads and each one became more and more narrow until the truck could not go any further without the paint being scrapped off by the encroaching vegetation. The front doors barely opened enough to allow them to squeeze out. "Dang Doc," was all Shelby said. Ross figured Shelby was in some kind of culture shock or maybe it should be called nature shock.

They proceeded to unload everything from the truck on to the ground. Ross slammed the tailgate shut, grabbed his small backpack and the rifle saying "You ready?"

As expected, Shelby's reply was, "Ready for what?"

"We need to scout out a good place to set up the traps." Ross handed him a military web belt with a canteen, first aid pouch, small hatchet and machete attached to it. "Put this on. We may need to clear some of the ground to get these fence panels to fit together properly."

Shelby took the web belt and mentally weighed it by lifting it up and down a few times. "This thing weighs a ton."

"As thick as this brush is, we won't have to go too far into the woods. Maybe just a few hundred yards or a half mile."

"Half mile!" Shelby repeated under his breath. Shelby was not an outdoor kind of guy. The furthest he ever had to walk was from his dorm to the shuttle stop on campus. However, once, while extremely intoxicated and a little high, he walked from the concert hall of the convention center to his hotel. It was eight blocks, maybe eighteen or eighty, hell he couldn't really remember but it seemed like a long way. He found himself wishing he were drunk and a little high right now.

Ross was excited. He actually enjoyed doing this kind of work. This was like being in the army again but without the IED's and hostiles shooting at him. "Let's go."

Ross scanned the woods and spotted a slight break in the trees and decided to start their trek there. He plunged into the woods with Shelby right behind. They walked in what Shelby thought was a random pattern for about thirty minutes before Ross stopped and said, "This is it. See the animal trail there?" Ross pointed. Shelby didn't see anything but more green, thick woods. "Something has been coming through here on a regular basis. Right here." Ross held his arms out pointing three-hundred sixty degrees. The state boys took their gear off and began clearing the area.

Chapter 14

That night, Whisper was in her cabin feeling all alone, more so than usual because she was missing Ross. It was a different kind of gnawing loneliness. Then the thought, what am I going to do when Ross leaves? She really tried not to think too deeply about it. Relationships never seemed to make any sense to her. While at the refrigerator to get a snack for distraction, she heard a bump on John Luke's porch. She ran to the window and peeked out. John Luke was sneaking back in to his own cabin again! "What the…"

She watched for a few more minutes but there was nothing to see. The cabin lights never came on. He was in the dark the whole time. John Luke was frightening to begin with but this behavior made him absolutely terrifying. Sleep was now the last thing on her mind. Eating her snack and peering out the window occupied an hour. Reading and peering out the window occupied the next hour. She went to the bathroom and glanced out the window. Before going to bed, she looked out. In ten minutes, she looked out again. This was repeated for most of the night. When the alarm went off at 3:30 am, she was asleep but didn't really remember going to sleep.

At the restaurant before the customers started to come in Whisper asked Molly if she saw John Luke last night. Molly hadn't seen him because she was preoccupied with the young hunter from Cabin 4. He checked in late last night and Molly just happened to bump into him when he was unloading his truck. She didn't leave Cabin 4 until 3:00 am that morning.

Whisper asked Molly if she thought Big Al would mind if they got the spare key and went into John Luke's cabin for a look see. Molly said, "Does Big Al really need to know? We can just get the key and go look." They agreed, Molly would "steal" the key before they got off work and they would rendezvous at John Luke's cabin at 6:00 pm sharp.

All day Molly and Whisper exchanged conspiratorial glances. Even though the day progressed like any other day at the Hill Top Hunting Lodge, it seemed to be progressing in geologic time. After forever, the evening college-girl waitresses arrived. The one John Luke screwed gave Whisper a special once over when she walked in. Whisper usually didn't let the stares bother her but this bitch wasn't staring at her with the usual simplistic curiosity wondering what she was. This bitch was judging!

Molly looked at Whisper and said, "You ready to get out of here?"

Whisper said, "Give me a minute. I'll meet you there." Molly left. Whisper went over to the dark-haired college girl and asked, "You got a problem?"

The college girl looked her up and down again and said, "I don't have a problem. But you do."

"What are you talking about?"

The college chick said, "John Luke told me about you."

"Yeah. What did he say?"

The girl leaned in really close and said, "He said since you were, you know...orange, he thought you would smell like citrus. But..." She left it hanging,

"But what?"

She leaned in again, "He said you smelled like a cross between tuna fish and head cheese. I don't even know what head cheese is but I bet it stinks." She sniffed and made a disgusting face. Whisper fumed. She had many choices and she was sure she was going to make the wrong one.

Whisper balled her fist and punched the college girl as hard as she could in the left tit. The girl bent over with an ear-piercing squeal. Whisper grabbed the girl's hair and drug her out of the restaurant almost throwing her down the front steps. "Don't come back."

Big Al came out of the office when he heard the dog whistle type howl. He got out there just in time to see Whisper throw the girl out. Whisper dusted off her hands and told Big Al, "She's fired. I'll work her shift."

"Okay. Can I ask why I fired her?"

"Because she's a bitch." Whisper put on an apron and started to clean up tables. Big Al went back to his office, bewildered as usual.

The other college girl looked at Whisper and said, "I'm Shanna. Can you tell me what she did so I don't do it too?"

"Don't worry, you're going to be fine."

"How can you tell?"

"Because you've said ten words to me and none of them were mean."

Whisper completely forgot she was supposed to meet Molly down at John Luke's cabin. Molly was on the porch looking up the hill towards the restaurant. With no Whisper in sight, she couldn't help herself and put the stolen key in the lock, turned it, sneaked in and shut the door behind her. Last time in this cabin, John Luke terrorized her.

Molly didn't really know what she was looking for but started snooping around, opening all the drawers in the kitchen, bedroom and bathroom. She found nothing, but fondled some of John Luke's underwear for a few seconds. She looked under the bed, rifled through the clothes hanging in the closet and opened a cedar chest at the foot of the bed. The chest was filled with quilts. *How out of character for a man like John Luke.* She decided to look in the kitchen pantry.

Molly closed the cedar chest, walked out of the bedroom and turned off the light. It was dark in the cabin and she didn't see John Luke standing in the hall. She walked right into him. Instantaneously, he punched her in the face. Molly fell to the floor on her back, arms bent and hands in the air. John Luke stood over her and watched her hands slowly lower to the side as unconsciousness settled in. He got some duct tape from a kitchen drawer and wrapped her hands, ankles and taped her mouth. Molly was helpless. He could do anything he wanted to her for as long as he wanted to do it.

John Luke was about to drag Molly out of the cabin when he heard a knock on the door. "Fuck." He looked out the window and saw the college waitress he screwed a couple of nights ago. *What the fuck was her name? Katy, Kiki?* John Luke opened the door, "Hey Honey." He stood in the door frame.

"Can I come in? I'm having a terrible day." John Luke thought, *you don't know how terrible.* John Luke swung the door open and stepped aside. The young waitress walked in thinking she was going to get some of that big manhood. Looking up at him hoping he would immediately start kissing her, he only smiled strangely. She started unbuttoning her blouse, looking down at her buttons and never saw the punch. He struck her on the side of the face. She didn't go down but was completely stunned. John Luke struck her again as hard as he could. She flew across the living room, landing on the floor by the couch, out this time. John Luke got the tape and trussed her up in the same manner as Molly. *What to do, what to do?*

Whisper was working the evening shift for the first time in years. She was also getting along famously with Shanna even though they had nothing in common. Shanna came from an upper middleclass family in Texarkana and had three younger siblings. She didn't really need to work but thought it was the right thing to do. Whisper mentally gave her two thumbs up.

About 8:30 pm, Whisper remembered she was supposed to meet Molly down at the cabin. She couldn't leave now because the local high school booster club's annual supper was in full swing. Molly would be pissed, but Whisper made a new friend, tips were good and the clientele stared at her but weren't overtly mean. Tomorrow she would deal with the wrath of Molly.

Sometime just before 11:00 pm, the girls were finishing the last chores necessary for closing the restaurant. Whisper walked Shanna out to her car and gave her a hug. Whisper wasn't really a hugger but Shanna probably hugged everybody. She was.... nice. Whisper had never been accused of being nice.

Shanna was medium height, had five to ten pounds of extra meat on her bones, brown haired pulled back in a pony tail and brown eyes. She was not the type of girl guys chased after but if a man was set up on a blind date with her the guy would be pleasantly pleased she wasn't ugly.

Shanna drove off in her hand-me-down BMW which she received from her father when he was done with it. It must have been seven or eight years old. She watched the car until the tail lights disappeared down the highway. Whisper slowly walked to her cabin wondering what she was going to say to Molly. She looked at Molly's cabin but the lights were out. *She must be asleep.* John Luke's cabin was also dark. The thought of John Luke slinking around the corner in the night frightened her and she began to move much more quickly. Within seconds she was in the relative safety of her own cabin, looking out the window seeing no activity and hearing no sounds. Whisper put on some flannel jammies and went to sleep.

Chapter 15

At 4:05 am the next morning, Whisper entered the restaurant with her badge on, this time. Big Al was sitting in his booth reading the Tyler Morning Telegraph. "Where's your partner in crime?" he asked without even looking up.

"Molly's not here?"

"Why would I be asking if she was?"

"Maybe she's just late. You know how she sometimes keeps late hours."

Big Al grunted. "If you mean she screws anything that has a penis, especially the guy in number four, then, yeah, I know."

Whisper was amazed with Big Al's psychic radar. Changing the subject before his radar tuned in to locating John Luke's spare key, she said, "I really like Shanna."

"I'm glad because you are going to be working with her until I can replace Kylie."

"Kylie? That's her name?"

"She's worked here since the semester started in September and you didn't even know her name?" Whisper didn't respond. "In your defense, I don't suppose you need to know someone's name to punch them in the face and throw their ass out of the restaurant."

"I didn't punch her in the face."

Big Al finally looked up from the paper. "Where did you punch her?"

"I tit punched her, okay?"

"Is that really a thing? Tit punching."

"Now that you say it out loud, it does sound a little weird."

Two customers came in and took a booth. They were dressed in suits. Whisper put on an apron and Big Al fired up the grill. She went to the booth and started to ask the men what they wanted but instead, "I know you guys, you were with Myles Carter the other day."

"Yeah, we were. Have you heard?"

"Heard what?"

"Myles Carter is missing."

"What do you mean missing?"

"He hasn't been in the office for two days. He doesn't answer his phone. His mom and dad don't know where he is. We were supposed to meet with him yesterday about some financial matters but he didn't show up. The cops are involved. Haven't you looked at the news on line or seen it on TV. It's gotten national coverage."

"I have no friends, no TV, no computer and no phone. You are my news source today. She walked over to Big Al's booth and flipped through the paper. Big Al was reading the sports page. Sports and the comics were all he ever read. The rest just got cast aside. The 'missing millionaire' story covered the whole front page with many pictures of the handsome hometown boy.

Whisper walked back to the guys while reading the paper. "Wow! What do you think happened?"

Both men just shook their heads, "Don't know."

"Did he have a secret girlfriend he could have run off with or maybe he just went to Tahiti or wherever the filthy rich go these days."

"You don't know, do you?"

"Come on guys, know what?"

The two men looked at each other, "Myles is gay as a three-dollar bill."

Whisper's jaw dropped open. "Is this common knowledge?"

"I mean he doesn't put it on his business card but he is 'out'."

"Oh my gosh. I feel like I should do something to help. Is there anything I can do?"

"Bring us some coffee and a menu."

Jerks she thought. She handed them two menus and went to get coffee.

The restaurant started to fill up and Molly had yet to make an appearance. When Whisper came by the pick-up counter, she dropped an orange in the trashcan someone left on the table and said to Big Al, "I'm really worried about Molly. What do you think the chances of her being with Myles Carter are?"

"What do you mean? Like being together sexwise?"

"Since he's supposed to be gay, I wouldn't think he would flip for someone as shallow as Molly. But I mean, they're both missing at the same time."

"Hold on there, Orange. We don't know if Molly is 'missing', she's only been out of pocket for a few hours. I bet if you go down to number four and bang on the door, you'll hear her scrambling around trying to get her skivvies back on."

Whisper shrugged her shoulders, picked up three plates of food and carried them out to waiting customers. The whole restaurant was a buzz with the popular millionaire's disappearance. Myles' company was considering offering a modest reward for information leading to his whereabouts. Speculation on the amount ranged from fifty thousand to five-hundred thousand dollars. The company feared the county might be besieged by an army of fortune hunters if the reward were too high.

Whisper worked a double because of the altercation with Kylie. Molly never showed up and Whisper couldn't wait until her shift was over so she could knock on Molly's door. Whisper and Shanna speculated all evening about what happened, running all kinds of disturbing scenarios through their heads. At the end of the night, they were nowhere closer to figuring out what happened than anyone else.

At the end of the evening when the last chores were completed, Whisper and Shanna headed down to Molly's cabin. Shanna seemed concerned and was the type of person who somehow always did the right thing. They banged on Molly's door. No answer, no lights. Whisper told Shanna about Molly and the guy from Cabin 4. They went and banged on his door.

They heard movement and a man and woman talking. A guy opened the door wearing boxer shorts with a robe loosely wrapped around him. "What do you want at this hour?"

Whisper said, "We're looking for our friend Molly. Have you seen her?"

The man stepped out on the porch pulling the door shut behind him. "What the fuck are you doing? My wife is in there."

"You married asshole," Whisper said. "Have you seen Molly since you screwed her?"

"I haven't seen that cunt since last night. Now you bitches get off the porch and go bother somebody else."

From the back of the cabin they heard a woman holler, "Sweetheart, what's going on?"

The asshole turned his head over his shoulder and hollered back, "Nothing Babe, just some treasure hunters asking about that missing rich guy."

They heard footsteps coming to the front of the cabin. The woman appeared before them in a silk robe. Her long black hair flowing down her shoulders. She was really attractive. "Does anybody know anything about where he is?" She asked with what seemed like genuine concern.

"No ma'am," Whisper said. "We know Myles, ah Mister Carter has been out to the Hill Top Hunting Lodge several times recently because we waited on him. We're waitresses at the restaurant and we thought we'd try to help by asking around to determine if any of our guest might have seem him or know anything. We're sorry it's so late but we didn't get off work until a few minutes ago."

The woman looked Whisper up and down like most people did. "You're that orange girl everybody talks about."

"The one and only," Whisper said waiting to see which way this would go. There were three ways, mean, neutral or nice and that's the precedence in which the comments usually came.

"Your coloring is beautiful in the moonlight."

Nice.

The lady looked at her husband, "Chad, have you seen Mister Carter since you've been here?"

"No. I haven't seen anybody."

Whisper stared at the asshole.

The wife said, "If you girls can wait a minute, I'll throw some clothes on and I'll go with you. I'd like to help however I can."

Whisper and Shanna looked at each other and Shanna said, "You were the last cabin to check. Since we don't know what else to do right now, we're going on to bed."

"Well okay, but let me know if there is anything I can do. I'll be here for another couple of days while Chad hunts. Chad loves his hunting trips." She reached out and put her hand on his shoulder. Chad smirked and looked away. "He's come out here the last five years but this is the first time I've been here. I just decided to surprise him."

"How nice of you," Whisper said, "We better go now, goodnight."

As the two waitresses turned to walk off, they heard the lady say, "Aren't they nice."

The two girls stood in the middle of the parking lot and almost simultaneously asked, "What do we do now?"

Whisper bit her thumbnail saying, "I don't know, but I'll make coffee if you come over."

"Okay."

"I live there." Whisper pointed to her cabin.

"I've never been in one of these. Worked here two months and never seen any of this place except the restaurant."

Whisper countered with, "I've actually lived here for five years and never knew there was a lake down the hill with ten boat slips. I went there with Ross a couple of days ago."

"Ross?"

"Yeah. He's here to do some work with the wildlife."

"He's a ranger or something?"

"Everyone thinks that. He does wear a spiffy little uniform, but he's a biologist veterinarian type."

"Huh, I guess I've never seen him."

"He eats his evening meal early so I can wait on him and then he stays in that cabin." Whisper pointed, "but he's out in the field for few days and then off to Austin. He should be back on Saturday if everything goes as planned. He's out there right now somewhere in the woods trying to catch a giant pig,"

"Good God, a giant pig?"

"Yeah, some big three-hundred-fifty pound hog with five inch teeth."

"Sounds dangerous."

"That's what I thought. He's got this cannon for a gun he took with him."

"Is he alone out there?" Shanna asked.

"No. He's got this graduate student helper. His name is Shelby, but I don't think Shelby is an asset. He's a year or so older than me but he has this high school mentality."

Shanna asked, "How old are you?

"I'm twenty-one going on thirty-five,"

"I'm twenty," Shanna said.

They went into the cabin and Whisper started putting on some coffee. Shanna, looked around, "This is quaint."

"If you mean quaint like an outhouse, then I think you are right."

They sat at the small table with mugs of hot comforting coffee.

'What are you studying in college?" Whisper took a sip.

Shanna set her mug down and seemed to be deep in thought. "I'm taking classes......" She started again. "It was a simple question and should have a simple answer but it's a not simple answer. I've taken all of my basic classes but need to pick a major really soon. My parents want me to get some kind of art history degree. I want to go into business. I love numbers, finance, accounting, management..."

"Do what you want. Your parents will love you anyway."

"I know. I just hate disappointing them."

Whisper laughed. "Do you want me to tell you about parental disappointment? My parents couldn't stand the sight of me and gave me away when I was about a year old. I grew up in a Nazi orphanage until I was sixteen and then I ran off. Big Al and Glyna found me on the side of the road, literally, and slaved me out here. I can't afford to breakaway unless I just run off again. So, I've been here for five years waiting on God knows what."

Shanna looked embarrassed. "I didn't know. I suck, don't I?"

They sat in silence for a few minutes until Shanna asked, "What do you really think is going on around here? John Luke is AWOL, Molly is lost and the rich dude is missing. What are the chances of all of them being together?"

"I was thinking the same thing. I wonder if we should be afraid?"

"Of what, is the question."

After some more deep conversation, the girls decided to call it a night. Shanna left and Whisper fell into the bed. It was after midnight and she had to be at work by 4:00 am. "God, I'm tired," was the last thing she said to herself before she fell asleep.

Chapter 16

Whisper rolled into the restaurant at 4:10 am. Big Al said, "You know if you lose your job, you lose your place to live too."

"Yes, Master," was all she replied.

Two customers came in. They were uniformed police officers and they didn't sit down. Whisper went to see what they wanted and what they wanted was to talk to everybody who worked at the Hill Top Hunting Lodge.

Big Al told them, "There's only three other people who are full time employees besides John Luke. Me, Orange here." Big Al pointed to Whisper. "Molly, the other day waitress. There are two part time evening waitresses, Shanna Borger and Kylie Morgan. We also have some contract housekeepers."

The tall police officer said, "You said Kylie Morgan, right?"

"Yeah, why?"

"A missing person report was filed on her very early this morning."

Whisper put her hand to her chest, "Oh my God, Al?" She looked at him. "What's going on here?" She sat down in the booth across from Big Al.

The police officer asked. "Do you know anything about her disappearance?"

Whisper sat quietly staring at the tabletop. "We had a fight."

"About what?" The police officer was now taking notes.

"We fought over nothing really. She was just being a bitch. It may come as a surprise to you, but sometimes people decide to make fun of me." The police officer snorted a little. "She just pushed it a little too far and we got into it."

"Define, 'got into it', please."

Big Al spoke up because he couldn't help himself, "Orange tit punched her."

The police officer looked baffled. For moment he thought someone called 'Orange Tit' punched her. Then he realized, Orange, 'tit punched' her. "Why did you hit her?"

"I told you she was making fun of me. She was being a bitch," as if that gave it absolute clarity. "After the incident, the tit punching, she quit and left."

The police officer let it go. Then he asked about the timing of the tit punching event. "Her parents said she didn't come home after work, but she left here about 6:00 pm when you two argued?" He looked at Whisper and she nodded. "She was due home about midnight but never showed. The parents called it in about 3:00 am when they couldn't find her. We have it on file and were waiting for a full twenty-four hours to pass before we started an official investigation but we thought since we were in the area, we'd ask a few questions."

Big Al told the police John Luke was scarcely seen anymore and Molly hadn't been to work since the day before yesterday. Now Kylie is missing and Myles Carter has vanished. The police asked a million more questions as Whisper tried to take care of the demanding hunters wanting food before their hunting adventure.

Big Al was worried about the missing people but he was also worried about keeping the Hill Top Hunting Lodge afloat. He was down a maintenance man and two waitresses. However, he had the feeling these missing people were going to be good for business. Very good.

The next few days flew by. The missing people were on the news everywhere. Droves of reporters came with their big satellite dish trucks. A county, state and federal police presence was constant. Myles Carter's company, Veritas International, offered a million-dollar reward for information leading to Myles' whereabouts. Good ol' boys from half a dozen counties filled the roads with their tricked out pick-up trucks and spot lights looking for their million dollars. Everybody wanted to find Myles Carter for one reason or another.

All of these do-gooders and reporters had to eat somewhere and most of them chose the Hill Top Hunting Lodge restaurant. Shanna and Whisper had their hands full. Shanna started coming to work right after class instead of waiting until the evening shift. All three of them, Big Al, Shanna and Whisper, working as fast as they could for sixteen hours a day just barely got the job done.

On the third day of the media frenzy, the reporters were running out of things to report. One TV channel decided to interview the Hill Top Hunting Lodge staff, starting with the orange girl. Whisper was sitting at a table all mic'd up for the interview. There were two cameras on tripods pointing at her from two different directions. She was sweating and didn't like being in the limelight. It was not her style.

The blonde skinny reporter said, "Look at me when you answer my questions, okay?" Whisper nodded her head affirmative. Then the reporter started counting backwards, "Three, two, one…

"Here at the Hill Top Hunting Lodge in the middle of nowhere East Texas, the missing persons mystery saga continues. I'm here with Whisper Orange Jenkins, one of the long-time employees at the lodge. Tell me, Orange, how well did you know the missing people?"

Whisper wished the reporter didn't call her Orange on TV. "I know all of them. But I know Molly the best. She and I worked the same shift for several years. We were neighbors. Our cabins were close. John Luke lives next door, but I didn't see him much." She was scared to death they were going to find out she slept with him, twice! "Mister Carter came in to eat a few times recently and I had the privilege of meeting him then. He seemed fairly nice. And then Kylie, I'd just gotten to know in the last few days. We were on different shifts and didn't have much opportunity to socialize." Whisper was still sweating, hoping the reporters wouldn't find out about their fight.

"So Orange, you're saying all four missing people have ties to you?"

Now Whisper was afraid she just became the number one suspect.

"Me and the Hill Top Hunting Lodge, open every day from 4:00 am to 10:00 pm for your convenience," she said not knowing why.

"You heard it yourselves, the orange girl from Hill Top Hunting Lodge knows.....Cut!"

The news crew quickly packed up the cameras and headed to their trucks. The reporter, Amie Lynn Sylvester, pulled out a compact and looked at her make up. "Thanks Orange," she said flatly. "If we decide to air your lame interview, it will be because you'll add a little color to the broadcast. Funny, yeah?"

Not funny, mean.

Chapter 17

On Saturday morning, Whisper went to work as usual, anticipating Ross' return after catching his pig. Shanna showed up at 6:00 am since she didn't have any classes. The reporters were still hanging around, several police were in the restaurant and the usual number of hunters were on hand. It was busy to say the least. At 2:00 pm the restaurant started to clear out. The first chance they got, Big Al, Shanna and Whisper sat in the booth and read the paper. There was a TV in the corner but it shorted out three and a half years ago and Big Al was too cheap to buy a new one, so all of their current news, via newspaper, was nearly a day behind.

The paper basically reported three pages of words that said nothing. It was status quo. Four people were missing and no one knew where they were or why they were missing. Whisper was rereading an article about local volunteers who were helping the police and wondered if she should also volunteer.

The front door opened and Ross walked in. Whisper was sitting on the inside part of the booth, pinned in by Shanna. Whisper never said a word, stood up on the booth seat, stepped on the table top and jumped off on the floor. She ran to Ross throwing herself at him with no inhibition whatsoever. He hugged her back as they swayed slightly as if dancing.

Shanna couldn't help but say, "Aw."

Big Al didn't say anything but was glad the Ranger Boy was back.

After twenty seconds of full body hugging in the middle of the restaurant, Ross started to get a little aroused. He quickly pushed away, grabbed her hand, walked to the booth and sat down. Shanna moved over to sit with Big Al and Whisper slid in first and then Ross. Whisper held on to his leg which wasn't helping Ross' situation any. Ross looked over at Whisper, then at Big Al and Shanna sitting across from him. Big Al and Shanna were both staring at the couple. Ross said, "Let me guess what you were talking about. The missing people. It's all over the news in Austin."

"Molly," was all Whisper said with a contemplative voice.

Ross squeezed her hand. "I know."

Seven reporters, camera technicians and drivers banged through the front door and started looking for a place to sit even though every seat in the dining room was vacant. "Hey, can we push these two tables together?" They started doing it anyway.

"Sure," Big Al said. The customers never heard his reply over the screeching of the tables and chairs sliding over the wooden floor. Big All lifted his girth to go to the kitchen and prepare to handle the influx of orders. Shanna got her order pad and went to the table. Ross reluctantly let Whisper out of the booth so she could get water and drinks. Ross was momentarily left by himself.

These news guys just arrived from Houston. All were young and eager to "break" the story to the world. Of course, all they were really doing was waiting for the story to "break" and then tell everybody else about, hopefully being the first to do so.

Ross was thinking that exact thought and decided he had two choices, sit and wait to see if the story broke and let the reporters tell him about it or he could try to help in some way and be the person to break the story. He decided to be an active participant and do something. Decision made, he would go to the Incident Command Center in Jacksonville as soon has he had his late lunch and volunteer his services. Shelby walked in the restaurant looking for a meal also. To Shelby's chagrin, Ross didn't stop to eat while driving on the way back from Austin. Ross wanted to get back to the Hill Top Hunting Lodge quickly. He missed Whisper. Therefore, Shelby hadn't eaten since breakfast.

Shelby sat across from Ross. "I'm hungry," he said.

"Good," said Ross. "Eat a big meal and get your energy up. We're going to go volunteer at the Incident Command Center this afternoon."

Shelby looked terrified, "Volunteer for what?"

"Anything they need us for but if they have any sense, they'll let us do what we do best."

"What's that exactly?" Shelby had no clue what Ross was about to say because Shelby wasn't really good at anything except playing video games, sleeping and eating. He was pretty sure those skills weren't in high demand.

"Leading a search team, water rescue, tracking, manning road blocks, anything that's outdoors. We could really be helpful."

Shelby's enthusiasm was less than positive but it didn't curb his appetite. While Shelby ate lunch, Ross was on the restaurant phone with his headquarters and received permission to stay at the Hill Top Hunting Lodge as long as necessary if he was asked to help with the official investigations and searches.

Ross told Whisper he was going to volunteer over in Jacksonville. She looked at him with a 'you just got back' glare. "The good news is, I get to stay here, while I'm volunteering."

Whisper didn't want to smile, but she did. "I feel bad that I'm happy you get to stay because the reason you'll be here longer is a horrible one."

"I know. Maybe we'll find them quickly and they will have all been partying together on a five-day bender at one of Myles' hideaways."

"Maybe. If anybody could party for five days it would be Molly."

"I've got to go. I want to get up there before they change shifts at the Command Center. All the guys who are really in charge will be there during the day."

"You'll be back tonight?"

"Sure, well, I'm pretty sure."

"I'll be in my cabin at eleven. Naked on the bed with my legs spread." She walked off to wait on customers.

"Fuck." Ross watched her saunter away. He thought her hips swayed an inch or two further to the side than normal. She looked back over her shoulder and blinked her big blues at him and he almost made a squealing noise. He quickly cleared his throat, yelled at Shelby to finish eating and meet him at the truck.

Chapter 18

Ross and Shelby drove to the Incident Command Center in Jacksonville and sought out the boss. The Commander was sitting with two other men in the room with six large-screen computers. The computer screens showed various components of the operation, weather, a local news channel, a spreadsheet with an accounting of assets, an organization chart and a couple of word documents.

"Hey Fellas," Ross called out. They turned their heads and introductions ensued. After a lengthy discussion of the incident status, which was basically square one, the Commander gave Ross an assignment, grid search the area around the Hill Top Hunting Lodge.

In the last five days, the Incident Command operations teams have interviewed family, friends, church acquaintances, set up a hotline and posted the enormous reward. They checked airlines, bus companies, trains and rental car companies. They contacted hospitals and morgues. They made daily pleas for help using multiple media: television, radio, internet and the good old fashion newspaper. They reviewed phone records, verified credit card use and bank statements.

They interviewed nearly everyone at Veritas International, Myles Carter's company. They reached out to business partners and competitors who were no help. Hundreds of police officers, dozens of agencies and an army of volunteers found nothing. The time was right to go out into the isolated places and look for clues or bodies. A long shot but other options were becoming scarce.

The Incident Commander arranged for a dozen volunteers to show up at the Hill Top Hunting Lodge at 6:00 am the next day. Ross was going to organize a search in an expanding semi-circle pattern on the east side of the road. That area was basically the woods and lake behind the lodge. Another team made up of professionals would search the west side of the road. The professionals, for their services, were receiving $45.00 an hour from the county emergency fund paying for the Incident Command operations. Ross wasn't sure if he was going to be compensated for his search efforts or not. He didn't care.

Ross and Shelby spent another three hours in the Incident Command Center planning the search grid with times and check points. The Operations Chief issued Ross a satellite phone, a military grade GPS and a list of names and numbers of key Incident Command staff. Ross was to report at each check point and when each grid was cleared but no later than every two hours. The Commander told him a Public Information Officer representative would be at the lodge everyday form 6:00 am to 6:00 pm until the search was completed. Only the Public Information Officer representative should talk to the media.

Well after dark, the state boys started driving back to the lodge. Shelby wanted to eat as soon as they got back but Ross wanted to go to the cabin and take a cold shower, several of them, until time to see Whisper. In Jacksonville, between every break in conversation or lull in planning, Ross thought of Whisper lying naked on her bed. Her thin colorful body writhing around in agony, waiting for him to come satisfy her. *Damn, I need a cold shower.* He drove faster.

Somewhere around 8:00 pm, Shelby entered the restaurant. Whisper saw him and smiled knowing Ross was back at the lodge.

Her thoughts were the same as Ross', her lying on her bed, naked, writhing around in agony when suddenly a strong, taut muscled man walks in, naked, with a huge beautiful angry cock bobbing up and down in front of him as he stalks his prey. *Damn, I need a cold shower.*

Chapter 19

When the last customer left the restaurant, Shanna and Whisper were flying around cleaning and making ready for the next day. Shanna didn't know the plan about being naked but she knew Whisper was anxious about seeing Ross. At last, they were done, it was 10:42 pm. Whisper grabbed her old sweater with holes in it and ran down the hill to her cabin, leaving Shanna to turn out the lights and lock up. *Hurry, hurry.* She was so afraid she wasn't going to be where she was supposed to be at the right time.

She burst through her cabin door, threw her clothes in the hamper, peed, brushed her teeth and jumped in the shower before it had time to warm up regretting getting in so fast but there was no choice. Soap, soap, soap, rinse, rinse, rinse, underarms, crotch, feet...ready. She hung the towel on the shower curtain rod and ran to the bed. The time was eight minutes until the hour. Just right. Plenty of time to lie there and think about what was about to happen. She hoped her expectations and anticipation didn't lead to disappointment. Now she started worrying about it not working out the way she planned at all.

At 10:59, she heard the front door open. No knock. She stiffened in the bed. Hearing a few footsteps and then silence, she arranged herself on the bed. Propped up just a little, legs spread, one leg bent at the knee, her essence aimed at the bedroom door. She heard the floorboards creaking slightly. Her breath caught. *I wish I peed again.* Too late.

Then there it was. Not Ross, but Ross' cock, preceding him into the room. A raging hard on led him around the corner. Then he stood tall in the doorway. Hands high on the door jam. Just for a moment, he stared at her and she stared back at him. He thought, *that is incredibly sexy.*

She thought, *get that fucking massive cock over here and get it in me.*

He moved to the bed, his cock swaying back and forth with each step. She spread her legs wide open already wet with anticipation. He didn't need to warm her up, no foreplay, no nothing. He fell on top of her. His dick sliding in with ease. *Yes!*

Their bodies were roiling across the bed in a sensual dance of hot breaths, groans and orgasms. Whisper was being plied like kneading bread, pulling, pounding, twisting, stretching, squeezing and rolled over to be done again. Whisper briefly wondered where Ross picked up all of these amazing tricks. Then she thought, *where did I learn how to do all of this?*

Ross eventually came twice although he really struggled with the last one. *Poor baby must be tired,* she laughed to herself. Whisper had cum more times than she had fingers and toes. She glanced at the clock as Ross settled in beside her, 3:30 am. They had been doing it for four and a half hours straight! *Oh God.*

It was time for Whisper to get up and go to work! She thought, *okay, I'm young. I'm only twenty-one. I can pull an all-nighter.* Ross was lying face down in the sheets. She climbed right up on him, being mindful of his scarred back. She whispered in his ear. "I've got to get ready for work. You just sleep."

Ross mumbled something and groaned. As she slid off him, she reached between his legs from behind and gave his sore balls a gentle squeeze. He groaned again, rolled to the side on his elbow. "Do you really have to go to work today?"

She just looked at him with her hands on her hips. "I guess that's a 'yes'," he said.

"Come take a shower with me."

Ross stood, "Alright, but no funny stuff. I've got to be somewhere in a couple of hours also."

"Yeah? Where are you going to go?" She was afraid he was leaving again.

"Just out back of the lodge to do a grid search. The Incident Command Center is sending some volunteers down at 6:00 am and I'm supposed to lead them."

She waved her hand for him to follow and went to the bathroom. She turned the shower on and got a fresh towel for Ross. "What do you think you'll find out there?"

Ross shrugged his shoulders, "To tell the truth, I don't think I'm going find anything."

She stuck her hand in to test the water and stepped in. Ross followed. The first thing she did was take a squirt of body wash from the plastic bottle and start washing his genitals. "Hey, no funny stuff, remember."

"I'm not messing with you. I just want to make sure it's all cleaned up. You were a very dirty, dirty man."

She kept washing his cock and balls, reaching way back underneath and like lightening shot a finger up is ass for a brief second." It slid in easily with all the soap.

"Whoa! I think that's funny stuff now."

"Maybe a little." She was just plain jacking him off now. He was hard again. *Third time!* she thought.

Ross leaned his back against the shower wall and let her play with him. When he was raging hard, he spun her around, her hands braced against the wall and he took her from behind. Whisper came easily which was unusual for her, unless…this was really the right man.

Her hands were on her knees now, bending over. He held her hips and made quick, deep thrusts trying to make himself cum quickly. Muscles strained, a grunting moan and he pulled it out letting his cum dribble down her leg. He was just about jizz'd out. She washed off quickly and jumped out of the shower stall. "I got to get out of here or I'm going to be late."

Dried off, dressed in her waitress uniform and headed for the door, she said, "Take your time. You know where I'll be." Whisper shut the door and swiftly walked to the restaurant thinking about how tired she was and how wonderful all that was. Smiling and not even knowing it, she entered the restaurant.

Ross toweled off and tried to decide if he could lie down for a little while before he had to get ready. Slowly dressing, the decision was made, he's up for the duration. He walked around her cabin for a few minutes just looking at the décor. Of which, there was none. There were some condiments on the small kitchen table. They looked like they were stolen from the restaurant. There was a magnetic calendar on the fridge, a cheap clock on the wall that was standard in all cabins, a toaster and microwave on the counter, also standard in all cabins. The living room had nothing, just the furniture that came with the cabin including the TV/DVD player. Big Al was too cheap to spring for cable but he bought tiny TV's and used DVD players for all the cabins and had a hundred or so used DVD's that could be checked out for $1.00 a night. The bedroom had three paperback books on the night stand. The bathroom had towels and toiletries. She lived here for five years and it looked as if she hadn't moved in yet.

Ross left her cabin at 4:30 am and went to wake Shelby for the search. Shelby was deep in sleep and Ross made several attempts to get him up. Eventually, Shelby went to the bathroom to get ready but only because he had to pee.

"Dress in your hiking clothes and boots. Layer yourself. Take all of your hiking gear. We'll be out there all day."

"All day?" Shelby looked up from pulling on a pair of jeans.

"Yeah, you know, sunup to sundown."

"Why are we doing this?"

"Shelby, there are four missing people. We're trying to find them. If nothing else, we'll be able to say where they ain't."

"What good does that do?"

"It's like hide-and-seek. You look in the closet. They're not there. You go look someplace else."

"But they could be anywhere. The woods is ridiculous around here. Have you seen it?" A rhetorical question Ross hoped. "They could be in Mexico, Canada, India, or anywhere. This is going to be such a waste of time. What's this got to do with my studies anyway?"

Ross waited to see if he really wanted an answer or if it was a rhetorical question also. Shelby stared at him. *Ah, a real question.* "You're assigned to me to learn what a wild life biologist does in the field. I'm in the field and this is what we've been asked to do. It will give you untold bragging rights among your peers."

"What good does that do?"

"Experience is probably more important than education. They'll be talking about these disappearances for twenty years and the value of being the leader of one of the search parties by itself will get you a job. If we happen to find a clue or actually find them, you'll be a hero."

"A hero, huh?"

"Yeah, a hero. Get your shirt on and let's go eat breakfast."

Ah, breakfast. That was something Shelby understood.

Chapter 20

Ross and Shelby sat at one of two open tables in the restaurant. The place was packed with media, law enforcement and students from Stephen F. Austin University. Ross figured the students were going to be the members of his search party. Shanna came over to wait on the guys. "What'll it be boys?"

"One Big Breakfast to be shared. Coffee and water, please."

"You got it."

Shanna and Whisper ended up at the service counter at the same time. Shanna said, "The Ranger sure is cute." Whisper couldn't agree more. The girls were busy slinging hash and Whisper never noticed when the state boys left. Then the college crowd left and a second shift of breakfast seekers sat down. The process started all over again.

Ross saw a gaggle of students milling around in the parking lot by the cars. Ross and Shelby went over to them, "Are you all here to help with the search for the missing persons?"

They all talked at once but Ross heard they were the search team and hailed from the Delta Chi and Chi Omega fraternity and sorority.

Ross didn't know which was which. While they were making introductions, three large, crew cab pick-up trucks pulled into the lot. Four
men got out of each truck.

Twelve hard men were wearing what was virtually combat gear.
Each man wore boots, cargo pants, a tactical vest, hydration systems
and identical ball caps with *Veritas Security* printed on the front. As
soon as they dismounted, they put pistols in their tactical leg holsters
or in their vest holsters. They pulled out assault rifles, all looking like
M-4's, and hooked them to cross-body slings.

One of the armed men came over to Ross and introduced himself
as Adrian, the search team leader. Adrian said, "We're Search Team
One if there is a need to call us on the radio. Our sat-phone number
is on the information sheet they gave you at the Command Center.
If nothing goes wrong, we'll see you at sundown." He turned away,
waved his hand in the air in a circular motion and his men formed
up in two bunches, marched off across the road and disappeared into
the woods.

"Impressive G. I. Joes, aren't they?" Shelby said.

"I've seen their type before." Ross looked back at his team. None of
the college students was wearing anything heavier than a light jacket.
Two of the boys were wearing shorts. Most of them wore some form
of sports shoe but others wore slip on loafers that resembled a sports
shoe, no hydration systems, no packs, nothing. Shelby looked them
up and down. Even he realized they were in trouble.

"What do we do with them? They look like a mistake," Shelby
looked back at Ross who was scanning the group. Seven of the dozen
were looking at their phones and unsuccessfully getting a signal of
any kind. If one was lucky, a signal could be accessed from the top of
the hill near the restaurant but not actually in the restaurant.

"I'm going to let you lead them. You'll look like a rock god in their
eyes. I want you to search the immediate area. Start down by cabin
ten, work your way around each cabin, the parking lot and around
the restaurant. Go a hundred yards deep into the woods. Got it?

One-hundred yards, no further and then go over the hill behind the restaurant to the barn down there about fifty yards on the far side of the restaurant. Look for clues..." Ross thought a minute. "Look for jewelry like an earring that may have been pulled off during a struggle." Shelby pulled out a pad of paper and a pen. "A discarded cell phone, a jacket or other clothes, or parts of clothes that could have been pulled off or torn off during a struggle. Shoes, purses or purse contents. The girls in the search party will know what to look for. Look for pools of blood or blood splatter, broken windows or broken locks on any of the cabins, busted locks on sheds or other out buildings. Anything that looks out of place like a blanket or picnic basket in the woods."

"Picnic basket?" Shelby questioned.

"I know, that was a terrible example but look for anything that may indicate someone was there before and now they're gone. An axe leaned up against a tree, an abandoned ATV, a walking stick, tracks on the ground. If you find anything that really seems like a clue. Go to the restaurant and call the Command Center number on your sheet. Tell them what you found. If it's something doubtful but could possibly be a clue, like a gum wrapper or cigarette butt, then record the location, bag it up and we'll report it at the end of the day. If you don't find anything, call in to the Command Center and give a negative report. Got it?"

Shelby finished writing in his pad. "Got it."

"Okay, get your gear on."

Shelby went over to the state truck and pulled his backpack out of the bed. It was well stocked with all kinds of emergency items, including lunch in case he was away from the lodge at noon time. It had a hydration system and a machete strapped to the back. Shelby thought he looked rather macho wearing his gear.

Shelby looked at Ross who said. "Go have your way with 'em."

Shelby walked over to the group. "Okay, listen up. We've been given a very important job to do today. We'll be looking for the four missing persons, their bodies, clues to help find the missing people or we'll just find where they ain't." Ross smiled.

Ross grabbed his large pack out of the truck bed and went to get his rifle from underneath the back seat. He locked the door and watched Shelby give a lecture concerning what to look for, where they'll search and what they'll do if they find anything. Ross donned his pack, slung his rifle over his shoulder and walked north of the restaurant to grid number one. Let the search begin.

Chapter 21

Ross pulled out the GPS and switched it on. It had a device that could track him so he was going to hurry, making sure each grid was covered as sufficiently as one man could in the allotted time. If the Command Center plotted his movements, they could see a suitable pattern. He was going to take each grid and serpentine from one side to the other moving about thirty yards away from the previous line on each turn. He would be able to see a vehicle, a body, maybe some clothes or other large unusual items but he would certainly miss a wallet or a pair of glasses or something that small unless it was directly in the path of his search. It was the best he could do alone.

Shelby was lording over the college group, barking instructions like a drill sergeant. Two or three of the dozen searchers were actually looking for something while the others just chatted, flirted and talked very foul mouthed about the cold, the early hour and what they were going to do that night. In fifteen minutes four of the group went to the restaurant to use the restroom. Ten minutes later, two more left to warm up. None of them came back. When the search party neared the restaurant, three more basically just quit and went to get latte's "if this stupid cowboy restaurant serves them."

When the search was completed, Shelby's team was only three strong, two guys and one girl. He thanked them for sticking with him through the whole thing and they met up with the others in the restaurant. They were all drinking coffee and eating donuts and pastries.

Shelby gave the group his pad and pen and asked them to sign in so he could submit it to the school as proof of community service. "Who knows, it might mean extra credit," Shelby said. When he got his pad back, he put a check mark by those three who stuck with him, an 'X' by the names of those who quit near the restaurant and a double 'X' by those names who went to the bathroom and never came back.

He looked at the group and said, "I bet you're glad it wasn't one of you who was lost with help like we provided today. You are released." Shelby used the restaurant phone to call the Command Center and give his report.

The students filtered out of the restaurant and went on their merry way not knowing that nine of them would be recognized in a letter to the university president for their utter uselessness in the search for the missing people. However, the three of them who completed the search would get a glowing letter of appreciation for their service. After Shelby ended his call, he went to the cabin to type his letters. *Holy shit, working with students sucks!* As soon as he thought that, he realized he was a little less than helpful also. *Time to man-up.*

Ross was busting brush at a steady pace. He felt confident he wouldn't find anything but he was going through the paces, keeping a sharp eye out for the unusual. At 7:55 am, he completed the search of the first grid. He pulled out the satellite phone and called in a negative report, no time to waste. He took a big drink from his old school canteen and continued at a faster pace. Grid two was smaller and the terrain was flatter so he should be able to beat his time for the previous grid. Small and flat was good.

In less than an hour, he called in a negative report for grid number two. And so his day went, grid by grid, hour by hour. In grid seven, he heard a noise through the brush. The tree leaves were turning brown and falling but the cover was still thick enough he couldn't see what was making the noise. He heard leaves being disturbed on the ground, then a distinctive grunt. Nothing threatening, just the sound a happy hog makes when he's knee deep in something good to eat. Ross pulled his rifle off his shoulder and held it in front of him for a moment while he listened. He heard another grunt, a different pitch than the first. Two animals at least, maybe a sounder of hogs. If what he was hearing was a mother pig with a litter, he needed to give them a really wide birth. If the sounder was made up of young male pigs.... it didn't matter, give them a wide birth, too.

Ross took three large cartridges from the leather butt stock ammunition holder and slid them into the loading tube of his rifle. Moving to the left, he thought, *this part of the grid will not be searched today.*

At 3:30 pm, Shelby entered the restaurant wanting some lunch. The time was late for lunch but after he wrote his letters, he fell asleep for four hours. Shelby and two county deputies were the only ones in the restaurant. Whisper waited on him, asking if they were through with the search. Shelby told her he was through. He only had to search a small area with the students. Nothing further than a hundred yards out.

"Where's Ross?" she asked a little worried.

"He's out in the woods somewhere."

"Alone?"

"Yeah, he can take care of himself."

"He's alone?" she asked again.

"This is what he does. He's got that big gun with him."

Whisper almost went to tears, worried. Worry was a new feeling for her. She never worried about anybody before. Instantly, she was mad at Shelby for no apparent reason. Standing by Shanna at the condiments counter, she said, "Go wait on that string bean. I'm mad at him."

"Why are you mad?"

"I don't know."

Shanna went over, took his order giving it to Big Al in the kitchen. "What did he do? Did he call you a name?"

Whisper stood with her arms wrapped around herself, chewing on her thumb nail. "I think I love him."

"Shelby?" Shanna was in shock.

"No, Ross. You know, the Ranger."

"Oh, spill the beans."

Whisper threw her arms up in the air and sat in the corner booth. Shanna slid in with her. Big All hollered from the kitchen, "Don't say nothin' until I finish this order." He heard everything from the grill. Shanna and Whisper looked at each other and shook their heads.

Big Al set the plate on the counter and yelled, "Order up!" Shanna got the plate and almost ran it over to Shelby and hurried back to the booth. She and Big Al sat down at the same time. "Okay, spill."

Whisper took a deep breath. "There's not much to tell."

Big Al was having none of that. "No, no, no, you're starting from the beginning and telling us everything." Shanna and Big Al leaned forward in anticipation.

"He's funny. He's got a good job. He's smart and educated. He's nice to me. He hasn't called me names, not even Orange. He thinks I look like a sunset…" and with that she started to cry. Shanna moved around the booth and put her arms around her.

"Is that something you should be crying about?" She looked at Big Al.

In a few seconds Whisper straightened up and wiped her nose on her sleeve. "It's just he's only here for a while and then he's back in Austin or another Hill Top Hunting Lodge someplace else in the state and now he's out there all alone."

"Out where?" Big Al asked.

"In the woods. Roaming around like some lone wolf."

"What's he doing roaming around in the woods?" Big Al asked.

"He's searching grids," Whisper made the air quotes with her hand. "They assigned him a dozen grids to search with some volunteers but Shelby used the volunteers for something else and he's out there all alone."

Whisper had her head in her hands. Big Al looked at Shanna and gave the 'what are we going to do' shrug. Then he said, "Look, the Ranger in the woods alone is no different than me being in the kitchen alone or you being out front in the restaurant alone. It's what we do and we're comfortable with it. Right?"

It made sense to Whisper. "I know you're right."

"Then why are you crying?" Shanna asked.

"Because I don't know."

"I think you're in love for the first time and it's just overwhelming." Shanna looked at Big Al.

"Sure," he said. "You're just in love."

Shelby cleared his throat from across the room. "Can I get something to drink?"

Shanna jumped out of the booth, "Crap."

Whisper laughed.

The restaurant phone rang and Whisper got up to answer it because whoever was on the other side of the line would have hung up before Big Al could have wrenched himself out of the booth to answer it.

"Hill Top Hunting Lodge restaurant," she said into the phone.

"Hello, this is State Trooper Carl Starling. I have a message for a Ms. Jenkins."

Whisper's heart leaped into her throat. "That's me."

"I'm working at the Command Center for the missing people. We got a call on the satellite phone from a...Ross Evans who I believe is out with a search party right now." Whisper was about to scream.

"Ms. Jenkins, he just called to say he was going to spend the night out in grid seven and resume the search in morning. Ma'am, he will not be coming home tonight." There was a long pause. "Ma'am, did you hear me?"

"Yes. Yes sir, I did. Thank you." She hung up, turned and looked at big Al and Shanna, "The jerk isn't coming back tonight. He's staying in the woods."

"See, he's fine. Pig in shit." Big Al had a way with comforting words.

"Al! Have you seen those pigs out there? Oh, God! He's going to get eaten by a giant pig."

Shanna stood up, put her arm around Whisper and laughed a little. "He's not going to get eaten."

"But those pigs are so big. He caught one the other day that weighed over 330 pounds." Whisper subconsciously pointed at Big Al when she said that.

Big Al chuckled. "Why you looking at me?"

They all laughed and the girls began preparing for the evening shift.

Chapter 22

Ross stopped the search fairly early. The woods get dark quickly in the winter and he needed to set up camp. In his pack was this new triangular hammock tent he was excited to try out. Once tied to the trees, the hammock tent hung about three feet off the ground. He stocked the tent with water, a thin sleeping bag, a poncho liner and his rifle. He took his big back pack fifty yards away, ate two energy bars and hung the pack up in a tree ten feet off the ground.

Ross climbed in the tent which bounced up and down like a trampoline. Ross wasn't sure this was the time to try out his new tent but here he was. He rolled around for five minutes trying to get in the sleeping bag with his blanket on top properly. Once in the bag and relatively comfortable, he realized his rifle was working its way underneath him. Ross tied the heavy gun to the nylon straps used to secure the tent window. He put his flashlight in a nylon pouch on the tent wall and was ready for sleep. The time was 7:09 pm.

Whisper was waiting on three tables simultaneously. Shanna had four tables but with less people. Big Al really needed to get off his ass and hire some more waitresses. He was interviewing some girls tomorrow. Maybe one of them will work out.

In a few minutes, the Veritas Security crew came in, fully armed and dirty from the field. Whisper has seen many men with hunting rifles or even assault rifles come into the restaurant before but these guys were armed to the teeth. They all had an assault rifle with dozens of extra magazines, pistols with extra magazines, big knives on their belts or vests and some had small knives hanging around their necks. They all were about six feet tall, bearded and heavily tattooed with skulls and gruesome scenes of violence. They looked more like a gang than a security team.

The armed men pushed some tables together and doffed their rifles and some other gear on the floor. They owned the place. The guy at the head of the table waived Whisper over as if she didn't know what she was supposed to do. He said, "Hey there, Crayon." All the men laughed. "We'll start with two racks of ribs, three pounds of brisket, six whole sausages with jalapenos, two quarts of beans, two loaves of bread, oh yeah, bring out some smoked turkey, potato salad and coleslaw for Jimmy 'cause he's a pussy." The guys laughed again staring at Whisper to see what reaction she would have.

"Anything to drink?" she asked.

"Six pitchers of beer. We've had a hard day saving damsels in distress like yourself. Well, maybe not like you." He put his hand to the side of his face as if he were thinking. "I've got to admit, I've never seen anybody like you before. How 'bout you Jimmy? Ever seen anyone who looks like pureed carrot baby food?"

Then men laughed in unison. "No sir, I haven't." Jimmy was giving her the once over, trying to think of a snappy retort. He leaned forward with his elbow on the table, chin in his hand, "You think there is a pot of gold at the end of that rainbow?"

Whisper shut them down by saying, "We don't serve beer if you are armed."

They were incredulous. "We're out here saving lives at the risk of our own and we can't get a beer?"

She pointed to the pistol holstered on the leader's vest. "Big Al doesn't like mixing alcohol and guns."

"We are professionals. Even drunk as skunks, we can out shoot any man in this joint."

Whisper looked around at the 'other men in the joint' and saw six guys including Big Al. Two were at least eighty years old, one she knew to be a local dentist and the other two looked like college professors. Big Al looked up at her through the kitchen window. Whisper laughed. "Yeah, Okay. What do you want to drink?"

"Tea," the asshole said. He removed his pistol from his vest holster and set it on the table. "I guess you don't have to worry about us killing anybody because we're drunk."

Whisper gave big Al the order and tried to take care of her other guests. However, the mercenary types kept calling her over for stupid stuff, more barbecue sauce, extra napkins, tooth picks and when they ran out of things to ask for, they asked, "Are you orange all over? Can we see? Show us your tits. Do you smell like an orange?"

What assholes! Big Al called up the order and Whisper carried mounds of food to the table. Before they were through eating, they ordered another side of ribs, another pound of brisket, two more sausages more tea, more sauce, more beans, more napkins and two dozen orders of peach and cherry cobbler with coffee to follow up. Finished, they leaned back in their chairs like people do after a Thanksgiving dinner. They patted their stomachs and three of them lit up cigars.

Whisper brought the leader the check and told him there was no smoking in the restaurant. "We'll make an exception since you are such heroes and let you smoke on the veranda if you'd like." She was trying to be accommodating to avoid trouble but she may have said it a little too facetiously.

"You are going to…let…us smoke on the veranda…" His thought trailed off. "Hey, if I squeezed you real hard, would juice come out?" The men roared.

Whisper walked off. Big Al never came out of the kitchen to help. She didn't know if he was afraid or if he just knew it was pointless. The men smoked for a few minutes until the leader stood up and grabbed his gear. Everyone else did the same. They filed out of the restaurant, the leader standing at the door. He yelled at Whisper, "Little orange girl, put this on the county tab. They're paying. We're still on the clock." He walked out. The bill was $278 and change. No tip.

A little after 10:00 pm, the restaurant was empty. Shanna and Whisper were talking by the condiments. Shanna said, "Sorry you got stiffed. We can pool our tips and split them if you'd like."

Whisper was touched. She reached out and put her hand on Shanna's arm, 'No, you earned that money. You keep it. I've got to go to bed." The girls put on their coats and left.

Whisper threw all her clothes on the floor, fell face down on her bed and for a fleeting moment thought about Ross. Whisper contemplated masturbating but fell asleep. Sometime around midnight she woke up not remembering if she rubbed one off or not, got under the covers and really took the bus to dreamland.

About the same time Whisper was sliding naked under the covers, Ross was thrashing around in his sleeping bag, hovering three feet above the ground in his newfangled bouncing trampoline tent. He needed to pee. He thought briefly about trying to pee out the opening in the tent while lying down but decided against it. If he missed, he might fill up the tent and it was miserable enough. He clambered out, stood two feet away and peed. While in midstream he thought he heard a noise not natural for the woods at midnight.

After he finished, he stood in the cold night air listening, thinking he heard it again, only fainter. The noise was definitely not one heard in nature. It could have been a hundred yards away or it could have been a half a mile away. Sounds were tricky when one was alone in the woods at night.

He listened until he was too cold to listen anymore. He got back in the tent, covered up sufficiently and untied his rifle, sleeping with it by his side the rest of the night. In Iraq, he walked in the valley of the shadow of death and this felt a lot like that.

Chapter 23

The sun was up. Ross slept longer than he anticipated. Within thirty minutes everything was packed up and he was on his way to grid eight. Two hundred yards into grid number eight, the old familiar rock house appeared through the foliage. This is where the noises were coming from last night. He unslung his rifle from his shoulder and approached the house. Walking right up on the porch he tried the door but it was still locked. Nothing could be seen through the windows. The ground around the cabin didn't seem to be disturbed any more than when he and Whisper were there earlier.

Going behind the house, he scanned the woods for feral hogs. He had an uneasy feeling or maybe a slight case of paranoia. Seeing nothing in the woods, he walked up on the back porch and tried the door. It too was locked. The wood floor of the porch showed no signs of anyone walking around there recently, but there was one strange anomaly. Only five rocking chairs were on the back porch. Last time there were six! The one sitting to left of the door was gone. Someone moved the chair or stole it.

Now Ross was on Iraq patrol level alert. Levering a round into his rifle, he backed away and sought concealment in the woods. All was quiet as he moved stealthily and kept his head on a swivel. Pulling out his satellite phone, he called the Command Center, reporting definite signs of human activity at the rock house. The coordinates were accessed through his GPS. The Command Center ordered him to abandon the rest of the grid search and go back to the lodge. He couldn't cut across the lake without a boat so the alternative was walking all the way around.

He gave the rock house a wide berth and quickly hiked out of the woods. By noon, Ross was coming into the lodge area from the south side cutting between cabins to get to the parking lot. Passing by Whisper's cabin he could actually smell her. In the middle of the parking lot, there were several reporters, the Public Information Officer assistant from the Command Center and Adrian, the leader of the Veritas Security goon squad. When they saw Ross coming in, the PIO assistant jogged over to him. "Don't say anything."

The press quickly surrounded Ross, "What did you find?" they asked in unison. Ross remained silent.

The PIO assistant talked, "The eastside search team discovered some signs that may lead to a breakthrough in the case. We can't tell you anything more at this time. We'll hold a press conference at the Command Center at 4:00 pm today. Thank you very much. We'll see you later this afternoon."

The reporters left to prepare for the press conference later in the day. Adrian looked at Ross, "So Bro, what did you find?"

Ross looked at the PIO assistant, "Can I talk now?" The PIO guy nodded. "There is an old homestead, a stone house, a mile or so back in the woods behind the lake. I was there several days ago and noticed six rocking chairs on the back porch. Today, there were only five chairs there. One was missing."

The PIO guy said, "That's the big evidence. Someone stole a rocking chair off the porch?" Adrian gave a little grunt.

Ross elaborated. "Somebody has been back there. There are no roads to drive up to the house. The were no ATV tracks around it. I don't think anyone carried the chair on their back several miles out of the woods to the Hill Top Hunting Lodge parking lot. It's made of heavy wood and weighs fifty pounds at least. I personally don't think anyone stole the chair at all. I think it's inside the house."

"Why would anyone want to move it inside the house?" The PIO assistant had no idea what Ross was thinking.

"I don't know, maybe to have something to sit on," he said flippantly. "All I know is we're looking for four missing people and we now have proof where some unknown person has been. I think it deserves another look. I'll ask Al for a key and go back this afternoon, take a boat across the lake and have a look inside the house. "

"Hold on there, sweetheart," Adrian said. "We've been assigned that exact duty for tomorrow. You're out, we're in. This is a job for a professional team. Not one ...one uh." He couldn't come up with a quick put down. "One state hack," he finally said.

The PIO assistant said, "Well that's it, Reggie. We won't need your services anymore."

Ross threw his hands up. Within 30 seconds he had been called 'sweetheart' by a mercenary and 'Reggie' by a useless twit. *Screw this. I'm getting some lunch.* He went to the state truck, opened the door and levered three big bullets out of his rifle on to the back seat. He placed the cartridges into the butt stock ammo holder and put the rifle in the floor board, locked the truck and went to the restaurant, excited to see Whisper.

Chapter 24

Ross walked into the restaurant smelling a little gamey wishing he'd gone to his cabin and taken a shower before seeing Whisper. And there she was. Her back turned picking up two plates at the service window. Ross stood at the door. When Whisper turned to deliver the lunches, she saw Ross standing there looking... *very, very manly.* She froze for just an instant and then set the plates down on the closest table to the surprise of three older female curiosity seekers having quiche and listening to gossip.

One of the ladies at the table said, "Oh, this is going to be good."

Whisper ran across the restaurant and threw herself into Ross's arms. They hugged like long lost lovers reunited after an extended separation. Hugging long enough to get the attention of every patron in the restaurant, she pulled away. "Are you alright?" she asked looking him over as if she were going to find some wounds.

"Of course I am. All I did was spend the night in the woods."

"But there's missing people and giant pigs and deep lakes, darkness and…" Her thoughts trailed off as they embraced again.

Big Al's booming voice sounded from the kitchen, "Orange! Leave the Ranger alone and get this food out."

Whisper looked Ross in the eye, "How embarrassing. Sorry. Take a seat over there." She pointed to Big Al's booth. "I'll be there in a minute."

Ross sat in the booth and Whisper went back to the table where she left the two plates. One of the old ladies grabbed Whisper's arm when she reached for the plates. "How long has he been away?"

Whisper laughed. It sounded silly to say it but she did, "I saw him just yesterday."

"Oh my word…" the old lady said.

"Yeah. He's that good." Whisper smiled at the ladies and delivered the lunches.

She went to Ross and asked, "What'll it be Tarzan?"

"It wasn't the jungle. It was the woods, not too far from where we saw the rock house. And…I think someone has been in the house since we were there." She sat down beside him all ears. "When we were there, I remember seeing six of those big wood rocking chairs on the back porch." He looked at her for confirmation.

She shook her head up and down, "Yeah, three on each side of the door."

He reached over and put his hand on her thigh while he was talking. All of a sudden, his voice sounded far away, miles away, and his hand seemed really close, which it was. Only six inches away from…she couldn't think about it. She was trying to listen, really, she was.

All she could remember from the several sentences he said was one of the chairs is missing. "A chair was missing?" she recapped for her own benefit.

"Yes. I was going to get the key from Al and go back this afternoon but I was stopped by Veritas Security and told I was out."

"Good," she said. "If it's dangerous in any way, I'm glad they will handle it. They are mean assholes and they can spend the night out there."

"Sounds like you know them."

"I had the privilege of serving them last night. Nearly a three-hundred dollar supper bill and no tip. Plus, the usual..." She kind of waved her hand in front of herself. Ross assumed she was indicating her color.

Ross continued, "They are not going back out until tomorrow. I feel there is some urgency to this. I know there are search parties all over East Texas looking for them and the chances of them being in that rock house are small but if they are held captive, being tortured, raped, starved or... I can't even imagine. Shouldn't I get back out there as quickly as possible and at least eliminate that location?"

She didn't say it, but she thought it, and meant it, *my hero.* Then she recoiled. "You're going back out this afternoon anyway, aren't you?"

"I'm thinking about it."

"Doctor Evans! I'll swear. If you go back out there...I don't know what I'll do."

"I'm just considering it. I didn't say I was going to do it."

"I'll make you a deal. You eat your lunch, take a shower, please."

"Sorry," He said. "I couldn't wait to see you."

"Good answer. You're forgiven. Take your shower, have a nap and at precisely 4:30, we'll meet at my cabin for a quickie." She squeezed his thigh and maybe a little more than just his thigh.

"You keep your hand down there, I may have a quickie right here."

She slapped his shoulder and stood up. "What do you want to eat?"

Ross smiled, "Club sandwich, fries and a diet coke."

"You got it, stud."

Three young women entered the restaurant obviously looking for somebody or maybe the restroom. Whisper went over to them and asked if she could help. The girl in front said, "We're looking for a guy named Big Al. We're applying for the waitress jobs." Whisper hugged her.

The restaurant was starting to thin out. Ross ate and left to comply with his instructions: shower, nap, rendezvous. The applicants were now occupying Big Al's booth, drinking tea and talking among themselves. Big Al told Shanna and Whisper to help him interview the applicants during the dead time before the supper crowd. He would start the interviews about 4:00 pm. Dangerously close to her scheduled afternoon delight. *This interview thing may not work out.*

At 4:10 pm, Big Al came out of the kitchen wiping his hands on the greasiest rag anyone has ever seen. He threw it on the condiment cart. Big Al stood by his booth staring at the girl who was sitting in his place. They blankly stared at each other until it dawned on her what he wanted. Without a word, she stood up and Whisper drug a chair over from the nearest table and let the girl sit down at the end of the booth. Big Al grunted his way into the booth, belly pinched against the table.

"I'm hiring three more waitresses on a temporary basis. As you know, we are in a bit of a crisis here. You've seen the news. We'll start the interview process with questions from Orange. Go ahead Orange, ask them something."

Whisper dropped her hands to her side from her hips, looked at the clock on the wall and said, "…the fuck. Ya'll are all hired. I'm taking a break." She turned and walked out of the restaurant.

"Where's she going?" asked Big Al.

Shanna said, "I think she's got a date with the Ranger."

The three applicants simultaneously asked, "The Ranger?"

Big Al answered, "We're kind of like Gilligan's Island around here. We have names for everybody, the Ranger, the Bad Boy, the Millionaire, the Orange Girl," he pointed to himself, "Big Al."

The blonde applicant said, "I want to be the Movie Star."

"That makes me Mary Ann," said the dark-haired girl.

The third one said I guess I'm the Professor. I don't want to be Gilligan."

The blonde said, "Beth, you are the Professor since you're the smartest one of us."

"I only have a 2.4 grade point average."

"See," the blonde said. "Smart."

Shanna, who really was smart said, "Big Al, why don't we hire them all. We need the help."

The girls looked at Big Al, "Alright, show them the ropes. You start tomorrow."

The girls squealed with excitement not knowing what the hell they were getting into.

Chapter 25

Whisper made it down to her cabin with barely enough time to get a shower. She dried off and was standing in front of a steamed-up mirror trying to make herself look beautiful when there was a knock on the front door. "Yes!" She opened the door wearing a white towel covering her breast and hanging down to the top of her thighs.

Ross was standing there not knowing what to expect. He sure wasn't expecting that. His eyes widened. She dropped the towel, stepped out naked on the porch in the evening sun and stood inches away from him. He damn sure wasn't expecting that. They stood for only a couple of seconds but it felt like one of those moments frozen in time.

Finally, he said, "Maybe we better go in before someone sees what I'm about to do next."

Shelby also had a moment in time. He shut the door of his cabin to get an early supper when he saw the action in front of Whisper's cabin. Long after Ross and Whisper disappeared into the cabin, Shelby stood replaying the moment in his brain like a favorite scene from a favorite movie. He'd only seen one other girl naked before and that was Margie Blankenship from the Audio/Visual Media Club in high school. She lured him over to her house with the promise of letting him use the newest sixth generation digital camera to make a science fiction short for class. What Shelby filmed was Margie stripping naked in front of the camera with the hopes of Shelby going for it, which he did.

Margie Blankenship's body looked nothing like what he just saw on Whisper's porch. Margie had grayish pasty skin, dark hair, not black and not brown but burnt oil sludge looking, inch long hair circling her nipples, dead dark eyes, an unruly pubic region going all the way down her inner thigh and she was twenty pounds overweight. Make that thirty. Orange, on the other hand, was thin, had shiny yellow hair on both top and bottom, orange skin with reddish highlights on nipples and lips and eyes so sparkly blue, he could see them across the parking lot. Shelby forgot he was hungry, turned around, went back into the cabin and proceeded to have his way with himself, using Whisper with an occasional side of Margie for stimulus.

Ross followed Whisper into her bedroom. He stood in the doorway as she crawled onto the bed looking like a big African cat, a lioness. Her moves were smooth and slinky. She turned over on her back and rubbed her knees together like two sticks trying to start a fire which was about the truth. She was scorching hot. "Hurry," she said. "I don't have much time."

Ross snapped out of it and started removing his shirt. "Don't worry. This won't take long. I'm half way there already."

He dropped his clothes in a pile which was the closest thing to neatness he could muster at the time. Standing with muscles rippling from anticipation, his large cock literally bounced in front of him as if it had a mind of its own. "I may cum just looking at you."

"I'm going to need a little more than that."

She sat on the edge of the bed and Ross walked over, his big manhood swaying back and forth with every step. When he got near enough, she reached out and grabbed the shaft, pulling him in close.

Her mouth was wrapped tightly around the head before he knew what happened. She couldn't get more than the head in her mouth but she was working that a mile a minute with her tongue swirling in circles around the smooth warm tip. "I'm really going to cum if you don't stop," he said as she looked up at him, her mouth still gobbling him up.

"No, you're not." She slapped his nuts hard enough to make him yelp and bend slightly at the waist. She spun around on the bed on her hands and knees, her butt right at the edge in front of Ross. All he had to do was put it in. He grabbed both sides of her hips and aimed at the perfect spot and it slid in all the way. He held her tightly, his big dick captured inside her. Grinding it into her ever so slightly, she could feel it way up in her belly. Her head thrashed up and down with every thrust, yellow hair flying. He could tell she started to cum because she tightened her grip on his cock. With each bob of her head she let out a groan, loudly at first, then tapering off as the orgasm waned.

As soon as she finished, Ross took two long deep strokes, conjuring all of his control not to pound away. On the third stroke, Whisper could tell he was going to cum and there was no way he could stop it even if he wanted to. "Get it, babe," she said.

He started to shoot his load. He went up on his toes and actually lifted her up off the bed with his dick. She could tell he was lost in the orgasm. There was no conscious control of anything as his massive balls unleashed their burden in her.

She gave him thirty seconds to recover and come back to earth before she said, "Well it's about time. What took you so long? I've got to go back to work." She looked over her shoulders at him. She was still on her hands and knees and he was standing behind her, inserted, throbbing in her and barely able to stand. "I think you better sit down," she said.

He pulled out of her with each of them making their own kind of moaning sound. Immediately, his juice flowed down her leg. He spun and sat on the bed as she went to the bathroom to clean up.

Whisper wet a wash rag with warm water and threw it out to Ross who was lying back on the bed, his thick resting cock slung over his thigh. Amazing how sexy that looked, especially knowing she was the one responsible for putting that magnificent dick to sleep. "Big Al is hiring some new girls," she said from the bathroom. Ross grunted a response. She laughed.

"Maybe you won't have to work so hard," he finally said after saving up enough energy to respond.

"That's what I'm hoping. Something else I'm hoping…"

"What's that?" Ross, hands behind his head, looking at her dressed in her waitress uniform.

"I was hoping I could get some more of that after my shift tonight."

"I'll have to check my schedule, but I think I can squeeze you in."

"Asshole," she said as she bent down, roughly grabbed his cock and kissed the head of it good-bye. "Let yourself out or stay as long as you like. If anything is missing, I know where you live."

He jumped up and chased her out the front door. She went flying off the porch on her way to a miserable dinner shift but bolstered by the pleasant thought of a rematch at the end of the night. She was really starting to like this guy.

Chapter 26

Whisper got to the restaurant a little after 5:00 pm. Shanna met her there with a smile. "How was your break?" she asked.

"Shut up," was Whisper's response, also said with a smile.

"How does it feel knowing this is your last double shift?"

"I'll let you know tomorrow if those bitches really show up."

"A glass half empty kind of gal, are we?"

Whisper stared at her for a second and then the door opened. The mercenaries barged in, dressed in their usual full combat gear. Whisper and Shanna looked at each other and Shanna said, "I'll take them tonight." Whisper nearly cried thinking how nice Shanna was being to her.

The guys crashed around in the restaurant dragging tables and chairs across the floor and stacking weapons, field packs and tactical vests on the nearby booths. They were acting like they owned the place. When settled, Shanna went over with a tray of filled water glasses and started distributing them. "What can I get you guys?" She set the tray down on an empty table and pulled out her pad and pen.

Adrian, the mercenary leader, grabbed Shanna's arm and said, "I want a piece of white cake with some orange on the side." Whisper was watching intently and heard the comment.

Shanna jerked her arm away. "Keep it civil, now. What food do you want to order?" Whisper walked over and stood beside Shanna. Big Al was watching from the kitchen thinking, *it used to be so peaceful around here. A couple of deer hunters, a few wives, a snide remark about Orange and then we all went home.* Shanna and Whisper glared at Adrian almost daring him to make another comment.

Adrian was about to say something when one of the new girls walked in for her first evening shift, ready to be trained. Not very often did Adrian show any common sense but he held his tongue. "Bring out the same order from yesterday and don't forget a damn thing. We want it all. The county is paying boys!"

The guys all cheered and the girls huddled at the service counter. Whisper and Shanna told Beth Ann, the new girl, about these assholes and they made a plan to interact with them as little as possible. Whisper told Beth Ann not to talk to them at all. Serving this bunch would not make for a good experience on her first day at work.

Adrian started calling Whisper 'Orange Crust'. He thought it was a clever play on words referencing the popular carbonated beverage. He called Shanna 'White Cake'. A few other customers came in and the girls were busy. Just before the mercenaries finished their desserts, a news crew entered with a camera.

The reporter was the same one that interviewed Whisper. The segment with Whisper never aired because the TV station brass thought showing the orange girl would distract from the story of the missing people and they sure didn't want a distraction because ratings were the highest in station history. A freak girl in the midst would derail interest in the main attraction, which was the magnificent Mister Myles Carter.

The reporter was barking instructions to the camera man as he set up over in the corner of the restaurant. The reporter took a few sound bites and the camera guy adjusted the lighting. The perky reporter looked around the restaurant as if trying to find someone to interview. She was obviously there to talk to the mercenaries.

"How about you, sir?" she said to Adrian. "Care to be famous for fifteen minutes?"

"Well, Little Darling, I was born to be famous." He stood up and donned his gear including his AR-15 style rifle. "Where do you want me and how much of me do you want?" His compatriots laughed hysterically.

"Stand over here just to my right." He stood in his position posed like soldiers do when they are trying to look tough in a picture to be sent home.

"You ready?" she asked the camera man. He counted her down and the interview commenced.

"I'm Amie Lynn Sylvester at the Hill Top Hunting Lodge with…" she put the microphone over in front of him.

He leaned in really close to it, "Adrian Walker."

"And what is your role in this unfolding drama?"

"I'm team leader of Veritas Security assigned to search the area of operations around the Hill Top Hunting Lodge. We're twelve experienced men who can get the job done. As a matter of fact, we discovered evidence of unusual activity in and around the lodge and we will be going out on night patrol to ensure all is safe. At midnight, Veritas Security will deploy from the parking lot and sweep the woods completely around the lake lying to the east. It will take us most of the night but someone has to do it."

"You appear to be heavily armed. Are you expecting trouble?"

"We're ready for anything. This could be a dangerous mission. If you want to, you can embed with the team and see us work first hand. I'm sure the viewers would love to watch American heroes in action. What do you say, pretty lady?"

"There you have it, American heroes heading out into the unknown at midnight tonight. Heavily armed and ready for action. Should we go with them? Tune in tonight at midnight and see what this reporter has decided to do. Amie Lynn Sylvester, signing off."

The camera man said "cut." He slapped the camera tripod legs together and left the restaurant pissed off at the thought of the possibility of filming live coverage of the patrol until the wee hours of the morning.

The reporter pulled out a compact and straightened her makeup. Adrian said, "Well Darlin', do we have a date tonight?"

"Honey, you don't realize what you just did for me. If this works out right, I'll have a job in New York or L.A. by the end of the week. What's this evidence you discovered? Is it something juicy?"

"I'm afraid not. It's hardly anything at all. Some jackass thought he saw something in the woods and we're going to follow up."

"Why the big deal about it then?"

"Darlin', I make $45.00 an hour for the first eight hours and then it goes to $67.50 an hour plus $90.00 an hour bonus for anything over forty hours in a week. If I can spend 16 hours a day looking for these meat sacks, I'll make over $11,000 a week. I hope we never find that bastard Myles."

"You're in it for the money," she said.

"And you are doing this to bring truth and knowledge to the world?"

"I'll see you at midnight and it would be really beneficial if something happened tonight while out playing Boy Scout."

"What do you have in mind?" Adrian asked.

"How should I know. I just know both of us would benefit greatly if something significant occurred."

Adrian thought for second. He wasn't very bright and needed extra time to process the proposal. "I think something is going to happen tonight. But we need to seal the deal. Nationwide incidents don't come cheap."

Amie Lynn knew exactly what he wanted. "Where and when," she asked.

"In my truck, now."

I knew it, she thought.

Adrian and Amie Lynn walked out to the parking lot and climbed in his big crew cab truck. They drove to the far corner of the lot and Adrian told her to get in the back seat, raise up her dress and take off her panties. She did as he requested. He climbed on top of her, slipped his dick in, grunted about five times and had an orgasm. Amie Lynn laid there with her legs spread up over her head until he pulled out and hitched up his pants. He backed out of the truck and said, "Get out." She got out, pulled her dress down, kept her panties wadded up in her hand and went to her car. Adrian drove off thinking about what he was going to rig up tonight to make him look like a hero and give the reporter her story. He also wondered if she would be willing to give it to him again if the story was a good one, *you know, like a reward.*

Ross stepped out of his cabin showered and dressed in clean clothes. He saw the reporter walking briskly across the parking lot and saw Adrian by his truck. He knew something was going on but didn't really care enough to give it another thought. He went to the restaurant for sustenance and to see Whisper.

Whisper saw Ross come in and smiled so big she nearly looked guilty of something. Who knows, maybe it was guilty pleasure. Ross sat at a table and Beth Ann went to wait on him. Shanna grabbed the girl's arm and stopped her. "That's Whisper's new boyfriend."

"He's a…yeah, he's…"

"I know." Shanna and Beth Ann both stared.

Beth Ann was trying to say he was cute, but that didn't exactly cover it. She wanted to call him handsome, but that didn't describe the ruggedness of his features. *What was he?* Beth Ann thought.

Without knowing what Beth Ann was thinking, Shanna said, "He's hot as fuck."

"As fuck." Beth Ann confirmed as she was gawking.

"Get this," Shanna said. "He's ex-army. Brave right? He's a doctor! Educated, right?" He's got a good paying steady job with benefits. And for real, he's a nice guy."

"No shit?"

The Veritas Security crew yelled for 'White Cake' to give them the bill so they could sign it. No tip included and none left on the table. The guys started milling around and gearing up.

Ross asked Whisper, "What's up with the toy soldiers? I just saw their boss and the reporter in the parking lot in what I think was a compromising position."

"You talk so funny. You mean you caught them screwing in the car?"

"In their defense, it was a large pick-up truck."

Whisper stood beside Ross who was sitting in a booth, her hand was on his shoulder. She bent down and spoke softly into his ear, "The Veritas boss guy gave an interview and said he was going out in the woods tonight to follow up a lead. Your lead, I think. The reporter is thinking about going with them."

Ross looked up, big blue eyes staring down at him. He had to focus intently to keep on track. Then she said, "They're leaving at midnight and making a sweep around the lake. Sounds all military."

"He said that in the TV interview?" Ross appeared to be all business now.

Whisper shrugged her shoulders, "Yeah. Why?"

"If they air this on the six o'clock news, they will have told anybody involved that they're coming. Not very OPSEC."

"OPSEC?"

"Operations Security. You don't announce your tactical plans to the enemy. If anybody really is involved in this, they now have a six-hour head start on tying up loose ends, getting out of Dodge or finishing whatever job they started. It was a stupid thing to say on the air."

"It may have put people in danger?" Whisper said.

"Including asshole Adrian and his team. They know he's coming. That is, if anybody really is behind all of this."

"Don't you think there is 'foul play'?"

"I do," said Ross. "It's too coincidental, but it could be something else. I don't really know what to think."

"John Luke, Myles, Molly, Kylie. What do two waitresses, a rich guy and a lodge maintenance man have in common? Who knows all those people?" Whisper thought for a second and said, "That's a bad question because I do."

"So do I," said Ross. "So does Big All. I think I should call the Command Center and let them know about what's going on tonight." Ross got up to make the call.

"What do you want to eat?"

"Plain burger and fries. Iced tea."

Chapter 27

Ross came back from using the restaurant phone. Whisper met him at the table. "The Command Center said the piece was airing right now as a 'Breaking News' segment. This is bad."

"What can you do about it?"

"Nothing." He thought for a moment, "I suppose I could meet them at midnight and make a plea to postpone this maneuver. But I'm sure they'll go out anyway."

"Oh yeah they will."

Ross looked at her a little sideways, "What do you want to be doing at midnight?"

"Sleeping," she said, "Because when you come over at eleven, you won't last that long. Kinda like this afternoon."

"Hey, that's not fair. This afternoon was supposed to be a quickie."

"It certainly was," she said smiling at him.

"Orders up!" yelled Big Al.

"That's your burger." She brought Ross his food and returned to grab some other completed orders.

Beth Ann met her at the service counter. "Wow," she said and tossed her head in Ross' direction.

"I know. I can't believe this is happening to me." Whisper was beaming.

"Why? Is it hard to get a guy because you're colored orange?"

Whisper was analyzing what she said, trying to determine if she was being mean or not.

"Well it's harder to weed out serious guys from assholes. Same as women friends." Whisper's eyes burned a hole in the poor girl.

After an awkward, long moment, Beth Ann said, "I'm not sure what to say now."

"I'm sorry. Most people treat me mean and I never know who will or won't."

"So, how did you and this guy…what kind of uniform is that anyway?"

"He's with the State of Texas Parks and Wildlife. Big Al calls him the Ranger."

Beth Ann stared at Ross, as did Whisper. They watched his muscular arms flex as he ate his meal. Whisper looked at Beth Ann, "I never in my life ever thought a man was sexy while eating a stupid hamburger, until now." Beth Ann just nodded and fingered the pearl on her necklace.

A booming voice from the kitchen broke their trance. "Stop staring at the Ranger and get to work." Both girls jerked and scattered to prepare tables, embarrassed that everyone in the restaurant heard Big Al. Of course, he wanted everyone to hear him.

Supper customers started coming in steadily and the waitresses were busy. There were very few hunters because law enforcement restricted the use of the hunting leases due to the searches being conducted. Big Al at first protested because he thought he would lose a crap-ton of revenue but the cabins were completely rented out to news crews, law enforcement, Incident Command staff and reward seekers. The reward for information leading to the recovery of Myles

Carter doubled to two million dollars. The restaurant was constantly full of incident personnel and locals who came in for the show. Big Al was killin' it.

At 11:15 pm, Whisper finally got out of the restaurant. A party of seven and three State Troopers would not leave. She ran down to her cabin only to find Ross sitting on the steps to her porch. She looked at Molly's and John Luke's cabins with the yellow police tape across the door feeling sad for the missing people and their families but she struck gold with Ross and her life was going to go on.

"You're late," Ross said.

"I couldn't get away." She sat down next to him and put her arm around his broad shoulders. She could tell something was wrong. "What is it?"

"Can we skip tonight? These guys are going to show up in a few minutes and I'd like to try to talk some sense into them. I've got this really bad feeling. Somebody was at that rock house in the woods and if they are still there, then there's going to be trouble. What kind? I don't know but Veritas Security…" Ross shook his head. "Can we take a rain check? You said you were going to be done with me in a few minutes and then kick me out so you could get some sleep. What do you say? Save it for tomorrow?"

Whisper was disappointed but could see the worry in Ross' face and she had been up most of the night. "Alright," said reluctantly. "You go save the world. I'll stay up with you if you want?"

"No, I got this. Go to bed." He stood and raised her up to him. She was standing on the step above him so they were the same height. They kissed, chests pressed together and arms squeezing the breath out of one another. Juices gushed between her legs as she spun her tongue around his. He pulled away before he became erect. "Wow, you better go in…now," he said as he stepped out into the parking lot.

"You gonna leave me like this?" she asked playfully but not really.

"You go on in now. I'm going to try to avert a potential disaster."

"Hero to the bone," she said.

"If you don't go in right now, I'm going to be a hero with a bone."

"You better be available tomorrow to spread some of that hero bone around." She circled her hand in front of her concentrating on her lower region. "You feel me?"

Ross felt her alright. His burgeoning cock was twisted up in his underwear and pubic hair. The sensation was uncomfortable to say the least. Painful, was a better description. Ross turned to walk out into the parking lot. He waved his hand over his head, "Goodnight." Whisper grinned, he was walking bowlegged. She went in to shower away the day and get a good night's sleep.

Chapter 28

Within minutes, the three big Veritas Security trucks pulled into the lot followed by three news vans and a half a dozen other cars and trucks loaded with local rubberneckers. Why watch this on TV when you can be a part of it.

Amie Lynn, the reporter, was dressed in something that could best be described as 'safari chic'. She looked more ready for a runway photo shoot in South Africa than a walk in the East Texas backwoods. Adrian and the other mercenaries were dressed in their usual combat gear but this time they had their faces blackened out with camouflage.

Amie Lynn ordered the camera guy to set up the shot with one of the Veritas trucks in the background. When ready, the camera man counted her in and…action. She stood with Adrian and began a quick orientation.

"I'm Amie Lynn Sylvester at the Hill Top Hunting Lodge with Adrian Walker, the head of the Veritas Security team. Tonight, they will sweep the woods behind the lodge where unusual sightings have been reported. With any luck the team will locate and rescue the venerable Myles Carter, their boss, and the other missing people. How will things proceed tonight?"

"My men will be divided into two fire teams of five men each. I will be in command of both teams. One team will move forward and set up an overwatch then the next team will do the same. Leapfrogging until the area is thoroughly covered."

"Sounds like precision tactics. I see you are completely camouflaged and heavily armed."

"Yes Amie Lynn, if there is anything bad out there, we want to make sure we meet the threat with every possible advantage." Adrian smiled into the camera and raised his AR-15 style rifle in a childish pose.

Amie Lynn moved a few steps away from Adrian and continued to speak into the camera. "Tonight, we will follow these brave men into the woods, filming every step of the way. Our camera man, Gary, (his real name was Larry but she didn't care to learn it) will be using high-tech infrared lighting so you can see all of the action without exposing us to any unnecessary danger. One of our vans will be picking up our signal and transmitting it out to America."

Several more cars and trucks pulled into the parking lot. One SUV was filled with personnel from the Incident Command Center. Two police cars pulled in, one a Deputy Sheriff and the other a State Trooper. Their lights were flashing. One car sealed off the south entrance to the lodge and the other sealed off the north entrance.

Ross looked at this and thought, *what a shit show*. He sought out Adrian who was checking ammunition and other paraphernalia. "Do you really want to do this?"

Adrian looked up, "Well if it ain't Ranger Rick."

"Hey get it right! Ranger Ross." he joked back. "I know you're looking for a lot of publicity for some reason, but I really do think there's somebody out there."

"Oh, I know there is."

"What are you saying? Do you have fresh intel?"

Adrian smiled, "I just know there is somebody out there."

Ross had a very strong feeling that something wasn't right. He didn't trust Veritas Security as far as he could spit. "Call this off. Somebody is going to get hurt. The reporter will probably sprain an ankle the first hundred yards. She's wearing high-heeled patent leather boots for God's sake."

"You don't need to worry about her. I'll take care of that little filly."

Ross walked over to plead with the Incident Command Center staff. They said it was out of their hands. It was a private undertaking and they had no control plus Veritas international just gave them the SUV they were driving and three others like it back at the Command Center. *A good old fashion bribe.*

The technicians set up a sixty-five inch TV on the side of the van and dubbed the live feed into it. Ross went to his truck, grabbed a folding canvas chair, set it up right in front of the screen and settled in. Some of the police officers did the same.

With as much fanfare as possible, Adrian and the rest of the mercenaries started tactically moving out into the woods. Amie Lynn and Larry, the camera guy, followed behind with the reporter continuously commenting about anything that popped into her head, the darkness, the danger, the excitement, how America was lucky to have this opportunity. Ross watched the men on TV as they entered the woods. He noticed they were formed into two groups of five men plus Adrian. Earlier, these guys were a twelve pack. Somebody was not present. Men like this didn't miss these kinds of opportunities to dress up like commandos, carry weapons in the woods at night, show off for a pretty girl all on national TV. *Nope, unless the twelfth man died earlier today, there is no way he would miss this.*

Ross went to the Command Center staff and asked about the twelfth man on the team. They didn't know or care. All they wanted to do was watch the show. Ross sat back down and ran his hand through his hair.

The patrol was moving slowly through the thick brush. Amie Lynn was making asinine comments and Adrian would face the camera every now and then and explain what maneuver they were doing, checking a flank, clearing a defilade or readjusting an azimuth. It all sounded very military. Amie Lynn even fell right down on her ass once which brought chuckles from the men in the parking lot but it probably endeared her to a national audience. Brave soul she was, enduring such hardships in the search for truth and knowledge.

About two in the morning, the team made it to the far side of the lake. They regrouped and were making plans that sounded a lot like an assault on the rock house. Ross couldn't understand why they hadn't gone out in the daylight yesterday afternoon so they could see what they were getting into. It didn't make sense.

At 2:30 am, the team was in place to make their assault. The camera was on Adrian as he checked his watch, as if they were synchronized with some other unit like artillery or air support. *What a show.*

"It's time," Adrian said as he stood, waved his hand in a 'follow me' kind of gesture. *Good grief,* Ross thought. The men moved forward, rifles at their shoulders, barrels pointed toward the house.

Amie Lynn stumbled along behind giving color commentary on every move they made. "Cautiously inching forward. Weapons ready. Focused on the objective, securing the house and saving the victims of this horrific tragedy."

At fifty yards out from the house, the group stopped for dramatic effect. Amie Lynn said, "This is it America. The assault begins."

No sooner did she finish those words when a shot rang out coming from the rock house. Amie Lynn's head literally blew the fuck up. The .308 caliber, 168 grain Hornady bullet struck her just to the left of her nose at 2800 feet per second and exited the base of her skull spewing bone, brains and blood vapor six feet into the air behind her. Larry, the camera guy, was covered in her gore. The microphone fell from her hands and her body stiffened from the blast, she fell like a tree to the side.

Larry was done. Screaming like a two year old, he dropped the camera and ran off into the woods not knowing which way he was going. After three steps, the headphones he was wearing jerked off his head nearly taking his ears with them. The camera on the ground spun in a half-circle and pointed toward the trunk of a tree. It didn't really matter which way the camera pointed, blood splatter covered the lens and no one could see anything anyway.

Adrian and the mercenaries were stunned. Most of them had sense enough to get down on the ground or seek cover behind a tree. Adrian yelled, "Derek! What the fuck are you doing?"

There was no answer. "Derek!" he called again. The mercenaries looked at their leader.

One of the team members asked, "Adrian, what the fuck did you do?"

Adrian shook his head. "It wasn't supposed to happen like this."

"What the FUCK did you do!"

"I sent Derek ahead of us to the house. He was supposed to snap off a few rounds in our direction and show up at the lodge acting like he was late for the mission. Now he's shot that bitch right in the head and the camera man has run off. Derek! Derek! Come on out. It was an accident. We can fix this." Everyone was yelling Derek's name, "Derek, don't shoot!"

Chapter 29

After 1:30 am, the group of people in the lodge parking lot dwindled to just a half a dozen. Ross was one of those. He was in his chair with a blanket draped over him trying to stay awake. Two hours of listening to Amie Lynn talk to herself was about to put everyone asleep. When they got close to the rock house, Ross rubbed his hands on his face and sat up straighter. When he heard her say, "This is it America. The assault begins," he was staring directly at the TV. Then boom! A rifle shot with a simultaneous sound like a baseball bat hitting a watermelon and Amie Lynn's head splashed across the screen. The camera was down and a male scream of terror was heard. The sound of the actual rifle report rolled across the lake and rumbled through the parking lot.

Ross jumped up and the blanket went flying. "Did you see that?" he yelled or maybe it sounded like he yelled in the quiet of the night. "Come here," he waved to the group of guys near the van that brought in some truck stop coffee. "Did you hear it?" He held his finger up as if listening for another rifle shot.

The guys crowded around the TV. The van technician was trying to retrieve a better transmission but the camera was obviously on the ground and no one was operating it. They could hear Adrian and the other mercenaries hollering at Derek. Ross asked the technician if he could play that back and enhance the sound.

Two painfully long minutes later, the technician pushed 'play'. He ran it forward and backwards a dozen times but everyone agreed they could hear Adrian confessing to setting up a hoax and the hoax going terribly awry.

In the woods, Adrian gathered what he thought were his loyal men. Discussing what to do next, they decided to go root out Derek from the house and kill him. The story would be he was killed during the assault. They'd clean the house of evidence suggesting anything else happened and of course, the big bad perpetrator will have gotten away.

The mercenaries went full on tactical forming a skirmish line and assaulting the house expending dozens of rounds of ammunition each. When they got into the house, they found Derek dead on the floor with his throat cut from ear to ear. They stood over him and reevaluated their plan.

Ross stood at the TV van with a dozen people now. Two of them were the deputy and the trooper assigned traffic control at the lodge. They were discussing the number of arrestable offenses committed by the Veritas Security team. In the middle of their discussion, a loud roar of continuous gunfire came in a wave across the parking lot. Ross heard that sound before. It was definitely a firefight. The two law enforcement officers called for the cavalry and within minutes, every police car in the county was on scene. Some got there quickly because they were watching TV at the time and saw Amie Lynn's murder and started rolling immediately. Ross turned to get out of the crowd and think when he looked up to see Whisper running out of her cabin. She was wearing some flannel pajamas and barefooted.

She ran right into his arms. "Are you alright?" she asked while hugging him.

"Yes," he said as he hugged her back.

"What's happening? I was dead asleep until I heard all of the sirens."

"You won't believe this."

"Try me." He picked her up and carried her back to her porch. They went in the cabin and she put on a pot of decaf coffee.

Ross told her all he knew. Whisper looked shocked. "So," she said still processing. "Adrian set this up and Derek killed Amie Lynn or something else we don't know about happened. And…they're still out in the woods shooting up the place."

"That's as close as I can figure it right now. Until the security idiots get back and can be interviewed, nobody will know anything more."

"What a mess." She sipped coffee holding the mug with both hands. "What are you going to do about all of this?"

"Wait and see. I know I can help if they'll let me. My credentials aren't exactly a good fit but I do know the woods and we've been to the rock house. Maybe I could guide or track. I'm a pretty good tracker." He took a sip of coffee.

"Why don't you lie down a while? It's three in the morning and I have to be at work in an hour. We can lie down together. No messing around, okay?"

They went to the bed. Ross stripped down to his underwear and slipped between the sheets. Whisper followed, wearing her red flannels. Within thirty seconds, Ross had her bottoms down to her knees, spooned her and slid his manhood up in her from behind. He grabbed her shoulders and pushed her down on him over and over. They began to cum at the same time. Each fighting one another to better enhance their own orgasm. It was a sensual dance of moans and jerks and rigid muscles until nothing was left but hard breathing and relaxation. They fell asleep with him still in her. For the thirty minutes of sleep they got before her alarm went off, she dreamed she was getting fucked.

The alarm was jarring and she reached over and slapped the snooze. They were still in the same spooning position and incredibly, his cock, as flaccid as possible, was still big enough to stay in her all night. All night really being twenty-eight minutes. *Impossible*, she thought. The snooze button allowed her nine more minutes before the next alarm.

She decided to squeeze his cock inside her to see if it would wake up. She was not an expert at doing this but she tried and it must have been working because she could feel it jump to life. It swelled with astonishing rapidity. Two minutes into the snooze they were pumping again. Maybe even hungrier than before. It took Ross nearly five minutes but he got there and cried out when he came. Whisper did not reach a simultaneous orgasm this time but had three little tremors before he finished. She needed to pee too badly to really let herself go. As soon as he was finished, she slapped the alarm clock, beating the snooze alarm by a full minute, and jumped up to pee and shower.

Whisper did her usual 'I'm late' bathroom routine and was out and dressed in record time. Ross was lying on top of the covers with his underwear on. She was talking a mile a minute about him being careful today, checking in with her but only after he got some sleep. Slipping on her shoes, she was ready. Ross raised up on an elbow to get a good look at her. She walked over to the bed and pushed him flat on his back, rolled his underwear down, pulled out his limp cock and gave it a kiss goodbye. Kissing him goodbye that way seemed to be something she was going to do with him. Never had she ever done it with any man before. It made her tingle all day long.

Standing in the door she said, "Stay as long as you want. You know where I'll be and today..." She smiled broadly, "I'm off at 5:30 pm." Her blue eyes flashed at him. He couldn't help but smile back. His cock jerked by itself as he started to get hard again. She giggled and closed the door behind her.

The parking lot was filled with cop cars and other emergency vehicles. There were several groups of armed men dressed in tactical gear instead of police patrol uniforms and they weren't the Veritas Security guys. Whisper figured them for local SWAT teams. News crews and their vans were being held at bay on the highway that fronted the lodge. They weren't allowed in the parking lot. The live murder on national TV drew the attention of the entire world. Every media outlet was covering this story.

When she got to the restaurant, Big Al was shouting orders to the two new girls who weren't responding because they didn't know anything. "Get the big coffee urn out of the back storeroom."

The girls asked, "Where's the back storeroom?"

Whisper chimed in, "I've got this. Put the 'OPEN' sign in the door and start taking orders. It's going to be a busy day."

Ross wasn't sure what to do with himself. As he was trying to decide, the best thing that could have happened to him, happened. He fell fast asleep. He could hear commotion in the parking lot but it was a dull roar and lulled him deeper into sleep like white noise.

After an hour and a half of slumber like death, Ross dressed just enough to stumble over to his own cabin. He sneaked in trying not to wake Shelby. Showering and dressing in his uniform, Ross went out to face the madness.

Big Al made a large urn of coffee and wheeled it out into the parking lot. He had the girls set up a table of pastries and coffee condiments. The police army was swarming around it. Ross fell right in line. *Coffee!* He introduced himself to the new waitress assigned to keeping the pot full and the pastries abundant and welcomed her to some level of hell but he just didn't know which one.

Ross sought out the guy in charge and asked what was going on. The guy in charge was a Texas Ranger and explained the situation. Amie Lynn, the reporter was assumed to be dead since her brains splattered all over national TV cameras last night. Larry, the camera man, was presumed missing. Derek, a member of the Veritas Security team, was given the task of entering the woods, finding the house in the area of concern and firing 'warning' shots at the approaching Veritas Security team to make an interesting story. Something went wrong and Derek or someone else shot and killed the reporter. The Veritas Security team returned fire to defend themselves and they have not yet exfiltrated to the lodge. The SWAT teams are here to help facilitate the arrest of the entire Veritas Security team until all of this can be sorted out. He finished his speech with, "The biggest cluster fuck with which I have ever been associated."

"If there is anything I can do to uncluster this fuck, let me know."

The Texas Ranger gulped the last hit in his coffee cup and said, "If we can detain these Veritas assholes without an incident, I want you to lead us into the woods so we can work the scene. Maybe help us find the camera man if he doesn't come out with the team."

"I can do that. You know the shortest way to the rock house is straight across the lake. It will save an hour each way and it'll sure make lugging equipment a lot easier. I can call my guys and have a couple of boats down here in no time."

"Get on it." The Texas Ranger went to the courtesy table to get another cup of coffee. The pastries and coffee were free to first responders but Big Al kept count of how much was sent out to the parking lot. The county was getting a bill for this. *What a gold mine.*

Chapter 30

At an hour past sun-up, the Veritas Security guys began coming out of the woods. They were surrounded by three SWAT teams who made the men drop their weapons and lie face down on the ground. The Veritas guys acted incredulous. They were heroes, why were they being treated like this. Each member of the Veritas Security team quoted a surprisingly similar story. They said, "As they approached the house, an unknown perpetrator fired on the team. The reporter went down first and later Derek was killed during the assault phase. The perpetrator got away. Oh yeah, Larry the camera guy, ran off and is still missing."

They loaded the Veritas Security lying sacks of shit into six police cars and sped them off to two different county jails. The Texas Ranger sought out Ross and said, "We've got a couple of jobs for you now. Get us to the scene so we can work it and recover the bodies. And…find the camera man. He didn't return with the team. I hope he's not dead."

"Okay. The boats are on the way." Ross made the call earlier from the restaurant phone while he was sneaking sideways glances at

Whisper. Ross spoke his mind to the Texas Ranger, "This all seems cut and dried to me. Veritas Security is guilty as hell of some crime. I mean people are dead, right? But I'm sure it will take you forever to process a scene spread out over a hundred yards that involves two dead bodies, hundreds of expended rounds and now a fifth missing person." The Texas Ranger was shaking his head in agreement, wondering what Ross was thinking. "You'll be out there all day and maybe into the night. You'll need at least a six pack of bottled water per person. You'll need food for one meal and maybe two. A cold front is blowing in from the northeast this afternoon and temperatures are supposed to drop twenty degrees by 3:00 pm. Take layers of clothing and you may want some warming fires. You'll need lights if you're out there past 4:00 pm. It gets dark in the woods early. I can guarantee you there will be aggressive reporters trying to get to the scene so perimeter security is a must…."

The Texas Ranger held up his hand. "I get what you're saying. We'll put a full team on the planning and logistics. Anything else?"

"You don't care if I take my rifle with me when I go traipsing through the woods, do you?"

"Your call. I know I would take something reassuring with me if I were going out there."

"You're not going?" Ross asked."

"Oh, hell no. I'm too important," he said facetiously. "I've got to stand here in this parking lot, drink coffee and eat…" He looked at the pastry he was holding in his hand. "…whatever the shit this is." He threw it in the trashcan set up by the courtesy table.

The boats arrived in a few hours and Ross went about giving instructions, coordinating the loads, planning the number of trips across the water and generally taking over the operation. Just before noon, the first set of boats blasted across the lake with Ross guiding them. The boats were filled with nothing but armed men assigned to clear the area and set up a perimeter. They all had assault rifles and semi-automatic pistols, lots of ammunition, flash-bang, tear gas and smoke grenades. Ross was holding his big bore lever action Marlin rifle. He looked like a dinosaur compared to the other men.

Once across the lake, the police teams swept through the woods. Ross sent the boats back to the staging area at the edge of the lake nearest the lodge. They began loading and ferrying supplies to the far side in a constant stream of people and equipment moving back and forth. As soon as the police gave the all clear, Ross started his quest to find Larry, the camera guy.

Ross easily found the camera on the ground some fifty or sixty yards away from the house. The camera was ten feet behind the gruesome dead body of Amie Lynn. This was the last known location of Larry since he was carrying the camera when the shit hit the fan. Ross circled around the camera a few feet and found what he thought were Larry's tracks, heading away from the action at a high rate of speed.

Ross wasn't the best tracker but with some luck, maybe he could find this city slicker before the poor bastard froze to death tonight. Ross felt sure Larry was not shot or his body or blood would be around. The only blood was from Amie Lynn.

Ross set off with his canteen, snacks, some small binoculars, the state issue GPS, sat-phone and some cold weather gear in a large pack strapped to his back. He carried his rifle in his hands. Ross couldn't find any tracks or other signs after about a hundred yards. Ross decided to take the easiest route thinking Larry would run as fast as he could on the most level terrain putting as much distance as possible between him and the bad guys in the shortest amount of time.

Once out of sight and earshot of the police contingent, Ross loaded his weapon with six cartridges from his spare ammo leaving his butt stock ammo holder full with six additional rounds. The rifle only weighed about eight pounds but it sure felt heavy. He moved quickly and quietly through the woods, paying maximum attention to the sounds and sights. He was home in the woods but he didn't think he would ever get used to hunting men.

Sometime around 2:00 pm, he sat down under a tree and ate a power bar that tasted more like a chocolate bar than a protein bar. He drank copious amounts of water, shut his eyes for a moment and thought of Whisper's beautiful orange body with that wonderful yellow hair and red nipple highlights. *STOP!* He couldn't let himself get distracted. He pulled out his phone and called in to the tactical operations center in the parking lot and told them he was going to spend the night in the woods and he should not be expected in until the morning. Could they please send someone to the restaurant to tell Whisper Jenkins that he would not be home until the morning? Telling her he wasn't coming home via a third party was becoming a habit. A bad habit.

He put the gear away and resumed his trek. There was little hope of finding Larry but his plan was to continue on this route until hitting the highway and calling for someone to come get him. Every hundred yards, like the last twenty times, Ross hollered out Larry's name on the odd chance he would answer.

At 3:00 pm the wind began to blow cold. Ross put on his field jacket and watch cap. At 4:30 pm the woods began to grey out and by 5:30 pm, it was dark as the hubs of hades and freezing. Ross hollered Larry's name for the last time. He collected a ton of wood, started a fire and pulled his thin sleeping bag out of his pack and settled in for a miserable night. While cocooned in the bag, he ate another snack of jerky and nuts. He used the pack as a pillow and hoped no animals came to camp wanting to share the rest of his snacks because they were right underneath his head.

Every hour he woke up and threw another log on the fire. When the sun finally lit the woods enough to see, he packed up, heated some water and made instant coffee that tasted like mud but had enough caffeine to do the trick, plus, it was hot. After the coffee, he couldn't make up his mind if he wanted to try to take a crap in the woods or not. The thought of a full-on squat in the cold just didn't do it for him. Ross wandered around a little, looking for a log, stump or low hanging branch with which to brace himself for the squat. To the east there was a deep gulley so steep he couldn't see the bottom. He never saw it in the dark last night and was thankful for not walking right over the side.

He edged over to it and looked down. At the bottom was Larry, contorted in a garish manner, ashen grey in color, long dead. "Fuck." Ross drew back, a little sick to his stomach. He slept within twenty yards of the body last night and never knew it. Ross ran to the far side of camp, pulled his pants down and purged.

Recovered from the shock, he mentally made a quick plan to call the tactical operations center at the lodge, report his findings and fire up his GPS so the Command Center could take a reading. Ross would stay and guard the body until the forensic and recovery teams arrived. Fire rebuilt, he tried to make himself as comfortable as possible for the long wait.

Hours passed before the forensic team arrived with all of their gear. As soon as they were briefed, he headed back to the lake, rode a boat across, hiked up to his cabin and took a long hot shower. Shelby had been hanging around all morning waiting for Ross to tell him what to do. They both went to the restaurant for lunch. As soon as Ross stepped into the building, Whisper went flying across the room into his arms.

"I guess you heard," Ross said into to her ear.

"Yes."

They continued to hug in front of everybody in the restaurant and it was packed. Whisper wasn't going to let go. They moved over to the service counter so they could talk and still hold each other. Ross explained in detail what occurred last night and this morning.

Whisper summed it up, "Three people died in the woods last night because of Veritas Security's plan to become famous and we are no closer to finding the missing people. This is getting out of hand."

"I couldn't agree more."

Chapter 31

The truth came out about Veritas Security because of the live recording. Adrian unknowingly confessed on tape to perpetrating a hoax which led to the deadly outcome. Adrian was personally charged with manslaughter in the second degree for Amie Lynn, criminally negligent homicide for the death of Larry and Derek, conspiracy, obstruction, fraud and a half a dozen other lesser crimes. The Veritas Security Team members were charged with conspiracy after the fact, obstruction and a few other minor offenses. The courtroom drama was going to be another shit show.

Ross was summoned to the Sheriff's Office to give a statement not knowing when he would be back. Whisper was destined to spend the night in her cabin alone, which was probably a good thing because she hadn't slept in two days. She needed a break.

After the national TV exposure, reporters and fortune hunters from around the world came to East Texas. Big Al, was charging four times the going rate for cabins. He threatened to throw Whisper out of her cabin because she was costing him $450 a night. Ross got to stay in his cabin at the State rate because Big Al signed a contract with the State of Texas several years ago trying to boost the off-season sales. Now he was regretting it. However, he did run a couple of extension cords out of his barn to the field behind the restaurant where several RV campers hooked up to power. The occupants had to get water from a hose in the back of the restaurant. Big Al charged $200 a night for this service. Also, every item on the restaurant menu was marked up a dollar. His revenue was $5,000 a day and he was trying to figure out ways to increase that. He was starting the slide into home. 'Home,' being retirement.

Ross got back to the lodge at midnight and noticed Whisper's lights were off. He really wanted to see her but she was getting up in three and a half hours and needed some sleep. For that matter, he needed some sleep pretty badly also. At 4:00 am, Whisper rolled out of her cabin, looked for Ross' truck and spied it up near the restaurant. She saw no lights on in his cabin. He was right there, lying in his bed and she missed him so badly she ached between her legs and…in her heart. The heart part was a totally new sensation for her.

At almost noon, Ross and Shelby strolled into the full restaurant. There were no seats. Even Big Al's booth was taken up with out-of-towners. Whisper was at the service counter and swamped with orders and pick-ups. She managed to give Ross a wave and a smile but that was it. The state boys went out on the veranda to grab a table out there. Most of the veranda tables were taken also.

"When do you think this will end?" Shelby asked almost rhetorically.

"I think 'how' it will end is a better question."

They sat in the cold air and looked for a waitress. Instead, they got a guy about six-foot-two who weighed in at 300 very soft pounds. The guy had an unruly beard.

"Help ya'll?" he asked without looking at them.

Ross was a little stunned. "When did Big Al hire you?" After asking he realized it sounded a little rude.

"Three days ago but I didn't show up until today. I'm supposed to be the new maintenance man but due to the number of fucking people wanting to be here for the action, I got assigned waiter duties on the porch so the girls wouldn't get cold. Now what do you want?"

"Ah," Ross managed to say. "We haven't seen menus yet."

The big guy reached behind him and pulled out a handful of menus and held them out for Ross to grab one. Ross thought the big guy had them stuffed in his pants which meant the bottom of the menus were in the proximity of his butt crack. Ross didn't take the menu from him but put his hands up like he was surrendering and said, "I'll take a bowl of beef stew and hot tea."

Shelby grabbed a menu and perused it for what seemed like a full minute. The big guy was getting irritated. "Me too. A bowl of beef stew but I want a large Coke." The big guy snatched the menu out of Shelby's hand, stuffed them in the back of his britches and headed into the restaurant. The menus, sticking out of the big guy's pants made him look like he had turkey feathers waving back and forth as he waddled away.

In a moment the big guy came out carrying a tray with the food and drinks. He set the tray down on a nearby table, disturbing the patrons eating there, and grabbed the two bowls of stew. He set Ross' bowl down in front of him without incident but bounced Shelby's bowl off the table because the stew was hot and he accidentally stuck his thumb in it. Stew sloshed on the table splattering Shelby's lap. The big guy sucked the stew off his thumb and set the drinks on the table, threw down some spoons, turned and waddled back into the restaurant, turkey feather menus waving goodbye. He never returned to check on them.

Shelby began to eat but said, "Was it my imagination or was that guy a terrible waiter?"

Ross laughed out loud and began to eat.

When the boys finished, they looked around for the waiter to bring the ticket. They looked at the other diners who were looking for the waiter also. Some of them stood up as if it were going to make the big guy respond faster. The door swung open and Whisper came out, arms wrapped around herself.

She went straight to Ross. "I see you've met Big Al's nephew."

"That explains everything."

She looked around. "Is everybody waiting for a ticket?" she asked. People grumbled, "We need more water, silverware, bread, more coffee, the bill, a menu, ketchup…."

Whisper stormed off. In thirty seconds, she reappeared, shoving Big Al's nephew in front of her, yelling, "Get your lazy ass out there and take care of those people." He balked and tried to go back inside. Whisper literally beat him in back with the palm of her hand guiding him out to the customers.

The crowd cheered and clapped. Whisper ran around taking care of three times as many customers as Big Al's nephew. Ross made a mental note, Whisper was good at what she did and probably would be good at anything she put her mind to. *Wasted potential.*

In a few minutes, the crowd was current with their needs and Whisper rejoined Ross and Shelby at their table. "Impressive," Ross said.

Whisper played off the compliment, "That dude is just a blur of excitement and energy."

"Ain't he though," Shelby said. "I think I could be a waiter as good as him."

Ross and Whisper looked at each other and laughed.

"What's on the agenda today," Whisper asked.

Ross said, "I've got a new assignment."

Whisper looked visibly shaken. "What is it?"

"I don't know. I was told to report to the Command Center this afternoon for a big announcement and my new assignment. I don't have a clue about either."

"If it's something dangerous, I'll kill you myself. You've done enough."

"Don't get all excited. I don't even know what it is. Who's getting this tip? You or the big guy?"

"It's his table."

Ross took half the money he was holding and dropped it on the table. The other half went back into his pocket. Whisper calculated it in her head. *Still 18%, even with terrible service.*

"I've got to get back to work," she said. "Will I see you tonight?"

"Yeah you will," he said standing up.

"I get off at 5:30 pm so don't....."

"Orange!" Big Al was hollering from the door.

Whisper looked at Ross, "I bet I just got snitched on."

"Family, go figure."

Ross and Whisper were standing close and he could tell she wanted to physically reach out to him somehow. They settled on five seconds of hand holding as they walked back inside the restaurant. Whisper went to see Big Al at the kitchen. Ross and Shelby left to go to the Command Center.

The state boys snaked their way through all of the vehicles parked haphazardly in the lodge parking lot. Two news crews were making statements and four police vehicles with occupants were protecting and serving by playing games on their iPhones.

Shelby slept in the truck on the drive to the Command Center. They checked in at the front gate which was now guarded by three men in military uniforms. The men appeared to be unarmed but Ross noticed bulges on the righthand side of their waists under their uniform blouses. Concealed carry handguns. They had Texas flag shoulder patches and name tapes that said, 'Texas State Guard'. The Governor apparently activated part of his private army. Ross knew some of these State Guard types and they were good guys. All volunteers who stepped up to the plate during emergencies.

Ross said, "The Governor must think things are pretty bad if he activated you guys."

"Yes sir. But only the standard Emergency Operations Center package." The guard checked their ID's and waved him through.

Ross and Shelby entered the Command Center and sought out the Incident Commander. All the Command and General Staff were settling in for the afternoon briefing. There was standing room only but Ross and Shelby squeezed in anyway. The briefing was the standard boring logistics nightmare with no real news about the missing people.

After the briefing, the Incident Commander approached Ross and thanked him for quickly finding the camera man's body and said, "You were right."

"About what?"

"The medical examiner gave us a preliminary report on the causes of death for the reporter, the camera man and the Veritas Security Officer. The reporter was obviously shot in the head with a powerful bullet, the camera man died from injuries consistent with a fall but the security guy..." The Incident Commander paused a moment. "He had his throat cut. That's what killed him and then he was shot several times post mortem."

Ross was sorting this in his brain. "So, there really was somebody else there who killed the security guy and shot the reporter?"

"Exactly."

"Who? A kidnapper?"

"Fuck, I don't know."

Ross asked, "What do you want me to do?"

"I want you to go back to the scene of the shooting and try to track the unknown party. I know it's a long shot but we don't have any other ideas. We thought about getting dogs but they have no idea who to search for. There were no less than a hundred people in the area. Basically, your instincts are the only thing we have to go with."

"That's not much."

"We've got shit. National media is spinning up ghost kidnappers and conspiracies, the Governor's breathing down our necks, Veritas Security is completely out of control. We're grabbing at straws."

"And I'm a straw?"

"Yep. I got to get back to the madness. Oh, by the way, Veritas International raised the reward for finding Myles Carter."

"It's already two-million. What's it going to?"

"Five million dollars."

"Everybody and their grandmother will be out in the woods looking for Mr. Carter."

"As will you, I hope."

"I'll be there too. Same deal as before, GPS, sat-phone?"

"Check in daily by 1300 hours so we can get your report in the afternoon briefing."

"How long will I be roaming around out there?"

The Incident Commander thought for a moment, "Until you're satisfied you won't find anything. Could be a day, could be a month."

Whisper is going to be pissed. "Okay, when do I start?"

"Today. Now."

Oh yeah, she's going to be pissed.

Back at the lodge, Shelby was helping Ross get prepared. Ross had his big primitive camping pack by the bed with gear laid out all over the floor and spare clothes on the bed. They heard the front door bang open.

"What in the hell is going on?" Whisper definitely sounded pissed. Ross looked at his watch, it was 5:23 pm.

Shelby headed for the restaurant, leaving them alone.

Ross started to explain what was happening but Whisper interrupted him. "You're going out in the woods again."

"Yes."

"How long?"

"Indefinitely."

"I don't suppose I can stop you?"

"No, I have to do this."

Whisper bit her lip. "Okay. But you're going to give me something to tide me over until you get back." She shut the bedroom door, scraped off everything Ross neatly arranged on his bed into a pile the floor. She started taking off her clothes.

Ross swallowed hard and proceeded to disrobe. She laid down on the bed and he slid in on top of her. He was erect by the time they finished their first kiss. Zero to ten inches in thirty seconds. If Ross were a car, he would definitely be in the Ferrari class. *God, this boy can fuck!*

He slid down her thin body, gently kissing between her breasts. He held her arms so she couldn't move except the arching of her chest. He kissed in circles around each breast but never touched the nipples with anything other than his hot breath. She thrust her chest forward, fishing for his mouth using her red swollen nipples as bait. After an excruciating amount of time, Ross flicked the left nipple with his tongue. Whisper moaned so he did it again. He engulfed her nipple with his mouth making her cry out, sucking it like it was made of the finest Belgian chocolate. Thrusting her chest forward, he let her fuck his mouth with her elongated red nipple, while her legs involuntarily spread.

Leaving her breasts aching, he slid further down and kissed her smooth, flat belly as her chest still pumped into the air searching for his mouth. He rolled his tongue across the area between her belly but- ton and her golden pubic hair. Ross could feel the hair tickle his chin.

She could sense his big dick on the inside of her thighs. As his face lingered above her shiny hair, cheek rubbing against the softness of her skin, she pushed her hips up begging him to go down. Ross could smell her scent. Whisper growled in frustration and Ross ended her agony by parting her lips with his tongue and easily finding the swol- len clit. She was cumming before he could circle his tongue around it. She screamed internally and pushed Ross' face into her. His tongue flashed across her clit as she exploded with an oral orgasm, her body shaking from head to toe. Finished, she shoved his head aside, too sensitive to take anymore.

He laid on top of her, his cock throbbing. Kissing her deeply, she could taste her own juice on his lips. He positioned his big phallus above her, spread her legs further and slipped it in, her moistness oozing out as it was driven in deeply.

Moving his hips in big sweeping, rotating, slow undulations, she wrapped herself around him waiting for the inevitable. She clawed and kicked and squeezed but Ross never broke his slow deliberate strokes. *I'm cumming*, she either said or thought, she couldn't tell. She gripped him fiercely, trying not to sink her nails into the scars on his back. Her heels were digging into his legs. She cooed a soft sound and the orgasm splashed across her like a wave crashing on a beach. And just like the waves, they never stopped, pouring over her one right after another. She pitched and squirmed, grunted and gasped, slapped and pulled but he kept the same slow, penetrating strokes. It was wonderfully frustrating.

Ross never faltered, holding her tightly against his body. He could feel her knotted nipples piercing his chest, taking him to a place no other woman had ever taken him. He felt every inch of his long cock being swallowed up, over and over again. It felt so good, there was no way he was letting this moment slip away too quickly.

He kept going, like a piston on a big ocean liner slowly making its way home. She came again, making a grunting sound as she reached up and pushed some of her hair out of her face because she was breathing hard and sucking in the ends. He could tell she was tired from straining against his assault but the feeling of his big dick being raked by her hot flesh on every plunge drove him to the edge of losing control.

She was so beautiful and incredibly sexy. He was ready to let go. Whisper could sense an almost unperceivable change of speed and motion of his large cock up in her. She knew he couldn't last much longer. He gripped her tighter. *Here he comes*, she thought. *Oh no.* She started to cum again too. She finished first, mouth and throat dry from so many silent screams of pleasure. She was trying to recover so she could enjoy his orgasm with him. He bolted upright on his knees, grabbed his big manhood and shot a river of juice on her belly. He jerked back and forth like he was stabbing the air with his dick. The muscles over his entire naked body were rippling. Whisper instinctively put her fingers to her clit while watching. She probably couldn't have rubbed another one off if she were paid a million dollars but watching Ross lose his load like that…she had to at least rub herself.

Ross got off the bed, went to the bathroom and grabbed a hand towel. He threw it at her as he walked by. "Sorry about that," he said pointing to the mess all over her tummy.

"Are you kidding? That's what it's all about." She wiped herself off.

Ross came back from the kitchen with a glass of water. He stood in the door for a moment watching her clean herself on the bed. He was leaning against the door jamb with the glass in his hand. His dick was still swollen and out in front of him. It bobbed on its own and a little droplet of cum rolled out of the end and dripped, stringing down a foot before it snapped off and fell to the floor. Whisper smiled, he was still cumming and didn't even know it.

He walked over and handed her the water. She nearly gulped it all down. Ross took the glass and drank the last few drops setting it on the nightstand. He slid in the bed beside her. They propped the pillows up on the headboard and sat up, leaning back. Ross' dick was still poking up. She scooted down the bed, laid on her stomach, feet in the air and her face at Ross' thigh. She bent his dick over and put the head in her mouth. Ross stiffened and made some kind of strange noise. They both laughed. After he let her suck him for a while, he asked, "How is this going to work?"

She took his dick out of her mouth, shook it a little and said, "What work?" Back in her mouth it went.

"Ripping our clothes off every time we see each other."

She pulled it out of her mouth again and jacked it while she talked. "The only answer I can come up with is we have to see each other more often."

Ross didn't respond. He was breathing hard and flinching every time her hand circled across the head. She could tell he was going to cum again. She didn't know what to do…suck him, jack him, ride him…. *Ride him*! She straddled his body and inserted his cock all the way into her and held on because he started bucking like a bull. He thrust his hips way up into the air. Whisper was riding for all she was worth. His eyes went blank, staring somewhere through her and his mouth fell open. *He's cumming.* As soon as she thought that her face contorted and her eyes went blank and she was cumming again. She wanted to NOT cum but couldn't help it.

When they both finished, Whisper fell to the side and said, "Get your ass up, get a shower and get dressed. I swear to God…."

"I hope that means you're satisfied."

She chose not to address his comment. "I'm going to my cabin. You're coming over in thirty minutes and taking me to dinner. "

"Where," he asked.

"I don't know. Somewhere in Jacksonville."

"Okay."

"And," she was pointing at his dick tilting over, "If that thing pops out again…." She never finished her thought. She wiped the hand towel between her legs, bent down and kissed the head of his dick, covered it with the towel, dressed quickly and left the cabin.

Ross wanted to take a nap but should be getting ready for his walk in the woods…*screw it*. He was putting all that aside and taking his girl to dinner. First date! Unless you call the canoe ride across the lake a date…probably was but not in the conventional sense.

Chapter 32

They were driving to Jacksonville in the state truck not saying a word to each other. Every few seconds they would glance over but only for a moment. Ross felt like he was back in high school. Whisper, on the other hand, had no such reference. She did feel nervous in a very good way.

"Where do you want to go for dinner?" Ross asked.

"Where ever you're taking me." She was all in. She rarely got away from the Hill Top Hunting Lodge because she only had one day off, had strange work hours, no car and almost no money. Plus, there was no real reason for her to go anywhere.

She sat with her back straight, looking at everything that came into view. It was mostly trees and more trees but they weren't the same old Hill Top Hunting Lodge trees she was used to. Finally, they came to the outskirts of Jacksonville. The lights were almost blinding. She felt the way small town people do when they walk the streets of New York City.

They drove around town a little looking at what Ross thought was nothing, but Whisper found wonder around every turn. Eventually,

Ross pulled into Sylvia Mae's, a soul food restaurant. The restaurant was filled with black people and one white millennial couple in the corner chowing down on some of the best smelling food ever. Ross' stomach rumbled as soon as he walked in.

The hostess put them at the only open table which was near the kitchen. Between bites, everyone, without exception, took a peek at Whisper, the orange girl. They'd seen, whites, blacks, yellows, reds, browns, but never orange. The hostess was also the waitress, she set two waters down in front of them and said, "I hope ya'll aren't in a hurry. We're two waitresses short and we got a full house. I'll be back in a minute to take your order." She laid menus on the table and was off.

Ross and Whisper looked the menu over but Whisper couldn't take her eyes off the overwhelmed young waitress. "I want the chicken and dumplings," she said as she laid the menu down and looked at Ross. Whisper stared at Ross as if she wanted to say something. She looked at the waitress again and back at Ross. She tried to form some words but they wouldn't come out.

"You want to go help that girl," Ross said.

"Yes."

"Well, bring me the meatloaf when you have time." He threw the menu on the table.

She jumped up and hugged him around his head. Her nipples were right in his face. He could feel them. He just got publicly motor boated. He pushed her away, "Go."

She walked over to the waitress and Ross could see Whisper offering help.

Looking Whisper up and down, the young black waitress asked, "What are you?"

"I'm colored," Whisper replied. "Haven't you heard? Orange is the new black?"

Within minutes a plate of meatloaf, mashed potatoes, green beans, rolls and peach cobbler on the side was ready for pick up. Whisper placed the food in front of Ross and hugged him again. This time he knew she was pressing her tits in his face on purpose. Ross tingled all the way down his spine. Then she was off.

Ross ate his meatloaf and watched the show. It was like a dance and Whisper knew the steps forwards and backwards. He watched as many of the patrons struck up a conversation and sometimes even reached out and touched Whisper's hand or arm. One older lady cradled Whisper's face with her weathered hand. They were fascinated by her coloring and didn't hide their curiosity. Not a single soul said a disparaging remark. Ross was pleased. He waved her over when she looked up at him. "Did you get to eat?" he asked.

"Yeah. I've been sneaking bites every time I go into the kitchen. I'm good." She started to turn away but looked back "This food is killer." Ross agreed and she was off.

She worked the rest of the night, even helping clean up and close. Whisper got to keep her tips and the lady paid her twenty dollars to boot. Ross and Whisoer said their goodbyes and the couple walked arm in arm through the cold night air to the truck. Whisper felt good about herself and Ross felt good about Whisper.

She looked at him and said, "I guess I still owe you a date, huh?"

"Oh, I think you're about to make up for that when we get back to your place."

"Really?" she said kind of playfully. "We're going to wait that long?"

They climbed into the truck and were burning down the highway through the dark when Whisper instructed, "Pull over somewhere."

Ross took his foot off the gas a little and asked, "Why?"

"How can we fuck while you're driving seventy miles an hour?"

Ross stomped the brake and pulled off a hundred yards down a very narrow dirt road that was in a serendipitous location. Before he got the truck completely stopped and placed in park, Whisper's jeans and red Victoria Secret panties were in the floor.

Ross jumped out of the truck, unbuckling his pants as he ran around to get in on her side. He climbed in the passenger seat as she sat on the huge console waiting for him to get his pants down around his ankles. She bent over and sucked him to a hard-on which took no time at all. She slid down on him and they began to twist and pitch and buck. Her head banged against the roof of the cab a few times before they were done, at least done with the first one.

Ross was blowing like a toad when he finished and Whisper broke a sweat even though the night temperatures were in the forties. After their extreme urgency was satiated by their first orgasm, orgasms in Whisper's case, they began to kiss passionately and deeply. She never got off of his pole and it never relaxed completely. She could feel it much less hard than it was before but still...*damn this boy can fuck.*

She started circling her hips and he responded by tightening his buttocks and thrusting up with every rotation. It was like he knew exactly what she wanted...needed. Their tongues swirled with the same speed as their genitals. Their entire bodies were in sync. She was close to cumming and couldn't kiss anymore. She grabbed his head and pulled it to her chest, his mouth captured a long red nipple through her thin blouse and he sucked and bit until it almost hurt... almost.

That's it. She couldn't hold back any longer and she was really trying. Why? She didn't know but it was there now. She let out a low moan, more like a growl, and shook while the waves ran their course. She couldn't help Ross get there, she was too lost in her own. When finished she breathlessly said, "Use me. I'm done."

Ross pinned her to him with his rough hands and ground himself into her. She put her hands on the roof because he was going to jam himself way up in her when he came. Right at the perfect moment for him, he threw his pelvis high into the air and once again she was riding him like a bull. She was shoved up so high, her back was against the roof. Even in the turmoil of a cramped truck fuck, she could feel his dick harden like a baseball bat every time he shot a stream up in her.

She wrapped her arms around his broad shoulders and held on as he settled from his second orgasm. This one must have been righteous because he continued to twitch and jerk every time she moved or involuntarily clamped down on him. Sometimes she squeezed him on purpose just to feel him squirm.

Holding each other tightly and breathing normally, Whisper said "Am I going to have to sit in the wet spot on the way home?"

Ross laughed and returned, "Unless you want to drive."

"I don't have a license."

"Wet spot it is."

She could tell he was going to try to get out and she started to move.

Ross declared, "I'm not sure I can pull out without..."

She quickly pitched forward, lifting her butt and Ross' flaccid cock fell out of her with a slight sucking sound. Love juice gushing out on the seat. He lurched as she slid off the head. She sat on the console while he opened the door and stepped out. He walked to the back of the truck and kiddingly hollered, "Don't look. I have to pee."

When she heard his water hit the ground, she put her foot on the brake and the lights came on. "Very funny!" he yelled.

She got out of the truck and went to the front. She pee'd quickly and they both got back in. Whisper sat on the wet spot and Ross suffered with soaked underwear. They both looked at each other and smiled which turned into a laugh. Ross backed out of the dirt road and they were on their way.

"That probably wasn't very smart but I was thinking with my little head."

"I know you guys think with the little mister. But why was that not smart?"

"There's a killer-kidnapper running around out there in the woods somewhere and we pretty much hung out a sign that said come kill us."

"Did you ever think I might be the killer? I do know everybody involved." Whisper looked at him, illuminated by the dashboard lights. He smiled at her as if he were really considering her as a killer.

"Never until just now," he said in a comical way. They both laughed.

They drove in silence to the lodge. In no time, they were standing on Whisper's porch. It was midnight. "Do you want to come in?" she asked, secretly hoping he would say 'no'. If she went to sleep right now, she could get three and a half hours sleep. If he came in, they would do it again and probably again.

"You need to be at work in four hours and I want to be in the woods at day break. Better get some sleep."

She inwardly gave a sigh of relief. "Then I guess our date is over. I'm sorry I ruined it by helping those people."

"Don't be sorry. I found the whole affair enjoyable. Oh, and our date is not over until this…" He stood close and stared into her beautiful blue eyes that still sparkled in only the moonlight. He wrapped his brawny arms around her, pulled her close, hand behind her head, tangled in her blonde hair and kissed her. Her back arched, nipples erect and pressed into his chest and she nearly went limp. He had to hold her upright and pulled her into him. When the kiss was over, he picked her up and carried her the last few steps to the door. She had her arms around his neck, head buried in his shoulder.

He opened the door because Whisper never locked it. He set her inside and kissed her one more time, just lips on lips. "Now the date is over. I'll see you in a few days."

"Be careful out there and…"

"And what?" Ross looked at her thinking she might say the "L" word for which he was definitely not ready.

"Just be careful," she countered thinking the "L" word in her mind.

"Go on in now and lock the damn door. There's a killer about."

"Yes, sir," she said. The door closed and Ross waited to hear the deadbolt slide. When it did, he turned to walk away.

Ross had to finish packing, get some sleep and make a plan. He had no idea what he was going to do.

Chapter 33

At the crack of dawn, Ross hiked out the back of the lodge parking lot with his rifle and a fully loaded pack weighing nearly 60 pounds. With the carefully packed supplies, he could stay in the woods for four or five days depending on how he rationed his food. He went to the lake and took the boat across to the rock house. As soon as Ross entered the area, he started getting this creepy feeling of not being alone. At least three people died after coming to this house, maybe more depending on the status of those still missing.

Ross loaded six shells from his jacket pocket into his rifle. Six more were in the cartridge holder on his rifle butt. Twelve whole bullets and a five-inch fixed blade Ka-Bar combat knife were his only protection. He would probably not win a gun fight. He remembered his time in Iraq when the Forward Operating Base was attacked. It was the only true combat experience he had. He fired over a hundred rounds and probably didn't hit anybody. The firefight lasted less than thirty minutes. The only good thing about his 45-70 rifle was, if he ever did hit somebody with one of those big bullets, it would certainly knock their dick in the dirt.

He walked around the rock house a few minutes to see if anything jumped out at him. There were so many people in the area after the shooting, any signs of someone cutting trail were obliterated. He expanded his search. About fifty yards deeper into the woods Ross discovered a game trail that looked a little more worn down than it should have been with just an odd deer or two walking down it. He wandered back and forth studying the patterns of disturbance. Someone or something definitely went down this trail in the last few days. He decided he would hike the trail. That's the plan, take the trail, not get killed. Good plan.

The trail or what he thought was the trail seemed to meander in no particular direction. After four and a half hours of studying every leaf, twig, blade of grass and dirt patch on the trail, he got tired. Even though it was a little early he decided to set up camp and call in a 'no value added' report to the Emergency Operations Center

He found a nice flat clearing with grass and laid out his one-man tent shelter, opting for it instead of the new trampoline tent. A half-inch foam rubber mat was placed under his thin sleeping bag. He had a blow-up pillow that he hated. Every time he moved his head, the air in the pillow shifted. It was like sleeping on a water balloon. The food was hung in a tree fifty feet away from his tent. Rifle inside, boots off and stripped down to his underwear, Ross slid into the sleeping bag. The sun was just setting, reminding him of Whisper.

He rolled around trying to get comfortable but the ground was lumpy. The foam mat prevented sharp rocks from poking him but it wasn't thick enough to smooth out the hard spots. He turned once more and ended up on top of his rifle which was much more uncomfortable than the lumps. He finally got himself between 'the rock and the hard place' so to speak and was at ease enough to fall asleep. His eyes fluttered shut just as the Whisper colored sunset faded. His last thoughts were on the beautiful orange girl with yellow hands and feet and long flowing golden hair. In his semi-dream, Whisper raised her head, opened her big blue eyes, parted her gorgeous cerise lips in a crooked devilish smile and said "I love you."

Chapter 34

Ross woke around daybreak. He reached to grab his boots and realized how stiff he was. After a few 'in place' stretches, he got his boots on and exited the tent to urinate. Standing by a tree wearing underwear and boots, peeing, he got the feeling of being watched.

Dressed quickly, he rolled up all his equipment and got it back in his pack which turned out to be a chore. He couldn't seem to get it rolled tight enough for it all to fit. After several attempts he was packed and marching on his way down the trail.

By noon he was tracking himself on his GPS because without it he was lost. He knew which compass direction he was traveling but didn't know how far it was to the next road or civilized area. As suspected, the GPS put him right in the middle of nowhere. He kept following the trail even though it was almost indistinguishable from the woods itself. At one in the afternoon, another negative report was provided to the Emergency Operations Center. As soon as the satellite phone was put away, he came upon a small pond. It was a natural pond, maybe spring fed with a definite trail at the edge of the water.

There were human tracks near the pond edge. Recent ones, maybe even from that morning. He chambered a round in his big bore rifle and started circumventing the water. On the most southern side he found a camp stool with three crushed beer cans in the grass. A fishing spot presumably. Continuing around to the east side, he saw more tracks, boots maybe. They were at least as big as his own feet. The tracks veered east and disappeared into the woods. Lots of foot traffic headed that way. Following the tracks for a half mile, Ross came upon a small cabin. A wisp of smoke was coming out of the chimney. Someone was home.

He hid in the thick brush to observe, not knowing what to think about this. He wasn't sure he was still on Hill Top Hunting Lodge land or not. The cabin could very well be owned by a local. Or worse, it could be owned by a local survivalist with gun barrels bristling from every window and booby traps all across the yard. He would sit and wait, getting as comfortable as possible by taking off his pack, grabbing two protein bars and leaning his rifle and himself against a tree.

He waited for hours. He thought he actually fell asleep once. The sun was starting to go down and the temperature began to fall sharply. He rummaged in his pack and came out with a blanket in which he wrapped himself. Gonna be a long night.

Both protein bars were quickly eaten hoping their digestion would generate a little heat, which it didn't. The wind picked up. *Crap!* He got out his sleeping bag and wrapped up in it the best he could looking like a homeless person on a city street. At midnight, he was thinking he needed to get his tent out and get in it to break the wind when a door slammed at the cabin. Ross raised up in time to see a shadow figure go around behind the cabin. His heart rate soared.

There were no lights on in the cabin and the moon was behind some clouds. Clouds that were showing signs of snow. He watched intently and saw nothing else but heard a large vehicle crank up in the distance somewhere behind the cabin. Intermittent flashes of headlights appeared through the trees as a truck drove off to the east.

Ross was not an indecisive man, immediately making the decision to do nothing. He would wait to see if the individual came back. If the guy didn't return by morning, Ross would approach the cabin and knock on the front door, just like that. Although no longer cold, Ross got in his sleeping bag and basically set up camp. He would try not to fall asleep.

Of course, Ross fell asleep almost immediately but roused rather quickly when the sound of the truck engine filled the silent night. It was 1:30 am, about an hour and a half since the man left. The engine cut off and vehicle doors slammed. Moments later, two shadow men came around the corner of the cabin and went in. Lights came on in the cabin, not electric lights but candles or oil lamps. Ross could tell they fed the fire because smoke and cinders from the chimney billowed forth into the night sky.

What the hell? What was he supposed to think about that? *Two male lovers having a secret tryst? Two hunters, one getting off a late shift at work and going out in the morning? Two criminals hiding from the law? A meth lab?*

Change of plan, Ross would give them some time to settle in and move forward to peek in the window listening to try to catch any conversation. He got disentangled from his sleeping gear and pulled a watch cap down around his ears, put on gloves with a trigger finger opening, grabbed his big rifle and began creeping toward the cabin. At the edge of the clearing before the cabin, he quietly checked his rifle for a chambered round, adjusted his watch cap and crept to the corner of the cabin. Slowly sliding up to one of the front windows, he tried to look in but the flimsy cotton curtain blocked his view. Crossing in front of the door to the other window and peering through a crack in this curtain, he could see half of the living room.

Two men were standing naked by the fire stroking themselves. *Oh, brother*, he thought. *Gay lovers.* He started to turn away when he noticed something oddly familiar. The big guy, both in stature and penis size, was John Luke. *Fuck!* He just found one of the missing four people hiding out in a cabin in the woods having gay sex. Ross backed away quietly. Little did he know but Molly, Kylie and millionaire Myles Carter were stripped naked, bound and gagged in the bedroom. John Luke and his unknown friend were about to have some fun at the expense of their captives.

When Ross reached the relative safety of the woods, he called the Emergency Operations Center on the satellite phone. A sleepy volunteer answered and took the message: one of the four missing people was found! Ross told the volunteer to read his location on the GPS tracker. "I'll wait here until someone shows up." He was feeling halfway proud of himself for solving some of the mystery.

Ross figured it would take an hour to roust everyone on the call list out of bed. They would need another hour to get to the Hill Top Hunting Lodge and another hour to get organized and another two hours to get to his location. *It will be morning before they get here.* Ross wrapped his blanket and sleeping bag around him, ate another protein bar and leaned against the tree, rifle in his lap.

Although very cold, he was still fighting sleep. While standing to take a leak, a faint, muffled scream came from the cabin. *It sounded like a woman!* He heard the noise again, even while peeing. The scream was much louder than before. He zipped up, grabbed his rifle and moved forward one more time. Looking in the window with the best view, he could see the unknown man standing by the fire and Myles Carter tied up on the couch. Both men were naked. *What the fuck?*

Ross processed the scene for a minute and came to the conclusion all of the missing people were probably in the cabin being held as sex slaves. It didn't make a lick of sense to him. *Sex slaves? Is that what all of this is about?* He heard a woman moan from what he thought was pain. She was somewhere in the back of the cabin with John Luke.

Ross had to stop this now. He banged on the front door with the butt of his rifle. Shouts came from the men inside and the cabin went dark. *Oh, fuck.* Ross started running as fast as he could to the tree line. Seconds before reaching cover and concealment, a blast from a shotgun rang out and Ross could hear the buckshot peppering the tree branches beside his head. He slid behind the nearest big tree trunk available, breathing hard from exertion and fear. He called on the satellite phone to the Emergency Operations Center to report finding Myles Carter and at least one of the missing women and two perpetrators. "Oh yeah, shots fired! The men were armed. Send help immediately."

Ross laid prone pointing his rifle at the cabin, afraid to return fire because of the hostages. Ross hollered, "John Luke! The cavalry is coming. Why don't you come on out?" The door opened and the buck shot from another blast of the shotgun dug up the dirt twenty-five yards to Ross' left. They didn't know where he was and just shot blindly. Ross wanted to keep it that way.

Chapter 35

A mass of law enforcement was gathering in the Hill Top Hunting Lodge parking lot. Red and blue lights were everywhere. Whisper woke as did everyone staying at the lodge. Throwing on a minimum amount of clothes, she went out to see what the commotion was all about. As suspected, it involved Ross, it always seemed to. She just prayed he was okay.

A non-law enforcement official told her all he knew, "Someone found one or two of the missing people, one of them, for sure, was Myles Carter. They were being held hostage and there was a gun fight of some kind. The place they were being held hostage was a cabin several miles off the grid in the woods."

No doubt in her mind, Ross was involved. He had this irritating knack of placing himself right in the middle of danger. *Damn him*! Now she was really worried.

She blended in with the rest of the first responders listening to the briefing. One group of armed men would leave from the parking lot and move to the cabin using the lake route. Another group would be transported by vehicle to a road on the other side of the lake and enter the woods there to move to the cabin. The two teams would converge on the cabin, locate Ross, negotiate and free the hostages. Simple plan.

Whisper was trying to figure out a way to hitch a ride with the road team. Ross was out there and she needed to find him. Watching the armed police officers scatter all over the parking lot, she noticed the arrival of several news crews. That's the ticket, get one of them to take her with the road team.

She went to the nearest news truck and found the reporter, another young good-looking woman trying to become the next anchor by delivering a national story in the middle of the night. Whisper said, "You want to go where the action is?"

The woman looked at the orange girl like she was nuts. The reporter didn't want anything to do with Whisper but her urge to get the scoop was too great. "Well, yes."

Whisper jumped in the van. "Can you broadcast as we go? Follow those cars."

"Yes, Chuck, get the camera going. Blaine, don't lose them." Blaine, the van driver, started following the police caravan.

Chuck, the camera man started firing up his shoulder held camera and pointed it at the reporter. Whisper told her the story in 30 seconds or less. The reporter said, "Chuck, on three, two, one…" The red light came on the camera and the reporter started broadcasting.

"I'm Rebecca Jameson and we're live and departing from the Hill Top Hunting Lodge in East Texas where a new development has just occurred. Myles Carter, the attractive multi-millionaire, who has been missing for a week, was just spotted at a remote cabin in the middle of the woods. He has been held hostage and we are following the team of brave police officers sent to free him." The camera panned out the front windshield to the line of cars and trucks with their lights flashing. "There have been reports of a gunfight at the cabin and we will be following this story closely and bring you updates as they occur." She nodded to the camera man and he stopped rolling. "Get that out now."

The camera guy went to the control panel and started doing his work. It was 3:00 am and the reporter didn't know how many people would be watching but she was sure glad to be the lead. The reporter asked, "What's your deal?"

Whisper looked at her a little funny, "My deal?"

"Yeah, why are you in this van right now helping me?"

"Oh, you mean, what's in it for me?"

"Exactly."

"I think the guy who discovered the hostages is my boyfriend."

"The reporter looked at her confused, "You think he discovered the hostages or you think he's your boyfriend?"

"Well, now that you put it that way, both. The guy I've been seeing lately may be the one who discovered the hostages. He went out searching for signs and clues on order from the Emergency Operations Center and I don't have any idea who called this in but I suspect it's him."

"And he's your boyfriend?"

"Yes, I think. We haven't discussed the exact terms of the relationship."

"Huh."

"Huh what?" Whisper asked.

"Oh nothing. I'm just surprised someone like you has a boyfriend." *Mean bitch.*

The police caravan must have driven twenty miles before they came to a stop on a deserted country road. The police piled out of their vehicles and started adjusting their gear. They looked ready for war. The weapons looked like something out of a science fiction movie with electronic sights, laser aiming devises, 1000 lumen tiny flashlights under the barrels, shoulder slings and scores of ammunition magazines.

Whisper thought of Ross out there somewhere with his old timey western lever action cowboy rifle. *What an asshole!* Not that Ross was really an asshole but going out there with a rifle 140 years behind the times pissed off Whisper and for pissing her off, he was an asshole. Actually, she was just worried sick.

The reporter jumped out of the van screaming at Chuck to get the camera ready. She smoothed her hair and held the microphone at the ready with the scurrying police officers in the background. Whisper sat inside the van with Blaine, the driver. The camera light popped on, blinding everyone within a hundred feet. The police screamed at her to turn the light out because it was ruining their night vision. She did not comply and started broadcasting. The police sergeant in charge came over to her with every intent of giving a stern reprimand but melted like butter on a hot July afternoon in Texas when she squeezed his arm and called him a hometown hero.

The reporter plied the cop with questions and compliments until every last bit of information was extorted. Whisper watched in amazement wondering why most guys, even the roughest, biggest, strongest, most macho types in the world, turned to putty at the bat of an eye. Whisper hopped out of the van and ran over to the reporter, "Are you going to follow them into the woods?"

The reporter looked at the orange girl a little too long, "Fuck no. It's dark and filthy out there and look at my shoes." The reporter preened getting ready for the next shot.

"I'll go with you." Whisper offered hoping to use the reporter as an excuse to get into woods.

The reporter stared at Whisper again, this time giving her the once over. "Are you stupid too?"

Whisper wanted in the worst way to punch the bitch in the mouth and knock out half a dozen or so of those perfectly capped white teeth, but there was something more urgent. Ross in the woods, at night with a gun that was technologically superior in the 1880's but was a dinosaur today. And what did he have, five or six bullets, she couldn't remember. She needed to get out there and made the decision, as bad as it was, to follow the police.

The police put on a big show of lining up in some kind of tactical order and moving out with a flurry of hand signals and verbal commands. *These guys are going to get dead*, she thought, even with their magic guns, body armor and night vision goggles.

Giving the guys a five minute head start, Whisper stepped into the darkness behind them. They would be easy to follow because of the tremendous amount of racket made by brush rubbing against their cargo pants, twigs snapping, metal clanking on metal, flashlights intermittently going on and off, verbal commands and curse words carrying through the night air.

Whisper, totally unprepared for a night walk in the woods, was only wearing a pair of jeans and long sleeve shirt. Her shoes were a kind of penny loafer with no socks and a light shawl she used to cover herself while sitting in the chair reading. Ross would not approve of her poor planning or her poor choice to come save him. She'd be lucky not to die out there.

Chapter 36

Ross, John Luke and the unknown man were at a stand-off. Ross was nearly buried in the dead, damp leaves behind a tree and the others were in the cabin. Ross was freezing, they were warm, they win. After ten minutes of nothing Ross yelled, "John Luke! Let's talk."

The cabin door came open. "We're coming out!" The three hostages, Myles, Molly and Kylie, were pushed through the door. All three were naked, tied together at the neck, hands and waist. The two kidnappers came out next using the hostages as a shield. "You better not shoot, asshole." John Luke and the other man were holding pistols to the heads of the hostages. The bad guys had long guns strapped around their backs. Ross couldn't tell if the long guns were shotguns or rifles.

Ross aimed his big bore rifle at the group but there was no way he would pull the trigger. He was a fairly good shot but in the dark with open sights at a moving target, with innocent people in the line of fire, no way. The group stumbled around the cabin, loaded in the truck and drove off. There was nothing Ross could do. *Well, fuck!*

As soon as the truck was out of earshot, Ross relaxed and realized he was cold. He took his gear into the cabin, lit some candles, threw a log on the fire and called the Emergency Operations Center confirming there were two armed perpetrators, one of which was John Luke, one was an unknown assailant and the three other missing people, Myles, Molly and Kylie, were being held hostage. He told them they drove off in a large, tan colored, crew cab pick-up truck, headed northeast using forest roads. Ross sat on the couch and started drifting off to sleep as he got warmed by the fire.

Interagency communications in East Texas were behind the rest of mainstream America and word there was no longer a threat at the cabin location did not reach the police closing in. The sergeant ordered all cell phones, there weren't supposed to be any on the operation, to be switched to vibrate and the one radio was turned off, for 'radio silence' purposes. They were making so much noise it didn't matter if the radio was blaring or not, but turning it off seemed tactical, so they did it.

Whisper followed along, oblivious to anything but being cold, scared and nearly blind. They walked for an hour and she thought the sun might begin to come up at any moment. She didn't own a cell phone and didn't wear a watch. Maybe she would be better off in an 1880 world like Ross and his gun.

Ross dozed on the couch, waiting there for whomever was coming. At some point. Ross woke up to what he thought were voices outside. The sun was coming up and he went to the door expecting to see his police rescuers. Peering out, he saw nothing. "Anybody out there?" He walked out on the porch and looked around. "Is somebody there?" asking in a command voice. Back inside, Ross grabbed his big bore rifle and sat on the couch contemplating his next move.

The two police teams finally linked up after each team got lost at least once. The team from the lodge got lost twice. Whisper followed along behind, obscured in the woods in a state of what she thought was actually freezing to death. She watched the two teams making plans and fanning out in a semi-circle in front of the cabin.

The sergeant in charge turned on the bullhorn which the junior officer had to lug out to the site. The speaker made a loud screeching noise. Ross' ears perked up. The sergeant cleared his throat and spoke into the microphone. "You in the cabin. You are surrounded. Come out with your hands up." All the police officers were aiming their assault rifles at the door of the cabin.

Ross said to himself, "Well okay then." He leaned his rifle against the couch and stepped to the door. "I'm coming out. Don't shoot." He cracked the door and looked out. He only counted a dozen or so men but it looked like an army. He swung the door the rest of the way open and stood in the middle with his hands held up. "I'm coming out. Don't shoot." He didn't move. He just stared at all the guns pointed at him. Just before he took his first baby step out of the door, one of the cops spied the rifle leaned against the couch behind Ross and yelled, "Gun!"

Everything slowed down to milliseconds. The cop who yelled fired the first shot. Ross heard the bullet buzz by his ear while he was diving to the left. As with all cops, when one shoots, it seems all of them feel obligated to shoot. They did just that. They shot...a lot. The glass in the windows was disintegrating, couch stuffing was flying everywhere and anything set up in the cabin was being chopped down...lanterns, pots and pans, a mounted deer head fell to the floor. Ross scrambled to the corner of the cabin. The bullets from the powerful police rifles easily came through the wood frame of the cabin but a stack of firewood was on the porch near the corner. Ross thought if he laid completely flat with the logs of the cabin and the stack of firewood for protection, he might not get too killed.

Ross was screaming obscenities but no one heard. The rifle reports were deafening in the quiet of the early morning forest. Each police officer emptied an entire magazine of twenty rounds into the cabin. Luckily, they all shot as fast as they could and needed to reload at the same time because Whisper was running forward at a high rate of speed, having heard Ross' voice from the door of the cabin. She ran right through the line of officers and straight up to the porch. She was screaming Ross' name. The sergeant was yelling "Cease fire," and something like "You can't do that."

Whisper paid no attention to the authorities. She ran through the door which was a solid wall of splinters. In two seconds, her eyes adjusted to the dimness of the cabin and she saw Ross in the floor to the right. He was covered in glass shards, wood chips and dirt. Sliding in beside him slightly cutting her knee on a piece of glass, she gently began removing the debris from his body and softly reassuring him and herself by saying everything was going to be okay.

The police recovered from their own adrenalin rushes and reloaded for a possible round two. The sergeant cleared his throat again and turned on the bullhorn which emitted another horrendous screech. "Hey you! The orangish looking girl. Get out of the cabin now." He turned to the officer standing next to him. "Who is that orange bitch?"

The officer replied, "What…is that orange bitch is a better question?"

Ross opened his eyes and looked up at Whisper. "Is it almost night?"

She thought he was delirious because it was maybe 7:00 am. She just held his head in her hands and stared into his eyes.

"I just wondered because I see a beautiful sunset."

She thought, *that's so corny…but I love it.* She pulled him to her and hugged him.

The voice on the loud speaker shouted, "We're coming in."

Ross said, "Help me up. Let's stand somewhere they can easily see us with our hands up and maybe we'll live through this." He was halfway kidding, but then again, over two-hundred rounds ripped through the cabin on his first attempt to surrender. He drew his hunting knife and tossed it to the floor. They stood by the fireplace looking as defenseless as possible. Whisper gave him the once over but miraculously detected no injuries.

The officers came flooding in with their guns at the ready screaming instructions that were impossible to follow, "Get your hands up!"
They already were up. "Get down on the floor!" "Don't move!" How
does one get down on the floor and not move? "Let me see your
hands!" Their hands were up over their heads. Finally, the officers
closed the space between them and rudely threw them on the floor,
nearly broke their arms wrenching them to their backs and putting
on cuffs. Once hooked up, the police snatched them up to a standing
position and herded them outside into the yard and the daylight.

Ross and Whisper stood next to each other looking at the police
sergeant. The other dozen men were guarding them. The sergeant
took a gigantic wad of Beechnut Chewing Tobacco and stuffed it in
his cheek. He was looking mighty satisfied with himself. He studied
Ross up close like Ross may have been John Dillinger. Then he stared
at Whisper and asked. "What the fuck are you supposed to be?"

Ross stepped forward in protest but two of the guards clubbed the
back of his legs with their rifle butts. Ross went down on one knee.

Whisper yelled "Stop! Do you know who this is?"

"Yeah. He's one of them son of a bitches that done this."

Ross got back to his feet. "I'm Ross Evans," he said.

"Doctor!" interjected Whisper. "Doctor Ross Evans who works for
the State of Texas and the Emergency Operations Center."

Distinctly but quietly, one of the police officers in the back said,
"Oh fuck."

The police sergeant spit a nasty gob of chewed tobacco on the
ground at Ross' feet. "That right, cowboy? You a doctor working
with us?"

"I am. I'm the one who called this in and I was waiting for rein-
forcements when you started shooting the place all to shit. By the way,
do you know who owns that cabin?"

The police sergeant just looked at Ross. "Me either," said Ross. "I
suggest we find out. There were two perpetrators, one was John Luke,
one of the missing four, and the other guy I didn't know. Maybe he

owns this cabin. If the perpetrator doesn't own the cabin, then you are going to owe someone a big apology."

The sergeant told an officer to check Ross' identification. Once confirmed, the sergeant made a sign with his hands and a police officer uncuffed both of them. Ross' arm immediately went around Whisper. She rubbed her wrists. Ross said, "We're going back into the cabin."

"Or what's left of it," Whisper said looking directly at the sergeant.

"And we're going to stand by the fire until we're warm. I'm grabbing my rifle and going back to the lodge and making a full after-action report to the Emergency Operations Center. Good luck with your end of the story."

Ross and Whisper went into the cabin and stood with their backs to the dying fire too shocked to say anything. Ross took off his field jacket and gave it to Whisper. She started to protest but he wouldn't listen. Ross strapped on his pack, grabbed his knife, picked up his gun and they hiked out of the area leaving the Keystone Cops to secure the crime scene.

"It's a long walk. You up for this?"

She looked at him sideways. "I swear I didn't know how boring my life was before you. I wake up at the butt-crack of dawn, prepare tables, serve food to ungrateful customers, go to the cabin, eat a sandwich, read a book, fall asleep and do it all over again. Six days a week for five years! And now…"

"And now, staying up all night in the freezing woods, getting shot at and chasing killer criminals is soooo much better?"

They stopped and gazed at each other. There was a long dramatic pause leading up to something. Ross just didn't know what.

Whisper spoke. "You've got about thirty seconds to figure out how you're gonna fuck me because it's happening right now one way or another."

Ross was standing with the rifle butt on the ground, holding the top of the barrel. The rifle fell from his hand and landed in the dirt. He threw the pack down, opened it and yanked out the tent, sleeping bag and blanket all at once. Three or four other things came flying out as well but he paid them no attention. He haphazardly spread the tent, sleeping bag and blanket on the ground, grabbed Whisper by the front of his field jacket, lifted her up like a child and placed on the padding. He flipped her loafers off and began fumbling with her jeans. She shoved his hand away and unbuttoned and unzipped her pants herself. Ross pulled her pants off by the legs nearly lifting her off the ground as he did. She was wearing her red Victoria Secret panties. "Don't rip them," she said.

She took her panties off herself. He stood up and pulled his cargo pants and underwear down to his ankles. There it was, already poking out in the bright morning sun. Whisper thought it might have been the most beautiful cock in the world. The thing bounced twice on its own. He knelt down, wrapped his cold hands around her little yellow feet and spread them far apart. He stroked her vibrant orange thighs and scooted forward, burying the head of his 'most beautiful cock in world' right in the middle of the warmth of her golden pussy hair. She groaned in anticipation. He inserted the head. She groaned in pleasure.

He fell upon her and kissed her like they almost lost each other. The perfect kiss considering the recent events. Her legs automatically spread even further. He slid it in halfway. She groaned in ecstasy. His massive muscles involuntarily pumped twice and she could already tell her orgasm was not far away. In full control, he started trying to make her feel good. He was succeeding, by stroking and twisting and thrusting until she cried out for more. Ross gave her more, every inch he had. Her legs and feet extended up, shaking in the air.

Ross was thinking with his brain right now but knew he couldn't last much longer. If she came, he was going to lose his load. No way around it. He kept thrusting, using the full length of his cock, mentally begging for her to cum. Ross was moving like a machine. The perfect rotations with the perfect timing at the perfect depths. She couldn't hold back. Her whole body tightened, eager to receive her pleasure.

In three strokes, she knew she would cum. She knew it and Ross knew it too.

One! *Oh my God! Oh my God! Oh my God!*

Two! She softly announced it. Not really meaning to, "I'm gonna cum."

Three! She screamed. It felt so good to her, it was nearly painful. She threw her legs up and actually grabbed her feet and held them up by her shoulders, exposing every inch of herself to him.

Ross was done. Her body's reaction to the orgasm pushed him over the edge. He pulled out in one smooth motion, stood up and stroked himself turning slightly to one side and shot such a big load it hurt his balls.

Whisper rolled to her side, placed her hand between her legs and rubbed her clit while watching Ross strain every muscle as he shot his considerable jizz on to the ground.

He looks like a sculpture, she thought. She came slightly once again by rubbing herself as she watched Ross stroking himself down from a climax. He straightened up from a crouch, relaxed his taut muscles and shook his phallus up and down knocking off the last droplets of cum. Ross stumbled over to her on wobbly legs and collapsed by her side, his huge dick laid against thigh. He held her in his arms and wrapped themselves in the blanket. Both falling asleep.

Chapter 37

Ross woke up in what he thought was only minutes but it must have been longer. Voices were coming closer. He shook Whisper and she startled. He put his finger to his lips to quiet her and whispered in her ear, "Some people are coming."

They frantically pulled their clothes on and shoved the gear into the pack. They were standing and looked presentable by the time the group of forensic investigators reached them. They greeted one another and Ross told them the thumbnail version of what happened and pointed them in the right direction to reach the cabin.

They parted ways with Ross and Whisper headed back to the lodge. Whisper said, "Big Al's going to kill me."

"Why?"

"I'm supposed to be working today."

"You can't work today. You've been up all night and you have a hurt knee."

"I don't think Big Al will much care. I've worked tired many times before and the 'hurt knee' is just a scratch. I don't think it even needs a Band-Aide."

"I've got a Band-Aid in my pack if you want one?"

"You're just looking for an excuse to get my pants down again. Come on, let's go."

They walked on, reaching the lodge by late morning. They stood in the parking lot holding hands and staring into each other's eyes. Whisper took off Ross' field jacket and handed to him saying, "You go to your cabin. I'll go to mine. I'll see you later."

"You're going to work, aren't you?"

Whisper didn't respond. She just went up on her toes and kissed him, turned and went inside her cabin. Ross went to his cabin, still wanting more of her but he was too damn tired to argue about it.

Whisper showed up at the restaurant before the lunch crowd started to come in. Big Al was sitting in his booth when she walked through the door.

"Orange!" he boomed.

She went over and sat down across from him. He said, "This better be good."

"Primo," she responded and proceeded to tell about the all-night operation and early morning gunfight. She told every detail using extreme animation and sound effects. The new waitress came over to listen. Whisper told everything except about the love making on the ground on the way back. She was disappointed not telling that because to her, it was the best part. She nearly got wet thinking about it right there in the booth. Whisper drifted off in thought.

"Orange!" Big Al brought her back to reality. "You're working the evening shift to make up for missing breakfast. It was a big crowd and my nephew had to work really hard."

"I'll bet," said Whisper sarcastically. The other waitress rolled her eyes.

At 1:30 pm Ross and Shelby came in looking for a hot meal. Whisper waited on them. Ross asked if she was doing okay and she responded with a perky affirmative. "But I have to work the evening shift to make up for missing breakfast." Not what Ross wanted to hear but he had to go the Emergency Operations Center and get debriefed. They agreed to see each other tomorrow and would try to get a good night sleep tonight.

Ross left the lodge to get debriefed, Shelby went to play video games and Whisper went to work. Sometime after 5:00 pm, her good friend Shanna came in ready for a shift. Smiles flew across both their faces as they ran to embrace. They only had a few minutes to catch up before Big Al would start screaming their names across the restaurant. "I'll tell you all about it after shift," said Whisper. Shanna couldn't wait to hear the latest stories. Besides the kidnapping and gunfights, Shanna wanted to know about what was going on with Ross, the Ranger hunk.

After the last patron left, the girls were cleaning up and preparing for the next day just like they always did when Whisper said, "Hey, I have a bottle of wine in my cabin."

Shanna was wiping a table and stopped in mid-stroke, "Why aren't we drinking it?"

"Because it's not here."

Shanna threw down her rag, took off her apron, "I'm gonna go get it."

"The doors unlocked. It's on the counter."

Shanna left and Whisper continued to clean up and clean up and clean up. She looked around and everything was nearly finished. A glass of wine while they gave the restaurant the coup de grace would be most excellent. She sat in a chair with her feet up on a table. *Dog tired.* She started to relax waiting for Shanna to return. She dozed off for a few seconds, maybe minutes she didn't really know. When she fully woke, she realized she was alone. Whisper went out to the front steps and looked down the parking lot. *Shanna should have returned by now.* Whisper took the steps two at a time and ran down to her cabin. Crashing through the door, she saw the bottle of wine still on the counter. Shanna never made it to her cabin. *Oh God no!*

Whisper ran to Ross' cabin and banged on the door. Shelby finally answered with a video controller in his hand. Ross was not back from the Emergency Operations Center yet. The parking lot was devoid of police, they were all out traipsing through the woods chasing ghosts. She ran back to the restaurant and used the land line to call 911. The dispatcher transferred her to the police to whom she reported Shanna missing. The desk sergeant asked how long this person had been missing and Whisper responded "Twenty, maybe thirty minutes."

The desk sergeant laughed and told her it would take twenty-four hours before they could file a report. Whisper interrupted, "Listen, asshole. She's my friend."

The desk sergeant cut her off. "I'm sorry but we are busy with the Hill Top Hunting Lodge murders and kidnappings. We don't have time to look for a woman who is probably spending too much time in the ladies' room putting on make-up."

"Look...sir." She used the term disparagingly. "She is missing *from* the Hill Top Hunting Lodge."

"Oh, that's different. What's her name again?"

It was all Whisper could do to keep from going down to the police station and beating this guy's ass. She went through ten minutes of narrative with him, repeating herself numerous times. The sergeant said an officer would be dispatched to the lodge and for her to wait there until he arrived.

She waited for thirty minutes and still no one showed up. *What would Ross do?* Pondering for only a moment she decided to look for clues. Whisper had no idea what could possibly have happened but she would look anyway. *Was Shanna captured and silently walked off into the woods at gunpoint? Was she forced into a vehicle and driven off in a trunk? They could be sixty miles away by now. Was she in one of these cabins? Did John Luke come back and get her?*

Whisper went to her cabin, put on her only winter coat, some boots and picked out a small kitchen knife to carry with her. A kitchen knife wasn't a gigantic rifle with a barrel so big one could put their finger down it but a knife was better than nothing. She wrapped the blade in an old, thin pot holder and tucked it in her belt. She got a bottle of water out of the fridge and stuffed it in her jacket pocket. *Ready.*

Her first item on the agenda was to check all of the cabins. She would go door to door and knock. If the registered occupants answered, she would excuse herself and move on. If no one answered, she would investigate further because all of the cabins were supposed to be occupied and it was after midnight now.

She started with John Luke's cabin, which was still cordoned off with police tape because it was a crime scene. This cabin was supposed to be empty. When she reached the porch, she noticed the yellow tape had come loose at the door. *A bad tape job or is somebody in there?* She was not Ross and became frightened, standing on the porch, wrestling with her fears. She reached for the doorknob but paused. *Nope!* Pissed at herself for thinking she was brave and then not being brave...at all. She spun around to climb down the stairs when the cabin door flew open and a man grabbed a hand full of yellow hair and yanked her into the living room and right down on the floor.

Whisper was stunned more than hurt and less afraid now because she was mad. She jumped up ready to scratch this guy's eyes out but as soon as she got righted, he slapped her across the temple, knocking her to the floor again. This time she stayed down because the room was spinning. Looking in the corner through the dark she could make out the image of woman sitting on the floor with her knees up to her chest. *Shanna!* Whisper laid her head softly on the rug and calmly drifted off to unconsciousness.

When Whisper awoke, she was sitting next to Shanna, in the same position, hands duck taped behind her back, ankles duck taped and a piece of tape across her mouth. Whisper leaned her shoulder into Shanna and they tilted their heads until they lightly bumped together, closest thing to a hug they could muster.

Whisper raised her eyebrows indicating a question. Shanna really didn't know what she was asking but pointed her head toward the front. Whisper listened carefully and heard light breathing noises coming from the couch. He was asleep on the couch.

Whisper didn't know how long she had been out but it was still very dark outside. The only light was coming from the one street light Big Al was forced to erect in the parking lot after many customer complaints. The light was on a timer and went out at 1:00 am. As Whisper was observing the windows, she noticed the flicker of red and blue lights approaching. *Now the policeman shows up!* As soon as the room filled with emergency lights, the man on the couch jumped up and went to the window. He looked out only to see a patrolman walk around the parking lot, get back in his car and drive off. Whisper could see a gun in the man's hand. *Who was this guy?*

As soon as the cop left, the man came over and cut the tape off the girl's ankles with a knife that was curved and had a serrated blade. It looked a hell of a lot more lethal than Whisper's paring knife she still had in her belt. He stood the girls up and said, "We're going," walking them right out the front door and down the steps into the woods. At that moment, Whisper realized they may be lost forever. After an hour of being halfway dragged through the woods, they came to the lake with which Whisper was familiar. At least she knew exactly where they were.

The guy got them into a boat and started rowing off toward the far bank. Even in the dark, Whisper could tell he was headed down the finger of water that led straight to the rock house. Again, at least she knew where they were. The man ran the boat up on the bank, got out and pulled them from the boat. Whisper managed to step out and only get wet up to the knees. Shanna tripped over the gunwale and fell into the water. The guy dragged her through the mud up on to the bank.

In a short time, they were at the rock house. Standing on the porch drinking a fucking cup of coffee was John Luke. He was wearing boots, cargo pants and a tactical vest of some kind with no shirt. His enormous arm muscles rippled in the moonlight.

John Luke put the coffee cup down on the porch rail. "Well, well, well, if it isn't the orange cunt and a friend." They stood at the bottom of the steps, a woman in each of the unknown man's hands. "I see you've met my cousin," John Luke said.

John Luke asked his cousin, "Where did you pick up these bitches? I mean, I don't mind. The more the merrier. But why?"

The cousin responded, "I came around the corner of your cabin and ran right in to this one," He shook Shanna's arm. "I had to snatch her. When we were in your cabin waiting for a good time to exfiltrate, this one came up on your porch." He shook Whisper's arm. "I had to grab her too. Look at this bitch, would you?" He shook Whisper's arm again. The cousin was giving Whisper the once over. He subconsciously licked his lips. Whisper thought she might vomit while her mouth was duck taped, which would be a really bad situation.

"Bring 'em in and join the party. I'm getting a little bored with what we have anyway."

The cousin pulled the girls up the steps and into the house. In the floor by the kitchen, a trap door was open that led to a basement. The cousin cut their hands free, for a moment, but re-taped their wrists in front of their bodies. "Off you go." He pointed down the stairs. Shanna and Whisper looked at each other in desperation but at this time, they had no choice. They climbed down into the unknown.

Chapter 38

The three other kidnap victims were in the basement too. Myles was trussed up in what appeared to be a sex swing. He was completely naked and looked loaded with drugs. Molly and Kylie were naked, staked out and spread eagle on mattresses on the floor. Each had duct tape on their mouths.

Whisper could see all hope drain from Shanna's face. Whisper admitted to herself there was nothing positive about this situation but she wasn't a quitter. Maybe there would be a moment of opportunity. She still had a knife. *If I can only get to it.*

The cousin strung the girls' hands above their heads and tied the ropes off on an exposed wooden joist. He pulled hard almost raising them off their feet. As Whisper stretched, the knife in her belt became exposed. The cousin pulled it out of her belt and poked her pussy with the sharp end. Whisper flinched although it didn't penetrate her jeans. He threw the knife on the floor in the corner.

John Luke joined his 'cuz' in the basement, carrying two cups of coffee, gave one to his kin and asked, "Do you want either one of these girls?"

The cousin paused looking back and forth between the two. John Luke spoke up again, "I've had the orange one. She's a terrible fuck. I think I'll try this one." John Luke reached out and cupped Shanna's face. Shanna turned away and Whisper fought hard against her restraints, realizing the futility and calmed down. John Luke turned to Whisper, "Did I mention, my cousin is gay and the only way he'll have a woman is if he fucks them up the ass. So, get ready." John Luke smiled and walked to the other side of the basement to check on his used-up captives and get some special equipment.

The girls watched their captors prepare tables on which they were about to be raped. Whisper looked over at the other victims and understood they had probably been sexually abused continuously since they're abduction. Her heart went out to them but she had to stop thinking about the victims and figure a way castrate these bastards.

After the tables were prepared, John Luke got right in Whisper's face. "We're going to go upstairs and get a few hours of sleep before we have our way with you. We're tired and we want it to be done right. Plus, you can hang around down here and think about how lucky you are that it's us giving you such a good time. It could have been some ugly motherfuckers." He laughed and as they went upstairs John Luke said to his cousin, "I told you the police wouldn't come back here after they processed the place. They wouldn't think anyone would be so dumb, which is smart, right Lonnie?"

Whisper and Shanna were nearly hanging off the floor. He pulled the rope holding their hands up really tightly. They were touching each other and the position felt awkward. Whisper was trying hard to figure a way out of this when Shanna grunted into her tape. Whisper looked at her but couldn't understand what she wanted or what she was doing. Shanna began rubbing her taped mouth against her upper arm trying to fold the tape back. Whisper saw what she was doing and tried it herself. Whisper was having no luck but Shanna started a tiny roll at the edge of her tape. Another hundred attempts and it might come off and it did just that. The tape was only rolled back about halfway but far enough for Shanna to talk. "Keep trying with yours." Shanna went back to rubbing her mouth against her arm. Shanna finally got hers rubbed all the way off.

Whisper had a small edge on her taped rolled up. Shanna said, "Lean over like you are going to kiss me." Whisper's eyes widened. "Do it." Whisper leaned in the best she could being hung up by her arms and Shanna reciprocated. Whisper's eyes were shut because it was a creepy feeling and she didn't need to see it. Shanna groped around on Whisper's cheek with her tongue until she got the edge of the tape in her teeth and pulled. Whisper winced as the tape came off her lips. Shanna spit out the tape with some difficulty because it kept sticking to her lips.

The first words out of Shanna's mouth. "Did you really have sex with that guy?"

"Really? We're hanging up here about to be raped every ten minutes for the rest of our short lives and that's what you want to know?"

Shanna stared at her. Whisper responded reluctantly, "Yes, I did. Now how are we going to get out of here?"

They looked around the room for ideas. None came to them. Quietly, they called the names of the other victims but they truly seemed drugged out of their minds. Myles, Molly and Kylie all remained immobile.

Chapter 39

Ross got back to the lodge about 1:00 am. The 'hot wash' debriefing, as they called it, lasted an entire eight hours. It was a fucked up operation. Ross was surprised the governor didn't show up and fire everybody.

Ross parked the state truck in one of the few available spaces and walked to his cabin. He tried to be quiet so not wake up Shelby but Shelby was on the couch playing video games. Shelby had reverted to his college hours since the kidnapping. Ross didn't have him on a schedule so Shelby ate, stayed up late and slept in. He liked this assignment.

"Good, I didn't wake you," Ross said as he entered.

Without looking up from the video screen, Shelby said, "The orange girl came by earlier looking for you."

Ross wished he wouldn't call her that but nearly everyone did. "What did she want?"

"Didn't say. But I figured she wanted you. Ya know what I mean?"

"When did she come by?"

"Let's see, I was on Level 2 when she interrupted me and I'm on Level 8 now. Ah, six levels ago."

Ross tried to figure out if Shelby was being a smartass or if he actually lived in video game time. Shelby might be quirky and dumb, but he wouldn't be a smartass to Ross. *He lives in video game time.* "That would be what in minutes?"

"Oh, 'bout an hour."

"Thank you." Ross went straight to Whispers cabin, knocked on the door and knocked again a little louder thinking she may be in a deep sleep. Neither of them had slept worth a flip since all this started. There was still no answer. He twisted the door knob and walked in. The door wasn't locked but that was not unusual. Ross turned the light on and started calling her name, lowly at first and then yelling it as he quickly went through the cabin. She was not there.

This was very disconcerting to Ross. She had to be at work in three hours. *Is she sleeping with somebody else? Where'd that thought come from?* Ross went to the restaurant, the only other halfway logical place she might be. The restaurant was locked and dark. He went back to her cabin, focused this time, determined to figure it out.

Looking at everything it was obvious that nothing was turned over or out of place. No struggle. He went into the bedroom and saw her dirty work clothes laid on the bed. *So, she changed clothes.* He went to the closet and rifled through the hanging clothes. No winter coat and her boots were missing. That was enough for Ross. She evidently dressed to go out in the cold for a long period of time. He knew from experience she would run outside barefooted and wearing a flimsy blouse if she didn't think she was going to be out there very long.

Now the question was, where would she go and why? Ross sat on the edge of the bed thinking, but for the life of him, he couldn't channel any Sherlock Holmes. He got up and went through the rest of the house and nothing seemed amiss. He was worried. Going out on the porch he couldn't make himself pull the door shut. He leaned his head against the door jamb holding the knob in his hand. *Where is she?*

Taking a deep breath and softly closing the door, Ross sat down on the steps trying to gather his thoughts but he had no clue what to do. He stood, stretched his back and looked both ways before he walked several steps into the parking lot. Each one a little slower and shorter than the previous. Completely stopped, he looked back at John Luke's cabin. The yellow police tape was no longer across the door.

Bounding on to John Luke's porch, Ross reached out and turned the knob. The door opened and he rushed in, turning on every light he could find, running through all the rooms half way expecting to find Whisper's dead body on the floor. He had to quit thinking like that. No one was present but someone had been there. Some of the furniture in the living room was a little out of place and John Luke's smut magazines had fallen off the coffee table and were askew on the floor. There was a struggle but not a knock down drag out.

He started searching the outside of the cabin and instinctively began looking for trail signs, clues, tracks, anything. After going all the way around the cabin, he found the distinct markings in the dirt and grass indicating fresh travel by something other than wildlife. The signs were hard to see in the dark but they were there. To him, the way the earth was disturbed, indicated more than one person recently traveled this direction. *Did Whisper see someone and follow them?*

Since Ross started staying at the Hill Top Hunting Lodge, his whole demeanor changed from a mild mannered wild life biologist to something a lot more like a movie character. Every other day he seemed to be headed off into the woods hunting men. Not what he wanted to be doing.

Ross went to his cabin and dressed for military night maneuvers. Shelby never looked up from the video game. The last piece of equipment Ross strapped on was a web belt with a canteen, six extra bullets in a pouch and his knife. He almost said something to Shelby, then he asked himself, *why?*

Ross got his rifle from the truck and began reading the trail signs behind John Luke's cabin. After a few yards of tracking it became obvious the trail led to the lake. Ross quit being cautious, no longer needing to read the signs and made a dash to the lake. Once at the pier, he instantly noticed the rowboat was gone. He checked the other boats to see if he could 'borrow' one but they were all secured by pad locks to their moorings. The canoe he and Whispers used was sent to Austin with the other boats after the police assault several days ago. He would have to circumvent the lake on foot adding an hour to the journey. He wasted no time and took off at a trot.

* * * * *

Shanna and Whisper were sick with dread, unable to think of a way to free themselves. They wiggled and twisted but all they accomplished was wiggling and twisting. After exhausting themselves, they just hung by their hands and talked softly. "How do you think they'll do this?" asked Shanna.

"Several things have to happen. They've got to get us from here to there," pointing with her head to the tables. "They have to tie us down and get our clothes off."

Shanna processed her statement and said "Maybe, sometime between getting moved, stripped naked and tied down, they'll get lax and we can get away?"

Whisper replied, "If they take us down at the same time, we'll have a better chance of doing some kind of damage to them but if they take us one by one....I'm not so sure."

"What if we can coordinate an attack, two on one at the same time. We might have a chance. We need a signal for us to start fighting back simultaneously. You know, you hit 'em high and I hit 'em low kind of thing. We need a code word or phrase."

"Like a safe word but the opposite. Instead of stop hurting me, start hurting them."

"Right."

Whisper smiled, "Don't make the phrase 'you cock suckin' mother-fuckers' because I'm going to be yelling that right from the beginning.

Shanna smiled too. "How can you be making jokes at a time like this?"

Whisper didn't respond to her question. "If they take us over to the tables together, whomever is the closest to getting tied down first will say the word "blueberries" and we'll go to wailing on them. If either of us break free, make a run for it. Don't think twice, just run, save yourself, bring back help. "

"Okay."

"If we go together and they tape our mouths before they transfer us to the rape tables, as soon as the first one of us hits the table, go to kicking ass, break free, run, etcetera."

"Okay."

"If they take us one by one, as soon as you have the best opportunity, fight back as much as you can. Each of us do the same when our time comes."

"Okay."

Whisper nodded her head. "A plan."

They hung there in silence, eyes wide with fear, hyper alert. They were miserable where they were but they didn't really want to hear anyone coming down the stairs to move them to the tables.

In about ten minutes, Whisper asked Shanna, "Have you ever been in a fight before?"

"Never."

"This isn't going to be rolling around on the ground pulling hair like some girl spoke to your boyfriend the wrong way kind of fight. I mean anything is fair game. Scratch their eyes out! I don't mean scratch either, I mean dig your thumbnail in there and pop that son of a bitch right out of the socket."

Shanna was listening.

Whisper continued, "Their balls are good targets. Kick 'em in the balls, hard and continuously." Whisper thought for a minute, "Biting's good too. Chomp down. Bulldog it, don't let go until they knock you off with a stick and when they do, make sure you take whatever you had in your mouth with you. Bite it off. God please let them put a dick in my mouth. I'll swear if they do, it's gone."

Shanna's eyes widened but she was still listening.

"I don't know if we're going to get out of this. In all reality, chances look pretty slim but they are going to wish to hell they never messed with us. By God, I promise you that. I promise Shanna, they are going to regret this."

Chapter 40

Shanna's hands were stretched so high breathing was difficult. "How long has it been?" she gasped.

Whisper's eyes were shut, doing the best she could to be someplace else mentally. "I don't know. Three hours?"

They heard a distinct bump upstairs. Both girls panicked but what could they do? They heard more noises from the men walking around. The captors were finished with their naps, well rested for their rape session. The girls heard what sounded like the front door slam, the truck fire up and drive away.

The girls looked at each other and asked, "Did they leave?"

Their question was answered in a moment when boot scuffling was heard on the top of the stairs.

"Oh, God. Which one is still here?" Shanna said, choking back the fear.

Slowly the man began to walk down the stairs. He was doing the 'slow walk' on purpose. Step-by-step. Shanna's heart was in her throat. Whisper was trembling.

Two quick steps and it became apparent. Lonnie! The cousin was coming to take Whisper up the ass. Shanna said, "Oh God Whisper, he's here for you."

Whisper's face hardened like steel. She took two deep breaths and expelled a blood curdling rant, "You cock sucking motherfucker! You motherfucking, cock sucking, motherfucking fucker!" What she was screaming didn't even make sense but she was letting him have it the best she could.

Shanna lost her mind too. She chimed in with a growl and started screaming at the top of her lungs, "Blueberries! Goddamn Blueberries! Blueberries motherfucker! Come here you motherfucker and get some fucking blueberries!"

Lonnie climbed down to the floor and stood with his hands on his hips. "Got your tape off I see." He walked straight over to Shanna who was still spewing forth a blueberry tirade and punched her in the mouth as hard as he could. Her head snapped back and her lips made a gurgling noise as she expelled excess air and three teeth from her mouth. Two teeth slid down her chin on a river of blood and one stuck to the corner of her mouth. Blood bubbles were forming on her lips as she was still attempting her verbal attack. Her eyes were not in focus and consciousness was fading.

Lonnie grabbed Shanna's hair and held her head up staring into her glassy eyes. "Blueberries to you bitch."

Shanna made a "twa" noise as she spit blood in his face. He threw her head back and she slumped unconscious, hanging by her hands. Lonnie wiped his face and turned to Whisper. "Now, are you going to give me any trouble?"

"You cock sucking motherfucker!" She said the only thing that would come out of her mouth. She was terrified.

"Don't make me hit you in the face. I will if you don't shut up. Look at your friend." He grabbed Shanna's hair again and held up her head. "She doesn't have any teeth anymore. John Luke's going to be pissed. He won't like fucking a toothless whore. Now you're a different matter.

I won't mind knockin' all of your fucking teeth out 'cause I'm gonna get you from behind anyway."

Whisper wanted to say it one more time but her brain kicked in. *Cock sucking motherfucker!* She just thought it. The only way she was possibly going to survive this was to be compliant, wait for an opportunity, then maybe do something. *Poor Shanna.* Whisper was so sick she thought she may throw up.

"Okay," she said. "I'll do what you want."

"Good girl." She hated him saying that.

Lonnie started untying the rope at the stud. He got the knot undone, held the rope in his hands checking to see if she was still complacent. He wrapped the rope around his wrist a few times for a good grip. The rope was still tied to her hands which hung in front of her. He jerked the rope. Her arms raised but she gave no other reaction. He did it again and her arms pulled forward but she didn't do anything. "That's better. I like 'em docile." He untied her feet. "Need you to be able to spread your legs, you know."

Lonnie guided her over to the table leading her like a pony. "You're gonna take your bottoms off and bend over that table. I'm gonna stretch you out real good and tie your hands on the table legs on the far side. Got it? Start taking your pants off." He gave her a little slack.

She really wanted to go after him but didn't have the strength or ability to fight him with her hands still tied and him holding the other end of the rope. She didn't want to take a beating and still get raped. No advantage in that.

Whisper reluctantly bent over and took off her boots. She used her shoulder to wipe away a tear at the corner of her eye, angry at herself for letting one get away from her. Boots were off.

"Socks too," Lonnie said. "I want to see your feet."

Whisper pulled off her socks.

"Yellow!" Lonnie exclaimed. "I knew it. I sure wish you had a cock and balls. I'd really like to see what color they would be. Plus…"

Whisper stood and looked at him.

"Plus, I'd rather have a cock and balls of any color than your fishy smelling cunt. Get your pants off and be quick about it."

Whisper undid her pants and wriggled them down. As she stepped out of them, she turned around and bent over the table.

Lonnie looked at her. "Get your panties off."

"Nope."

"What?" Lonnie couldn't believe what she just said.

"If you want them off, you come take them off." She wiggled her ass a little.

Lonnie thought about it for an instant and decided what could it hurt to pull her non-descript pink nylon panties down. "Don't do anything you'll regret." He moved over closer and reached out with one hand while holding the rope with the other. Just as he got his hand inside the waistband, Shanna revived enough to blurt out, "Blueberries motherfucker!" Spitting blood all over everywhere as she did.

Lonnie turned his head in surprise. Split second decisions sometimes change one's life forever. Whisper spun and threw her arms over Lonnie's head. Her hands were still tied and she was trying to strangle him using the rope binding her wrists as a garrote. It wasn't working very well because he was strong and she was a really small woman.

Whisper was behind him to the side, he was spinning trying to get her to the front. Whisper had one of his ears in her hand, twisting and pinching the shit out of it and had already bitten off a portion of the opposite ear. Lonnie was screaming and pulling her hair trying to get her off his back.

Whisper stuck an index finger in his eye. The nail was not long but hard and sharp as knife blade. She dug in and damned if she didn't get one. Didn't pluck it completely out like she instructed Shanna but a good chunk of his eye came out under her nail.

Lonnie bent over in excruciating pain and flipped her to the floor. He let go of the rope and grabbed his face screaming obscenities. Whisper jumped up and kicked him in the groin but he didn't have any reaction. *Did he have balls?* She kicked him again and struck pay-dirt. He screeched and an immediate expulsion of bile flew from his mouth. *God, he threw up a nut!* She ran towards the stairs. Her hands were still tied, the rope dragging behind her.

She missed the first stair and stumbled. Panicked and stumbling up several more stairs, she reached the top and was nearly into the house when the rope yanked and she sprawled on the floor. The rope pulled taut and she was being dragged back down the stairs, bumping and rolling down each one. Battered and bruised, she landed on the basement floor.

Whisper looked up from her prone position to see Lonnie standing over her with a torn, ragged ear, mangled eye and holding his crotch. She laughed, "Like John Luke said, I'm a terrible fuck, huh?"

Lonnie became enraged. He grabbed her by the ankle and dragged her over to the rape table. She was kicking and screaming "Cock sucking motherfucker!"

Once again Shanna revived enough to yell "Blueberries bitch!" Then she faded.

Whisper was encouraged and inspired. She was fighting with all the strength she could muster. Scratching! Kicking! Biting! Punching! A furious onslaught.

Lonnie was actually losing the fight and he knew it. He had to get the upper hand so he reared back and punched her on the cheek with all the strength he had left. The blow stopped Whisper in her tracks. Everything went black but she knew she wasn't unconscious. Blinking twice, she shook her head and a little light started to comeback, then her eyes came into focus. She was on the floor, still, with Lonnie standing over her, ready to deliver another blow.

Whisper knew she couldn't take another punch like that but her body was unable to move. *I'm going to get raped up the ass and killed and there's nothing more I can do about it.* She just looked at her assailant waiting for him to strike again. In a low guttural tone, Shanna spit out the word, "Blueberries" one more time.

Whisper repeated, "Blueberries." She shut her eyes, took in a long deep breath and blew it out resigning herself to a horrible end.

From the top of the stairs an explosion rang out nearly bursting Whisper's eardrums. The concussion caused dust to puff forth from the ceiling and walls. Lonnie's head burst open like a water balloon popping. His body slammed to the ground and smashed down against the side of the basement six feet away. His head was glued by what was left of his brain to the bottom of the wall. Blood spatter and the remaining brains were sprayed in a ten-foot circle behind him.

Whisper's ears rang with a high-pitched whine. She stared at Lonnie's contorted face with its shattered bones, gouged out eye and partially missing ear. His face looked wide and flat, which it was considering it had just absorbed a shot from a Model 1895 Marlin 45-70 rifle dispensing a 405 grain bullet traveling at 2000 feet per second. A cannon!

Whisper tore her gaze away from the body and looked up the stairs to see her wonderful Doctor Ross Evans, looking ever so rugged, handsome and heroic. He just put an end, with and exclamation mark, to her worst nightmare. "God, I love you," she said but no one could hear it for the ringing in their ears.

Ross crept down the stairs looking in all of the corners for another threat, that threat being John Luke. When he realized no other bad guys were there, he put down his rifle and went straight to Whisper. They embraced like there was no tomorrow. Whisper wanted to stay in his arms forever but she pushed him back. "Help Shanna," she yelled.

Ross got up, took his knife and in one stroke from his powerful arms, sliced clean through the rope. Shanna fell over his shoulder. He laid her gently on the table and checked for other injuries besides the obvious one to her face. Her lips were moving. He bent down to her so she could speak directly into his ear. "Blueberries." was all she said. She shut her eyes and went limp.

Whisper, still in her underwear and bare footed, went to Myles and started to unbuckle the sex swing restraints. He was in bad shape, bruised and heavily drugged. Ross went to the Kylie and Molly, cutting them loose. Kylie was completely out of it but Molly was mildly coherent. Molly hugged Ross, more like clung on to Ross but somehow her hand went to Ross' crotch.

Whisper saw this and came over and replaced Ross with herself. "Damn, Molly. Even raped, beaten, drugged and semi-conscious, you're still a horny bitch."

"I know," Molly managed to say before she closed her eyes and laid her head on Whisper's shoulder.

Ross went upstairs and called the Emergency Operations Center with his satellite phone. He reported freeing all the hostages, the rescue of an additional two women, the elimination of one of the kidnappers and the escape of the other, John Luke. He told them he was at the rock house and to find it by tracking his GPS. He needed lots of medical services, enough to transport at least five live bodies and one dead pile of shit.

While Ross was on the phone, Whisper was at Myles' side trying to make sure he didn't slip into a life-threatening situation. Hs eyes opened momentarily. "Hey," she said.

"Where am I?" Myles looked around barely able to keep his eyes open.

"Doesn't matter, but you're safe. That's all that counts."

"Safe," he repeated. He tried hard to focus on Whisper, "I know you, don't I? Yeah, you're the girl from the restaurant and you're here to save me?"

"You're safe," she repeated. "We're all being saved."

He started trying to get out of the swing. She encouraged him to stay there but understood completely when he said he wanted out, now! She tried to help but ended up calling for Ross. Ross came running at her beckon and helped Myles to the mattress that Kylie was on.

Myles' naked body rubbed all over Ross. "Jeez, ya think we ought to find some clothes for these guys?"

Whisper looked down at herself. Ross looked down also. Whisper said, "I would have worn sexier underwear if I'd known I'd see you today." She put on her pants and boots and checked Shanna who was still out on the table.

Whisper brought down some of what she thought were John Luke's clothes from upstairs. Myles and John Luke were about the same height but John Luke was thicker. Ross managed to get some of John Luke's pants on Myles. Whisper put one of John Luke's shirts on Molly and Whisper's coat fit over Kylie enough to cover the essentials.

Ross and Whisper stood surveying their work. He put an arm around her and looked at the bruise on her face. "Was it a good fight?" he asked.

"I was kicking his ass until you showed up and shot the shit out of him."

"Sorry, I would have waited if I'd known you were enjoying it so much." She started to cry and buried her face in his chest. He held her tightly.

They heard the helicopter overhead. Separating, Ross ran up the stairs to the front yard to try to guide them in. The trees were thick and landing seemed impossible to accomplish. The bird circled several times and flew off aborting a nearby landing attempt.

Ross went back down to the basement and saw Whisper and Myles sitting on the edge of the mattress. He was reasonably awake now. Kylie was even showing signs of coming around. Ross gave them all a drink out of his canteen. Ross sat on the mattress by Whisper passing the water back and forth when Shanna raised up on the edge of the table. She was looking at the body of Lonnie stuck to the wall by his head, or what was left of it. Whisper jumped up and ran to her, swollen cheek throbbing all the way.

"You're back," Whisper said.

Shanna was still staring at Lonnie's body. "You blueberried the fuck out of him!"

"Yeah, we did, didn't we?"

Shanna leaned in for a hug, lisping with her ruined mouth, "Are you alright? Did you get raped?"

Whisper said, "I'm fine. He got my pants off but that was as far as it went."

"Did I get raped?" asked Shanna.

"No."

"Our plan worked then? Although I don't remember a damn thing about it."

Whisper looked her friend in the eyes, "You were fearless."

They continued to hug and stroke each other's sore faces. Whisper never had a friend like this before.

Chapter 41

Ross said, "Quiet!" And everyone went deadly silent and still. They could hear voices.

"You in the house. Police!"

They all started screaming, "Down here! In the basement! We're here!"

The emergency service personnel easily followed the voices and burst into the basement to be greeted with cheers. The uniformed guys went to work and within an hour, all of the victims were rescued, flown out on a helicopter. Ross and Whisper went to the Emergency Operations Center for a debriefing and the other four went to the hospital for treatment. All the media followed Myles to the hospital.

Ross and Whisper sat in separate rooms, each drinking a cup of coffee trying to stay awake. The debriefing felt more like a police suspect's interview but with such a high-profile case, the authorities wanted to get things right.

Whisper's summary statement: "I went to check on Shanna when she didn't return to the restaurant. When I couldn't find her, I called the police. They took so long to get there, I started looking around and got caught. I don't know why Lonnie was in the cabin at that precise moment. Bad luck for us, I guess. Shanna was already tied up when I got there. He tied me up too and took Shanna and me to the rock house where we were put in the basement to wait our turn to be raped. The other hostages were already there. Shanna and I got the tape off our mouth's and made a plan to escape. The plan failed but it had a zero percent chance of working anyway." Whisper smiled a little thinking back on it. *Blueberries!* "We heard Lonnie and John Luke upstairs milling around. A vehicle drove off and Lonnie came down to rape me. He said he would do it anally because he was homosexual and that was the only way it would work for him. He punched Shanna in the mouth because she was verbally fighting back. He hit her so damn hard." Whisper let a tear roll out of the corner of her eye. She wiped it away quickly as if she didn't want the interviewer to see it. "Lonnie took me down from where I was tied up so he could secure me to the rape table in a position that allowed him access to what he wanted. He made me take off my boots, socks and pants. We fought horribly. I bit his ear off, gouged out his eye and kicked him in the...scrotum...twice. Although I think I completely missed the first time. He was really mad. He hit me in the face with his fist." Her hand instinctively went to her swollen cheek. "He didn't knock me out but I couldn't see anything for a moment. He was going to hit me again when Ross shot him in the head. Ross called for help, I freed Myles and we took care of everybody the best we could until the first responders came. That's pretty much it."

Ross' summary statement: "I was at the Emergency Operations Center doing a hot wash for eight hours and didn't get back to the lodge until after midnight. My roommate told me Whisper came by looking for me. I went to see what she wanted. It was 1:00 am and I fully expected her to be in her cabin. She was not there. I noticed the police tape was no longer stretched across the door of John Luke's cabin. I went in and realized there had been some activity. I prepared myself for a walk in the woods…" The interviewer interrupted Ross asking what the preparation entailed. Ross answered, "A gun, a knife and some water. As it turned out, I used all three." Ross continued, "I trailed the group to the lake and found there were no boats available to take so I had to go around. It took and extra hour, even moving at a fast rate. When I approached the rock house, I heard a vehicle drive off. I never saw it. I moved in closer and could hear screaming like an argument coming from inside. I entered the house, gun ready, and determined all the action was going on downstairs. I crept down into the basement and saw a man standing over Whisper, who was in her underwear. I saw a woman hanging up from the ceiling with a bloody face, Myles fastened to a basket-swing thing and Molly and Kylie were tied up on the mattresses. Those three were naked. It was a lot to take in so quickly." Ross paused for a second. "I thought, 'this ends right now'. All but Whisper might have been dead already, I couldn't tell. I raised my rifle, snap fired, aiming for his head. I made a lucky shot. Unlike his captives, he didn't suffer for even a tenth of a second. After checking on Whisper and cutting Shanna down, I went outside to call for help."

"What happened after you called for help?"

"I went back down stairs. Whisper unlocked the restraints holding Myles and I helped him to the mattress. Whisper found some clothes for them, I gave them water and waited for help. There was a failed attempt to land a helicopter but an hour later, we were rescued."

Several hours after giving statements, multiple times, Ross and Whisper were driven back to the Hill Top Hunting Lodge. They held hands like teenagers in the back of the cop car in which they were escorted. Whisper fell asleep on his shoulder.

The police officer parked out on the highway because the parking lot was overflowing with police, media and spectators. There was a big show going on at the restaurant but Ross and Whisper could care less, they wanted to sleep. After dropping them off, the police officer went to the restaurant to see what was happening and to get a rack of ribs.

Ross and Whisper stood on the pavement among all the cars. They were holding hands and looking into each other's eyes. Whisper spoke first, "I'd invite you in but I really need a shower, at least ten hours of sleep, a cold compress and a Band-Aid or two."

"Sexy," said Ross. He kissed her on the side of the face that wasn't swollen. "I'll see you in ten hours," he said jokingly. He dropped her hand and they went to their respective cabins. Shelby was up at the restaurant seeing the show so Ross was alone to shower and collapse in his bed without having to relate the story one more time.

The Governor just finished his speech on the steps of the restaurant and invited the whole crowd into Big Al's to buy some barbecue. Big Al was really killing it. If he could do this for a couple of more weeks, he'd take the money and run, retire. Work never suited Big Al but the restaurant business, although hard work, allowed him to cook and eat as much food as he wanted. He probably could have retired years ago if he didn't eat up half the profits.

Short on waitresses, Big Al set up a buffet and charged an exorbitant, cash only, fee for a one-time trip through the line. The waitresses and Big Al's nephew kept the buffet full and bused the heck out of the tables. Over three-hundred meals were served and the line of customers was still out the door. Big Al noticed some of the larger boys were in line again for second helpings. Fine with him, they'll pay full price again.

Chapter 42

Whisper woke up in the middle of the night, somehow sleeping through all the commotion outside. It was 3:00 am and all was quiet now. After brushing her teeth and running a comb through her hair, she looked at her face in the mirror. It was beginning to bruise, one of those horrid purple bruises that turn yellow as they heal. No one, especially a woman, likes anything wrong with her face. Whisper struggled with this every day…orange face, grapefruit lips, yellow hair, blue eyes and now a purple cheek.

She stepped out on her porch in the cold, barefooted and wearing only her flannel pajamas. She wrapped her arms around herself and walked out far enough to look up at the stars. It was very dark and the sky was filled with diamonds. She took in a deep breath and let herself feel content.

The sound of a car door opening startled her. In one of the far parking spaces, she could see the dome light on in Ross' truck. She smiled from ear-to-ear watching Ross quietly close the truck door and walk back to his cabin.

In the middle of the parking lot, he looked around and saw Whisper on the edge of the porch. They were grinning at each other like Cheshire cats. He walked toward her with a black case in his hand, wearing a pair of slip-on Adidas, jeans and a field jacket, open in the front exposing his bare chest. He looked like he belonged on a calendar of urban guerrilla hunks. Whisper unconsciously squeezed her thighs together.

He strode up the steps, put his forearm on the porch column and hovered over her. They stared each other down for a moment. Whisper spoke first, "Are we going to do it right here or do you want to go inside?"

He leaned in and kissed her. Lips and tongue only, nothing else was touching. Her nipples were already erect from the cold but during the kiss, they tightened to the point of pain, needing to be rubbed. Her hand searched for the top of his pants and she fumbled miserably with the button on the jeans. He wasn't wearing a belt.

They broke their kiss and pulled away. This gave Whisper a chance to see what she was doing. She undid the button, found the zipper and pulled it down. His jeans were tight and she put her hand on his lower stomach to reach in and pull him out. His muscles were solid and made that wonderfully sexy 'V'.

She couldn't get her hand in so she grabbed his pants and started trying to pull them down. They began to slide, inch by inch. He wasn't wearing any underwear. She slid his pants down lower. All of his pubic region was exposed. She pulled down another inch or so. The base of his beautiful cock was in view.

She really wanted to get his clothes off and pulled more forcefully until the pants were at mid-thigh. To her surprise, the tip of his long cock was still stuck in the top of his jeans. She had forgotten just how big and beautiful and hard he was. She grabbed it with her hand, sending tiny, electrical shock waves through them both. She popped it out of his jeans, knelt down, held it with both hands hugging it against her bruised face. It felt warm and soft.

Ross cupped her chin and raised her up to a standing position. He shed his jeans right on the porch and placed the case he was holding on top of the jeans. While he was bent over, he grabbed her flannel bottoms and easily pulled them down to her little yellow feet. Whisper nimbly stepped out of them.

She reached out and took the head of his extended cock and pulled him to her. They kissed with arms wrapped around each other this time. He reached between her legs and felt her moistness. Dripping actually. He picked her up and pressed her against the side of the cabin. She enveloped him with her legs. He tried to insert himself but he couldn't get the angle right, daring not to use his hands because of the way he was holding her up. He was quickly getting frustrated.

She spit on her hand, grabbed the big head, rubbed it around and guided it right up in her. Four inches in on the first thrust. A slow deliberate retraction and a steady forceful insertion. Six inches in on the second push. A third drive brought eight inches of pleasure into her and the last push brought it home. All ten inches up inside her. It took her breath away.

Ross was an incredibly sexy animal but being mostly naked in public doing it, turned her on even more. She was aware of wanting to please him and tried to figure out if she was giving it to him or if he was taking it from her but either way one sliced that bread, she was about to cum and there was nothing she could do about it unless she stopped him from doing what he was doing. Fat chance of that happening.

She didn't know for sure but she thought she was going to say, "Ross, I'm going to cum." What she actually said was, "Ross...", and then she came. She shook like crazy and clawed at his back. Thank goodness he was wearing the field jacket or she would have torn his scars to shreds. She ended her orgasm with a moan and the release of a handful of his head hair she was grasping.

"C'mon, give me some more. I need it," she told him. She could tell he was so close to cumming. He was holding her tightly but tenderly.

He was forceful but careful. Instead of pumping into her, he was actually using her entire body to jack himself off. He was lifting her up and down on him. Ross was incredibly strong.

She could tell he was cumming….right….now! He pulled her down on him and held her, fully impaled. She saw him straining, shooting his load in her. He lifted her and jammed her down on him again. *Another stream*, she thought. He lifted her once more and ground her into his groin.

He pressed her up against the wall, her feet clear up by his shoulders. He was still in her but he was not made of granite like he was moments ago. She pushed his head back and looked him in the yes. "We gonna stay out here all night or will you take me inside."

Ross grunted a little and carried her through the door, big cock still up in her. She had to help him open the door and hold it. He carried her straight to the bedroom. "Put me down, I need to clean up. You go get in bed." She slid down his naked legs, feeling his wet dick slide up to nearly her chest. She pulled on it, squeezing out the last droplets of juice into her hand. Ross jerked as she pinched the head. "Sensitive, are we?"

Whisper went to the bathroom and ran a shower. Ross, being a man, fell asleep, naked, on top of the bed. She got dressed for work and checked herself in the mirror one more time. Most women would have put makeup on their face bruises but Whisper didn't use makeup. She was never able to find the correct color to accent orange. *A big purple blotch…maybe no one will notice.* Whisper touched Ross on the shoulder, "I'm going to work now."

Ross turned toward her. His dick flopped over as he turned. She'd seen him naked several times but the shock of seeing his cock was always unexpected. She kissed him on the lips and then the head of his dick. Ross opened his eyes when she went for the latter. "I'll see you tonight?" she said as a question.

"Yes, you will."

Chapter 43

At 10:38 am, Ross instantly became fully awake, sat on the side of the bed and scratched his head. He put on his shoes, jeans and field jacket, picked up his black case Whisper brought in from the porch last night and took a mini walk of shame over to his own cabin. Shelby was asleep on the couch with electronic gaming devices strewn about, headphones still attached to his neck. *A video battle royale.* Ross wondered if something was wrong with Shelby or himself. Shelby was obviously a geek and Ross didn't even really want to turn on a TV let alone play a video game. Shelby slayed thousands of whatever he was killing in the video game and then it hit him like a ton of bricks…

He just killed a man. The man needed killing, especially at that precise moment. But the way his head exploded…. Ross shoved it back in his mind, somewhere in the dark recesses where he kept the vivid imagery, smell and pain of him on fire in Iraq. *Live in the present*! He took a shower, dressed and walked up to the restaurant to see Whisper and get brunch.

The parking lot had a few cars parked here and there and the restaurant was empty. When he stepped in, Whisper jumped up out of Big Al's booth and ran to him. She put an arm around his waist and guided him to a seat across from Big Al.

Big Al was eating a sandwich. It must have been his first lunch because it was only 11:25 am. Big Al spoke with his mouth full, "I hear you fucked that dude up?"

Ross looked at Whisper. "Yeah, I guess you can say that."

"They say his head stuck to the wall like a two-year-old throwing a plate of spaghetti." Big Al took another bite.

Whisper could tell Ross was uncomfortable and maybe going to get mad so she changed the subject. She grabbed his arm and asked, "Can you run me over to Tyler tonight. To the hospital. I want to see Shanna and the others?"

"Sure, we can go." To get Al's goat, Ross added, "I know where you can get a job over that way if you want. They pay good wages and since you worked there before, rehiring you ought to be a breeze. Plus, they serve really *good* food." Ross got up to walk out.

"Hey now, wait a minute. What's this about working someplace else?" Food fell out of Big Al's mouth. Whisper laughed, winked and waved at Ross when he looked back before exiting the door.

As soon as the first evening waitress showed up, Whisper ran down the hill to her cabin. She cleaned up and got dressed in what she thought was the cutest outfit she had. Her wardrobe sucked. She was wearing her fake UGG boots, jeans stuffed in the tops of the boots, a white halter top covered by a flannel shirt. If the magazine Log Cabin Living had been shooting an advertisement, she could have been on the cover.

She walked over to Ross' cabin and knocked on the door. Ross answered wearing what Ross always wore, looking ruggedly handsome. He was carrying the black case. They walked to the truck and drove off towards Tyler. Being naturally curious, nosey more like it, Whisper asked, "What's in the case?"

Ross pulled it from under the seat while he was driving and put it in her lap. She opened it to reveal one of the biggest revolvers she had ever seen, not that she'd really seen any. "It's a Ruger 44 magnum. They kept my rifle as evidence. They may keep it for months and I need a weapon to be able to do my work safely."

Whisper ran her fingers over the cold steel. "It's a big one."

"It's not the biggest they make but it's about as powerful as I want to shoot. It'll knock a hog down if I hit him in the right place and he's standing still at about 21 feet away."

"Sounds like a lot to ask for"?

"Chances are, if I have to use it, I'm screwed. However, if I'm in a situation where I should use it, and don't have it…then I'm doubly screwed."

Whisper smiled at him, put her hand way up on his thigh, so high he jerked the steering wheel a little. "Let's make sure if there's any screwing going on, it's me that's doing it." Then she grabbed his dick and balls and gave a firm squeeze. This time, he not only jerked the wheel but he stomped the gas and raised up out of the seat.

Ross started looking off into the woods, left and right. Whisper said, "If you're looking for a place to pull over and give me a quickie, forget about it, I'm not going to visit Shanna and the girls smelling like fuck. Mark my words, Molly will know and start coming on to you. She will. Then she'll grope you and every doctor and orderly in the building." Ross kept driving, disappointed. Whisper could tell, not only by the bulge in his pants but the sour look on his face. "Don't worry. I'll make it up to you later." His expression eased.

They pulled into the hospital parking lot after looking up the directions on Ross' phone. The whole parking lot was filled with media and law enforcement. This is why Big Al's place was empty. They parked as closely as they could to the front door which was a hundred yards away. Whisper asked, "This is a silly question, but do you have a scarf or a hooded sweatshirt lying around? I don't want anyone to spot me on the way in."

Ross looked a little puzzled but reached back behind her seat and came out with a shemagh scarf he wore in Iraq. It was filthy. "Damn, Ross, ever wash anything?"

They got out of the truck. She shook the scarf a half a dozen times and dust flew everywhere. It was a desert tan color and absolutely clashed with her red and blue plaid flannel. Of course, *she* clashed with red and blue plaid flannel. *What the hell.* She wrapped it around her head and tied it. Ross said she looked like a Pennsylvania Dutch Muslim.

They walked into the hospital, getting by the guards because they looked somewhat like regular people and said they were there to visit friends not named Myles Carter. Once inside, Whisper removed the scarf and ran it through her belt. They went to the information desk manned by a blue-haired volunteer lady. She told them Molly and Kylie were in room 276.

They went up the elevators and found the room. It was a semi-private room occupied with their two friends only. Whisper stepped in the room which had the beds separated by a plastic curtain. Molly was in the first bed.

Molly looked up, saw Whisper and let go of the Physician's Assistant who was trying to examine her. The Physician Assistant ran out, embarrassed because he was doing a little more than examining, consensually, of course. "Orange!" Molly held out her arms. Whisper hugged her. When done, Molly held out her arms again. "Ranger!"

Ross looked at Whisper who nodded. Ross went in for a hug but nearly had to call Fire and Rescue to get extracted from her grip. At least it was all head and shoulders instead of other types of groping. Whisper thought it was funny.

Whisper sat on the edge of the bed as the girls caught up on what they remembered and how they felt. Ross stepped around the curtain to look in on Kylie. She was sitting up in bed with earphones on. She had no idea anybody entered the room.

She eventually looked up and saw Ross. Not knowing him very well she looked puzzled and then she recalled he was at the rock house. She took off her earphones and said, "I think I owe you some gratitude."

"An unusual turn of a phrase but you don't owe me anything. I'm just glad you're back with us and appear to be doing well."

"I'm uninjured. There was some sex stuff but fortunately for me, I was drugged so heavily I don't remember. It's only traumatizing if I think about it so, I choose not to dwell on it. They're keeping me here because I had such high doses of whatever drug they gave me. They want to make sure my brain looks okay. A scan or two tomorrow and if all is clear, I'll be released."

"Good for you," Ross said genuinely happy for her.

Whisper came around the curtain and gave Kylie a hug. "You look so much better today."

Kylie raised a hand to Whisper's face. "Ouch," she said as she touched the purple bruise.

"Ah, it's nothing. I see you have one too." Whisper could see the yellow remnants of a bruise on Kylie's face.

Kylie started to cry. "I think I owe you an apology for treating you so mean at the restaurant."

They hugged again. "Don't worry about it. You got fired for it."

"And tit punched," added Kylie. They both gave a short embarrassed laugh.

After they visited with the girls, Whisper wanted to go see Myles. He was on a different floor and heavily guarded. Ross thought the guards were there to keep the media out instead of anymore bad guys. They couldn't even get the elevator to go to the right floor. It had been programmed so a key card was needed for access. "Well, shit." Ross and Whisper went to find someone in charge of the hospital to grant them access.

As they were aimlessly walking through the halls looking for the administrative offices, Ross said, "Why don't we just call the hospital and tell them who you are and let them ask Myles if he wants to see you? If he says he wants to see you, they'll probably send a limousine to pick you up. Whatever he says will go. I promise."

Whisper snatched up the first house phone she saw on the wall and it started ringing. The hospital operator answered. "Hello," Whisper said. "My name is Whisper Jenkins and I'd like to pay Myles Carter a visit."

The operator rudely interrupted, "Ma'am, there is no Whisper Jenkins on the visitor list," and hung up.

"Bitch hung up on me."

"Try again," Ross encouraged. "Tell her you were a captive with him."

Whisper hung up the phone and quickly picked it up, getting it to ring once more.

"Hey again, don't hang up. I was with Myles when he was rescued. I'd really like to see him."

Click, nothing but dial tone. "Oh, this is pissing me off."

Whisper slammed the phone down and yanked it off the cradle. It rang.

When answered, "This Orange Girl is gonna come over there and beat your ass if you fucking hang up on me one more time!"

"Orange Girl?"

Whisper paused, "Yes."

The 'Orange Girl' is on the list of visitors.

"Well, that's better. How do I get up to his floor?"

"Come by the big glass window on the first floor with 'Finance' on the door. A Veritas Security Officer will escort you up. Bring a picture ID."

"Are you kidding right now? An ID that says 'Orange Girl'? Never mind. You'll know it's me," and Whisper hung up.

"What?" asked Ross. "You don't carry your 'Orange Girl' passport around with you?"

"Shut up."

They walked around the first floor until they found the finance office. When they saw the security guard, Whisper asked if Ross Evans was on the visitor list.

The guy checked, "Nope."

Ross spoke up, "What about 'Rugged, Outdoor Type, Ranger'?"

The security guy saw no humor in that what-so-ever. Whisper thought it was hilarious.

"I'll meet you in the main lobby," Ross told Whisper as she walked off with the security guy.

Whisper was quite impressed with Myles' room. It looked more like what she thought a hotel suite would look like. Myles was sitting in one of three lounge chairs. The other two chairs were occupied by an older couple. Myles' parents she assumed.

"Mr. Carter," she said as she stuck out her hand to shake his. He went right in for the hug. "Mom, Dad," he said. "This is the girl who saved me." The parents jumped up, at least as fast as older folks could jump out of lounge chairs and moved in for a group hug. The mom was crying.

When the initial hug-a-thon ended, Myles sat on the edge of the bed and the others sat in the lounge chairs. Myles recounted her bravery to his parents. Every word was embellished because, truthfully, he was so far out of it, he didn't remember a thing, only what others told him. When he finished his regaling them, the mom was in tears again.

Whisper said she was glad he was alright but she needed to get back to her friend Ross, who was the one who shot the kidnapper. "Oh yeah," Myles said. "Well done."

Whisper got out of the lounger with some difficulty and Myles walked her to the door. Whisper told him she just finished visiting two of the other girls who were captured with him and they were doing alright.

Almost as a second thought, Myles said, "Oh yeah." He bent in closer and told her not to worry about him. He was not as traumatized about this as the media was making out. He told her he was gay and of course, had men before, many men. Being "raped" by a man was not the worst thing that could have happened to him.

She thought he was trying to explain to her in some weird way that maybe he enjoyed being kidnapped, restrained, drugged and raped up the ass. Whisper just said, "Okay. I've got to go now."

Myles opened the door saying, "We'll be seeing you later." The parents waved goodbye and thanked her for saving their son.

The Veritas Security Officer was still standing outside the room with several of his compatriots and he escorted her down. Whisper easily found Ross and told him how flippant Myles was about the whole situation.

After Whisper expressed her concern over his aloofness, Ross added, "I don't know about rich people. They have everything to begin with and if something bad happens to them, but they still have everything when it's over, then they think 'what's the big deal?' If this caused his stock to go down by 50 percent he probably would have thought it was a tragedy and caught the vapors or something."

"Caught the vapors? Oh my God Ross, how old are you?" she said laughing.

"I don't even know what the vapors are, I just said that."

Whisper and Ross went back down to the volunteer desk and asked about Shanna. Unfortunately, Shanna was transferred to a Dallas hospital for emergency oral surgery. Whisper bit her thumbnail and had a faraway look in her sky blue, sparkly eyes. Ross didn't know her really well but he was pretty sure that look meant he was driving to Dallas. She looked up at him, brow furrowed....

"Do you want to go tonight or in the morning?" Ross asked.

"Yes!" She jumped on him hugging him with pretty much every part of her body with which she could touch him. He walked out of the hospital, carrying her wrapped all over him. Everyone in the lobby gawked. "Tonight, please," she softly spoke into his ear.

Chapter 44

As they were driving down the freeway, Ross said, "You know it will be after visiting hours when we get there. They won't let you in to see her."

Whisper grunted acknowledgment.

"I guess that's not going to stop you, is it?"

Whisper grunted acknowledgment to that also. He could tell she was thinking. Plotting more likely.

Following the directions from the phone, they drove directly to the hospital, a sprawling complex. They went in to find one of the volunteer ladies but none were there at 11:00 pm. A few people in scrubs were walking down the hall who Ross asked, "Where would someone be who just had extensive emergency oral surgery?" The scrub folks agreed, every surgery patient would end up on the sixth floor.

Whisper and Ross got in the elevator and Whisper pushed the button for six saying, "So help me. If we need a key card to get up there, I'll explode." The elevator went straight to the sixth floor, no stops. Whisper looked at Ross with a degree of satisfaction on her face. The elevator door opened and they stepped out.

The nurse's station was a little bit around the corner and no one saw them exit the elevator. Ross asked, "What's your plan?"

"You're going to go up there and give them a line of bullshit. Figure out what room she's in and come back and tell me."

"Me? I'm going to do that?"

"Yes. Now go." She started shoving him out into view of the nurse's station. None of the nurses looked up. They were too busy charting all the activity from the day.

Ross walked right up to them as if he belonged there. "Hello."

The nurse nearest him looked up. "My name is Doctor Ross Evans. I'm here to see Shanna Borger. I work for the Emergency Operations Center and the State of Texas. Can you tell me what room she is in?"

"She's in room 632 but visiting hours are over for the day."

"That's fine. I just wanted to make sure I was in the right place. What time are visiting hours in the morning?"

"They start at 09:30 am and end at 11:00 am. They pick up again at 3:00 in the afternoon."

"That's good. Fine. I'll be back in the morning." Ross walked off.

Whisper was anxiously waiting around the corner. "Six-thirty-two." Ross said.

Whisper grabbed his face and kissed him on the lips. "Wait in the lobby. I'm going in. Get comfortable. I may be a while if she's asleep." Whisper crouched down, so low it was almost a duck walk and scooted into the ward, right by the nurse's station and down the hall. She even waved 'bye' to him when she was safely passed the nurses view.

Fearless, he thought. He exited the ward, stepped off the elevator on the first floor and took up residence on a horribly uncomfortable tiny couch.

Whisper quietly entered room 632. She could see Shanna asleep on the hospital bed with bandages wrapped around her face. Someone slept on a roll-away bed next to Shanna's. It looked like a woman, Shanna's mother probably. *Must be nice, wonderful actually. To have a mother who cares.*

Whisper sat in a chair and waited and waited and waited. At 3:00 am, a nurse came in to get Shanna's vital signs. Whisper pretended like she was asleep on the chair and had every right to be there. The nurse asked Shanna several questions about pain, vision, nausea and such. Shanna answered with yes or no, not being able talk very well.

Halfway through the nurse's visit, Shanna realized Whisper was sitting on the chair. Shanna's eyes widened. Whisper put her finger to her lips to shush her. Shanna caught on quickly and let the nurse finish without raising suspicion.

As soon as the nurse left the room, Shanna raised her hands, shoulders and eyebrows silently questioning, 'What are you doing here?'

Whisper went to Shanna and hugged her saying, "I came to see you."

After the hug, Shanna picked up a pad and pen off the night stand and wrote, 'How did you get in?'

"I sneaked in."

'Just like that?' she wrote.

"Yep. Ross drove me over and helped me find your room."

Shanna drew a dick and balls on the paper.

Whisper snatched the pad and tore the sheet out, "If you're asking if we're doing it….." Whisper thought for a second. "I think I love him."

Shanna sat up straighter and wrote a '?' on the pad.

"I don't know. I lose my breath when I see him. I miss him when he's gone. I miss him now and the big bastard's just down in the lobby sleeping in a chair or something, waiting on me. He saved us all from that horrible place. He helps animals…" She started to cry.

Shanna drew a heart.

"Yeah, but he lives in Austin and I'm a slave at the lodge. When all of this is over, he'll go back to a normal life and I'll serve food and get oranges as tips for the rest of my life.

'Move to Austin.'

"I think I'm afraid."

Shanna wrote, 'Ha Ha! You're afraid of nothing.'

Just then Shanna's mother stirred, sat up and looked at the two girls conversing. "I know you," she said. "Shanna's told me about you."

"I'm Whisper Jenkins."

"How'd you get in here?"

"Pretty much broke in."

"Sounds just like you. She said you had guts….and heart."

Shanna and Whisper looked at each other. "I'm moving to Austin, bitch," Whisper said to Shanna.

Shanna wrote, 'That's my girl.'

"Nice to meet you Mrs. Borger. But I need to go and find Ross. Shanna, will you come back to the lodge to work after this?"

Mrs. Borger said, "No, she won't be working anymore. Not while she's in college."

Whisper looked down at the pad where Shanna wrote, 'Of course I'll be back.'

Then she wrote, 'Tell him you love him.'

"I've got to go." She kissed Shanna on the forehead and walked out not caring if she was caught.

Down in the lobby, Whisper found Ross trying to sleep, halfway hanging off a loveseat sized sofa. He looked horribly uncomfortable. "I truly love that son of a bitch."

She bent down and touched him on his shoulder. He roused and sat up, rubbing is face. "Everything alright?" he asked.

"Better than alright."

"What now?" He looked at his watch and it was approaching 4:00 am.

"Let's go home."

Chapter 45

They arrived at the lodge well after sun up. Whisper told Ross to go to bed and she would check in with Big Al to see if she still had a job. "You can't work today," Ross said more like a question.

"It's just handing people plates of biscuits and gravy. It's not like brain surgery."

Ross picked her up like a man carries a bride across the threshold, her arms around his neck. He carried to the steps of the porch, "Say the word and I'll take you right in there and put you to bed."

Whisper was thinking she was always in the air around Ross. If he wasn't physically holding her off the ground, she was floating all on her own. "Put me down. I've got to go."

Ross gently placed her feet on the ground, but he didn't let go. They gazed into each other's eyes. Ross spoke in a low sexy voice, "I am doing unimaginable things to you in my mind right now......"

"Oh, I can imagine." She put her hand on his chest and pushed away. "Go get some sleep."

"I think I have to." His eyes were halfway shut.

"Dream about me."

"I will…I do…all the time."

They turned and went their separate ways.

Ross was showered and asleep within fifteen minutes.

Whisper went to her cabin, got her name tag and kicked off her fake UGGs. She slipped on some comfortable work shoes and headed to the restaurant. Bursting through the front door, she saw Big Al and his nephew sitting in the booth. Nobody else was in the restaurant. "Packin' 'em in, are we?" Whisper said sarcastically. Big Al grunted. His nephew never looked up from playing a game on his iPhone.

"Where you been Orange? You missed three customers, two cops and a guy who came to see the murder hotel."

"This will blow over. There's a nation-wide manhunt going on for John Luke. As soon as they find him, everybody will be back. Even more….they'll want to see the murder hotel." Whisper smiled but Big Al didn't think it was too funny….unless there really was a buck in it.

Whisper passed the time by folding napkins, arranging the condiments and wiping down everything that had a surface. She was extremely sleepy and stuck in geologic time. Torture, pure torture.

At noon, several customers came in and asked Whisper questions. Mostly they wanted to know if Whisper got raped. *Assholes! Did they think she would really talk about something like that?* The customers knew rape was traumatic for most women but wanted to know if it was bad for her or if maybe she enjoyed it. *Why? Because I'm orange colored? Assholes!* She did not receive a tip from any of them. They were lucky she didn't get after them with a coffee pot.

Late in the lunch service, two suited men came in asking for the proprietor. "Well, for goodness sake, I'll go fetch him for you." Whisper was goofing on their formality. She told Big Al these guys wanted to parlay.

Big Al waddled out from the kitchen still wearing his greasy apron that may never have been washed. "Help ya?" he asked.

"Are you the proprietor?"

Big Al wasn't a hundred percent sure what that meant but he replied, "I own the joint. If that's what you mean?"

"We represent Veritas International, Myles Carter's company. In three days, he will hold a press conference on the steps of your establishment. The press conference will be aired on TV by national networks. We expect over five-hundred people will be in attendance. All you have to do is say 'yes' and we will handle everything but the food. Of course, we would expect you to cater the event. Say twenty dollars a plate, five-hundred people. We are willing to pay ten thousand dollars up front and settle up any cost overruns on the backend."

Big Al was stunned. The Veritas gentlemen waited for an answer.

"Yes."

One of the men opened a briefcase and handed Big Al a check for ten thousand dollars. The men stood and walked out in silence. Big Al went to the booth and showed his nephew and Whisper the check. They all looked at it like it was alive. Big Al finally said, "I have to figure out a way to feed five-hundred people for less than five thousand dollars."

"But you have ten thousand dollars," Whisper said.

"Yeah. I want half as profit."

Cheap bastard.

For the rest of the afternoon, they planned, plotted, cut corners and decided it was doable. Big Al had plenty of meat or could get more if needed, his nephew could prepare the fixin's and Whisper would do most of the work. *Great.*

After the evening waitresses showed up, Whisper went straight down to Ross' cabin. Shelby answered the door. Whisper must have looked disappointed because he said, "Sorry, It's just me."

"Where is Ross?"

"He got called to the Emergency Operations Center,"

"Again?" Whisper instantly became pissed.

"Yeah. That's exactly what he said."

"Okay, thanks Shelby. If he gets back, please tell him to come by my cabin."

"Sure."

Whisper went to her place, threw her clothes in a pile, showered off all her worries and collapsed on the bed. She wanted to dream of Ross and his huge, strong arms holding her but instead, she quickly thought of his equally big, beautiful dick slipping inside her and then she fell asleep. A deep sleep.

Chapter 46

Ross was at the Emergency Operations Center which had expanded immensely for the manhunt. Media was all over this now. It was a worldwide search. John Walsh even made a sound bite asking for the public's help. They switched leadership and the Incident Commander was a US Marshal. Some blue suited law enforcement guy grabbed Ross and took him to an isolated room with a mirror.

"I hear you have had some success with tracking fugitives."

"Who are you?" Ross asked.

"You don't need to know."

"Bullshit. I'm not doing this spook shit." Ross stood up. The man in the suit stepped forward. They were eye-to-eye. Both men were built like brick houses and a fight would have been muy grande. However, the man with the suit put his hands on his hips, which opened his coat exposing what Ross thought was a 9-millimeter Sig Sauer pistol.

"Who are you?" Ross asked again.

The door opened and another gentleman came in wearing an identical suit. "My apologies," he said. He reached in his pocket and pulled out an FBI identification wallet, opened it and showed it to Ross. "I'm Special Agent-in-Charge, Phil Lowenstein, and this ball of confusion is Agent Blanchard from the Dallas office. We would like your help in finding John Luke Thibodeaux, the FBI's number three most wanted fugitive."

"What if I say no?" Ross asked.

"You're free to go. We're just asking for help." The Agent-in-Charge remained silent while Ross thought it over.

When the Agent surmised Ross may really say 'no' he chimed in, "A man who served his country in the Army, received a purple heart in Iraq, might want to serve again."

All Ross could think about was how badly Whisper was going to kill him. "You don't have to sell it. I'll do it."

"Good. I had no doubt." Although he really did. "Any gear you need let me know…body armor, night vision devices, range finding digital picture capable infrared binoculars, automatic weapons?"

Ross thought for a minute. "I'd like my own rifle. It's held as evidence by the Smith County Sheriff's office, I think."

"Done. We'll have it for you this evening. Anything else?"

"Can you tell my girlfriend I'm going back out on a manhunt so she'll beat the shit out of you instead of me?"

The agent laughed and said, "Sorry. We don't solve domestic disputes. Although I can get a deputy to escort you for your own protection."

"Better not. I don't want her arrested for assaulting a police officer." They both smiled…a little.

"We'll swing by the lodge at 8:00 pm with your weapon. That will be the last time you can request help or equipment before you deploy. I can even get you satellite coverage if you want. This thing is big and they've thrown a shitload of assets at it."

"No, I just need my rifle. I'm really low-tech. I walk around on the ground and look at stuff."

"What will you do first?"

Ross said he would start at the rock house and go from there. No plan really, just let the clues take him where he needed to be. Ross told the Agent-in-Charge the manhunt would last as long as there was something to go on but he'd call it off the instant the leads ran out.

"Call in once a day between noon and 2:00 pm. We'll get your report on the afternoon daily briefing for the boss. Good luck."

Ross and Agent Lowenstein shook hands but Ross ignored Agent Blanchard. Now the question was, how was he going to tell Whisper. Ross drove back to the lodge feeling something he thought could best be described as dread. He parked the truck in the empty lot and took a few deep breaths. He went to Whisper's cabin and knocked on the door.

She answered in her flannel pajamas, reaching out and pulling him inside by his jacket. Two feet inside the door, she started taking his jacket off and unbuttoning two of his shirt buttons, just enough for him to get the idea of what was about to happen. He started taking off his own clothes.

The flannel pajama bottoms dropped right there in the floor and she took off her top off on the way to the bed. She jumped in the middle of the bed with her legs spread, knees bent, sitting up on a mound of pillows. Ross couldn't take his eyes off of her as he stripped.

His underwear hit the floor and there it was! Sticking out in front of him, pointing toward the ceiling. She made some noises while sitting in the bed. Ross thought she might be cumming already. *Can a woman cum by just looking at it?* He may not have known it, but the answer was 'yes'. She was cumming just by looking. It wasn't a monstrous scream until you pass out kind of orgasm, but she was cumming just the same. One of those buzzing little tingly things that wouldn't stop on its own.

He walked over to the bed, big dick wagging back and forth with each step. She slid down on the bed and grabbed her feet pulling them up to her chest. The buzzing in her pussy increased. "Hurry up! Get it in and fuck me!"

He climbed up between her legs. Instead of sticking it in, he buried his face in her shiny yellow pussy hair, his tongue landing perfectly on her clit. Her buzz turned into one of those real orgasms as she moaned from the pleasure.

Her orgasms always started at zero and increased in intensity to ten over time. Usually it took her about fifteen seconds to hit the peak. That wasn't true with this one because this one started at about four instead of zero. As pleasure was building quickly, Ross stuck a finger a little way up her ass and two fingers all the way up her pussy. He continued to swirl his tongue around her swollen clit in the most amazing way. When he slid his tongue to the side for just a second, her body begged for him to get back on point.

Right before reaching the strongest part of her climax, she reached around between her legs, grabbed his hand and made him push his finger all the way up her ass. *Now I'm filled up.* She concentrated on nothing but cumming and cumming. It wouldn't stop, not that she wanted it to but she couldn't catch her breath. *I'm going to pass out.*

She forced out a final scream, expelling all her air while pulling a few times on Ross' hair in a faux effort to get him to stop but then shoved his face against her, grinding it in. Whisper hadn't taken a breath since he went down on her. It had been a minute, maybe two. Her orgasm was peaking but somehow became even more intense making her scalp tingle and then she fucking fainted. Ross was shocked. He just ate her unconscious. He pulled away, wiped his mouth and said her name, "Whisper?"

She didn't respond but she was breathing and…he thought she had a smile on her face. "Whisper?"

She moaned and her eyes fluttered. *She's coming around.* He rubbed her arms trying to get some blood going to the upper parts of her body. She opened her eyes. "Please tell me you didn't eat me until I passed out."

"I can tell you that, if you want."

"Oh God, that's so embarrassing." She sat up on the bed holding her face in her hands.

"Why?"

"I don't know."

Ross smiled at her and joked, "I'll tell you what. I'll let you eat me until I pass out."

"Deal," she said.

They pretty much traded places. His big thing was still hard as a rock, poking directly up in the air. She contemplated for a second, trying to decide what was the best way to approach this. She figured most guys thought any blowjob was better than nothing and the worst blowjob was still 'good'. So, how could she deliver a special 'pass out' blowjob to the man she loved. The longer she waited the more purple the head of his cock became. *If I wait long enough, he'll cum by himself.* It was just a comical thought but the more she waited the more a hands-free orgasm seemed possible.

She started tingling again watching his huge pole sway and pulse through the air. She moved forward and lifted his balls in her hand. He jerked ever so slightly, closed his eyes and turned his head to the side as if he couldn't watch. She rolled them around with her fingers giving them a gentle massage.

His poor dick was spasming. *He's trying to cum. His dick wants to cum but his balls aren't ready.* She encircled the base of his cock with her index finger and thumb, pulling a little harder on his balls with her other hand. She couldn't put her finger and thumb together around the base because he was too big.

Whisper pulled the base down, stretching his skin tight, turning the head even more purple. His hips started to involuntarily move up and down. *He's fucking air!* Juice ran down her thighs. She was truly hoping she could finish him before she was lost to a hands-free orgasm herself.

The hand wrapped around the base could feel every throb as he was trying to squirt. He was breathing hard, legs were out straight and stiff, toes were pointed. He was gripping the mattress. Whisper made a moaning sound trying to fight off the wonderful sensation between her legs.

When she thought Ross was about to go off, she leaned forward, stuck out her tongue, and touched the tip to that special spot just below the head, licking it with as much force as her tongue could muster. She didn't want to tease him, she wanted him to feel it. And he did.

He made noises like he was enduring something incredibly painful. She had him right where she wanted, tongue on the tip, one hand on the shaft and one squeezing his balls. He took a deep breath and she knew he was about to push out a load of a lifetime…*but not before this*! She dropped his balls and stuck her middle finger all the way up his ass at the exact moment he started to cum. The added finger pressure on his prostate along with his own massive muscle contraction, shot a stream in the air right in front of Whisper's eyes. She never took her tongue off the head and squeezed her hand gently on the base. She felt his ass tighten when he squirted. He let out a horrid sounding roar.

If she had heard that sound outside in the night, she would have been frightened, but in the bedroom…music to her ears. He shot another impressive stream and then another. And more! *This boy's a veritable fountain*! She continued to massage him up the ass until every last contraction ceased. She pulled her tongue away and withdrew her hands.

Ross was blowing like a beached whale. He was in great shape but that full body clenching was draining, kind of like when you can't stop throwing up, but in a good way. She reached out and picked up his dick which was lying against his cum soaked belly. It was still hard, just not 'first time' hard. She rubbed it up and down but when she hit the head, Ross shot a hand down to hers to keep her from touching it. She kind of giggled.

"Okay stud. If you don't want it touched, that's fine." She climbed up on him and slid it up in her slippery wet pussy. *My God, he's big.*

She leaned forward, her erect, red nipples digging into his chest. Fuck juices gluing their bodies together. *If he moves, I'm going to cum.* Of course, he was going to move. His dick was in the hot, wet, tight pussy of a gorgeous, sexy woman. Oh, he moved and in such a perfect way.

It was like a steam train starting from a dead stop. Chug! In it went all the way to the bottom. Slowly out, raking every nerve along the way. The head was almost exposed, maybe it came out. She couldn't tell. Then….Chug! back in to the hilt. Slowly out…and chug! Pulling out…chug! Again out…chug! Out…Chug! Chug! Chug! Chug! Then the train was going a hundred miles an hour careening toward Cum Town. Chug! Chug! Chug! Whooo! Whooo! Her screams echoed the whistle in her mind as the train slammed into the station. They both arrived at the last stop simultaneously….Cum Town.

She collapsed on his chest, which was heaving up and down. He held her in his arms as his cock still pulsated up in her. He was squirting but there just wasn't any juice left. She loved that. His cocked throbbed in her for a full five minutes before he started to settled down and relax. She could feel it shrivel inside her. Even fully flaccid, it remained several inches up in her. *What a cock. What a man.*

After a while she said, "You're not going to like this." He opened his eyes and looked at her. She jerked her pelvis up and his soft dick fell out on his balls.

He flinched, "Ah! You're right."

She was on her knees with her crotch hovering above his. Juices dripped from her pussy to his dick. "You are the messiest man."

He looked down. "You started this one." She couldn't argue with that.

Whisper went to the shower and turned on the water. "I'd throw you a towel to clean up, but in this case, I don't think it will be enough. You better join me in here." Ross reluctantly got up and met her in the hot shower. First thing, she reached down and soaped up his dick and balls. He started to get hard again. "Well look at that would you?" she said holding it in her hand.

"You planned this," he teased. They kissed with his big dick nearly reaching up to her chest. He bent down with the water rushing over his face and sucked on each of her long red nipples. He reached a soapy hand between her legs and 'washed' her holes, both of them. Really, he was just fingering her but she didn't object one bit.

Chapter 47

After some wonderful sex play in the shower, Ross got dressed. Whisper put on her PJ's. She could tell something was weighing on his mind. *He better not tell me he's married! Or he's leaving to go home to Austin!*

Ross sat her down on the bed. "I've got something to tell you that you won't like." Whisper didn't say anything. "They've asked me to go back out and help find John Luke." Ross waited for a thunderstorm response. "I'll be back as soon as I can."

Whisper was happy he didn't say he was married or leaving for good. "Okay." She waited for the rest.

"I'll go out in the morning and start looking at the rock house. My guess is I won't be able to find anything useful and after a day, I'll come back." She didn't respond. Ross thought she looked vulnerable, sitting there in her flannels, bare feet crossed on the floor, chewing her thumbnail. He reached up and pulled her hand away from her face and leaned in to kiss her.

They kissed this incredibly soft, rolling, moist kiss that normally would have launched Ross' cock to the sky, but this time it felt more like the 'at the train station, saying goodbye and going off to war' kind of kiss. When they pulled away and opened their eyes, they both felt light headed. Ross wanted to make an appropriate remark but he was struck dumb. Whisper was screaming 'I love you!' in her head but no words came out.

"I've got to get some sleep." Whisper walked him to the door. He stood, sheepishly with her beside him. She was feeling warm all over. Not from the flame caused by a sexually charged lightning bolt but that glow one gets with a shot of whiskey on a cold winter night or sitting by the embers of a once roaring fire or crawling under the safety of the covers of your own bed after having a great day...*Shit, snap out of it!...I need to tell him I love him...I can feel it all the way down to my toes...*

'I'll get back as quickly as I possibly can. I promise," he said never lifting his gaze from her blue eyes.

"You better." *You Better! That's all I can come up with?*

Ross kissed her on the lips and stepped out. She closed the door and leaned against it. "I'm so stupid." She was shaking her head, almost in tears, really wanting to run after him and tell him how she felt but.... *he'll be back. He will.*

At 4:00 am Whisper was in the parking lot ready for work. She stared at Ross' cabin. All was dark. He said he was going out in the morning but 4:00 am was ridiculous. He must be in there. She started up the steps to his cabin but noticed his truck was gone. *Damn! He's already left.*

Ross decided to drive his truck around to the far side of the woods where the second tactical team entered earlier. He had a full pack and his trusty rifle which was delivered to him as promised. Ross had two thoughts as to John Luke's whereabouts. The first being John Luke fled the area, maybe even the country and was laying up on a beach somewhere sipping Margaritas. Or, he's right back at the rock house after the police processed it a second time thinking the police were too stupid to think he would come back to the scene of the crime... again! *Would he really do that?*

After an hour or so of walking, Ross could see the rock house through the woods. The house had so much police tape around it, it looked like it had been toilet papered at Halloween. Ross decided to circumnavigate the house looking for the tire tracks of the truck in which John Luke escaped. About 400 yards to the northeast, Ross found some tracks. He followed them for nearly three miles down the narrowest of forest roads. The road was actually two ruts in the ground the same width as vehicle tires.

To his chagrin, the forest road popped out on the state highway. The same highway on which his own truck was parked, only two and a half miles away. *Well, crap!* He started hiking to his truck. When he arrived, the time was close enough to the lunch hour to go ahead and eat. His meal: beef jerky, some kind of Country Quinoa Cracker that tasted better than it sounded and a canned diet Coke.

Finished eating and starting to load up again, he felt exhausted. He'd been up since 3:30 am and walked six miles fully loaded. Deciding to hike to the rock house again, Ross would set up camp and look around for clues near the house. Ross thought briefly about sleeping in the house, out of the elements, but quickly dismissed the idea. Nothing but bad memories were in there. Hell, the whole area was nothing but a bad memory.

Ross walked about halfway to the rock house and found a beautiful clearing, an East Texas grassy meadow. The grass was brown now, but still a good, soft, flat spot for a tent. He shed the heavy pack and set up camp. Deciding to do a recon of the house, he carried his rifle and wore a web belt with canteen, knife, ammo pouch, first aid kit and flashlight. He had protein bars in the ammo pouch because he carried his six extra bullets in his jacket chest pocket. He had the sat-phone and the GPS in the other pockets of his jacket. He felt light compared to carrying the full pack of camping equipment. Ross approached the house with no tactical sense what-so-ever. He was actually whistling the theme from *Andy Griffin* as he walked with rifle slung over his shoulder.

A hundred yards out, Ross became a little edgy. He felt sober, like he needed to be respectful, the way you are when you're in a cemetery. People were tortured and died here. Ghosts were everywhere, the camera man, the reporter, the Veritas Security officer, the kidnapper...Ross swallowed hard, nearly scaring himself thinking about it.

He unslung his rifle and held it at the ready. A shell had not yet been levered into the chamber. *Can't kill a ghost with a gun.* Ross could see the rock house standing solemnly, isolated in the woods as it had for the last hundred or so years. Streamers of police tape hanging off of it. The ends blowing in the wind.

He approached, although, at that particular moment, he thought it was a terrible idea. Fifty yards away, right where the woods started to clear, he waited and observed. He didn't know what he was waiting for, other than trying to punch down all the horrid memories of literally blowing a man's head off inside the house.

Just an instant before he took his first step toward the house, he heard a noise. He backed up behind the trunk of a rather large oak tree. The banged up front door of the house opened and, as casually as you please, out walked John Fucking Luke, drinking a cup of coffee, an AR-15 rifle tactically strapped across his chest.

Fuck! Ross pulled back behind the trunk of the tree trying to gather his thoughts. *I want to get the fuck away from here!* was his first thought. Then he calmed down and decided to get the drop on him. He peeked out around the right side of the tree and raised the rifle and jacked a round into the chamber making a rather loud noise in the quiet of the forest.

Ross' intentions were to chamber a round and yell 'Hold it right there!" or some similar directive. However, as soon as Ross levered in the round, John Luke dropped his cup of coffee, raised his automatic weapon and fired three shots before the cup hit the ground. John Luke steadied himself behind a porch column and fired seventeen more rounds in quick succession.

The first fucking bullet hit Ross in the upper right thigh. It was 'just a graze' as they would say in movies but it felt like it tore his whole thigh muscle off. Ross staggered back behind the tree trunk, recoiling a little too far from the impact, exposing himself on the other side of the trunk. Another bullet went into his left side about even with his belly button. It entered his jacket pocket and hit the sat-phone causing the bullet and the phone to disintegrate and penetrate his side. The impact was more like a small explosion rather than a bullet entering. It was like being hit with shrapnel.

Although damaged badly, Ross was still in the fight. He spun around the right side of the tree, took aim while John Luke was reloading, and fired. The boom from the big bore rifle was deafening. Ross' bullet struck the column behind which John Luke was standing. The column broke and the right side of the porch roof partially collapsed. Splinters from the bullet strike peppered John Luke's face with a few smaller pieces sticking into his right eye.

John Luke retreated into the house. Ross collapsed, leaning against the tree trunk. Both men addressed their wounds. Ross' biggest concern, besides the pain and the probability of imminent death was his ability to communicate was destroyed. His sat-phone was shot to pieces. He couldn't walk out, at least not easily, and he couldn't call for help. He was stuck there for the duration. The duration being until they shot the shit out of each other or until John Luke escaped out the back.

Ross was fiddling with his tiny first aid kit hoping something was in there that would ease the pain, stop the bleeding or keep infection away. John Luke was standing at the bathroom mirror looking at himself hoping the dozens of splinters sticking out of his face wouldn't hurt his good looks. He pulled the ones out of his eye first. Once done, he could still see, but everything was fuzzy. He started pulling the others out.

John Luke was pulling out the last big splinter when he heard Ross yell, "Hey John Luke. You ready to give up?" John Luke thought it was funny. He actually cracked a smile. *Guy's got balls.*

John Luke went to the edge of the door yelling back, "You shot me in the fucking face."

"Good," Ross answered. "However, I was aiming for your ego. It's so damn big, I figured I couldn't miss."

"Funny man, huh? How you feeling?" John Luke checked the magazine in his rifle.

"I got a few new holes in my body. I'm going to name them after you."

"Yeah?"

Ross smiled to himself. "I'm calling them my new assholes!"

"Laugh at this!" John Luke raised his assault rifle and fired half a dozen shots at the tree. Ross tried to get really small. "I got a million rounds of ammunition in this house. I can shoot all day. What do have?" To emphasize that he fired half a dozen more rounds.

When the shooting stopped, Ross yelled out, "I got eleven bullets." He heard John Luke laughing.

"You're the most honest, bravest, dumbest son of a bitch I've ever met."

Don't I know it.

Chapter 48

Whisper and Big Al were discussing what they needed to do to get the place ready for Myles' big press conference. The lunch crowd was light due to the fact Myles was being discharged from the hospital today along with Molly and Kylie but who cared about them. The press corps of the world seemed to have descended upon Tyler, Texas…The Rose Capital of America.

As they were speaking, six business-clad customers entered the restaurant. Whisper went to help them but they needed no help. The business people were sent from Veritas International to prepare the Hill Top Hunting Lodge for world fame, courtesy of Myles Carter. The suits pretty much shoved Whisper back into the booth and started measuring, inspecting and discussing things as if no one else was there.

Whisper looked at Big Al to see if he would protest but he just took a bite of hamburger with a fried egg on top of it and watched the show. Whisper sat longwise in the booth, her feet on the bench and her back to the wall. Finally, a tall, *Bay Watch*-quality blonde came over. The tall woman was wearing heels so high Whisper didn't know how she walked in them. The woman looked at Big Al and then at Whisper.

Whisper always had that game show mentality when it came to first impressions--Deal or No Deal--but it was--Nice or Not Nice. She could tell in ten seconds which deal a stranger would take.

The beautiful Amazon looked at Al, who was staring at *Bay Watch* boobs like most men would. "Are you the proprietor?"

Big Al, literally, with egg on his face and now knowing what proprietor meant, just shook his head up and down. The tall woman leaned over with her hands on the table top exposing everything except the nipples. "Now, you don't mind if we sort of run the place for a couple of days, do you?"

Big Al shook his head back and forth. The woman sat down next to Big Al, arm around his shoulders, hand on his thigh, *Bay Watch* boobs pressed against his chest. She spoke breathlessly in his hairy ear, "You've got to say it, Honey. Tell us we own the place for three days. Go on sweetheart. Say it."

Big Al's lips moved but nothing came out. "Come on Honey, you can do it."

Finally, Big Al cleared his throat and said, "The place is yours for three days."

"Good boy." She patted him on the back and squeezed his thigh. Whisper's eyes rolled so far back in her head she thought they may have spun completely around.

The woman stood up and said, "Okay, you heard him. It's a verbal contract and we're in charge." She walked off to join her staff.

Definitely Not Nice. Whisper looked at Big Al. "Is it really that easy?"

Big Al was still staring in the Amazon's direction.

"Earth to Al." Whisper was snapping her fingers.

Big Al's glazed eyes turned to Whisper. "Really?" she said. "All she had to do was show a little tit and you caved in."

Big Al looked pathetic, "In my defense, it was more than a 'little' tit. Did you see those things?"

"Good grief, Al." Whisper crossed her arms and leaned back against the wall watching yet another shit show in the making.

After five minutes of apprising the situation, the tall blonde turned to Whisper, "Hey, Red and Yellow, come here!"

Whisper caught Big Al's eyes, "I'm going to coffee pot this bitch before it's over."

Big Al told her, "No more chucking coffee pots at anybody. You hear me Red and Yellow."

"I'm going to beat your ass too. Or better yet, I'll tell Glyna you've been rubbing up against that walking set of udders and she can beat your ass for me."

Big All shook his head suggesting, 'You better not,' because the one thing he was afraid of in the entire world was the wrath of his wife, Glyna. Whisper stood up slowly, straightened her uniform and strolled over to Miss Mammary, USA.

Whisper stood face to face with her. More like face to boobs because the Amazon was so tall in those heels. "My name is Whisper but if you feel compelled to denigrate me, call me Orange."

"Orange it is. I'm leaving now."

Not soon enough, Whisper thought.

"Roscoe will be in charge. Come here, Roscoe!" she yelled.

A man came over wearing a perfectly tailored suit. Hipster tight legs and flamboyant tie.

"Roscoe, this is Orange. Anything you need Roscoe, this…girl… will get for you." The Amazon left the building.

Whisper was standing, waiting on the ten second rule to determine if Roscoe was going to be Nice or Not Nice. He looked her up and down and said, "What's your real name. It's not really Orange is it?"

"Whisper," she said.

"Damn, Girl. I like that." She could tell not only was he Nice, but he was gay. "Okay," he continued. "We usually handle these things on our own. Anything we need, instead of asking you guys for it, we just buy it. Myles is stinking rich and gay as a three dollar bill so he wants things just so and has the money to do whatever he wants. So, Whisper, why don't you take off and go have a spa day."

Whisper was stunned.

"Sweetie," he said. He put his hand on her shoulder. "We got this. Go have some fun."

"Okay. Thanks. If you do need me, I'm in cabin number eight."

"You go on now, pretty girl."

She turned and walked to Big Al, staring down at him blankly, "I'm leaving now. I was just given the day off by our new bosses. See you tomorrow." She turned and walked out the front door all the way down to her cabin.

Chapter 49

Ross applied some pressure bandages to his wounds. That was about all he could do at this point. He was pissed as hell because both his cargo pants and field jacket were now ruined. *I'm going to have to buy new clothes.*

He wanted John Luke to keep talking mainly to confirm he was still in the house. "John Luke! What made you do all of this?"

John Luke was trying to decide what to do. He really wanted to walk straight out the door, firing every step until he got face to face with the Boy Ranger and then shoot him full of holes like Swiss cheese. "Money," John Luke yelled. "Simple as that. Myles Carter, that queer fuck, has more money than God. What does he need all that money for?"

"What do *you* need all that money for? Gonna start a charity? Open a halfway house? Oh, I know. An orphanage!"

"Don't be a shithead. I want the good life. Big houses on the beach, fast cars, women!"

"Working at the Hill Top Hunting Lodge about three hours a day, a free place to stay, free food and screwing everything that walked or crawled wasn't good enough for you?" Ross adjusted the bandages on his side because there was too much blood to secure them tightly.

"Yeah, the pussy was good. I've got to admit that. I had them all you know?" John Luke was still trying to get all the splinters out of his face. He'd pull one out, rub his hand gently over the area until he felt another and then try to pluck it out. Some were really deep. *Boy Ranger was shooting a man-sized gun.*

John Luke continued, "Molly threw herself at me. I took Kylie whenever I wanted, right here in this house. I even fucked Myles up the ass once just so I could brag about it later. I had several college girls from the night shift. I think they were the most fun. You know what I mean?" He asked rhetorically. "Those girls have never been with a real man, especially one with a dick as big as mine." He laughed to himself. "You should see the look on their faces. It happens every time. And then the wives of the hunters, the old ladies from town." He paused almost sighing at his reminiscence.

Ross had no response to that. *Just let him talk. At least I know where he is.*

John Luke started back up on his favorite subject, himself. "Oh yeah. They all had a treat. Sometimes they didn't seem to appreciate what they were getting. You know, Grade A prime American fifteen-inch dick." John Luke took the liberty of exaggerating. Just a little, but still…

Ross rolled his eyes. *Just keep talking Big Dick.*

"I think the one I was most disappointed in was that orange bitch."

Ross felt like he took a bullet to the gut.

"Yeah, that colorful piece of ass just didn't get it. God she was hard to look at. She should have been more appreciative. You know what I mean? Fucked up girl like that. Tiny, fucking little strange titties. Orange ass and those stupid looking hands and feet. She should have been happy…no…grateful, to get fucked by someone like me." He laughed loud enough Ross could hear him.

Ross didn't know what to think. The news was certainly a punch in the face but he would never mention it to Whisper. He had to worry about not bleeding death, not getting his ass shot to hell and not freezing when the sun went down which was just an hour or so away. He figured John Luke would make a break for it after dark.

John Luke yelled, "When will the cops get here?"

Ross responded, "Any minute. It takes them a while to gather up half a dozen professional SWAT teams."

"You're full of shit. A helicopter would have been here by now if they knew. John Luke waited for a response. None was forthcoming. "You can't contact anybody, can you?"

"As long as we are being honest with each other. You're right. You shot me in the sat-phone. It basically blew up in my pocket and my cell doesn't work this far out. There you have it. Just me and you."

John Luke smiled knowing he definitely had the upper hand. "I think I'll just walk out the back and disappear into the woods. What do you think about that?"

"Go ahead if you think you can out run one of these 45-70 rounds. I will be right behind you."

John Luke was in a situation he had never been in before. He was unsure of himself, pissed, frustrated and his face was swelling so much his eye was closing. It was the eye he aimed with making him even more unsure. *"Fuck!"* He was feeling like a caged animal. "Why such a big gun, Boy Ranger? Making up for other inadequacies?"

Ross thought the conversation was a little school-yard but having him talk was better than silence. "I need it for my work, to kill pigs you know." Ross checked his wounds again. No bleeding, but damn they hurt. John Luke's response was cutting loose with five rounds at the tree behind which Ross was concealed. The shots were all scattered as if he wasn't aiming. "You're shooting at the wrong tree, dumbass. I moved down to the big tree to your left while you were inside crying about your face."

"I don't believe you!"

"Believe what you want, but know this, I'm going to put a bullet up your ass if you go out the back door."

John Luke fired five more rounds at Ross' tree. After two seconds, he fired ten rounds at the big tree to the left. *He really doesn't know where I am.* A good tactical victory for Ross.

John Luke slipped another twenty-round magazine into his weapon. Most of what he said was bullshit but he wasn't lying about having a crap-ton of ammunition. He went to the rear of the house to look out the back door. There was fifty yards of open ground before he reached the nearest cover. Then another hundred yards through dense brush before he got to his truck which he camouflaged with tree branches.

John Luke's brain wheels were turning a mile a minute. If he could get to the first line of cover, he really thought it would be safe. *Seven seconds.* That's all he needed. How long would it be before Ranger Boy's help arrived? Surely someone was reporting all of this gun fire. John Luke was paralyzed with fear and indecision.

Chapter 50

The Emergency Operations Center was waiting for Ross' first daily call. When it was twenty minutes late, they called his sat-phone number dozens of times. Nothing! At fifty minutes past the deadline, they called the Hill Top Hunting Lodge. Big Al struggled to answer the phone before it quit ringing, telling them he hadn't seen the Ranger all day.

Big All sent his fat nephew down to Whisper's cabin to see if they were both holed up in there. Whisper was reading a book when she heard the footsteps on the porch. Fear was her first reaction. Then there was a knock. *A killer wouldn't knock, would he?* She opened the door to greet the wheezing nephew. He asked if Ross was there. "Of course, he's not. He's on a mission." The nephew explained that Ross didn't report in.

She ran to the restaurant not waiting for the fat nephew to catch up. Bursting in and heading straight for the phone, she called the Emergency Operations Center and demanded to talk to the man in charge. After explaining herself to two different people, the Incident

Commander finally answered. She told him Ross went out early this morning and was heading to the old rock house, the scene of the first shooting and the hostage situation.

"His GPS puts him in the middle of the woods?" said the Commander. "It hasn't moved in over an hour."

"Come get me. I'll take you there," she said. "Hurry."

"We'll send someone to meet you at the lodge. But...you're not going with us."

Bullshit. Whisper was nervous. Patience was not her strong suit and she was considering taking off by herself, ahead of the army of men who would surely charge off into the woods.

Somehow, she contained her anxiety and sat on the steps of the restaurant, waiting. In fifteen minutes, a black Suburban with flashing lights drove into parking lot. She ran down to greet them before they finished parking in one of the spots facing the highway. The cop, agent or otherwise peacock with a badge just rolled down the window. He wouldn't even get out in the cold. "I assume you're the girl who has been down to the target area before. They said you looked different...you know...like orange sherbet. Fuck if I didn't believe them." The primary thing on Whisper's mind was Ross' safety which was mentally rated at 100%. Kicking this motherfucker's nuts up into his stomach hit the chart at 99.99% with a bullet.

The officer started to unfold a map. "Now, Buttercup, can you just show me on this map the best way to get to the target area?"

Please step out of the vehicle. If he got out, she would attempt a 42 yard field goal with whatever little marbles he had in his scrotum. "You don't really need a map officer...?" She was just trying to get his name for a later ambush if necessary.

"Well now, Pumpkin. I'm Special Agent Big Ed Callahan from the Big D. They don't call me Big Ed for nothing you know."

"We already have a Big Al who owns this place. He's just fat so... never mind. Let me show you where the trail to the target area begins.

She used air quotes to emphasize 'target area'. It starts right over here between these cabins. She was pointing.

"Show me," Big Ed instructed. He cranked the vehicle and turned around and pulled into a parking space facing the woods.

Whisper walked along beside the SUV. *What an asshole.*

She pointed between the cabins and said the trail started there and led down to the lake. They could take a boat across the lake, take the third finger and come out very near the target area, the rock house. I suggest you send somebody now...a team...a squad...whatever you call them, on land around the lake. Just in case it takes a while to get the boats down there. You can also drive around and walk in the back way. The local police have done this exact same thing before. Why don't you coordinate with them?"

"Sweet Potato, you're sure full of ideas. Why don't you let Big Ed and the boys handle this?"

"You pompous ass. Are you really a Federal Agent?" She had serious doubts.

"Don't make me show you my badge and gun." He grabbed his crotch when he said the word 'gun'. "I'll be seeing you later. You live here, right? Which cabin? As soon as we go save this yokel, what say you and I get together and celebrate me being a hero?"

"What does your wife think about the idea?"

"I'm not married."

"Why do you wear a ring?" She pointed to his big bear paw left hand.

"Oh, that? I'm married alright, when I'm home, but when I'm on a mission, it's like Vegas. What happens on mission, stays on mission."

"I see," she said. This guy was nothing but John Luke with a badge. There was no way she was going to rely on this ball bag to help Ross, deciding right then to do it herself. She started walking to the restaurant without saying another word to the dude in the vehicle.

Big Ed drove off confident of a rendezvous later that evening. Going to bed with the orange girl would bolster his swordsman reputation around the water cooler. She was definitely the type of girl you wanted to notch up but you could never marry something so ridiculous. People, including himself, would make fun of her all the time.

Whisper went into the restaurant and told Big Al she was taking off. The nephew was sitting in the booth, still breathing hard from the walk down to and all the way back from the cabin. He was proud of himself for not having to stop and rest. She asked the nephew to drive her to the far side of the lake. The nephew didn't know where that was exactly. Neither did Whisper. "Just get your ass up. We're going." The nephew looked at Big Al hoping his uncle would stop it but Big Al nodded an affirmative.

Big Al was quickly learning Orange was a force to be reckoned with. The young fat man scooted out of the booth, grunting his disapproval. He grabbed his coat and out the door they went. "Meet me at my cabin," she said.

Whisper ran in, pulled out a back pack purse. She threw in two bottles of water, a wool cap, gloves, a cigarette lighter she used for candles, a small advertisement flashlight she got from a restaurant supply salesman and a six-inch kitchen knife wrapped in paper towels. Whisper put on her only winter coat, snatched up the purse/pack off the bed and walked out the front door as the nephew was pulling up.

He was driving a red Ford Fiesta. *Good grief.* She didn't know how a man that large could fit in a car so small. Whisper got in the passenger side and sat among all the old hamburger wrappers and bags, pizza boxes and assorted other organic and non-organic garbage.

"Sorry 'bout the mess," he said. "Wasn't 'specting company tonight."

"Don't worry about it. I just appreciate the ride." She reached over and patted him on a very flabby upper arm.

"Where exactly do you want to go?"

"I don't really know. But if we take a left out of the parking lot and keep taking lefts, we should circle around the lake, right?

"Sounds plausible"

"Dennis?" she asked. "Your name is Dennis, right?"

"Yeah."

They drove away in silence.

Whisper wondered what Dennis had on his mind, because she was thinking…*what the fuck am I doing*?

Dennis was thinking how much he really wanted a sandwich.

Chapter 51

John Luke went to the front door. "Where are you now asshole?" he yelled out. Ross was still in the very same spot, behind the very same tree, in the same body position, not having moved a single muscle. Ross decided not to answer to see if he could get John Luke to make a mistake or at least get him doubting himself. "Did you bleed to death?" John Luke yelled.

John Luke stuck his head out the door. The door was only hanging on by some ancient nails from the 1800's. The door had been shot to shreds in the earlier gun fight. John Luke had to stick his head out far enough to see with his left eye because the right one was completely swollen shut. John Luke pointed his rifle towards the wood line and fired ten rounds at Ross' tree, five rounds at the other tree and three scattered shots into the woods.

Ross thought he counted twenty rounds fired. If so, John Luke would need to reload. Ross rolled to the right side of the tree in a prone position, aimed and fired. His big gun boomed, sending leaves flying in front of the barrel. John Luke rapid fired the remaining two rounds in his magazine. One shot went wide and the other hit the tree above Ross' head. The impact of the bullet sent tree bark flying like tiny missiles from the trunk of the tree and caught Ross above his left eye on his forehead. Ross rolled back behind the tree and put his hand to his head. He was bleeding from yet another wound.

Ross' single bullet hit low on the door and knocked it out of its hinges. The heavy oak, four foot wide door spun inwards and fell on John Luke's right foot. The corner of the door hit him squarely on the toe next to the big one and clattered to the floor.

John Luke's toe was severely smashed, almost severed. It was hanging on by skin only. The pain was incredible. John Luke fell, dropped his rifle and curled up holding his leg. He was wearing his slip-on work boots. No steel toes, he didn't think he needed them working at the Hill Top Hunting Lodge. John Luke took off his boot with an effort that almost made him pass out. His white crew sock was turning red. *Fucking Ranger Boy, I'm gonna kill that son of a bitch.* He took his sock off and the toe almost came off with it. John Luke rolled to the side and puked some bile.

Although bleeding profusely, Ross surmised he wasn't actually shot in the head which made him feel a little better. He jacked another round into his rifle and waited not knowing if John Luke was dead or around the corner laughing. Ross couldn't hear any noises coming from the house.

Ross had no idea where his bullet went because as soon as he fired, the tree exploded in his face. He peeked around the edge and noticed the door was missing. Well crap, *I killed the door.*

John Luke hollered, "I'm going to kill you Ranger Boy. I'm going to kill you real slow."

Ross could tell John Luke was injured by the strain in his voice. Ross hoped John Luke was gut-shot and on his last legs. Little did he know, John Luke was only wounded in the toe of all places. Ross stood up, wobbled some, and took off running to another tree. He ran like a zombie, all twitchy, jerky and bloody. He hobbled by the first big tree and continued on to the next. He slowly eased himself into the most comfortable position as possible considering he'd been shot three times. He waited.

John Luke didn't know what to do now. He'd taken off his boot and probably wouldn't be able to get it back on. His second toe was flopping around like a bloody dish rag and he needed to make an impossible run to the truck. John Luke crawled to the front door opening. The door was actually in the middle of the living room now. "Where are you? You son of a bitch." Ross remained quiet. The stand-off continued.

Chapter 52

Whisper and Dennis traveled six miles down the road before they found the first left turn. Turning left, they traveled four more miles until the next left turn. Whisper said, "I don't know shit about geometry but I think in a few miles we might actually be behind the lake. What do you think?"

Dennis just drove. He had no thoughts, well…the sandwich.

In five miles they saw a vehicle on the opposite side of the road. As they approached, Whisper recognized it as Ross' state truck. Her anxiety went through the roof. "Pull over, pull over."

Dennis pulled the little car up to the truck, front bumper to front bumper. Whisper jumped out and tried to open the driver's door. The truck was locked. She went to the passenger side and tried the door. Not surprisingly, it was locked too. She wrapped an arm around her waist, elbow in that hand and her other hand went to her mouth. She bit her thumbnail. Dennis could tell she was thinking.

Whisper walked back to Dennis sitting in the car. "Do you have a tire iron or something I can use to break the truck window?"

Dennis stared.

"Well?" She was tapping her foot.

"Back floor board. There's a tool box."

Whisper opened the back door and found the tiniest tool box in the world. "It's for computers," Dennis said. Whisper pulled the box up to the seat and opened it to find it was filled with what she could only describe as Hobbit tools. Nothing was bigger than three inches long. She dumped the box on the seat and spread the 'tools' out, finding a fairly normal sized crescent wrench. It would have to do.

Whisper walked to the passenger side of the truck and banged the window with the wrench. The window spider cracked but didn't smash out like in the movies. It also hurt the shit out of her hand. She repositioned with determination and banged it again. The window cracked all over but didn't fall out. She dropped the wrench because her hand was hurting too badly to hang on to it. Frustration was starting to overcome her when the door of the Ford Fiesta open.

Dennis wriggled out and waddled over to her, already breathing hard. Putting his hands on the cracked window and leaning his considerable weight against it, the window slowly melted into the truck as Dennis groaned with exertion. Then it snapped and shattered into pieces on the seat. He reached in and opened the truck door. Whisper stood up on her toes and kissed him on his hairy cheek. He turned to go back to his car thinking himself a hero and how much he deserved a sandwich.

She gave the truck interior a once over, looking for anything that might help her. The truck was remarkably clean and organized or maybe it only seemed that way after being in Dennis' car. She felt under the passenger seat and found nothing. She jumped up on the passenger seat and reached under the driver's seat. *There it is!* It was black case containing the Ruger 44 magnum revolver.

She carried it back to Dennis' car. Once seated, she opened the case to expose the gun. "Do you know how to use this?" she asked Dennis.

"In theory. I've never shot one. My guns are all on video games." He reached over and lifted the gun. It was heavy, even to a man as big as Dennis. He opened the cylinder and dumped out six shells. Big shells! He spun the cylinder. Snapping the cylinder shut, he handed it to Whisper. She hefted it a little trying adjust to its weight.

Dennis sad, "You can pull the trigger or cock the hammer and pull the trigger. Go ahead and practice."

At arm's length, pointing over the driver's side dash, she held it with both hands. It was too heavy to hold it up one handed for any length of time. She used both index fingers to pull the trigger. It took an effort.

"Now cock it and pull the trigger," Dennis encouraged

She reached up with both thumbs and pulled the hammer back. She pointed the barrel over the dash and pulled the trigger again. "Oh, that's better," she said.

Dennis leaned over and looked in the case. There were no extra bullets. "I'm going to reload this with six bullets. Ain't no extra cartridges so there's no use me teaching you how to reload." He put the bullets into the cylinder and closed it, handing the gun back to Whisper. "I guess I can't talk you out of this?"

"No. But thanks for trying." She opened the little back pack purse between her legs and stuffed the revolver in. When she zipped it shut, the grip of the gun was still sticking out. "I'm going to the rock house. Go back and tell anybody who will listen."

"Will do. By the way, if you shoot that thing, hang on tight. It'll kick like a mule."

Getting out and slinging the heavy purse over her shoulder, she again said, nervously, "Tell them where I am." Sun going down, she scooted off into the darkening woods.

Chapter 53

When Dennis got back to the lodge, the place was swarming with law enforcement who wouldn't let him into the parking lot. Parking on the highway with all of the media trucks, he made his way into the milieu and found a uniformed officer, telling him the orange girl had gone out to the rock house on her own with a 44 magnum. The officer made Dennis leave the area. The policeman was from Dallas and never heard of the orange girl and believed Dennis was talking nonsense.

Dennis huffed and puffed his way down the road and went into the parking lot from the other entrance. Finding a local county deputy, Dennis told him the orange girl went into the woods with a 44 magnum. "How do you know this?" asked the deputy.

"I drove her out there and showed her how to use the gun."

The deputy went to find the Agent-in-Charge who was about five levels above the deputy's paygrade. The agent listened carefully as the deputy explained the situation. The agent asked, "This orange girl is one of the good guys, right?"

"Definitely. She's been serving me breakfast for five years now."

"What the fuck possessed her to go out there at sundown with a 44 magnum?"

The deputy pushed his Stetson up, scratched his scalp and replied, "Who knows what gets into these orange girls' heads." Like he knew several of them.

The Agent-in-Charge went to brief the four heavily armed SWAT teams. They were going to advance down the trail behind the cabins to the lake and then circumvent the lake to the rock house.

Dennis watched for a brief moment until he realized he had no more responsibility. Shrugging, he entered the restaurant to get a sandwich. *Finally, a sandwich.*

In the meantime, Whisper was stumbling all over the woods trying to find the rock house. If she reached the lake, that would be too far but she could figure it out from there. It was getting really dark and considered hollering Ross' name but scared herself off the idea. She didn't want anyone knowing where she was. *What am I doing out here?*

Ross stayed quiet behind the tree, letting the darkness surround him, figuring John Luke would make his move soon. An escape out the back door was most likely. Ross could see some of the back but not all of it from his new position. If John Luke exited the back door and took a hard left, the asshole could get away without Ross ever seeing him. Another move was in order.

John Luke was in the cabin, trying to figure out how to get his boot back on. There was no way. He'd have to make his break for it with one bare and bloodied foot. He hobbled to the back door and looked out. His one good eye was straining but it was much too dark now to see anything except the night sky against the tree tops.

Ross was slowly ambulating to the next big tree, moving as if he were stalking an animal. It was slow going and painful, but deathly quiet. When the back of the cabin came into view, he went prone behind another tree. The night was very dark and actually seeing anything in the shadows was almost impossible.

John Luke hopped on one foot to the front door opening. "Time's almost up Ranger Boy. I'll be out there in a minute to kill you."

Ross hoped John Luke didn't go out the front. *Christ, I don't feel like running after him.*

John Luke pointed his assault rifle out the front opening, aiming the best he could with one eye in the dark and fired ten rounds at where he thought Ross was hiding. Before the last casing hit the floor, John Luke spun and limped out the back door.

As soon as the back door opened, Ross fired his rifle. The flash looked like a strobe light in a night club. Ross' position was compromised. The bullet struck one of the rocking chairs on the back porch and spun it around into John Luke's escape path. John Luke stumbled over it, stubbing his bad toe and fell down four steps off the porch. The assault rifle slipped from John Luke's hand and rattled on the ground.

Ross stood, braced against the tree, levered in another bullet and took steady aim. The front sight of his rifle was barely visible in the dark. John Luke scrambled to get his assault rifle. Ross fired. The huge flash momentarily blinded him. John Luke cried out. There was some more commotion on the ground. Ross heard it but couldn't see a thing. The stand-off continued, again.

Chapter 54

Whisper heard the shootout. She panicked and began running in the direction of the sound, falling to the ground twice. On the second fall, she took time to retrieve the revolver from her pack, resuming her quest at a little slower and more controlled pace.

Ross was quite sure John Luke was no longer on the ground. He couldn't really see, but didn't detect any form or lump. John Luke was loose in the woods, headed for his vehicle. *Damn it!* The worse thing that could have happened.

John Luke limped off in a direction away from his truck, thinking he would circle around to get to it. Going straight for it would take him too close to Ross' position and Ross was turning out to be a pain in the motherfucking ass. Ross shot off John Luke's left ring finger as he had reached for his assault rifle on the ground. *Son of a bitch!* Now John Luke was wounded three times also.

Not feeling the least bit like walking, Ross wanted to lie down and take a nap. He was tired and in pain. *Just lie down a minute.* Knowing he couldn't do that, he started moving in the direction of John Luke's escape, trying to stay between the outlaw and his truck, where ever that was.

John Luke felt that bile come up in his throat again. *Goddamn Ranger Boy shot off my finger.* John Luke bent over and puked. Mostly dry heaving but he strained enough to make his splintered-up face start to bleed. He was wiping his mouth with his good hand when he heard leaves rustle. Somebody was only a few yards away! John Luke crouched behind a tree and waited. God, he hoped it was the Ranger Boy. He pointed his rifle toward the noise.

The noise persisted and was definitely footsteps. John Luke was poised to fire in ambush. Then he heard the soft voice call out, "Ross?"

It's the orange bitch!

Whisper took a few more steps. "Ross?"

"No, Darling. Better than that."

Oh God! John Luke! She raised the revolver and fired blindly into the dark. The gun gave off a tremendous explosion and flash. The recoil was so bad, the weapon flew back and hit Whisper in the forehead, knocking her down and nearly rendering her unconscious. She was on her back seeing stars and not the those of the night sky.

John Luke had been shot yet again. This time the huge 44 magnum bullet went through his right hip. It hit the pelvic bone at the belt line and shattered a small section sending the flattened bullet and bone fragments right out his back jeans pocket. *That fucking hurts!* John Luke went down to the ground on one knee. His rifle slid out of his hand.

Ross was moving in the direction of the shot. Obviously, there was someone else in the woods, with a gun. Whisper got to her knees and was groping in the dark and mental fog for the revolver. She grabbed it with every intent on shooting John Luke in the face.

John Luke sensed her determination and lurched to the left, stumbling, rolling, and picking up his rifle. He continued to hobble off into the darkness, dragging the rifle behind him by its sling. Whisper, on her knees, got the gun in the correct firing position and was blinking away the cobwebs hoping to get a clean shot, but John Luke was long gone. He just faded away into the dark.

Whisper settled to the ground, gun in her lap. She was feeling her forehead. *Another purple bump*! There was a loud rustling of leaves coming from the opposite direction in which John Luke escaped. She raised the revolver and pointed. "Who's there?"

"Ross Evans. Is that you Whisper?"

"Ross!" She jumped up, forgetting for a second she was still dizzy. When steady, she ran and threw her arms around Ross knocking him to the ground. Falling on top of him, they both grunted loudly.

"Well, hello," Ross said, her head buried in his chest.

When she raised up to say something sarcastic about saving his ass, she realized his face was covered in blood. "Oh my God, you're hurt." She rolled to her knees and started checking him out. *Oh my God. He's a bloody mess*! "What happened?"

"He shot me in the leg first," Whisper's hands automatically went to the wound. "Then he shot me in my side." Ross pointed. Whisper opened his field jacket and shirt to expose a bruised and bloody spot the size of her hand. It was poorly bandaged with a light layer of gauze. "Then a bullet bounced off a tree and caught me in the head. She pushed back his hair, took his head in both her hands and gently turned it to the side so she could see better.

Ross said, "It looks bad. I know. But John Luke's still out there. I need to stop him."

"*We* need to stop him," she said. She picked up the big revolver and showed it to Ross. "I shot him with this."

"Where did you get that?"

"I sorta broke into your truck."

"How'd you find my truck.....Oh, never mind. You can tell me later. Get me up and let's go asshole hunting."

Whisper stood and pulled Ross up behind her. "Are you sure you're up for this?" she asked.

"I'm good." He bent down and tried to kiss her but they bumped heads in the dark. "Ow!" they said simultaneously.

Whisper rubbed her forehead knot. "When I shot him," she said, "the gun flew back and hit me in the head."

"Ouch," Ross responded.

"I'm going to have another purple bruise on my face."

"A little color never hurt anyone."

"If you hadn't just been shot three times, I'd punch your nuts."

"You can punch my nuts later. Let's get going. Which way did he run off?"

"I don't think he actually 'ran' off. After I shot him, he went down. Well, we both went down because, you now, I hit myself in the head so hard it nearly knocked me out. He recovered a few seconds before I did and staggered off in that direction." Whisper pointed.

"Let's go, slowly. I'll lead, Okay?"

Ross moved out. Whisper following close behind.

Chapter 55

John Luke was hurting...badly. But, he knew if he could make it to the truck, he could get away and implement plan B which included medical attention from a nurse practitioner he'd been screwing who lived up in Kilgore. In a few hours, he'd be laying in her bed, under the covers with stitches and a whiskey. John Luke smiled thinking about it.

Whisper followed Ross, watching him move with ease through the dark woods. Even wounded, he moved with grace and purpose. He belonged out here. *What a man.* Her thoughts turned to sex. She envisioned him naked in her bed, ready for her to crawl on top... *Wait! I'm turning into a guy!* She was on a manhunt to kill John Luke and couldn't keep her mind off sex?

They walked silently along. Ross more silent than Whisper. After a couple of hundred yards, Ross waited for Whisper to catch up and bent down close to her ear.

"I think I hear something up ahead. It doesn't sound right for just one person. I don't know what we're walking into. Stay at least five yards behind me."

She barely heard a word he said. All she could do was feel his hot breath blow in her ear and the sensation of her nipples hardening. *Definitely turning into a guy.*

Ross moved in front of her and when they reached the correct spacing, he waved her forward. Moving very slowly, one measured step at a time, Ross was listening intently, shutting his eyes to enhance the other senses, even though he couldn't see ten yards in the dark.

After advancing only a few feet, Whisper heard a sound also. Her mind finally left Ross lying nude in her bed and came back to the cold, dark, dangerous woods. She looked up at Ross who was frozen completely still, rifle halfway up to his shoulder. He was searching off to the right. Whisper looked that way also even though she didn't know from which direction she heard the noise. She was relying on Ross' instincts. They stood immobile for the longest time. Whisper became conscious of the throb in her head and how heavy the gun felt in her hand.

Fifty yards in front of them, they heard a voice. Gun shots rang out. Half a dozen or more. Ross hit the dirt. Whisper followed suit.

John Luke's screams were mixed with squeals of wild hogs. John Luke surprised a large sounder of wild hogs and they were not happy about it. John Luke killed two hogs with the six shots he fired but the biggest hog of the bunch, a three hundred pounder, ran from behind the truck and flattened John Luke. The big boar's tusks entered John Luke's right thigh, ripped up and across his body, exiting under his left rib cage. John Luke was disemboweled and his prized penis was severed.

John Luke fell to the ground whimpering. He didn't care that part of his intestines were hanging out, nor did her care his femoral artery was sliced wide open. He only cared about his big dick lying in the dirt in front of him. He reached out and picked it up, cradling it to his chest.

Ross yelled, "Get ready!" He got to a kneeling position with his rifle up. Whisper sighted her weapon and was determined to hang on to it better if she had to fire. A small stampede of wild hogs was running their direction. Seven hogs came at them, four ran wide, two veered completely off track but one came directly toward Whisper. The animal was a male juvenile but still weighed a hundred fifty pounds. Bigger than Whisper.

The hog ran right by Ross. Four feet away! Ross stuck the barrel of his big rifle right up to the hog as it passed and pulled the trigger. The blast was deafening. The hog tumbled head over hooves and bounced to a stop right in front of Whisper. The animal grunted. Whisper stood and fired the revolver almost straight down into the animal's head. The recoil nearly lifted her off the ground.

"You okay?" Ross asked. She didn't answer. "Whisper?"

"Yeah, I'm fine." She felt all her nerves tingling. Being with Ross, whether it was in the bedroom or the back woods, was always exhilarating.

"Let's move forward." He stood and started his slow, deliberate pace.

Whisper stepped around the dead pig and fell in behind Ross, matching his movements. Within a few minutes, they came upon John Luke's truck. There were two dead hogs in the area and John Luke's body lying within ten feet of the truck. John Luke was ten feet away from his escape and his next reign of terror.

Ross checked the body to make sure he was dead. John Luke was dead. Officially, he had been killed by the hog, in a very horrible way. Ross thought John Luke probably bled to death while clutching his own penis. As much as he disliked John Luke, he felt sorry for him. It's like any man's worst nightmare.

Whisper came over and looked down at the body. "Is he holding his own dick?"

"Yep." Ross stood up from his squatting position. Whisper noticed Ross touched his crotch, just to check it she supposed. "I'm going to go over here and sit by this tree a moment and think about what to do next." Ross halfway collapsed by a tree trunk and leaned against it.

He laid his rifle down beside him. Whisper sat next to him, her big revolver on the ground beside her.

Ross turned to look at her. "I think it's finally over. Really over this time." Whisper took his arm and leaned her head against his shoulder. She didn't realize she was cold until just then.

Chapter 56

Ross slid down the tree trunk into a supine position. Whisper went down with him. He wrapped his arm around her and she threw a leg over his and asked, "I'm not hurting anything am I?" Ross just pulled her closer even though she was rubbing against his side wound.

She snuggled in close for warmth and affection. Not exactly the most romantic scene. Both of them beat up and bloody, dead pigs all around and John Luke's mangled body in a heap by the truck. But she was in Ross' arms. Nothing else mattered.

Ross spoke first. "I didn't call in because my sat-phone got shot up. If they are on the ball, they'll figure out something's wrong and come looking for me. I have a GPS in my pack, which is back at the rock house. They'll go to it first. Let's see, it's been nearly eight hours since I didn't call in. They should already be here."

"They called me to see if you were with me when you didn't call in. That's how I knew to come find you. An agent came to talk to me about the best way to get to the rock house but all he wanted to do was get in my pants. I got Dennis to bring me out here and sent him back with the information. That was six hours ago."

"Who's Dennis?" Ross looked at her out of the corner of his eye.

"Big Al's nephew. You know the horrible waiter? He's really a nice guy in a slovenly, computer nerd, lazy kind of way."

"He drove you to my truck? And how did you know where it was parked?"

"I knew you went to the rock house. Your truck wasn't in the parking lot so I assumed you took it. I got Dennis to drive me around the lake on the most likely roads and after ten or twelve miles we found your truck. I broke out your window and got this gun. The rest you know."

"Thanks for coming to help me. I'd like to say I had it all under control but…" He squeezed her into him and she hugged back.

"You did the same for me…" They caressed again.

How's your head?" Ross asked.

"Swollen but okay."

"Can you build a fire?"

Whisper never built a camp fire before. "Can you talk me through it?"

"Sure, first you…." And he began to talk her through it. Within minutes, Whisper was holding her cigarette lighter under the small slivers of kindling at the bottom of the strategically placed sticks. As the fire caught, she added bigger sticks until it was roaring. The heat was wonderful. The light was comforting.

Ross spoke, "Maybe our rescuers can see this? I have a feeling they will need all the help they can get."

"Shouldn't they be close by now? There's been plenty of time. I mean it's the middle of the night, right."

Ross had a terrible thought. "Maybe they won't start searching until the morning."

"Should I go for help?" she asked.

She was standing by the fire. He reached up and pulled her down to him. "You're not going anywhere. Hand me your gun."

She reached down and picked it up. "What are you going to do?"

"Fire a shot in the air. If they are within a mile, they'll be able to hear it."

I'll do it." She took a few steps away. She pulled the hammer back and used both hands to point the gun up at a tall tree. "Hold your ears." Ross did and she fired. The blast was powerful and very loud.

Whisper lowered the weapon, stuck her finger in her ear and wiggled it around. "God, that's loud. They should have been able to hear that back at the lodge." They actually could hear it that far away if anyone was listening.

She sat back down next to Ross with the gun between her legs and waited.

Whisper kept the fire going, they drank water from Whisper's backpack and every thirty minutes she shot the gun in the air. Sometime around 4:00 am, they heard voices. Ross and Whisper began shouting and men shouted back. Two minutes later, four SWAT teams converged on their position. They were rescued.

Chapter 57

Ross was taken to the hospital. Whisper refused medical treatment because she thought she didn't need it and her crappy Hill Top Hunting Lodge insurance had something like a two-thousand dollar deductible. She visited Ross every minute they would let her on the ward and then some because she kept sneaking back in.

Ross' wounds were not superficial but they were not serious. The media called them 'non-life threatening'. Ross was due to be released after two nights. He would get out the same day Myles Carter was having his big press conference. What a show this was going to be, a nationwide broadcast.

The FBI would open the pageantry with the chronology of the events from beginning to end. This would take thirty minutes. Then there would be thirty minutes of studio analysis and commentary by each of the networks. The governor would talk next. Why? Because he's the governor. This would take fifteen minutes. Then back to the studios for more expert commentary and opinions. Next a representative from Veritas International would speak about the company and all the good things it does for the community. After what would basically be a paid advertisement, they would introduce the dashing Myles Carter. Myles would talk for forty-five minutes with graphs, charts, schematics and pictures put together by the Veritas International Information Technology Department.

Ross and Whisper were walking out of the hospital arm-in-arm. Ross had thirty-eight stitches in his leg, several subcutaneous and a couple of dozen surface stitches in his side and three stitches each closing a couple of cuts on his forehead. Not bad for being shot three times.

The FBI impounded Ross' truck for evidence so they Ubered from the hospital back to the lodge. Law enforcement stopped them well short of the parking lot because the Myles Carter extravaganza was about to begin. They walked a half mile to get to their cabins.

The parking lot was filled to capacity with media and law enforcement vehicles, people, *my God the number of people,* several mounted Texas Rangers which were part of the Governor's personal security team and Big Al serving up expensive barbecue. They started to go into her cabin but she asked, "You want to watch this show?"

Ross hesitated a minute. "I think I do."

"Me too."

They walked hand-in-hand through the crowd to the restaurant steps which an army of carpenters turned into a grand stand overnight. The governor was in the middle of his speech. He was praising local law enforcement, the State Troopers, the FBI and most of all, himself. Ross and Whisper kept squeezing each other's hand when the Governor said something that wasn't true or was just plain political. It was constant and they started to giggle. The governor finished to thunderous applause.

The smell of smoking barbecue wafted over the crowd. "Are you hungry?" Ross asked.

"Starving," Whisper replied.

"Me too. All I had in the hospital was red Jello."

"That's not true. You had some green Jello too."

"Has anyone called you a bitch today?"

"Not Today."

They walked over to the serving tables, paid twenty dollars a plate and got a fair-sized helping of brisket, sausage, potato salad, beans and bread. The sauce was at the end of the table as was a glass of tea. They could help themselves.

Still having a job after this was doubtful because Whisper hadn't really worked in a couple of days. Plus she was supposed to be helping with this fiasco. Ross was the priority. If Big Al fired her, so be it. She did notice Big Al hired a professional catering company to set up and serve. *Good move Big Al.*

When they finished their meals, an announcer came on and told the crowd, the live show would begin again in five minutes. "This ought to be interesting," she said more to herself as she wiped sauce off her face.

They threw their trash in a barrel and wormed their way through the crowd to the front of the stage. A man in a headset counted down and a Veritas International public relations man started talking about the company and after a long build-up, introduced Mister Wonderful himself, Myles Carter.

Myles took the stage by bounding up the stairs showing his virility and youthfulness. He waved to the appreciative crowd. When the moment was right, he shushed the audience and began his tale. Although Myles Carter was drugged, strung up on a sex swing and raped up the ass continuously, he somehow sounded like a hero in his telling of the story. The way he told the tale, he didn't really need saving at all.

Ross and Whisper were stunned at his version but they were not surprised. The couple was looking at each other when two men approached them and escorted them to the stage. Whisper was placed on one side of Myles and Ross on the other. Whisper was shaking with stage fright. Ross was wishing he didn't have

Band-Aides stuck on his forehead. "These two people helped me escape," Myles spoke into the microphone. "I'm not sure who was the most instrumental but the first face I saw was this colorful one right here. They call her…."

Ross stepped up to the microphone cutting Myles off. "She's Whisper Jenkins. The Sunset Girl." He stepped back. A thousand clicks of digital cameras could be heard.

Whisper smoothed her blonde hair back and licked her lips. It was just a nervous gesture but what the world perceived was a new standard of beauty and definition of sexy. "Say a few words Sunset Girl." Myles stepped back and relinquished the microphone. A thousand more clicks sounded.

Whisper positioned herself behind the podium. She was shaking like crazy, looking at Ross for some help. He leaned forward and spoke into the mic, "She shot the villain John Luke Thibodeaux with a 44 magnum while chasing him alone at midnight in the deep, dark woods and she's afraid public speaking."

The crowd laughed. "Well, that helped," Whisper said sarcastically. The crowd laughed again. She faced the audience trying to think of something to say.

"We love you Sunset Girl!" someone yelled. The crowd roared approval.

She held up a hand to quiet them and began.

"Whatever part I played in the release of the hostages and putting an end to John Luke's reign of terror, I couldn't have done without the support and inspiration of this man." She grabbed Ross' sleeve and pulled him close. "He is fearless, strong, kind and filled with a sense of right and wrong and has the backbone to set the wrongs right again. And ladies, he's hot as…. Well, you can see foryourselves."

The media was eating this shit up. A million camera clicks were going off now. The women in the crowd and television audience were waiting to see if she would say it.

Whisper continued, "This man, Doctor Ross Evans, a humble state employee, a war veteran, a good man, the best of men....has stolen my heart. I love him more than life itself."

She said it. The place went nuts. Myles Carter's story just landed on page two.

Whisper looked up at Ross with a tear glistening on her orange cheek. She was hoping she hadn't made a terrible mistake.

They stared into each other's eyes for the longest moment. The crowd held their collective breaths. Cameras were poised. He took a step forward, wrapped both arms around her, bent her back and kissed like the war was over and he was coming home!

Cameras and the crowd went crazy. Myles stepped in front of them and said, "Ladies and Gentleman, I give you heroes, lovers and media darlings, The Sunset Girl and the Ranger! The crowd continued to applaud. Ross and Whisper kept kissing.

Eventually, Myles broke it up by saying, "You're cutting into my time."

They split apart. Both saying "Sorry" and wiping their mouths. They stood behind Myles holding hands and casting gazes in one another's direction.

Chapter 58

Myles continued the show, determined not to let anyone upstage him. He resumed telling about his heroic exploits. Whisper looked out in the crowd and saw Shanna, Molly and Kylie standing behind the serving line. Molly was chatting up a young uniformed police officer, Kylie had her sights on bigger fish, a Vice President of Veritas International. Shanna, with a purple and yellow face accented with a bloodshot eye, was smiling at Whisper with her new implanted teeth. Whisper ran down the back of the stage and gathered up the three girls, leading them to a spot right behind the podium.

Myles gave a slight irritated look in their direction but kept talking. Shanna and Whisper held each other. Kylie incessantly pulled down on her short skirt. Guys were looking at her when she navigated the parking lot in her high heels but she was now standing on a raised platform and there wasn't much left to the imagination. Molly was wearing a summer waitress uniform, skirt rolled up as high as she could get away with, white blouse with the top two buttons undone and a bra that must have been made out of something as sheer as

Kleenex. Molly was attempting to make conversation with a State Guard officer with a star on his uniform standing next to her.

Whisper was bursting at the seams with excitement, trying to be 'in the moment'. What a hell of a 'moment' it was. She was soaking in everything, the crowd, the trucks with satellite dishes, the smell of wood smoked barbecue, the blue sky, holding on to her first friend ever and peering over at the man she loved. She couldn't stop smiling.

Her meditation was broken when Myles put his hand over the microphone and asked her, "Who are these people?"

He didn't even recognize his fellow captives! Whisper once thought of Myles as a reasonably nice guy but he was turning out to be nothing more than another strutting peacock. Ross stepped forward once again and spoke. "With us today at the invitation of Mister Carter are the other hostages who were with him through his ordeal." Ross raised his hand and pointed, "I'd like to introduce, Molly in the black and white, Kylie in almost nothing." The crowd laughed and once again the digital picture barrage resumed. Kylie gave a few poses. "And next to the Sunset Girl herself, is Shanna. The angels who survived hell." Ross stepped back. Ross wrote another headline for them, The Angels Who Survived Hell.

Myles took his position on center stage. Whisper gave Ross a look and said, "You silver tongued devil." Ross just shrugged and shuffled his feet. *I love that big lug.* Whisper slowly moved over to Ross and they went at it again, a full body press kiss. Shanna let out a sigh and started crying. But it didn't take anything much more than a Hallmark movie to get her going. Myles threw his hands up and said, "I think they need to get a room." The crowd cheered, applauded and the cameras clicked.

When Ross and Whisper pulled apart Myles scolded them, "If you guys can keep your hands off each other for two minutes, I have an announcement to make." They both apologized for ruining Myles' big moment.

Myles cleared his throat. "After thorough research of the records of the investigation, including eye witnesses, interviews with participants, Emergency Operations Center logs, video evidence, law enforcement notes, ballistic studies and other forensic findings, Veritas International is pleased to present the five million dollar reward to…." Myles checked his notes to make sure he got the name correct because he really didn't give a shit enough to remember anybody. "….Doctor Ross Evans."

Whisper and Ross were stone faced. Myles continued, "Now, who would like to hear a few words from Texas' newest millionaire?" The crowd cheered again, professional photographers were clicking a mile a minute and all the iPhones were recording. Ross stood with Myles at the podium in the handshake pose until the world had enough time to see Myles' generosity. After a minute of a pasted-on smile and a creepy hand holding episode with Myles, Ross prepared to address the crowd.

Ross was holding a cashier's check for five million bucks. He held it up a little and said, "I don't think I can accept this. I'm a state employee and I was just doing my job. I'm already paid to do this. As long as I work for the state, I think it's unethical." He said it like a question.

There was a deathly silence in the crowd. At the perfect moment that couldn't have been scripted any better, the governor yelled, "Bullshit. You're fired! No conflict of interest!" The crowd nearly rioted. Cameras panned across the mayhem to the Governor and back the Ranger.

Hollywood could have spent a hundred years trying to write this script and it wouldn't have turned out any better. Myles was thinking, *what great television, I'm going to be the next reality star. I'll host my own show!*

Ross quieted the crowd. "I guess since I'm unemployed, I'll need this money." The crowd loved this guy. To hell with Myles Carter, they liked the Ranger and the Sunset Girl.

Chapter 59

Myles began speaking again. The media didn't care about Myles anymore and wanted individual interviews with the Ranger and the Sunset Girl, her best friend Shanna, and the two slutty-looking hostages.

Ross and Whisper stood face-to-face. "Can you wait right here for a minute? There's something I've got to do." He didn't wait for her to respond, leaping off the back of the stage, regretting it as soon as he landed. His leg, side and head all throbbed in unison.

Shanna asked, "What's he doing? He's not running off, is he? He does have five million dollars."

"No. He wouldn't do that." Whisper placed her arm across her waist, rested her other elbow on it and put her thumb nail in her mouth. Shanna put her arm around Whisper's shoulders and waited. Myles concluded the program and the crowd was starting to mill around. Whisper couldn't see Ross anywhere and was beginning to wonder what he was up to. Reporters were yelling at Whisper for an interview.

When the crowd thinned a little more, Shanna saw Ross walking toward them. "There he is," she said and pointed so Whisper could find him. Whisper dropped her hands to her side. Shanna backed off a few paces. Ross bounded up the steps two at a time again, regretting it as soon as he did it.

She hugged him when he got close enough for her to get her hands on him. He hugged back which eased her mind a little. Shanna was almost in tears again. "Where'd you go?" Whisper asked. "I was hoping to go get laid by a millionaire but you ran off."

"So that's it. You just want the money." She couldn't tell if he was being playful or not. "I'm sorry to say but you will never get what you want. This guy can't do it." Whisper was starting to get worried because she didn't understand what he was talking about. Shanna was about to pass out listening to the conversation.

"What do you mean?" Whisper asked.

"You're not having me as a millionaire." Ross could tell she was bewildered. Certainly not expecting this from him. Her eyes pleaded with him. "I mean, I'll take you down to your cabin right now and wear you out, but I'm not a millionaire."

Whisper wasn't sure what was going on. "They didn't let you have the money?"

"I got it alright," Ross said.

"You gave it away. To a charity?"

"Nope, not that either."

"Well you couldn't have spent five million dollars in the last ten minutes."

Ross looked at her with a dopey face.

"How could you spend that much money so fast?"

"I bought the Hill Top Hunting Lodge from Big Al."

"What?" Whisper asked, trying to let it soak in.

Ross heard Shanna say, "Oh my God."

Ross said, "Since I don't have a job, I needed something to do. I can run the range, guide the hunters, you know, properly use all of the acreage. You can run the new, modern Sunset Girl Grill and Shanna?"

Shanna looked up at Ross, eyes watery and glazed over, living her own Hallmark moment. "Shanna," he said again. "We need someone we can trust to be a business manager. I know nothing about finance as evidenced by the fact I couldn't hang on to five million dollars more than ten minutes. Will you be our partner?"

Shanna cried out a feeble, "Yes."

"Good," Ross said. "You can start now because we are broker than church mice. Big Al's even keeping all the profits from the barbecue sale. We are starting from square zero, if there is such a thing."

Chapter 60

A week after the broadcast, Whisper was approached by *Elle* and *New Beauty* magazines. They wanted to do a photo shoot. Her picture was in virtually every newspaper in America but not with an in-depth interview and photo outlay. She agreed as long as they did the shoot at the Hill Top Hunting Lodge. *Cosmopolitan* and *Vogue* followed suit with the articles, 'Unusually Beautiful Women of the World' and 'A Change in the Status Quo of Beauty' featuring women with freckles, bald women, tall women, curvy women, an amputee and of course, the Sunset Girl. Whisper Jenkins was now famous.

The Hill Top Hunting Lodge was famous too, especially after a three page write up in *Texas Monthly*. This magazine focused on the team of Ross, Whisper and Shanna. Molly was even in the background of one picture.

Whisper couldn't have been happier. Ross permanently moved in the cabin he occupied during his assignment at the lodge. Whisper stayed in her cabin. They didn't move in with each other because they weren't ready but that didn't keep them from screwing like rabbits, sometimes two or three times a day.

Molly remained in her cabin and continued to earn tips on the side. Whisper's only rule was 'no married men'. Shanna took John Luke's old cabin. Whisper loved having 'her girls' as neighbors.

Shelby went back to Austin and was hailed as a hero in the graduate program circles. Big Al and Glyna moved to Florida. Dennis just disappeared. Kylie met an author who wanted to write a book about her experience. After going to bed with her twice, he was never heard from again. Kylie is now a popular waitress at a Hooters near Dallas.

Whisper was standing on the veranda as the workmen finished installing the new orange and yellow neon sign: Sunset Girl Grill. Whisper thought it was a little gaudy but Shanna assured her it was a good move. "You watch and see." Shanna said. "A new round of pictures of this thing will be everywhere."

Shanna was right. A renewed interest developed in the story of the Hill Top Hunting Lodge with its world-famous Sunset Girl. Whisper hired two chefs to run the kitchen. One was a fairly renowned chef from Dallas who handled all of the non-grilled/smoked dishes and the other was an older black man named Little Moe whose pit smoked meats were regionally famous in East Texas. Of the two, Little Moe was by far the most popular. He was only five feet six inches tall but what he lacked in stature, he more than made up for in character. This guy was a gold mine and a good friend.

Valentine's Day was coming soon and the restaurant was booked to the gills. They were opening early at 4:30 pm and taking the last reservations at 9:30 pm. Every table was booked all evening. Little Moe's grilled Steaks-for-Two was the special. Forty-eight pre-ordered meals were already on the books. It was going to be Whisper's big night. Local media was even going to be there.

Shanna approached her partners with a new proposition that might not be looked at favorably. When they were all gathered at Big Al's booth (old habits die hard), Shanna said she had been approached by numerous interested parties wanting the lodge to provide guided tours of the rock house. "A torture house tour."

Whisper nearly convulsed at the idea. Ross was appalled. "Let me explain," Shanna said. "I know it sounds cheap and tawdry. But the people I spoke with said they would be willing to pay a hundred dollars per person for a tour. They have over thirty people on their waiting list right now. Big Al left us with a mountain of debt. Even with the magazine modeling money, the cost of the repairs and upgrades to the restaurant and cabins and the employee costs and being months until hunting season, we're strapped. We're broker than broke. We have less money than we had when we started. I say we do this at least until initial interest runs out."

Whisper was biting her nail again. Ross was hanging his head in his hands. He spoke first, "Since I have less to do than anyone, I guess I would run the tours?"

"Yes," Shanna responded.

Ross looked at Whisper. "We need the money. It's easy. No overhead."

Whisper shook her head "yes" and just like that Ross was tour guide.

Chapter 61

Shanna set up the first tour for Saturday morning at 10:00 am. Ross was in the parking lot early waiting on the 'tourists' to arrive. He looked up and saw Whisper walking down from the restaurant. Since Shanna took over as business manager, the new restaurant hours were 6:00 am to 10:00 am, 11:00 am to 2:00 pm and 5:00 pm to 9:00 pm. The hours varied with the season and holidays, an earlier breakfast opening during hunting season and later closing on holidays like Valentine' Days.

Whisper had her arms wrapped around herself still having the habit of going outside without a coat. She walked right up to Ross and stood against is chest. He opened his field jacket and she nearly got in with him saying, "You know you're out here thirty minutes early, don't you?"

"I don't want to be late. As broke as we are, a one-star rating on Yelp or Trip Advisor wouldn't do our new tour business any good."

"Ross, you're thirty minutes early!" She stared at him. He was bewildered. She finally jerked her head toward the cabins. "You can do some damage in thirty minutes."

Ross caught on. He picked her up, as was his habit, and carried her to her cabin. The door was unlocked as usual and he set her down on the bed. They began stripping off clothes as fast as they could. Fully naked, he laid on top of her and they began kissing, tongues spinning furiously.

She felt his big meaty cock on her thigh. With every second of the kiss, it elongated down her leg getting harder and harder. When fully erect, she said," You better get that in me now. I want you to cum twice and you have less than thirty minutes."

"Nothing like a little pressure." Ross said as he adjusted his position. She was wide open for him. He spit on his hand and rubbed it on the head. He aimed his big thing into her beautiful blonde mat and started to slide it in. The noise she made as it filled her up gave him goose bumps. His cock felt electrified.

She was holding her legs open with her hands. She almost had to so his large cock could get in. Her nipples sprouted out of her chest as he bent down to suck one up in his mouth. The red nipples were elongated, very distinctive like everything else on her body. He moved his mouth up and down on it like she would do if it were a tiny dick.

They hadn't had each other since yesterday morning which was a long time for them. Ross raised up so he could get the last inches in her. He had to be a little careful until she got loosened up and wet, but when she was ready, he could pound it. All the way in, she could feel his big, full balls bouncing off her ass.

She could feel everything. Everything! The wave of orgasm was just about to flood across her. "Ross….fuck," was all she could muster. The orgasm went roaring through her body, head flying back and body arching, pushing him deeper into her.

Ross tried really hard not to cum while she was writhing beneath him. Knowing he was the one making her feel that way was just too much for him. Her climax almost complete, he couldn't stop his now if he wanted to. Pulling out, making her flinch, he went up on his knees, hovering over her beautiful colorful body all twisted in ecstasy, and he stroked his big shaft. Milking it of all its juice.

Whisper felt his warm love extract rain down on her as the after-glow of a powerful orgasm consumed her. Ross collapsed beside her, his big cock lying in an awkward position across her thigh. She put her hand on it and could feel it still throbbing, trying to give her some more nectar.

She heard Ross fall into deep breathing like one might just before falling asleep. "Whoa, boy. You better not fall asleep. You owe me another one and then you need to get a shower, all in less than twenty minutes."

Ross groaned, "Work, work, work. That's all I do around here." He rolled over.

"Alright, lazy ass. I'll help you." She went down on him without warning. The head of his dick was so sensitive, she had him jerking around like someone was poking him with icicles. He was grunting as if in pain. She thought it amusing and loved her control over him.

She squeezed his giant dry balls trying to work him up for another go. He never lost his hard on and after a few minutes of magical suck-ing, he started to get into the rhythm. She worked the head forcefully for nearly five minutes all the while jacking the shaft or caressing his balls. He was hard as a rock again.

She pulled her mouth away, leaving some saliva on the head, strad-dled him and eased the big thing up in her. She was tight because her lips were still fully engorged. She worked it up, down, and around until she was sitting on it. It felt like a board up in her. He reached up and put his hands on her chest, red extended nipples poking through his fingers. He squeezed his fingers together trapping them, pulling a little. She felt the sensation run through her body all the way down to her toes. She ground into him, his dark pubic hair mixing with her blonde.

He could see by the look on her face an orgasm was forming, some-where deep inside her at the tip of his dick which was hitting bottom in such a magical way. She could feel the climax building, spread-ing through her entire body. She would swear later she could feel a flame-like sensation travel up his shaft and ignite her clit. Once her clit caught, she exploded, throwing her head back, making her tits jerk out of his grip. This movement pinched her nipples at precisely the right time with the right pressure to extend the orgasm through her chest.

Ross was mesmerized watching this creature fight through the grips of an all-consuming orgasm. She was momentarily lost to this world and launched to Planet Ecstasy. She pushed down on him hard with her full weight until it was over.

Placing her hands on his chest and leaning forward, her blonde hair flowed around him like a dream. She was breathing deeply, not like after running a race, but like one does when they are trying to settle their nerves.

Ross was starting to breathe deeply also. Whisper realized he was about to cum and said, "Use me."

Ross picked her up, spun her around, still impaled on his cock and placed her on her knees. He grabbed her hips and started with deep, long strokes in and out from behind. The cadence sped up. She reached between her legs and felt his big balls swinging under her and squeezed them. He went faster. She squeezed harder. He was pounding the shit out of her. She heard him make a guttural noise. He shoved her forward, flat on the bed. She instinctively put her hand behind her neck and flipped her long blonde hair up on to the pillows, right before she felt his hot cum shower down on her butt and lower back.

When the flow stopped, she turned on her elbow and looked back. Ross was still on his knees, jacking himself as fast as he could. Nothing was coming out but it still must have felt good. She sat up and stroked his nuts while he was slowing down. He eventually let go of himself, but she continued to rub his balls and kiss the head while it bobbed in front of her face. He was taking deep breaths now.

Whisper looked at the clock by the bed, "Don't you have a tour in seven minutes?"

"Oh shit!" He jumped up dragging his balls right out of her hand and ran to the shower.

She giggled. *He did it. Two in a row in twenty minutes. What a fucking stud.*

Chapter 62

Ross barely dried off, threw his clothes on and kissed her on the forehead as he ran out the door with two minutes to spare. There was a group of six people standing near the street lamp telephone pole, obviously, the tour group. "Hello! I'm Ross Evans, your tour guide."

Everyone in the group raised their cameras simultaneously and snapped pictures. *This is going to be worse than I thought.* "If you'll come with me, we'll start the tour."

Ross wrote a script and practiced diligently for days. The tour started in the parking lot with Ross explaining about who lived in which cabin. He was just finishing the cabin portion when Whisper came out on the porch. Ross said, "This group is very lucky. The timing is such that you have a chance to meet the Sunset Girl herself. Look behind you everybody."

The group turned and saw Whisper on the porch. They raised their cameras and ripped off a dozen pictures each. Ross waved her over. Whisper shot him a deathly stare and approached the group. Every step she took was covered in pictures. She said hello to everyone and told them all how happy she was they were here and invited them to have some lunch after the tour and said the lunch was on the house. Each of the group squealed with delight at the thought of free food, especially gifted from the Sunset Girl herself. Whisper took selfies with them and excused herself to go prepare their lunches.

Ross continued with the tour, marching them down to the lake, making the boat ride across and taking a solemn approach to the 'the torture house'. The people were eating it up. He pointed out every gruesome detail and he knew lots of them.

After an hour at the house with all of the areas identified.... where the mattresses were for Molly and Kylie, the torture swing for Myles, the place Shanna and Whisper were tied and hung up, the rape table, the place the Veritas Security Officer was killed, the exact spot where the beautiful young reporter was murdered, the trail leading to the camera man's contorted body, all the bullet holes in the house and finally, the cursed ground where the arch-villain, John Luke Thibodeaux lay after the giant wild boar disemboweled him and severed his penis, which he 'clutched to his chest as he bled to death'.

The group asked questions, stayed engaged, took literally thousands of pictures and enjoyed every minute of the three-hour tour. Once back at the parking lot, Ross told them to go on up to the restaurant and the beautiful Sunset Girl would take excellent care of them. They tipped Ross one hundred twenty dollars.

Shanna was on the porch of her cabin, watching as Ross finished with the group. She bounced down the stairs and asked, "How'd it go?"

"I think you are a genius."

"Good then, huh?"

"Better than good." Ross handed her the tip money.

"What's this?"

"Tip money."

"It's yours, I can't take this." She fanned it out in her hands. "Damn, that's a lot of money."

"You put it to good use. It was a joint effort. You booked the gig, Whisper took pictures with them and gave them free meals by the way, and I did the tour. Joint effort."

"Okay, but only because we really need it." She wadded the money up and stuffed it in her pocket.

Within the week, all of the original thirty people who requested the tour got to go on one. Ross received $580 in tips which he donated to the team. The Hill Top Hunting Lodge 'tour option' earned 18 five-star ratings the first week. After that, the tour became so popular, Shanna booked two tours a day Thursday through Sunday. The only change was, at Whisper's insistence, a free meal was added to the price permanently. Including tips, they were clearing $14,000 a month just on tours. With the tours, the cabins started to fill up with people who came from far away to take the tour. The free meals exposed many new people to the food and it was so good they always planned to come back. The willingness of Whisper, Ross, Molly (who especially loved it) and Shanna to take pictures with everybody who wanted one added to the popularity of the lodge. Even Little Moe had to pose several times a day while tending his pits.

All law enforcement, any military in uniform and other first responders got a 10% discount on everything including food, lodging, tours, hunting/fishing packages and unofficially, Molly.

Chapter 63

In late March, Ross was out on his morning tour. Shanna was in her cabin going over the books, which were looking really good and Whisper was in the empty restaurant. She liked being there during the morning break between breakfast and lunch. Today, her quiet time was taken up in the kitchen contemplating ways to get another oven installed to appease Elton Swenson, her fancy chef from Dallas. He was really good but never got the recognition Little Moe received mainly because Elton had no personality or flair. Elton just cooked great foo-foo cuisine. Whisper could barely pronounce some of the stuff on her menu, having to Google many of the sauces so she could train the wait staff how to describe them.

Whisper heard the front door open. As per her habit, she never locked doors. Coming out from the kitchen she saw a good-looking man wearing a ball cap. He wasn't tall but not short, his hair was in need of a cut and he looked outdoor-ish. Whisper cordially said, "We're closed right now but I can get you a cup of coffee."

He just nodded his head and sat at the nearest booth. She looked over her shoulder while brewing a fresh pot. "Are you here for a hog hunt or maybe some fishing?"

"Naw. I'm here for that creepy tour."

"I know. It is rather macabre but it's very popular."

The stranger looked around the restaurant. Everything was brand new, Spic and Span clean, yet it still looked rustic.

When the coffee was scalding hot and finished brewing, she carried the pot over to the stranger's booth. Turning over a cup from the set up already on the table, she looked at him sitting there, face covered with the bill of his cap. She noticed a pistol in his belt. This being Texas, handguns, concealed or carried openly, were quite common. She didn't panic but suddenly became super aware, mentally checking access to the front door, considering a retreat out the back and even contemplating a dash to the kitchen to grab the biggest knife Elton had in the rack, which he kept razor sharp.

She was close to him and was just about to pour when he said, "You're the orange cunt, right bitch?"

She froze. Goose bumps feeling like needles broke out all over her body. "Who the fuck *are* you?"

"I'm Bobby Lee Thibodeaux, John Luke's brother come to set things right." When Whisper didn't run or say anything, Bobby Lee figured she was going to submit quietly. A lot of the women he raped were like that. He just got them isolated, with no hope of escape and told them what he was going to do to them and they became putty in his hands, to be molded in any way he preferred. If the victim didn't comply, he used force, the old fashion way. "I think you'll pull those jeans down now, bend right over this table and I'll knock on that back door. Go ahead, get those pants off."

Bobby Lee made a move as if he were going to get out of the booth. Whisper, without hesitation and with no meekness about it, coffee potted the shit out of him. She raised the pot way back over her head and brought it down at an angle on the side of his face. It was a direct hit to his ear. The pot broke into a million pieces and scalding coffee splashed across his face. She dragged the pot downward and the jagged glass nearly ripped his ear off.

Bobby Lee didn't expect that. She looked so acquiescent. "Fuck!" he yelled as he grabbed his face. "Fucking orange cunt! I'm going to kill you." Holding the handle of the pot in her hand which still had a ring of glass attached to it, she tried to stab him in the face with the remnants but only managed to cut the back of his hands which he held to his steaming face.

She dropped the pot handle and ran to the front door. It was locked! The asshole locked it behind him when he came in. Whisper fumbled with the lock twice before she got it open. Bobby Lee couldn't see out of his left eye and kept blinking trying to make it work. She burned him blind! His ear hurt as he reached up and felt the shreds. Looking at the back of his hands which were seriously cut in several places, he let out a scream and went to the front door, blinking some more as he watched Whisper run down the hill into Shanna's Cabin.

Shanna was working at her 'home office' desk when Whisper burst through the door. Shanna jumped and papers flew off her desk, "Oh my God, what's wrong?" They fell into each other's arms.

"Blueberries!" Whisper shouted. "John Luke's brother."

Shanna went to her desk and called the police on her new office land line she installed. The cops were on the way. She opened the top right-hand desk drawer and pulled out a container of pepper spray, a tactical knife, a big Maglite the size of a billy club and a .38 Smith and Wesson revolver. She handed Whisper the pepper spray, the Maglite and attached the knife scabbard to Whisper's pants. Shanna hefted the revolver, opened the cylinder, spun it, and slapped it back shut. It was loaded with five, plus-p hollow points. "Blueberries, bitch," she said as she raised the gun.

They went to the door and looked out. Bobby Lee was in the parking lot, standing behind the nearest car. Shanna could see he was already bloodied and burned. "Did you coffee pot him?"

"Yep."

"What do you think he's up to?"

Whisper shook her head. "I don't know but if he stays out there much longer, the cops will catch him."

The girls waited until they heard sirens in the distance. Bobby Lee heard them too. He was out of time. Drawing his pistol, he charged the cabin, firing all the way. He was shooting a Glock 19, a very good weapon for such a low-life. There were fifteen rounds in the magazine in the gun and eleven rounds in another magazine. That's all the bullets he happened to have at the time. He wasn't much of a deep thinker and didn't bother to load the maximum number of rounds. He figured she would start to cry and strip off her clothes as he asked. Most of them did. If they didn't, he knocked them out and raped them while they were unconscious. This was not supposed to end in a gun fight.

Shanna fired one round out the door which went wide and hit the car Bobby Lee was standing behind. The girls slammed the door, locked it, and ducked to each side protected by the big logs of the cabin. His bullets were ripping through the hollow door. They heard his boots stomp up on the porch and he ran right into the closed door, banging it open. The little dead bolt never stood a chance against the force of his running body.

The door swung open and hit Shanna with a great amount of force. Shanna went to the floor backwards. Bobby Lee stepped in to be greeted with an eighteen-inch long flashlight smashing down on his head. The blow knocked his cap off. Whisper sprayed him in the face with pepper spray. Bobby Lee ran into the room wiping his eyes and screaming. Whisper chased him around the couch continuing to spray at his head. The pepper spray was so thick in the room, all three of them were having a hard time seeing and breathing.

The spray gave out and Whisper began to whip his ass with the flashlight. Shanna got to her feet and was pointing the gun in their direction but she didn't have a clear shot in the melee. Bobby Lee went to his knee and dropped the gun. Whisper quit beating him because she was tired, not because she was being merciful.

"Twitch a fucking muscle and I will shoot you in the dick," Shanna sounded serious. Whisper was impressed. The cops were pulling into the parking lot slinging gravel all over the customer's cars. Whisper was going to kick the gun away from Bobby Lee when he grabbed her leg and pulled her down to the floor. He wrapped his arm around her neck and they began wrestling as she refused to submit.

Whisper pulled the knife from her waist and slashed him up the thigh as she tried to roll away but he tightly held on to a handful of blonde hair. Whisper squirmed to get away. Shanna moved forward, placed the muzzle of her .38 right between his legs and pulled the trigger. She shot him in the dick as promised. He let go of Whisper and grabbed his crotch, screaming in a high pitch. Whisper and Shanna stood together watching Bobby Lee cry and wiggle helplessly in his own blood.

Whisper looked at Shanna, "These Thibodeaux boys don't have very good luck with their penises, do they?"

The police heard the shot and eventually confirmed where it came from. They raided the cabin and hand cuffed everybody until they figured out who was who and what happened.

Ross heard the shooting while he was down at the lake. He ushered the tour group back to the lodge as quickly as he could, getting there a little after the ambulance arrived. Whisper and Shanna walked out of the cabin breathing fresh air. Whisper saw Ross rapidly approaching and leaped off the porch into his arms. He picked her up. The tour group was taking continuous pictures. Shanna sighed, being a sucker for romance and would have cried if she weren't already crying from pepper spray.

After Ross confirmed Whisper and Shanna were alright, he said, "I don't much care for your perfume."

He was still carrying her with her arms and legs wrapped around him. Whisper bit him on the ear which made him feel a little tingle between his legs. As Bobby Lee was being carried out on a stretcher, Ross let Whisper slide down his body to stand beside him. Whisper looked over her shoulder and saw Little Moe with a cleaver so large it looked like a medieval weapon in his hands. He heard the shooting and came running to help. "I am blessed to be surrounded with heroes and friends," she said almost to herself.

Ross was engrossed in Bobby Lee's appearance. The rapist asshole was burned and cut about the face, definitely coffee-potted, bludgeoned with a Maglite about the head and shoulders, thigh ripped open with a knife and, Ross cringed, shot in the dick with a .38 at point blank range. These girls were dangerous.

Ross looked over at Whisper, "Did you say something?"

"Not really."

Chapter 64

After the shooting at the lodge, the 'Torture House Tour' became even more popular. Shanna raised the price to $150 per person and booked two tours a day Tuesday through Friday and three a day on Saturday and Sunday. She also bought Ross a bigger boat so he could take twelve people across the lake at a time instead of only six. She told him when the tour popularity waned, he could use the boat for fishing excursions. Ross wasn't going to argue with that.

On Monday, their day off, Whisper, Ross, Shanna and Little Moe all sat in the booth discussing, "What's next?" The money from the Torture House Tour, the Sunset Girl Grill and the Hill Top Hunting Lodge cabins was pouring in. Shanna had the place all classed up in rustic chic and converted one of the barns into a spa. The staff provided yoga, massages, wet and dry saunas, meditation and a dozen other services that Whisper never heard of before. The food was top notch and they sold an exclusive hunting lease for the first week of the season to Veritas International for a hundred thousand dollars.

They were paying their employees well and had more money than each of them could ever imagine. Little Moe was paying for three grandkids to go to the University of Texas at Tyler. Shanna was driving a new Lexus and was building a house near Jacksonville. Whisper was just watching her money grow because she really didn't know how to spend money. She'd never had any practice. Ross spent his money on one thing only.

They looked at Ross and ask him, "What are you thinking?" He was obviously off somewhere in deep thought.

"Shanna" he said. "Is there any profit to be made holding weddings here. You know, like out on the veranda at sunset?"

Shanna thought for just a second. "It depends on how much they would be willing to pay for the venue. Of course, we would cater the affair and provide the drinks. Yeah, I think we could squeeze some profit out of it."

"Good," Ross said. I wouldn't want it to be a burden." He stepped out of the booth. Pulled a little box out of his pocket and got down on one knee. Whisper stood up on the booth seat and leaned against the wall with her hands to her mouth. Shanna burst into tears.

"Whisper Jenkins. Will you marry me?"

Whisper shook her head up and down and a barely audible "Yes" came out. Ross stood and Whisper held her hand out while Ross slipped on the ring. She looked at it and jumped off the bench seat into his waiting arms. He spun her around once and kissed her. Little Moe handed Shanna a napkin to wipe her tears.

Molly walked in the restaurant just in time to see Whisper fly through the air into Ross' arms. Shanna yelled, "She's getting married!"

"You lucky bitch!" Molly began to cry. Little Moe handed her a napkin too.

"Don't worry, I'll plan everything," Shanna said. Whisper never heard her

Chapter 65

Whisper and Ross made their excuses and went straight to Whisper's cabin. As soon as the door closed behind them, Whisper fell to her knees. Ross was fumbling with his pants, she was trying to help, making it worse. She could see him growing inside and that big thing wanted to get out. Free at last, it sprang out by the side of her face. She grabbed his big balls with her right hand and the shaft of his handsome cock with left. She got the head in her mouth and stroked the base with her left hand. Ross leaned back against the door.

She normally closed her eyes when she performed felatio on him but this time she kept her eyes riveted on the large, one and a half carat diamond ring on her finger. Ross looked down and saw her staring at it as she manipulated him. "Do you like it?" he asked.

She stopped for a moment, looking at him. "The dick or the diamond?" She continued.

Ross didn't answer. He was beyond talking or even thinking clearly.

"Let's go to the bed." She led him to the bedroom by his dick, left-handed, of course. Stopping at the foot of the bed they stripped as quickly as possible. She told Ross to lie down and started rubbing herself between the legs with her left hand. She wanted to watch that immense rock weave itself through her blonde hair. She buried her middle two fingers inside her, leaving the shiny stone right on top of her clit. For some reason seeing that sparkly diamond right there on top of her most sensitive spot turned her on.

She crawled up on the bed and straddled him, going way up on her knees to get the tip of his long cock in the right spot for insertion. She was guiding him in left-handed, never using her left hand for anything before but couldn't help herself now. Angle correct, she sat down and the big slab of meat slid in poking at the front of her stomach. She put her left hand there trying to feel that huge dick up in her but mostly looking at the ring.

She leaned forward, hands on his chest and pushed back on his cock, still staring at the ring on her finger, then looking into his eyes and said, "I'm going to love you forever."

"Till the day I die, Sunset Girl. I will love you until the day I die."

She leaned forward, her blonde hair cascading down on him, shut her eyes, and surrendered herself. Diamond be damned, this man was her world.

The End

The End

Made in the USA
Middletown, DE
14 August 2020